Praise for *White Dan for 200*

White Dan For 200 is by far one of the best debut novels I've ever read—brimming with precise, insightful dialogue and indelible characters. Angela Wilson lovingly, deftly explores the interior and exterior lives of a demographic that has been long shamefully neglected in contemporary fiction—the veterans of our 20th-century wars. This is a must-read for understanding the politics, psychology and sociology of 21st-century America.

—Joy Dickinson Tipping, former staff writer/book reviewer,
The Dallas Morning News

Angela Wilson has developed her story into fine art in *White Dan for 200*. Brilliantly written and wonderfully expressed, this honest narrative captures the humanity of American strength with grace and courage. From a historian's background, this novel unfolds over decades with complicated and complex characters revealing their grisly, painful memories. Ms. Wilson's story adeptly weaves together loyalty, identity, and honest individuality where the reader must find out what will ensue. Through 'laughter and tears,' *White Dan for 200* is relatable in its soul and its ability to encompass the distinctions of mortality with a knowing heart.

—Lynne Zotalis, author of *Hippie at Heart (What I Used To Be, I Still Am)* and *Get Back Up (Once More)*

My own son, coincidentally named Liam, as is the young soldier in this book, fought and died as a U.S. Army commando (special forces/ Colorado National Guard) in the tragic wars in Iraq and Afghanistan. Angela Wilson's fine writing here brings both pride, sadness, joy, and tears to this "Gold Star" dad. Thanks, Angela for *White Dan For 200*.

—Bill Nevins, educator, journalist, poet,
Gold Star parent, anti-war activist.

Wow. Angela Wilson hits it out of the park with *White Dan for 200*, her debut novel. *White Dan for 200* is a powerful and brutally intimate look at how war can ravage a family and a town. The trauma that war inflicts on soldiers has long lasting repercussions. Repercussions that affect the soldier's relationship with themselves, their family, their partner (if they can keep one), and their communities, often for the rest of their lives. The flashbacks, the avoidance of triggering situations, the reactivity, the nightmares, the shame and the hypervigilance. All of these make it difficult for the soldier to reintegrate into society. Oftentimes they feel more comfortable living alone and on the fringe. Angela Wilson takes us into the minds of those experiencing this trauma. In doing so, she makes a compelling argument for peace.

—Jim Charleston, Executive Director Silver City Theatre

Angela Wilson's debut novel, *White Dan for 200,* presents a completely new perspective on life after 20th century military service. Presented as both fiction and memoir, her background as a military brat, professional playwright, actress and screenwriter lends a highly visual, dialogue driven, fast-paced work that cries out to be filmed. Soon.

—Pam Dougherty, actress, voice talent, anime, voice of Big Mom in *One Piece.*

A brilliant, rapid-fire, warts-and-all all last hurrah for a cantankerous member of The Greatest Generation.

—Matt Hader *Two-Seven Remainder, God Loves a Madman*

The trauma of American participation in 20th century wars, fabricated gender roles and toxic disconnectedness are threads that pull and fray in Angela Wilson's novel, *White Dan for 200*. What happens when the effects of war come home to roost? The book unravels the myths of the American Dream over four generations in small town Texas. But there are silver linings in the book. For example, the music. Soldiers have always had music. Their music is the voice of sanity, connection and reality and counters the broken, blurred and unreliable narratives in the world of White Dan. Music unites what the American Dream can't.

—Annie Benjamin, poet and songwriter

White Dan for 200

White Dan for 200

Angela Wilson

Mercury HeartLink
www.heartlink.com

White Dan for 200

Copyright ©2025 Angela Wilson
ISBN 978-1-949652-42-0
Publisher Mercury HeartLink
Silver City, New Mexico
Printed in the United States of America

Front Cover image: David Beebe III
Drawing of Soldier: Luke Tompkins, Texas artist, age 13
Part I Image: Vintage photo of the author's father
Part II Image: © Afif Fatchurozi, Dreamstime.com
Part III Image: The Baker Hotel, Mineral Wells, Texas
Part IV Image: © Saša Prudkov, Dreamstime.com
Author photo with bio: Wilson family archive
Author photo, back cover: Carl Savering
Layout and cover design: Pamela Warren Williams

WARNINGS:
PTSD, language, dementia, war, suicide, suicide ideation, violence against others, political opinions that may or may not make any sense, alcoholism, attempted murder, terrorism in a small town, the decline of American life in one man's opinion, adultery, lack of self-confidence, looking for love in all the wrong places, fathers and daughters, husbands and wives, draft dodgers, oddness, outside the box behaviors, songs and laughter that may or may not be at the appropriate time.

Mercury HeartLink: consult@heartlink.com

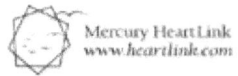

Mercury HeartLink
www.heartlink.com

To the loves of my life, Jennifer Collier and the girls.

And in honor of Army SFC Liam J. Nevins,
whom I only met in the writings of and
conversations with his father, Bill,
and in memory of my lifelong best friend,
Nancy Ann Martin of Dallas, Texas.

It is very difficult to know people and I don't think one can ever really know any but one's own countrymen. For men and women are not only themselves; they are also the region in which they are born, the city apartment or the farm in which they learnt to walk, the games they played as children, the old wives' tales they overheard, the food they ate, the schools they attended, the sports they followed, the poets they read, and the God they believed in. It is all these things that have made them what they are, and these are the things that you can't come to know by hearsay, you can only know them if you have lived them.

—W. Somerset Maugham, *The Razor's Edge*

I want you to feel what I felt. I want you to know why story-truth is truer sometimes than happening-truth.

—Tim O'Brien, *The Things They Carried*

All her young life she has tried to please her father, never quite realizing that, as a girl, she never could.

— Alice Walker, *By the Light of My Father's Smile*

PREFACE

The creation of this book took thirty years, and is infused with a love of reading, storytelling, movies, and American history. It began with writing a play.

In the nineties I was writing and researching American history, earning a master's in liberal arts at SMU in Dallas.

One assignment was to write a dramatic mashup of two well-known historical figures who would never have crossed paths in real life. I went with Typhoid Mary and Harry Houdini.[1]

Playwriting was so invigorating that I immediately took on another assignment—to write another, bigger play about war.

The second play, *Heart*, and its screenplay offspring, *Blue Eyed Son*, serve as the inspiration for this novel. Thirty years.

Heart, Blue Eyed Son, and now *White Dan for 200* are influenced by the brave soldiers I encountered while growing up in a military household. My father, Dan C. Wilson, served in peacetime during the 1950s until his separation from the Air Force in 1968. He was an instructor on bases in the United States and Europe, although he was not on active duty in combat zones. He cleaned up messes in war zones and later prepared young men for Vietnam.

Once he retired we moved to a small town in Texas. I spent my teenage years living near Fort Wolters Army Base, where nearly every helicopter pilot who flew in Vietnam was trained. I watched my high school classmates go off to Vietnam, and many were killed there. We lived in the haunted Baker Hotel, which is now the fictionalized Porterfield Hotel in the novel.

Our home had always been filled with soldiers, and with the draft looming over all my boyfriend's heads in the late 1960s and early 70s, there proved to be no end to the stories I knew I wanted to tell the world someday.

I moved from Dallas to New Mexico in 2019, three weeks before the Pandemic. It was Santa Fe author Rosa Rajkovic who suggested I turn my play and screenplay into this novel. And then I happened to meet Diana Gabaldon at a writer's dinner. She said

"I set out to teach myself to write a novel." That novel ended up being *Outlander*. The wisdom from these two lovely women changed my life! Writing 100,000 words eased the loneliness of moving to a strange new place. I taught myself to write about war, in the way that I observed those who served in war. I exhumed my dream of novel writing, buried since age eight when I had asked Santa to leave a new typewriter under the tree, and was rewarded with a dollar bill taped to an empty box marked "typewriter." My father, Dan, who thought his joke was funny, also thought it was character-building. Now I see that misguided attempt at humor to be the first investment dollar in the book.

My relationship with my precious dad was colored by our differing attitudes about the war in Vietnam. Americans experience war within their generations, influenced by their times, their exposure to stories, and their families. We share a residual pride from having won in World War II, a residual pain from whatever the hell happened in Vietnam, and maybe a residual numbness from unfinished business in Afghanistan and Iraq. I hope to honor the survivors and memories of all our soldiers by keeping their memories alive, even in fiction.

Of course, *White Dan for 200* is not just about war.

The book is fictional, in fact, it's enhanced fiction, since so many stories are based on private and emotional experiences of my own. To befriend, love, listen to, and care for someone, especially a family member, who has experienced war, PTSD, and huge loss such as the many characters in *White Dan*, will erode the ease of one's own life's journey. Suicide and the threat of suicide, raging behaviors, betrayals, lies, embellishments, alcoholism, drug addiction, and low self-esteem takes its toll on the witness. But life is meant to be experienced in highs and lows. Some days are lived in laughter, and some in tears, right?

Angela Wilson
Albuquerque, NM
2025

1. The Harry Houdini "Wild about Harry" fan club got wind of the play and wrote, "Here's one of the most unique takes on a Houdini story I've

ever heard."

And it was. It takes place in 1915. Harry Houdini shares a warehouse with his real-life brother, a doctor named Weiss. On one side of the warehouse the doctor experiments with "the healing properties" of an x-ray machine he's adapted for cancer treatment. "All he needs is a dying patient to try out the machine." On the other side of the warehouse Harry Houdini practices dunking himself in his Water Torture Cell. Both attract a certain Mrs. Churchill, who wants a way out of this life. She's suffering too much to live any longer. Her breast cancer has spread, so she becomes the patient of an unlikely trio of "physicians" that includes Houdini and his water torture cell, Leo Weiss and his x-ray machine, and Mrs. Churchill's own household cook, Mary Brown, better known as Typhoid Mary, who has her own methods for ending suffering. "Typhoid is three days of . . . not lingering on and on . . . like cancer."

TABLE OF CONTENTS

Part Four
Chapter

PART ONE ...

CHAPTER 1
The Old Man and the C

"I'm a man! Nobody, not you, not God, and ESPECIALLY not the blitherin' State of Texas, is gonna dictate what I do with my body!"

The storm outside was electric and wild, loud, so most witnesses inside the old folks' home could see, but not hear the argument Dan was having with Celeste. Dan, the ninety-five-year-old Drama King, was yelling, even spitting at her, and they saw him slap at her face once or twice. Watched her cower and turn a beet red color.

A couple of people close enough thought they heard Celeste scream out, "I cannot and will not help you commit suicide, Dad."

To which Dan, who always had to have the last word, replied . . .

Finally, a couple of Celeste's male friends intervened between the father and daughter, each placing a wager on what would prevail—Dan's notorious cowardice or his annoying bravado. Sure enough, Dan asserted his right to put himself at risk, scooted away, and wheelchaired outside onto the porch of the old folks' home, bumped perilously down the two concrete steps, and swept himself smack dab into the middle of the storm, like the hothead he was.

Then ZAP. Nobody knew if the sizzling, electrifying lightning bolt that, in that moment, zipped across the June sky and scorched the earth, was sent by God, or the State of Texas, or some deadly alien life force on a mission to destroy them all. But they saw Celeste run out to bring her father back to safety.

TWO WEEKS EARLIER

Awake.

First words Dan utters from his luxurious Tempur-Pedic bed in the old folks' home. "Dammit. Still here. Awwww."

"Hello world."

Gasped with a resolve only an old warrior who perceives himself to have grit and guts can muster.

He's been interred in the home for fifteen long years. The Rupert Rest and Care Home (known as the "RRC") is on the outskirts of town for a reason. It's unsightly, ugly, but it is surrounded by North Central Texas' beloved, ahem, breathtaking scenery, prairies and plains, including a dried-up river and smoky hills that are just ready to catch fire. It's half a mile from the Big River on the southwest side and half a mile from the hills on the northeast. The building itself is just crumbling red brick and a flat roof made of gravel and tar. It's an L-shaped, one-story building, with a rather Soviet-like appearance.

It's just ugly. Ugly 1990s Havana ugly.

And in sixty years, nothing has changed.

Well now, that's not true.

"Dammit. Hello world."

Perfect elocution, though. For someone ninety-five years old.

Old, what?

He waits for the daily laugh from the new nurse, "FN" (which stands for "Favorite Nurse"), who was assigned to him just two weeks ago. He affectionately refers to her as "EFFFF-N." (He can never remember her actual name, which is "Della.") He guesses FN to be around fifty, an old lady by any standard. If she's forty some, with that overly made-up face, then she's worn out from hard living. But he does enjoy her laughin' at his jokes.

FN isn't in the room with him this morning, though. Nobody is around at all. *Gotta pee*, he frets. *Could get urgent.*

Large picture window in his bedroom. Dan glances outside. FN has indeed gotten her ass to the building where she works, just not to his room. She's standing in the parking lot, where there's no shade and it's already ninety degrees, chatting up the driver of the DAV van. He's a new driver, come to the old folks' home to pick up veterans and take them to doctor appointments in Dallas. FN is out there sashaying her sweet rear end and giggling.

Well, she does have a sweet rear end for an old broad.

Dan wonders *who is this new man in her life?* The idea generates disgust, until he sees the muscular man open the back of the van, take out a pump, and go around the vehicle airing up tires in the heat.

Obviously a hard worker and fit, Dan approves of that.

FN follows the man as he goes from tire to tire, flirting her sweet ass off the whole time. She is obviously charming him, his face red as a beet, unsuccessfully fighting off her silly distractions from his work.

A shy, embarrassed older man, maybe, Dan thinks, *or maybe he's just suffering from the Texas heat. He's got the complexion of a Mexican, though, so this guy can surely take the heat.* The man pulls the kerchief from around his neck to wipe what must be sweaty brown makeup from FN's forehead. Dan hears the man belly laugh at something FN says, realizes that he's just a bit jealous that yet another nurse is going to be late tending to him, because of another damn man.

His pitiful caretaker daughter, Celeste is also running late this morning. Dan sees her clumsily climb from her car, breathlessly zip past FN, waving. She obviously recognizes the driver, too, because she shrieks, changes course, runs to the guy and hugs his neck, before coming on into "work."

Dan moves into punishment mode. When Celeste opens the door to his room, his spindly legs make an unusually fast trek to the bathroom. Of course he pretends to be fine on his own, until his morning cough starts up. Dan always wakes with a stiff larynx, and an annoying crackly cough, so when he first speaks of a morning he will speak in a menacing whisper, Clint Eastwood-style. But that voice is perfect for punishment mode.

Celeste throws her purse and backpack onto the couch, and apologetically offers assistance. Dan brushes her away, grumbling, "You forgot to turn off the hot water all the way when you used my shower yesterday, C. It dripped all night. Kept me awake. Which I am sure was your intention."

"I'm sorry, Daddy. My shower is still broken at home."

"You need to call a plumber, get that situation cleared up at your house. You need to shower there. Not here."

"I will, Daddy."

By this time FN has hurried in. She, too, discards her purse and laptop, turns to apologize and discovers Dan holding onto the bathroom door, smirking with disapproval.

He waits for both girls to literally stand at attention before assuming the tone of the badass Clint.

"Good thing I don't need any help, you two lazy asses. Fifteen minutes late. Unacceptable."

(Nothing pleases Dan more than passing judgment on others, while imitating Clint Eastwood.)

Celeste wipes tears from her big blue eyes, moves to sit in a chair as far away from Dan's bed and bathroom as she can get, reaches into her backpack for knitting. Mission accomplished, Dan then ignores his daughter, but is quite pleased with FN's stiff expression of terror. She doesn't move.

Dan pulls on the bathroom door, but leaves it open a crack.

He pees in the sink, only a drop, looks in the mirror while he waits for the flood. Drip. Checks his false teeth. Drip. Marvels at his full mane of silver hair. A few rust-colored urine drops dirty the sink, but he's indifferent to the ominous color. He hears footsteps outside the door and knows he is being spied on, that FN moved closer.

FN turns to C and whispers. "He's not using the toilet. He's using the sink. Maybe he doesn't realize that he is pissing in the sink, Celeste."

"I can hear you," Dan calls out.

Recovered, C rolls those big blue eyes. "A sad trickle's all," C says. "His kidneys don't work right. I'll clean up after him."

Dan frowns. He certainly does not realize that he is peeing in the sink. FN spotted the misstep, and tattled. Now he's become the 'child' in his daughter's eyes.

This is a win for C. Notes how quickly the tables can turn now that he's old. More and more C has the upper hand. Dan can't have that. But his foray into punishment mode wore him out. He'll have to be somewhat nice for the rest of the day.

Scrawny privates in hand, a little embarrassed, Dan treks the five torturous steps from the sink to the toilet. Drip. Drip. He flushes, leaves his fly open, moves back to the sink, and just to be ornery, runs the water, but doesn't wash his hands.

"Success," Dan says through the crack in the door. "It wasn't a mighty flow like the Amazon River, but it wasn't the Rio Grande!"

Proud to remember the name of two rivers.

From the bathroom back to the bed can be a ten minute walk if his arthritis is acting up. It isn't, but he pretends suffering at this point, and feigns extreme exhaustion when he plops down on the bed, his skinny ass sinking into the Tempur-Pedic. The girls watch him slither under the covers. He makes quite the ruckus coughing, and when finished, coughs up and spits out a hawk into a Kleenex and starts his day. Every day starts with coughing fits while he talks. Says, "Christ, here we go again. It's Tuesday. June. 2023. Name is Dan, (hark, spit, wheeze) almost ninety-five and I always dress classy. I live in the old folks' home, which is off the main highway, in the eyesore of a town named Rupert, Texas. Birthday is in a few weeks."

FN leaps into action, nurse stuff.

"All of that information is correct, except the eyesore part," FN says. "That's just your opinion."

Having passed the first part of the daily ritual, the "who are you and how old are you" test, Dan clears his throat and proceeds. "I'm sorry about this cough, FN. Hard work for me to create a more appealing, sss . . . sonorous sound. But I'm trying."

FN indulges him with a smile.

Dan continues. "Ever s-s-sin . . . (hark, hark, spit into Kleenex) Ever since I got struck by lightning (bark, hark, hack, spit) and was in a coma for months, (wheeze, relax) I've done this awful morning coughing. The VA doctors didn't know what to do about it. They never did know what to do with a soldier like me."

"That's a smoker's cough, any dumbass can hear that, even the VA doctors," FN says.

"I never visited the VA in the morning (clearing throat) so they never heard me cough. Course, I never admitted to (clearing throat again) smoking when they asked. I lied. I used to smoke. Two packs a day. Camels. And I miss it. But I did admit to inhaling oven cleaner from time to time." He looks at FN to test her reaction. "Liked the name. Easy-Off. My high of choice."

"Oven cleaner?" FN looks to Celeste for confirmation. Celeste shakes her head "yes" and adds, "Thus his failing kidneys, but he was never struck by lightning. That's just a lie he likes to tell."

FN offers hot tea and honey to Dan.

"Sit up. Drink. It'll help your throat, and your kidneys."

He obeys. "I know I'm a man looks like a coffee drinker, FN, but I love (sip, swallow, sip, swallow, big loud cough, and done) hot tea."

FN asks. "How did you sleep last night, you big fat liar, you?"

The liar answers. "Bad dream. About C's mother. Corrie. She was shaking like a leaf so I tried to put something warm on her. She kept slapping at me. Kept saying "clutch, clutch," like a lisping chicken. Had two dollar bills in her hand, rubbing them together."

There was the time her mother wouldn't let go of a couple of dollar bills and her father tried to force them from her mother's hand, almost breaking her fingers, and slamming her hard into the wall, cracking one of her ribs. But C doesn't mention such a memory. She knits quietly instead.

"Some women call a purse a 'clutch' bag, Dan," FN says. "Corrie wanted to put her two dollars inside the clutch bag."

Feigning satisfaction with FN's know-it-all declaration, Dan continues the recitation of his morning ritual. "In the eyesore of the town of Rupert, Texas. Birthday's in a few weeks. And Joe Biden is president. (pause for effect) I have no idea what your opinion is on that, FN. I know C loves him."

"No opinion whatsoever. Take your time getting up, Mr. Kellar," FN orders. "You took a very hard fall yesterday, remember?"

"Yesterday?" *No, I don't remember.* "Are you sure?" The question slips out of Dan's mouth before he can stop it. He knows better than to show weakness.

"Your pillow tumbled onto the floor, and when you got up, your toes got tangled in the pillow case, Dan."

Dan closes his eyes, hunkers down again, ready for a nap.

C smiles. "We're going to keep you safe, though. Getting you a roommate, Daddy."

Jolt. "I'd RATHER go back to PRISON than have a GD ROOMMATE," Dan yells, convinced that raising his voice and almost cursing, solves the matter.

FN places an unwanted hand under his head to help him sit up again but Dan slaps her away. "I can pick my damn head off the damn pillow by myself. I am tired of being humiliated by you two silly females."

FN retreats at the slight.

"Don't forget to tell FN about your troubled childhood, Daddy, when you were four years old and you didn't get that red wagon Santa promised you. Wha wha," Celeste taunts.

The old man glares at his daughter. His silly, getting-to-be-mean-ass daughter. And who made that sweet girl mean? Dan knows the answer to that.

Serves me right that she has to take care of me in my old age, he thinks. *I oughta be grateful. Ingratiate myself.*

"I'm sorry, FN, I know you're only doing your job. But C can take care of me so I don't need a roommate. I don't want a roommate. Before you say anything I KNOW I'm getting to be more like Corrie was at the end," Dan says, "Cussing all the time. Her math skills went first. Now mine are going. Yesterday, at Walmart, my bill came to $8.23. I had a five, and two ones, and change. I'm at the register. C was still over picking up paper towels. I start counting money to make it add up to $8.23. Sure, I got confused. Dropped some pennies. Started over. The cashier got mad at me. She made a scene. I just needed a few minutes to get it all in order. Nobody treats the elderly with respect anymore. We're gonna have (wheeze, gasp) off moments."

FN softens her tone.

Falling for his schtick.

"You're afraid of ending up like Corrie," FN says.

"I almost took a shower in my clothes yesterday, FN, but I didn't. I stopped myself. So seriously, I do not need a roommate, long as C is here. She takes good care of me, and I am so lucky she does."

C rolls her eyes.

"Well, we can order some new tests on your old brain if that will make you feel better, Dan."

"It will," he answers. "Can you put off getting me a roommate until after I have tests on my old brain? I've been through enough, FN. (confides, whispers) Good as she is at helping me, C hates me. C never helped with her mother. That was all on me. Corrie used to hit me; she drew blood. I bathed her every afternoon before work. Bathed her, put her clothes on her. And every day she socked me in the mouth. C wanted to put her mother in a home."

Celeste. Knitting needles clacking. Lips pursed. Heavy silence. Then again. Needles click. Feet tap.

FN takes note of tension she senses between Dan and Celeste, responds. "The elderly, especially those with established dementia, can be too much for the average person to handle."

"Well, I'm not average. Not only did I take care of C's mother while she declined into Oldtimer's Disease, I'm the one rescued her from the Nazis, too."

"Sit up for me, Dan." FN reaches for her stethoscope.

Dan cooperates. "You understand why I could not put her in a home. She was my wife and barely (coughing fit) fifty-five."

FN listens to his lungs, takes the earpieces out. "Dan," she orders, "why don't we forget about things that happened decades ago, they are unimportant, you need to get up, get dressed."

Dan, slighted. *Why don't WE forget? Unimportant?*

"I have no intention of forgetting any of the great stories of my life, FN. I am incensed at the idea. I saved Corrie from the Nazis. I have many adventures worth memorializing."

C smiles. "True dat, Daddy. Somebody oughta write down all your lies."

"None of my stories are lies. Some are embellished for entertainment purposes."

"Lies." C reiterates.

Dan, working hard to curb his fury, and his temper, then, intentionally takes things slow. The best form of aggression is passive. He's still mad at FN for flirting with that Mexican driver guy, and C's condescending know-it-all shit irks him to no end. He painstakingly raises his head, lifts one finger to his temple and presses. Blinks. "Eyesight appears to be unaltered, in spite of the fall yesterday," he claims.

"And my hearing's ok," he goes on. "I can always count on the hiss of tinnitus, and today it's more of a roar," he says.

Celeste, right leg jiggling, nostrils flaring, knows what's coming.

Dad's passive aggressive drill.

The goal of it is to deliberately delay FN from tending to her next patient, to make her late to her next patient. He cites a checklist of sounds, which Dan delights in naming out loud. Soft conversations, traffic noise, birds chirping, dogs barking, cell phones beeping, and trees rustling.

Wind howling, construction, and garbage collection. Car radios, "Jeremiah was a bullfrog" playing.

"And then there's intelligent lyrics that define the hippie generation. Jeremiah. Was a bullfrog," he sneers.

Then he starts in on an irritating series of personal noises: groaning, creaking, cracking, and crackling. Another vehicle passes by outside. Same boomer channel. "Good morning, Starshine . . . "Ah, glibby, glub, glooby, more memorable lyrics," Dan says.

And after Dan got back the fifteen minutes she owed him, and once he was sure she would be exactly fifteen minutes late to her next patient, FN is dismissed. She furiously gathers her things, flies out of the room, slams the door.

Here it comes, my turn for punishment, C thinks. And she dreads it.

But Dan, having tired of playing his passive aggressive game, puts on the ugly personality he shows only to those closest to him. His asshole personality. "Celeste, my little marlin, you need to finalize the plans for my birthday party."

"Mo and the rest of the staff are planning your party, not me," C says.

"I want a spectacular birthday party, C. Invite everyone. Because I'm setting you free on that day. I'm planning to die. By my own hand, and I want you to help me."

CHAPTER 2
Don't tug on that cape

Well, Celeste is certainly up all night after that little tidbit. Her Dad's threat "planning to die" "by his own hand" is a scary proclamation. No sleep whatsoever.

She heads to the RRC before the light of day. He's awake already, and full of snarls.

"Hello, world. Still here, C. For two more weeks. Have a gun under my pillow. Drugs in the drawer. Now leave me to strategize my salvation before I kill myself. Silence. Please."

All day long she's feeling worthless, unloved, hurt, confused, frustrated, angry, and unimportant. Celeste clearly sees that her father is practicing his signature stonewalling tactic—the silent treatment. He does that when he doesn't get his way. Regardless, C is determined to put a stop to her Daddy's nonsense talk about killing himself, and to do it before FN gets in to work.

At various times of the day she chatters at him. "First of all, you're in perfect health. There is NO reason to think you need to kill yourself."

Then. "Second of all, you have plenty of money to see you through."

"And third, your memory is just fine. You remember all your stories and everyone loves hearing them."

No response.

About dinnertime she starts to lift a fourth finger, but shuts up. He's not paying a bit of attention.

About nine p.m. Dan peels himself off the bed, and makes his way to the bathroom.

C can hear her dad peeing in the sink.

She tiptoes to his hospital bed. Carefully, she lifts up the pillow and sneaks a peek. No gun. Thank God. He lied. Of course. She hears a toilet flush.

No time to check for Ativan in the nightstand drawer. She braces for his return.

Her heart is pounding with fear. She waits for her moody, angry father to totter over on legs that are no longer as strong as tree trunks, and sink into the bed. Her father still seems intimidating, as old as he is, as frail as he really is, though he's still as tall as his hero, the long dead John Wayne, with a thick, hairy chest, and bulky arms that are surely still strong enough to slap the shit out of her. She'd been chattering nicely at him all morning, about this, that, and everything else. But now, scared as she is of the old man, it's time to get some courage, and dig into him.

C carefully broaches the elephant in the room. "You'll go to hell if you kill yourself on your birthday without God weighing in, Dad."

That did it. Hackles up, Dan sideswipes the box of Kleenex and a plastic water bottle off the nightstand. "Not afraid of going to hell. I've been there. Lived with your mother."

C finally leaves the RRC at midnight. After a sleepless night she returns the next morning to continue the argument with her brooding father. C's stomach lurches. Holds back tears. New argument. New tactic. "I will also go to hell if I help you."

"Pick up all that shit that fell off the nightstand, C." She obeys. "Glad you bring that up. Going to hell," he adds.

Dan delights in this new argument. "Hell. That's just superstitious balderdash, C. Romans 8:38–39. Nothing can ever separate us from God's love. Translates to 'you can kill me first, and then decide about yourself later.' I just need you to pull the trigger. God will always forgive."

"Forgiveness does NOT work that way, Dad. And it's not just about God. Assisted suicide's also illegal in Texas. And it would be murder anyway because there's not a damn thing wrong with your health, Daddy. Assisted suicide is for people who are suffering."

"I am suffering, C."

"I'll go to jail first. Then hell. Which is real. With you. And I don't want to go anywhere with you, Daddy, especially not for eternity."

"Then take me to New Mexico, C. They don't care how or why anyone dies there, and nobody gets arrested. Look, I've gone through half your mother's life insurance money living in here. I want to leave the rest of that money to you. I don't want to sell the house you live in. It's for you. I could live to 110. That's fifteen more years, C. fifteen more years of your mother's insurance money going down the drain, and most important, if I kill myself, I won't have to have a roommate. I'll still have some say over my own life."

Worn down, C lights up a forbidden but much-needed cigarette.

"So that is what this is all about. Of course you don't want a roommate (inhales) (exhales). Let's go to breakfast."

"We can't. It's too early. FN isn't even here yet, C."

"What's up with her? Is she late again, Daddy?"

"Yes, dammit, she is. But I know where she is. Out in the parking lot sashaying her sweet rear end and making dates with that DAV driver."

"With Jimmy? Well, good for him. I hope she brings Jimmy to your birthday party."

"Why would I want this Jimmy at my party?"

"Jimmy! The kid you practically raised. Jimmy Ramirez, Dad!"

"Jimmy! Who used to put out your mother's fires and make sure she was wearing clothes when people were around? I thought he looked familiar to me. Good boy."

"He's in his seventies now, Dad. But I'm sure he would do anything you asked him to do, even now, well, not help you kill yourself, don't ask him that."

"I need to warn FN, though. It's not just that Jimmy's too old for her. I'll have to warn her about his crazy shell shock sickness. I don't know a single soldier ever went as crazy as Jimmy did after Vietnam."

"Vietnam was hard on a lot of people, Dad."

C was sorry she said it the second she said it. *I can never keep my mouth shut,* she mourns. *Why am I compelled to remind my old Dad of what our family went through, his long-lost son, my beautiful, blonde brother, Tad, missing forever, in Vietnam?* The biggest reason her father would want to die. To die and go to heaven, and maybe find out what really happened to Tad.

A few minutes later he's already forgotten about Tad. Dan mumbles under his breath. "But maybe I won't warn her. She might not come back if I make trouble."

"What's that you say, Dad?"

"I'm not going to mention her tardiness when she gets here. I sincerely hope not to upset her, because the last thing I want is to break in a new nurse, especially as my reputation declines among the staff, through no fault of my own. And anything to put off getting a roommate. If I don't misbehave, maybe I can continue to live alone until you pull the trigger and end it for me. On my birthday. Please, baby girl, please."

C marvels at Dan's brain. He's lucid, able to scheme, and experiencing dementia all at the same time. Yesterday her dad was trying FN's last nerve. Deliberately. Today he's strategizing how to keep FN on his team in spite of her committing the same work crime two days in a row. Being late.

FN, or "Della," her real name, has only worked with Dan for a couple weeks. She had been warned early on, though. The twenty-two year-old trainer, Destin-ee, explained to her. "Dan Kellar, is one of the oldest residents, and is in "reclining" health. He is considered to be feisty, but is primarily immobile. (Not true) Up until recently he hasn't caused any major problems. Sometimes he runs over people's toes with his wheelchair. Sometimes he flirts with the nurses, only women, though, we think he's a homophobe. He only pretends to take his medications, so you gotta watch out for that. He spends his evenings drinking one glass of wine and playing Mexican Train, which is really just a simple game of dominoes so you should have no trouble playing it with him when he asks. For the most part, Dan Kellar prefers being outside, alone."

"You allow that?" FN, er, Della, is surprised that Dan has such freedom.

"Oh, we let him stay up late," Destin-ee says. "We let him sit outside under the trees. He can't get far. And he can't work his cell phone so he isn't getting in any social media trouble or watching porn or anything like that."

Della is a bit shocked. "Porn? Who here watches porn?"

"Who knows? Someone probably does. We're so short-staffed we have to hire just about anyone who walks in the door. There was an assisted living place near Dallas that hired a serial killer. I'd rather us hire porn watchers any day."

Later, Celeste met with the concerned FN (*Della, sorry, I'll try to call you by your real name*) off site for coffee. "Don't listen to Destin-ee. I'll train you. They don't just hire "anyone off the street," FN. They hired you because you've got skills to take care of old people. Do take notes, though. You'll need to reference them. And you'll need to recognize his impressions of old movie stars. Clint Eastwood. John Wayne. Gary Cooper. That will clue you in a lot about his frame of mind at the time. Dad spends his late-nights smoking outside under the stars, which is harmless enough, though nobody knows that he is out there planning his eventual departure from the earth. At midnight, he calls it "the hour of a thousand crazy questions." This is how his mind operates. (And now Celeste speaks to FN using her best 'Gary Cooper,' her impression of the awkwardly shy sounding, 'just-make-me-the-hero' primal man, who can chop down a giant tree with ease, and be ready to screw after. Gary. Cooper. Gary with a deliberately soft, seductive, homey voice, a trick Dan taught her to use to keep people interested in her "generally boring teacher drone," as he put it. She has mastered the Gary Cooper voice, first he speaks, then she.)

"'It's time fer the Lord to take me home an' fer me to put an end tuit.'

"Well, Dad, I say, are you gonna let God decide what has to be done? And Dad says 'Iffen He's right quick about it, shore I'll let 'em decide. He's the boss.' This was Dad's late acknowledgement of God's omnipotence, you see, FN, Dad just turned Christian a few months ago. Oh and FN, you look kinda confused. As Dad would say, 'Imma thinkin' ya don't have a clue who Gary Cooper was'."

"Gary Cooper? Nope."

"Movie star. Silent films all the way to 1950's. *High Noon*? *Sergeant York*? 'Mr. Deeds?' Like a black and white Kevin Costner, in his prime. Only taller?"

C notes that Della, errr, FN, is nodding 'no', and C thinks this is so sad, and thinks how culturally deficient FN's world is. "Well, that's okay. You'll learn. So Dad says 'He's the boss. He could take me by rapture on mah birthday. Not shore how fir I'll git flyin' up to heaven, he says, considerin' the ankle bracelet I've been a-wearin' for twenty years, which weighs me down by a vicious half a-pound.' Write this all down, FN. I mean, Della. Shit."

"Just call me FN, that's okay. Ankle bracelet? Gary Cooper, Kevin Costner, ankle bracelet? Serial killers getting hired, not getting hired?"

FN is genuinely confused, points to her patient notes.

"The ankle bracelet, now that one is important, it's a phantom; he hasn't been required to wear it for years," C explains. "But Dad was in trouble with the law a lot. Sometimes he thinks he still is. You'll have to pretend you see the ankle bracelet when he brings it up."

"Ok."

"There's more, just let him ramble. And," she hesitates, "well, in Dad's hyperactive mind, a SWAT team is always standing by, ready to take him down or, as he likes to say, 'die tryin'.'"

"Do I have to pretend I see a SWAT team?"

"No, he only sees the SWAT team when his medications stop working. By the time the SWAT team appears, Dad is really far gone and beyond your pay grade. Just let him ramble about the SWAT team, but pretend you see the ankle bracelet." She pauses to take a breath.

"So, back to his midnight musings. The old guy is actually pretty profound. His midnight musings, Dad is out there, coughing away like he's taking his last breath, and thinking about prospective fights he will no longer get to have as a soldier, and new enemies he will no longer get to hate. It is bad enough that he missed the war against terrorism in Afghanistan and Iraq. But not going up against American's true enemies, China or Russia, is unthinkable. He mourns that he will be dead by the time WWIII happens. And he might be dead. I tell him he's healthy all the time, but he's slowing down. And he kinda wants to end it all. Keep that to yourself. I think that's about all. Welcome aboard, Della."

CHAPTER 3
... *Smoke through the trees* ...

FN sashays her sweet ass into Dan's room, quite late. She's nervous, expecting punishment, but he's full bore into a new mood and a new story. Whew. Settles, listens. Dan is telling C about his first close shave with suicide.

"Six years old. A bungled hanging."

C writes it all down. Furiously.

FN's eyes bug out. C raises an eyebrow in FN's direction, makes a sad face, indicating that she's not sure she wants to hear all this. Whispers. "I negotiated this deal, FN. You don't have to sit and listen. He's made a mess in the shower."

"I'll listen while I clean," FN says.

He goes off. And now he's ninety-five, as he says. All things eventually die. This has been proven over and over. "So why not me? Eventually dying doesn't cut it."

Dan puffs up like a peacock. Oh, the many ways he's tried to bail out of living, how many reasons, all his life. Death by cop, inciting domestic violence, an attempt to be imprisoned, soldiering. The excuses for trying. Betrayals. Prejudices. Feeling worthless. Hopeless. A lifelong flirt with the Great Depression. Seeing things. Hearing voices. Finally, for effect, feigning self-awareness and blaming someone else for his faults at the same time, "I had a father who treated me similarly to the way I treat you, Celeste."

His father, Wyatt Dan Kellar, tall, handsome, moody, and randy, with a beautiful "coulda been on the Radio" singing voice, a Scrabble and Monopoly award-winning player, was a successful cobbler. Arkansas. His poorer-than-dirt neighbors lived by the motto "Use it up, wear it out, make do or do without." For Wyatt Dan, or "White Dan" as everyone called him 'cause of their southern accents, that meant shoes. Whether it was loose stitching, broken heels, flapping soles, or all those put together, he could transform a pair of shoes into like brand new. He could build an orthopedic insert, too. He actually changed some lives. Survived the Great Depression by having a very important job, repairing shoes.

His father would have been a great storyteller, and he may have been a great thinker, but he kept his thoughts and his stories to himself. Dan would find him in the barn, deep in thought, sipping on something. He'd ask "Whatcha doin', Dad ?" He'd say, "thinkin', sippin'."

"Thinkin' and sippin' on what, Dad ?"

"Somethin'." Dan understood that the story was somewhere between 'thinkin' and sippin' and 'somethin'. It was just up to him to interpret.

His bigger-than-life father just happened to pass by the barn when White Dan, Jr. was standing on a bale with a rope around his neck, reaching up to attach the rope to a rafter.

At six years old, he was way too short.

His Dad yanked the rope off, tossed Dan, Jr. to the ground and gave him a mighty whooping. Then went inside to eat supper and never mentioned the incident again.

That's how parents did things back then.

White Dan left the boy in a heap on the barn floor, to reflect on his behavior. It worked, too. White Dan Junior is ninety-five now, and still reflecting.

Dan insisted that the rest home throw him a 100th-themed birthday party—five years early. It wasn't difficult to persuade them to do it. It would be their first real gathering following the end of the horrible, life-sucking Pandemic.

His plans for after the party (to die, of course) included four different options for God to pick from. Die in his sleep (preferred), die by a natural, sudden death, depart by rapture, or (last resort) kill himself. This would require C's help, unless he opted for the last, last resort—shooting himself by himself, God forbid. (He'd tried that back in 2003, and all that got him was prison time.)

He started working to wear her down her around the first of June. "We need to talk, C."

"NO!!!!!!!! No assisted suicide talk, not today."

"I have thirty Ativan AND a pistol."

He has no idea that C knows he is lying about the gun under his pillow. "Then you don't need me," lies Celeste, her turn for her eyes to be popping out of her head. "If you're going to shoot yourself, take the Ativan first. It will relax you, take the fear out."

"Okay, good idea."

"I'M JUST KIDDING, YOU ASSHOLE."

FN shows up on time the next day. Throws her stuff down, rushes to Dan's bedside. Grabs her stethoscope.

"Birthday in a few weeks. Joe Biden is president," Dan begins.

"You forgot something," FN says.

" . . . Oh yeah, (hark, spit, cough) Hello world. Dammit."

Big, overly toothy Dan smile. FN doesn't laugh this time.

"Holding a grudge, are we, and why?" he asks. "I am not in the wrong wanting you to be here on time, FN. I'm getting might tired of all the negativity around here. I feel like I'm held captive now, not even allowed to watch television."

"Dan, the rules are we keep you in compliance with our 'no controversial television' policy."

"A submersible is missing near the Titanic's wreckage in the Atlantic Ocean. Is that controversial?"

"How do you know about the missing sub?" FN is alarmed.

"C told me. C updates me on world news. Only time she can get me to listen to her. I'm starving for news."

"Well news is not allowed. You know that, Dan."

Celeste, who has been in his room all morning, as she has been every morning for fifteen years (with the exception of 2020 and 2021, when the world screeched to a stop due to Covid), says, "It isn't politics or religion, just a human interest story, so I thought it would be all right, FN."

"Political opinions are divisive, C. Even human interest stories can start fights," says FN. "We're short-staffed, can't have any problems with the residents. So no news, no politics. Per the big boss, per Moiselle."

C stiffens. "The first amendment of the Constitution gives my Dad the right to his dumb opinions on the news. I am willing to defy oppressionary dictators, like Moiselle, in order for the old man to hear some basic news stories. Would give him such joy."

Celeste fluffs her father's pillows and jabbers at him, ignoring FN's warnings not to talk news. C goes on. "Now they are thinking that Titan sub might be jammed on debris, can't float up. Not much oxygen left. A man and his nineteen year old son are on board. Father made his son go with him. Can you imagine how that father feels knowing he's probably killed his kid?"

Well. The air in the room definitely changes. Other than that, no response.

"Daddy?"

C quickly realizes she is stepping into an emotional minefield. *Uh oh, go back to the silent treatment, please Daddy.* But no.

"You're always accusing me of something, yesterday you mentioned Vietnam, hard on everybody, you said, today it's that Titan disaster," Dan says.

C is near tears. "Daddy! I'm not . . . accusing you of anything, certainly not accusing you of . . . hurting Tad."

"I did not kill my son. He was a soldier. If he died, he died a soldier, not because of anything I did." Dan fumes.

"See? Moiselle was right," FN says. "Even human interest stories . . . causes fights . . ."

". . . Daddy, I'm not . . .," ". . . there is no possible way you can connect what happened on the Titan to what happened to Tad." C defends herself. FN defends C.

Dan nips this conversation in the bud.

"FN, fuck off. Tad is not a human interest story. He was my son. My heart. And C. Subconsciously you are connecting the Titan story to me and Tad . . . you believe I killed your brother? Cause I made him go to Vietnam. That's why you brought up the sub story. To get at me. Just shut up. Please."

Her heart stops. *Breathe.* "Good God. You are the worst Daddy ever, always flying off the handle, when all I'm doing is making conversation on relevant, contemporary topics that have nothing to do with politics, or my missing brother." Celeste jabs a pointy finger into the tip of her Dad's nose, half-kidding, half-not. "Bad Daddy. Bad Daddy."

Dan glowers. "Stop it, Celeste. You're seventy years old, not a baby. I wish I was dead, mostly because of you bringing up Tad all the time. You want me to feel remorse. He's the reason I shot Wayne. The reason I leashed Corrie to the piano. The reason I ended up in jail twenty years ago. The reason I fought with Buck that last night. He's the reason I want to meet God, to tell Him what He did to me, what He caused me to do to other people. I feel all the fucking remorse you could ever want me to feel, C. I could have been better to you if you didn't punish me all the damn time over Tad."

Hurt and embarrassed, C retreats to the safety of the couch. She glances at FN. FN's looking at the floor, embarrassed as well.

Dan knows he's shown his ass and revealed his weak spot. Retreats as well. "Don't you two get it? Why I wish I was dead. It's simple. I wake up every morning fighting a great disappointment. (cough, hack, spit) (hark, hack, grumph, kakakaka, spit)."

"Me," says C. *So sure it's me,* she thinks.

"No," Dan says, "you're way down on my list of disappointments, C. I just hate living. I hate being old. I never get sick. Why not? I'm ninety-five. I should at least have prostate cancer by now. My daily ritual is boring as hell. No stimulation. Hello world. Blah. Blah. Ninety-five years old. Blah. Joe Biden is president."

"In that context, stop it, Dan," FN says. "Joe Biden begets opinions. What did I just tell you?"

"Joe Biden might be a perfectly wonderful president. I wouldn't know. If the paramedics didn't ask 'who is the president' every time someone falls down, goes boom in this place, I wouldn't even know that Joe Biden is president. Hell, we don't even hear if a tornado is coming."

"We tell you if a tornado is coming, Dan," FN assures him.

Dan. "I wanna hear it from the weatherman. From Pete Delkus. Not you." (wheeze, relax)

"Well, I won't be telling you any more news, Daddy," C snaps.

He softens. "C, I shouldn't have to lie in this bed uninformed and ignorant. Not all news will be painful to hear. Not all news will make me mad."

"Agreed, everyone should be allowed to hear the news," C concedes.

"You can use your phone to go down all the rabbit holes you want," FN says. "Mr. Briggs, for example, knows how to use his phone. He can show you how. Then you two can watch all the conspiracy theories you want online."

Dan asseverates with amazing and exemplary lucidity for his age, in spite of the F's and S's, and the wheezing. "Waking up in a retirement home that doesn't allow sensible discourse, forcing residents, like that weasel Mr. Briggs, to seek out suspicious news sources on dubious technology, is appalling."

Impressive.

FN repeats and inserts a new headline. "Mr. Briggs, who is coming to be your roommate, knows how to use his phone. I suggest you let him teach you."

The room grows dark and cold once again. "If Briggs is going to be my roommate, why will I continue to wake up every day?"

"To urinate," FN teases. "Hopefully in the toilet."

Furious, but resigned. "Briggs is going to be my roommate? Are you sure? Jesus Christ. C, you gotta stop this thing. I might as well shoot myself now."

Defeated, Dan lies on the bed, turns away.

Celeste to FN, "Dad has a past with Briggs."

"He's ninety-five, it's a small town," FN answers, "he probably has a past with a whole bunch of old people in here. Look, C, nobody wanted Dan to know. We were just gonna move the old guy in. I'm sorry I blurted it out. Two weeks I've worked here, even though he scares the hell outta me, I'm already tired that Dan threatens suicide every time he doesn't get his way. You know I'm supposed to report each incident of suicidal ideation, and I haven't been reporting it. Because he scares me. Because alot of old people say stupid things."

"That's just what he does to make everything all about him, FN. He threatens suicide."

Tensing up. "We just had a suicide in this place! With no warning.

The police were here for a week, we could get nothing else done. This is serious, C. So are you assuring me that your father isn't serious about suicide, and that I should not report it? There's more in my notes than just that . . . bullshit stuff you made me write down when you trained me, about an ankle bracelet, C. Is your father thinking of taking his life? And how likely is he to act on those thoughts? Does he have a plan and does he have the means to carry out his plan?"

"I honestly can't answer that, FN."

"I need to report it then."

"No."

C turns to her father and speaks in the chirpy tone that most annoys him. "I can answer this, though. Why you wake up, Daddy. You wake up for another opportunity to see the sun rise and set, Daddy. To appreciate yourself. You were a great war hero, and I'm proud of you. For killing Nazis."

Dan loves that the conversation includes him again. "I have questions regarding my . . . ta . . . tenure as a war hero. Whether it is deserved," Dan reveals, surprisingly.

C raises an eyebrow. This time FN adds the eye roll. Staggering reveal to both women, but at least the subject is no longer Briggs, or suicide, or the lack of First Amendment freedom. Or Tad.

Dan. Sitting up. Glad to be talking about himself, notes their undivided attention. "I have alot to regret. But I never expected the end of my love of all things 'war' or a questioning of my, let's face it, arrogant appraisal of myself as a soldier. I never expected to need to be forgiven for being a soldier. There's other people I harmed over the years. I want to apologize to them, so . . . so I can go to heaven."

C is suspicious, even stunned.

FN is shocked and suddenly more alert.

"We can talk about all this after FN leaves, Dad."

"I want to go to heaven, C."

C's head shakes like a dog sloughing off a gnat. "No, you don't. Just yesterday you were still talking about . . . well you know what you were talking about, probably not seriously, but may I remind you that what you were talking about is a mortal sin."

FN is more and more alarmed.

"Suicide," she says. She knows.

Dan goes on. "I want to be in heaven with your mother."

"No, you don't, Daddy."

"I do. I loved her."

"Oh Daddy, I was there. I was always there. You two fought all the time. She hated you and you hated her. And you both hated me. But don't worry. Like all good Christians who completely ignore all of the commandments, you're going to heaven. You're a war hero. And the only person I know of who needs your apology is me. I also know I'll never get it."

Dan stands his ground. "Asking forgiveness late in life is not nuts, C."

Dan opens a book, puts on a pair of glasses. Reads aloud. "The significance of forgiveness at end of life is it can bring healing (hark, spit, cough) to the person who is doing the forgiving and to the person who is being forgiven. I plan on asking your forgiveness, C. On my birthday."

C chaws. She is a chewer, not gum, not tobacco, but inside her mouth, her cheek. C chaws when she is whipped. She chaws when she is filled with hate. The truth is, in this dysfunctional relationship, C chaws when she sees any faux spiritual development taking place in her father's soul. She can't trust it. It moves her. It scares her. It fools her. Celeste does not enjoy her father's decline into old-aged insecurity, for the most part, though he'll wager that she hopes to get the better of him at some point. There is no 'fun' in their family dysfunction.

FN, notebook and pencil in hand, begrudgingly asks. "Again. Is your father thinking of taking his life? How likely is he to act on those thoughts? Does he have a plan and does he have the means to carry out his plan?"

"I'm right here, FN," Dan says. "There's a pistol under my pillow and a bottle of Ativan in my dresser. You draw your own conclusions."

FN snaps the notebook shut, drops the pencil, pushes him aside, searches the dresser for Ativan, and under the pillow for a gun. Nothing. As phantom as the ankle bracelet. "You're just blowing smoke, Dan. Figures."

CHAPTER 4
No easy way out

No FN, but Dan's hungry. Dan and C's roll to breakfast of a morning is stopped by a loud commotion in the main hallway.

It's Briggs, visibly upset. He takes one look at the wheelchair-bound Dan and immediately assumes more of a disability than he actually has. He howls an expletive in Dan's direction, then bangs his cane on the wall. Tosses his walker so hard that the little tennis balls fall off the wheels. An aide from the staff comes running to assist, rescues the fallen walker and returns it to Briggs before he topples. In a loud, raspy voice, the old man wails. "I know, woman. I know I have to be moved. But that man's an ass and I do not want to live with him."

"Daddy," C whispers to her father. "obviously Mr. Briggs doesn't want to live with you either."

Dan struggles a bit, but manages to lift himself halfway out of the wheelchair, and asks, "They're moving you today, Briggs?"

"Looks like it."

"Well, stand your ground. I didn't ask them to move you. I'm against it, too. Or calm your old ass down. I only have a couple of weeks to live. Then you'll have the room, and my great picture window, to yourself. C gets the Tempur-Pedic."

Briggs does calm down.

Dan's arms quiver, he winces with some pain, and slowly lowers himself to the more comfortable seating position. "C, roommate or not, he's just a fly in the ointment of my old age, just like he was when we were young."

When the gurney bearing his bags passes by, Briggs realizes he is in a situation akin to being held captive, and bursts into actual tears.

Dan can't imagine why Briggs would be the one crying.

"Jesus, I'm not that bad, Briggs."

Dan and C wait while Briggs passes, either out of consideration for him or because he has the right-of-way.

Briggs moves around the wheelchair. Taunts. "You are wife-beating trash, Dan Kellar."

Dan orders C to push his wheelchair out in front of Briggs. Says. "Briggs, I'm gonna let that remark go, because I understand you have to lie. I know all about your affair with my Corrie. And you know I have the right to kill you in your sleep. Which I will do once you move into my room."

Briggs smirks. "She loved me, hated you. And you beat her."

Dan shot back. "I never beat her. I restrained her. Everybody knows that lying is a common trait that goes along with adultery, and you committed that sin often enough, with my wife."

C is embarrassed. "That affair was sixty years ago, Daddy. Let it go." Then she adds, "I'm sorry, Mr. Briggs. My father is out of line bringing up the long ago past."

"Not long ago, C. Remember how my brain works. I remember every day of my life like it was yesterday. Nobody has a brain like mine. And I never beat my wife, Briggs. Liar, liar, pants on fire," Dan says.

Dan glares at his traitorous daughter. "I bet it's you asked them to move Briggs in with me. To punish me."

He throws his arms up to signal to Briggs, C, and the laughing staff, that he intends to give up, to accept his fate.

C intervenes. "You know you two can be roommates peaceably, Briggs, Dad, you two can do it."

Briggs nods, but holds his ground, stands tall, hovers over Dan in his wheelchair. "I miss your wife. Best lay I ever had."

Dan responds to this insult with a flurry of prickly fury sounds. Briggs spits in Dan's face. "That's from Corrie, from the grave."

C gets in the middle of the two baby men. "Quit acting like white trash, both of you. You two WILL live together in peace, do you hear me?"

Briggs doubles up his fist and bonks Dan square on the top of his head, spits on him again, rubs the spittle into Dan's scalp with his knuckles.

"You will NOT spit on my father, do you hear me, you bloated piece of shit?" C pummels Briggs in the chest, then backs away, fists raised.

From his wheelchair Dan gives Briggs' knees a thwack, then another square on the nose. Briggs retaliates, pulls Dan out of his wheelchair and onto the floor, balls up his fist, smacks Dan on the right side of his head. Dan rises to the occasion and the two men bitch slap it out, both lying on the ground like kittens pawing at each other. C kneels down, vainly attempting to separate them.

It's quite the sight. From the floor, C commiserates with the amused staff. Moiselle and most of the kitchen staff hear the ruckus and barrel out of their workplaces to the hall. They head for the old men, but C stops them in their path.

Says, from the floor. "Two old white men mired down with eccentric personality disorders probably shouldn't live together, y'all. Can anything be done?"

"We have our orders, sorry," Mo says.

Dan yelps. "Briggs, you wee, small, stupid, dumb prick, shit, asshole, dick cunt, that hurt. Get me out of here, C."

She rises to her feet. Hauls her father off.

It takes three burly guys, and a reprimand from Moiselle to settle Briggs down. Mo puts the walker back together. He threatens, but Mo takes the cane from Briggs' frail, transparent hands. Briggs collapses in a puddle of tears.

Mo gets old man Briggs back on his feet.

"We'll try moving you again in a week," she orders.

Briggs smiles. "Grateful to you, Mo. But ain't there somethin' you can do to stop this madness?"

"Ain't no easy way out, Briggs. You asked for this a long time ago," Dan taunts.

Dan keeps rolling down the hall, gloats. Says. "I can turn this into a positive, C. I've got two bullets, and one of them can be for Briggs."

Win. Win. For today.

CHAPTER 5
. . . Spurred us on . . .

Breakfast over and crisis averted. Back to the room, back to the comfort of the Tempur-Pedic.

FN is now one hour and forty five minutes late. Dan's short fuse ignites. Her fourth day of tardiness clearly demonstrates her unacceptable lack of enthusiasm for rules. No big deal had Briggs not happened. Dan needs to take his frustration with Briggs out on someone. Dan's bad disposition is rooted in narcissism, but look out, world, on days when his narcissism combines with 'sinister'.

Narcissinister. Such a great word he's made up, Dan thinks. He's the best word maker-upper in the world.

He waits until the sun has set and all is quiet inside the RRC. Then FN catches him red-handed, smashing glass bottles on the concrete walkway. She confronts him. He responds that he is obviously hoping she would trip and land on the edge of a bottle, and bleed out until death.

He has no problem stating that FN "should be dead in retribution for your tardiness."

Rattled by the confrontation, FN tattles to Moiselle, who writes up the activity as a one-off "mishap," then reprimands her. "It's only your second week on the job. You have four tardies."

"This proves the stress level I am experiencing," FN argues.

"Let it go, kid. Be on time or you're fired."

So FN goes over Moiselle's head. She reports her concerns to the Administrator, a fifty-something year old bleached blonde with long fingernails and false eyelashes. She warns that Dan exhibits signs of both active and repressed anger that could escalate into more dangerous behaviors. After all, it's only her second week on the job, and she already has three tardies to prove the stress level she's reached. "I feel like I'm going to get fired for being late, but I'm late because of the stress." The Administrator states that she can hardly replace her. "There is no staff anywhere willing to be hired. We lost so many during the Pandemic and they are not willing to come back to work." The Administrator agrees to call Dan and Celeste into her office for a mild reprimand. "Just go back to work, FN, and try not to be late."

After the condescending reprimand Dan gets from Mo and the Administrator ("You're old, just stay in your bed, quit causing trouble."), Dan furiously lashes out at FN with a ninety-five-year old version of primal rage. "I choose my actions. I choose! If I want to kill, I kill. If I want to allow you to live, I will allow you to live. But you will not be late again."

"I'm quitting," FN says.

"NO! NO. I didn't mean it. I love you, you're the best nurse I've ever had," Dan answers. "I won't try to kill you again, I promise. Please do not quit."

She's late the next day, and stops first at the Administrator's Office to report him again.

The Administrator reiterates that Dan is just an old man with dementia. "Yes, he yells. He's reliving his glory days, experiencing delusions of grandeur, seeing things that are not there, making up shit, threatening shit. But Dan is harmless. He just thinks he's God. And that's not causing any harm."

The Administrator discounts the entire situation as amusing, but nevertheless uses it as an opportunity to bring in a few highly-paid consultants from Dallas, two of whom she sleeps with whenever they're in town.

A social worker appears in Dan's room the following day. Several more appear on a regular basis over the next week, to counsel Dan on controlling his anger, in preparation for the inevitable arrival of Dan's roommate.

"Think before you speak." . . . *Eff you*, Dan thinks each time a social worker begins the drill, smiling to himself, then starting in, "I still remember the first time I ever clearly understood why young people love to use that word "fuck" so much. It was on a bus, and . . . "

"We don't need another one of your stories, Dan. Now focus," one of the social workers says, nipping his tale in the bud. "Once you're calm, express your concerns." . . . *Calm, you say? That ain't gonna happen until I'm dead, or you're dead, asshole*, he thinks. Out loud he says, "I am nothing without my stories." So calm, so sweet.

"I'm sure your stories are very interesting," the therapist said, with a fake smile, "but don't you think you should get some exercise instead of telling your stories all the time?" . . . *Eff you.*

"Take a timeout." . . . *and do what? Eff . . .*

"Identify possible solutions." . . . *Hmmmm. F . . .*

"Stick with 'I' statements." . . . *I always do . . . the pronouns everybody likes to talk about these days, well mine are "me, myself and I."*

"Don't hold a grudge." . . . *but grudges are so much fun.*

"Use humor to release tension." *And. Fuck. You. There! Tension released. Any more from you, jerkoff? Good, thank you. Goodbye.*

"This was very helpful, really. Thank you." Dan lies each time.

Several social workers ultimately refuse to work with him, but before they fire him as a client, each one diagnoses him with the go-to 'God complex', and each meets with Celeste, along with the Administrator, to inform C of their diagnosis.

"Celeste, your father has a God complex, which is an unshakable belief characterized by consistently inflated feelings of personal ability, privilege, or infallibility. He is highly dogmatic in his views, which means that your father speaks of his personal opinions as though he is always right."

Celeste laughs until she cries at these meetings.

"Well, he does think he is always right," C giggles.

"He needs a purpose, something to do," the last social worker suggests. "Okay," Celeste says. "I'll give him a project. He wants to die. Time to write an obituary."

C waits for the suicidal ideation speech.

But it doesn't come, so C accuses the social worker of not caring whether Dan lives or dies. "He's old, yes. And unpleasant. But, I suspect you are sorely overworked, and that you really don't care," she says. That's not entirely true, though. Lethargy, tiredness, all left over from Covid, created staff shortages, which created overwork. The COVID-19 pandemic pushed the small town nursing home staff beyond their ability to cope. The RRC residents, many with memory issues, were in lockdown. Isolated, lonely, fearful and listening to all kinds of news reports and conspiracy theories on their televisions (back when it was okay to watch television at the RRC), lockdown proved to be hell. From the daily news, they realized that they, nursing home residents, were the highest of the high-risk groups, the most likely to die, and die all alone, from Covid. 160,000 lives lost in the nursing homes, at least, to say nothing of the numbers of staff endangered by Covid. The medical system prioritized hospitals over nursing homes, so the RRC staff nervously attended the vulnerable without adequate protective clothing or proper equipment. Finally, most were told to stay home. With so few to care for so many, the residents often experienced delirium, failure to thrive, and rapid onset of dementia. Sometimes there was no one to help the very old folks with food. Celeste was forbidden to visit the RRC for almost two years. She worried constantly about her father starving. Worried about his angry episodes, his hallucinations. Dan lost a lot of weight, but managed to survive, occupying himself with identifying sounds, learning the lyrics to boomer songs that reminded him of better years, and keeping company with a make-believe SWAT team that tried to capture and kill him on a regular basis. Most important, Dan was fine alone. But the pandemic left a lasting mark on everyone else.

Lockdown was a hard time, but it finally ended. One stormy Friday morning, soon after Celeste and others were allowed back into the RRC, she rolled her Dad to breakfast and found herself shocked at what she saw. The slow, shuffling oldtimers seemed so much older, barely able to move their Zimmers and Rollators.

And nobody spoke among the congested hallways. It was so oddly quiet that C shivered. It was as if Covid still dominated everyone's ability to interact with other people.

But the frightening truth came when memory-impaired Mrs. Feiner, finally free to come out of her room, mistakenly rolled into Shell Jurgens' room during the night. Always a light sleeper, Shell heard a soft noise, sat up and noticed an advancing shadow. Terrified, she grabbed a vase and beat Mrs. Feiner to a pulp, then ran into the foyer screaming.

Of course, chaos ensued. Sirens, alarm bells, staff running up and down halls.

Dan and all the other mobile residents came out in their nightwear and crammed their walkers into the doorway of Shell's private room. The police set up barricades, but everyone could still see what was going on.

Mrs. Feiner was slumped over in her wheelchair, head drooping down to her chest, bloody slashes and gaps all over her head.

Paramedics gently, expertly moved her to the floor, and did their best to resuscitate the poor, beaten woman. To no avail.

Nobody slept after that. Shaky residents walked the halls, scared, angry. Moiselle went into the kitchen and made cocoa for everyone. A resident named Felicia suggested they all settle down together in the common area and watch a program. On television. Confused residents, schedules undone, and nobody in charge except Mo, who tried in vain to find a program that nobody would argue over. She finally found an old black and white cop show on MeTV programming. The peace was only momentary, though. Someone screamed from the back of the room that she couldn't hear, others simply spoke, or yelled to the TV characters, commiserating with their criminal dilemmas, still others shouted to turn the volume up (or down). Everyone descended into arguing, crying, yelling, name-calling and hitting.

Moiselle had no choice but to turn the television completely off, and go back to the 'no-TV' rules.

"We're too short staffed to police you guys, keep you safe, so no television unless I'm there to supervise it," Mo explained.

"We want our own remotes back," Briggs said.

Mr. Briggs took Mo aside and chastised her - that the remotes in all the private rooms had been absconded for no reason, simply in order to facilitate Mo's stupid 'no news watching' rules.

"All we have is this one public television," Briggs said. "Moiselle, we should all have the right to watch whatever we want to watch in the privacy of our own rooms. Then there would be no fighting."

Mo had removed all the remotes shortly after three residents scuffled over Felicia's personal television, knocking it to the floor.

One had threatened to break it over another's head. A third resident rummaged through Felicia's kitchen drawers, going for a kitchen knife. The Police were called.

"No," Mo answered, then became distracted by two angry old ladies pulling each other's hair. "You two, stand here with me and don't move." She held each one by the scruff of the neck and turned back to Briggs. "This is why we can't get staff to work for longer than two weeks. You remember what happened in Felicia's room. You were in the big middle of it."

Briggs stated his intention to file a lawsuit against Mo for taking away his rights.

Mo's lower lip quivered, but before she could burst into tears, a policeman informed her that the Mrs. Feiner had died.

Mo let go of her two angry charges. "Go to bed, everyone. Mrs. Feiner is dead."

Dan, like all the residents and staff, was shaken to the core. He put his daughter's mind at ease.

"I have a gun under my pillow, C. I feel safe."

C pats his hand. She had often worried that her old Dad might get confused and find himself entering the wrong room. But . . .

Her little warrior Daddy believes he has a gun under his pillow. How sweet.

A year later, not so sweet.

CHAPTER 6

. . . Another sleepy, dusty, Delta day . . .

The outcome of the investigation into Mrs. Feiner's death was in Shell's favor. The determination was that Mrs. Feiner was an intruder. Shell had been asleep, woke up to an intruder. In a word, self-defense. But, even exonerated, a year later Shell hadn't gotten over what she'd done. She couldn't sleep, often walked aimlessly around the grounds at night. Dan ran into her a few times during his midnight musings. In fact, she interrupted his favorite kind of alone time, and he wondered how he could get his porch back. But she flipped her hair, batted her eyelashes . . .

. . . And Dan thought, well, for a ninety-two-year old, she was cute. He went for it, so to speak.

So, a year after Mrs. Feiner died, Shell secretly took to spending nights in Dan's room. (Briggs, most conveniently, had taken to sleeping elsewhere, who knows where?)She slept after dinner until about midnight, then she would shower and dress, put a little makeup on, and wait. About 1:00 a.m., on his way back from his treasured alone time on the porch, Dan would tap oh, so lightly on her door, then roll back to his room and get into bed. A few minutes later she'd knock and enter. There may have been a little clumsy fondling, not much. Mostly, he soothed her fears, and held her when she cried. And she listened to his stories.

Every night was different with Shell because she was curious about everything, still loved life, and adored Dan. "Tell me about your wife. How did you meet her? How did she die?" "Did you ever do anything you regretted?" "Do you believe in God?" "Do you love me?" "What do you think happened to your son?" "What is your daughter like?" "I want every detail of your life." "What is your happiest memory?"

"I'll tell you about my second happiest memory. It was a hot Saturday morning. July, 1967. Corrie and I were still reeling from the news about Tad being missing in action; we were living in a permanent fog of grief. But on that Saturday morning I almost felt normal, puttered around the house, did some 'honey-do's' from Corrie's list. She was scrubbing the kitchen floor. The door to Celeste's bedroom was cracked just a little and I could see her, sixteen or seventeen then, beautiful girl. She was holding a hairbrush in her hand, like a microphone, looking in the mirror, singing. Over and over, same song. Her little '45 player was on repeat so she could learn all the verses. ' . . . another sleepy, dusty delta day . . . "

"Ode to Billie Joe!" Shell knew the song. Giggling like schoolchildren, they sang together, all the words they could come up with.

If the two of them had been younger, could dream of sixty years ahead together, they would say they fell in love that night, singing that song. Something changed that night, at least for Shell. She crept back to her room before the sun came up, as she had been doing for months, and believed that no one was the wiser. And she was ready to make their relationship public news.

And then one night she knocked, and Briggs answered the door. Dan hadn't warned her that a roommate had moved into his room. Shell pretended she was lost, and said she was looking for Felicia's room. Briggs pointed her in the right direction. Of course, it was the wrong direction for Shell. And for Dan. Shell refused to come back into Dan's room with another man there. He tried to get her to reconsider. Shy, sweet, modest, decent Shell. This just wasn't done. She just stopped coming.

Dan missed her a little. But he'd found he could handle a life when one day runs into the next, and the nights are just plain dark. But Shell couldn't. She couldn't face the intense loneliness of old age. She tried for a whole week after their breakup.

The EMTs found a note that she left for Dan on the night she took her own life. They wrapped her up, put her on the gurney about seven a.m., rolled her down the halls to the parking lot. FN was already out there sashaying. They gave her the note. She ran in to give it to Dan.

He read the letter by the morning light, at his picture window. Briggs was still snoring away.

"I am sorry to miss your birthday party, my darling Dan. I hope you have a wonderful one-hundredth birthday. Thank you for you. For singing with me that way, that night, the greatest night of my life. See you on the other side!"

She had managed to hoard her nightly sleeping pills.

The residents and staff, even the Rupert police, were devastated by Shell's end. But Dan, more stubborn than ever, was determined to stuff his grief. He blamed Briggs for Shell's suicide. He focused more on vexations—FN's tardiness, and his irritation watching her out there flirting with Jimmy—Jimmy, whom he had known for seventy years! That guy was too old for her, Dan would judge, not right for her, downright bad for her, and Dan knew he would have to intervene. Breaking up yet another couple would make him feel better, even though it might make collateral damage of Jimmy, the little boy he had once loved, the wounded warrior who had already been through so much. Dan didn't care. He was always more wounded than the next guy.

Dan's need to screw with FN, since he couldn't screw with Briggs, would win the day. Besides, Dan Kellar believed that, except for killing Nazis, and saving Corrie, and maybe shooting Wayne that night in 1978, he really never had any long-lasting impact on anyone else's life.

CHAPTER 7
. . . Ride a painted pony . . .

Dan wakes up thinking about a horrible possibility—Celeste writing his obituary.

His obituary? Where should he start? He's a local icon, always the honored guest of the Veteran's Day parade. He is the best storyteller in the state, always ready for a party, always wears his trademark 1970s crimson-colored velvet dinner jacket, adorned with leather trim.

All-American hero that he was, Dan killed Nazis; in fact, rescued Corrie from Nazis. Showed her the American Dream (she hated it, hated him). Stood up for the flag in all situations (shot a civilian in the back because he dodged the draft). Owned his own business (until he got drunk and accidentally burned it down). Defended his belief that women didn't belong in the military (shot out the windows of the Army Recruiting Center and tried to kill the Sergeant).

Opined publicly on local current events (loud drunk). Great dancer. Considered himself to be Rupert's historian. Wanted nothing to change. Became a Christian late in life. Very late in life.

Dan can hardly wait to get started. He dismisses C, plants himself at his little desk, and begins to write. Sentence after sentence, and then more sentences. And joy to the world! Briggs is out for the day, so anytime Dan has to pee, he opens the picture window, pushes out the screen, and lets her rip. All day and all evening, not stopping for lunch, barely eating dinner.

Until it's midnight. Time for wee-hour musings. Dan puts his pen and a fresh piece of paper in his pocket. One of the evening staff rolls him out onto the porch (they don't trust him to navigate alone). And tonight's midnight musings reveal an acceptable new assessment of himself. War hero of three wars. Father. Rescuer. Defender of the American way. Public speaker. Businessman. Dancer.

Early the next morning when Dan's still asleep C comes snooping around. Finds the obituary project is mostly blank, a line here, one there. A few lines for ninety-five years.

Then she spies something titled "Manifesto." "Who I am and Why I am Here." *Dear God*, C whispers. Slang for *"What the fuck is he writing about now?"*

So she settles in to read, occasionally looking over at Dan to check for signs of impendent wakefulness. In the manifesto, Dan whines about "white entitlement," which, as he points out on page 1, has long been the source of contentious debate, and seems to provide the manifesto a basis in necessity. Also on page 1, Dan points out that since about age sixty he has been personally referred to as "entitled." In a derogatory sense. Generally pointed out by Celeste. The daughter who hates him.

Celeste rolls her eyes, eye-roller that she is.

Checks Dan who's still snoring softly, then reads on.

How? He is white. Conservative. Male. Christian.

All signs of privilege.

"That is all it takes to be labelled in this country," he writes.

"But being old and cooped up in an old folks' home doesn't feel like much of a privilege to me. If I was ever entitled, I'm experiencing a different end of the stick now. Saddled with an unremarkable daughter who never leaves me alone."

Celeste sits on the edge of her Dad's bed, waits for him to wake up.

When he does, she puts both hands on his shoulders, leans in close to his face.

"Your obituary is paltry."

"I don't need to list my sins for the general public," Dan says. "If people are really interested in my terrible crimes, they can read the old microfilm at the library. Now get out of my face."

"And I read your fucking awful manifesto."

C's face becomes a storm of hateful expressions as she rolls her father to the dining room. "I know I'll never get an apology from you, Dad, for any of the things you did. But I'll have the last laugh. I swear to God, Daddy, the minute you die I'm editing your obituary and getting myself married to someone you hate."

"You? Marrying? Is it a man of color?" Dan asks.

"It's just someone you hate."

"I don't hate anyone. I don't even hate Japs anymore," Dan says through a mouthful of bacon.

"Oh good grief, your whole life is about hate."

Dan swallows in momentary defeat. C is somewhat right. "Once upon a time I hated who the government told me to hate. Nazis. Japs. Charlie. Arabs. Draft dodgers. But if I raised you to hate anyone of color, C, if I raised you to be racist, well God forbid, I didn't mean to. The Americans I've hated were white. I have never hated an American of color. Never. You can marry anyone you want, you can marry any color you want, you can marry anyone . . . except Wayne Herd, that draft dodging, unAmerican mother trucker, who deserved to be shot. And I think your mother slept with him."

"She did not sleep with him. You made up a lie because you do hate him. If you really want to go to heaven, you need to apologize to him in person. Of course, he refuses to come to your birthday party. I already asked him."

"I did not ask you to invite him to my party."

"Too bad. I'm going to invite who I want. If you are really going to die that day, it will be my party, too. And why not invite him? You should apologize to him. After all, you shot the man IN THE BACK. And I am going to make sure it's in your obituary."

For a brief moment, Dan allows himself to contemplate C's utter and apparent hatred of him. But he quickly moves on. Subtle reminder to her that she isn't all that significant, Dan says, "Apology accepted. Let's not talk anymore today. Pass the bacon."

"I did not fucking apologize."

"I'm not talking anymore today, C. Get ready and go on. You'll be late for wherever you go. School?"

C's jaw quivers with rage. She knows that Dan finds enjoyment in pretending to be senile when it suits him. It's something he's done for decades. She knows when he is acting. He finds as much enjoyment in fucking with her as he does in having breakfast, pouring himself another cup of coffee, buttering a biscuit, eating heartily, watching his pathetic daughter purse her lips and hold back tears. "Go on to school, honey," Dan adds, to further torment her. "I'll be all right by myself today. Lunch will be a sandwich and chips. I can manage. I'll have only one cigarette, I promise. We'll talk more when you come home from school."

C bursts into tears.

Dan chews. Stares at her, lucid as ever.

"Wayne Herd, the man I shot, won't come to my party. Why the hell not?"

"Stop making me feel stupid, Daddy."

"Ask him if you want. I would love nothing better than to apologize to Wayne Herd. I lived in the kingdom of darkness, C. Before I found the Lord, I was grieving, grieving over Tad. I shot Wayne over Tad. I blew out the windows of the Army Recruiting Center back in ought-three because of Tad."

"That's your story now," Celeste answers.

"It's the truth. I'm a changed man. Born again. Which changes the story. I am justified. Declared righteous. Sanctified. Set free from sin's penalty; Set free from sin's power. These things I can never lose. Go ahead, invite that asshole to my party. Didn't you say Jimmy's gonna show up for it?"

"Yep."

"Thank God I don't owe him an apology for anything."

CHAPTER 8
Born to wave the flag

Jimmy

Nobody who graduated from Rupert High School in 1967 would have believed that their classmate, Jimmy Ramirez, would still be alive fifty-five years later. Everyone remembered Jimmy as the blindly patriotic 'poor kid who couldn't wait to go to war' for his country. After graduating, their beloved Jimmy hit the battlefield in Vietnam, where everyone expected him to insist on dying as soon as possible, gloriously.

It was a few years before the government finally acknowledged the horrific effects Jimmy suffered in that war. Post-Traumatic-Stress-Disorder, a mental health condition that didn't kill men's bodies; it killed their minds. When the government finally decided to take proper care of Jimmy, Rupert citizens considered him their "sweet embarrassment."

This new version of Jimmy Ramirez lasted for five decades.

Jimmy graduated from high school and married his high school sweetheart the same weekend. They spent three weeks married before he shipped out.

Their wedding was simple and inexpensive—cakes, nuts, punch, and a pelting of rice. They drove away in an old junkyard Dodge Dart with push button transmission, cans tied to the rear, "Just Married" painted on the back window. Sweet, all-American kids.

They drove six hours to their honeymoon destination in San Antonio. They visited the Alamo three times in one week, and made love every single night. What with all that vigorous honeymoon activity, Sarah had hoped she would get pregnant so that when Jimmy came home from war, he would come home to a family. But that didn't happen.

He was gone only a few short months when Sarah's older brother picked her up in his brand new Dodge Coronet and took her on her first trip away from Rupert. They headed to Washington D.C., to an anti-war protest at the Lincoln Memorial. At least 100,000 people were there, more people than Sarah had ever seen or imagined in her life. It was heady stuff. Abbie Hoffman dazzled. Hundreds of protesters were arrested for various acts of civil disobedience. Sarah witnessed her government acting out against its own citizens; wrongly, she thought. By the end of the demonstration, she was hooked on flower power.

Sarah came back from the protest a changed woman, still Jimmy's soft-spoken high school sweetheart, but with a new perspective on the world. Now Sarah was committed to the burgeoning anti-war movement, while her husband remained a war monger—crazed, irrational, ill-tempered.

Because Jimmy told his new wife nothing about his war time experience, and Sarah didn't tell him about the shenanigans in D.C., their union became tenuous, uneasy, a violent fallout waiting to happen.

One afternoon, while he was laid up in the bed, clearly on the road to mental illness, Sarah set out to prove to Jimmy that, as a U.S. Soldier performing in the Vietnam conflict, he was on the wrong side of history.

At first, she tried to do it in the kindest way. She blamed his upbringing. Now, Sarah had always been on his side before, but he was not receptive to this new line of thinking. And the stakes were much higher than the choices they made during high school, like deciding should they work at McDonald's or Burger King; should they train in Kung Fu; should he wear a ruffled shirt to prom?

They had known each other since first grade, had walked to school together every day for twelve years. Sarah began her attempts to change Jimmy's perspective by analyzing those early walks to school.

She proclaimed that Jimmy, by the age of seven, had been brainwashed by television, newspapers, and childhood games that promoted racism, misogyny and isolation. Gunslinging. Cowboys v. Indians. Wyatt Earp. Maverick. Superman. Paladin. And of course, the American mantra that "Commies are bad."

Jimmy didn't believe he had been brainwashed. Not for a second. Jimmy loved his cap pistols in childhood. What little boy didn't? He certainly loved the empowerment he felt when he held his first real machine gun.

Now, some media and public opinion bundled all American soldiers serving in Vietnam into raging baby killers. But Jimmy was proud of defending, and being part of, the overwhelming majority of American soldiers who served with honor and decency in Vietnam. To be honorable and decent was a feat.

His war record would make his hero, Dan Keller, proud of him.

His brotherhood deserved better than to be spit upon and diminished by an American public that had no idea what that war was really like.

Like so many soldiers, Jimmy kept the war experience locked in his heart, never sharing the terrors he felt, or the horrors he saw.

Calmly, softly, but in all ignorance, Sarah said, "It is certainly not your fault, Jimmy. You were bred a killer. You, all alone, killed an entire tribe of Hostile Indians every day on the way to school with your little rifle, remember Jimmy? You were taught to love violence, to seek out enemies. And that asshole Dan Kellar was the worst influence of all, because he was your hero." Jimmy whipped around, a nasty curl on his lips. "Dan Kellar was like a second father to me!"

Now, Jimmy hardly saw himself, or even Dan Kellar, as racist. He didn't even know what the hell the word "misogynism" meant.

"Oh, did I not pronounce that correctly, Miss Priss? We were seven, and you sang the *Have Gun, Will Travel* theme song with me, hell, sometimes you were the damsel in distress, begging me to save you, sometimes you pointed out where the Indians were hiding. They were games, Sarah. Games. What boys did."

"Exactly my point, Jimmy."

Jimmy sensed that she was going to go further with her incriminations, though, to lump him in with a few bad apples who brought real shame to America, on to accusing him of committing real war crimes and outright murder in Nam. He aimed to nip that in the bud, but he ultimately grabbed her by the throat, slammed her against a wall, and screamed out at her, "I did not kill children. I did not kill women. I did not kill civilians, I DID NOT BECOME AN ANIMAL IN VIETNAM."

Jimmy cried, punched himself in the face over and over, slid down the wall. "Sarah, don't make me talk about the war. I can't. I was honorably discharged, isn't that proof enough who I am as a man and a soldier?"

Sarah backed down, tried to regroup. Softly. A little scared. "Of course you did not become an animal. I was just saying . . . the childhood games. They were wrong. Your influences were wrong."

Mistake. Jimmy stood up. Slammed Sarah against a wall, not once, not twice, but crazy.

"The only/slam thing wrong is that now/slam you cannot slip and refer to a Daniel Boone cap/slam as a coonskin cap. That's racist. The only/slam thing wrong is that our friends and enemies change all the time. Lucy goosy. The only problem/slam with me is that I fucking missed fighting in the greatest war!"

He let her go.

Sarah slid to the floor, crying, stunned, dizzy.

Jimmy kneeled, contrite. "You would have been proud of me if I'd killed Nazis."

She understood, of course. "Dan Kellar killed Nazis. This country did not send YOU out to kill Nazis," she whispered.

Jimmy knew they were done. Went to the fridge for a beer. Nothing in there.

He tore cabinets apart looking for something to swallow. Found some kind of brown liquor and swigged it down.

"And Japanese," he added. "Killing Nazis and Japanese was good, too. I grew up waiting for my fucking turn, Sarah. You should fucking be proud of me regardless of who I killed!"

"War is not black and white, Jimmy.

"It IS fucking black and white, Sarah."

"I don't believe in this war, Jimmy. I don't believe in any war, anywhere."

"Then you don't believe in America and you don't believe in me. Pack your bags. Get the fuck out of my house."

He never saw her again. Yes, he cried. He was devastated. Reduced to stereotype, everyone thought he might kill himself when she left. Everyone thought he would die of a drug overdose during the eighties.

Everyone thought he would be driving drunk and die in a car accident during the nineties. And certainly everyone thought he was going to stay crazy by 2000. An embarrassment, the 'sweet' part long gone.

And then, after 9/11, when another war started, sentiments changed, moods changed and once again Jimmy became Rupert's beloved, sad story. Townspeople helped him with food and booze. Sometimes people gave him jobs.

Jimmy slowly became accustomed to the intrusive imagery and reliving of conversations that had haunted his brain since his return from Vietnam fifty years earlier. By 2023 he could manage himself.

If only the contents of his consciousness were not so vivid, so sensory! He remembered events from the seventies as though they occurred just yesterday. He didn't fully understand the psychological notion of "triggers" but he had enough enforced therapy to know that "shame" was his biggest trigger. And for Jimmy, "shame" was feeling devalued. Sarah had devalued his service to this country, had made fun of his precious little-boyhood, over which he had no control.

People spit on him at airports after his return from Vietnam. Protestors called him names. PTSD set in, and Jimmy went from bad to worse, for awhile.

One day Jimmy woke up, and started to heal. He pronounced "Shame on Sarah. Shame on all of them."

When he got a call from Celeste in June 2023, Jimmy was renewed. Confident.

Had long ago honestly assessed himself and his life, accepted his past, forgiven himself for things he could not control. Gained a hard-earned new perspective about life.

"Haven't heard from you in awhile, C. Now before you start in on me, just remember that everything you think you know about me is based on the stories that everyone in Rupert has always told. I'm ever bit a war hero as much as Dan Kellar."

"If they only knew the truth, right, Jimmy?"

"Damn right, C. And I'm one-hundred percent pacifist now. Always was, in a way. It was only a toy cap gun I killed Indians with on the way to school."

Another crazy veteran.

With trepidation, Celeste invited him to her father's one-hundredth birthday party.

CHAPTER 9
Sweet dreams and flying machines. . . .

Jimmy

Jimmy stares a hollow-eyed stare at the old framed black and white photograph that he keeps on his makeshift nightstand, whether at the Porterfield or at his mobile home—The three young boys, Tad, Jimmy and Wayne, three little boys wearing their little play hats, the cowboy hat, the army hat, the coonskin cap.

All three hats are always on display on a table near his bed, like a shrine. The three hats represent their upbringing, their patriotism for their country, and their need to sacrifice for the greater good. In the summer of 2023, there is a Jimmy who is capable and kind, funny and smart. Capable Jimmy. He drives the DAV bus. Lives in a trailer that his lifelong friend, Wayne, bought for him, parked out in the blissful middle of nowhere. He takes a cute nurse named Della out for meals.

But there's another Jimmy, leftover from Nam. The one who sleeps hard, almost not waking up, with nightmares that he barely remembers. The other Jimmy hunts down Capable Jimmy, and haunts him with vaguely reconstructed thoughts that are just THERE on the edge of memory, but never fully realized in his waking hours. Maddening. Debilitating.

On a good night he dreams of another boyhood friend, Tad. Jimmy envisions the three little boys, Tad, Wayne, and of course, himself, roller skating all around the world-famous underground spas of Rupert's extravagant, and only, Porterfield Hotel. A childhood memory, around 1957, when life was perfect.

They swim in the pool and nap on the meticulously manicured lawn. They play cowboys and Indians in the Sky Room on the fourteenth floor by day, where the big bands played for posh parties and proms at night.

And on a bad night he dreams of fellow soldier, Tad Kellar. The never ending movie of the moment Jimmy cracked replays in his dreams. The moment when Tad Kellar fell from a fiery Huey and disappeared forever, never to be found. He jolts awake, reaches for the bottle, any bottle, misses work, doesn't shower. Drugs himself to sleep, praying for the good dreams to come, or better yet, no dreams. Just. Sleep. Sleeps hard again . . . The dreams playing out like in a movie . . .

EXT. JUNGLE CLEARING—NIGHT

The signature THWUMP THWUMP of a Cobra helicopter.

JIMMY AT twenty, in full jungle gear clutching his M16, runs as fast as he can towards the distant Cobra that is already taking off. A yellow Labrador DOG on his heels.

INT. HELICOPTER—DAY

The thunderous sound continues overhead.
In the chaos, no one inside the helicopter sees Jimmy running towards them.

EXT. JUNGLE CLEARING—DAY

Jimmy and the yellow dog are left behind.
Soon the helicopter is high in the sky.
The whimpering, hungry dog looks to Jimmy for help.
Jimmy gives the dog a pat and feeds her something from his pocket.
Jimmy and the dog then run for cover in the jungle.
This area is crawling with shadow . . . vapors of the enemy.
Jimmy fires slowly and deliberately, sweeping his field of vision, but with no clear target.
He runs deeper inside the jungle, to hide. *A loud EXPLOSION.*
He looks to the sky—
The Cobra is flailing, but still flying, though twisting, and turning.
A U.S. SOLDIER falls from the Cobra. Jimmy RUNS to the edge of the jungle.

Tad?

The falling soldier, for a moment, is the only being in the world.

And then the world stops.

A silent landing onto the earth; the soldier's body makes a grisly BOUNCE.

Jimmy is SCREAMING. TAD!!!!

GUNFIRE erupts. Land to air and vice versa, everywhere.

Jimmy's concussed by an EXPLOSION but retreats back into the jungle. Sees—

The fiery CRASH to earth of the flailing Cobra.

Ears ringing.

Blasting pain in his brain.

Chattering NVA.

From his hiding place in the jungle, Jimmy sees the NVA descend on the body of the U.S. Soldier. Tad.

When he wakes up, alone in his trailer, he wakes up as *other Jimmy*, who has taken over his reality. No longer safe inside his mobile home on the outskirts of Rupert, other Jimmy believes he huddles in the corner of a room on the fourth floor of the condemned Porterfield Hotel where he hid himself away right after 9/11, long after a series of heartaches—first losing his wife, then a year later losing his job as a fireman, and two years later facing life on the streets. A few nights in jail here and there. Drugs. Alcohol. Somehow during the recurring dream of the falling soldier's body, Jimmy's sleeping body thrusts itself into the corner of that long-ago room where he'd hidden away, safe there because he was invisible to the outside world, in the condemned, empty, abandoned hotel that nobody took care of, that nobody wanted.

Even in this state, Jimmy seeks protection, knows to ask . . . *Why do we dream what we dream*, and how does the body protect itself during a dream?

He knows it is the lingering effects of PTSD. He knows he will never control waking up in different locations, in different decades. The multi-layers of sensory information causes his jangled mind to react—he is also tortured by remembering random things—small things like a girl soldier he watched get off of a bus, or a license plate on a motorbike zooming past him, or big things like finding his father's dead body on the front lawn of his childhood home.

Agony caused by the demons of his experience at war.

Was it real? Or was it a dream? Fuck. Medical science was constantly changing, the law belatedly changing behind it. The law so slowly caught up with Jimmy's particular medical condition that for decades he was not considered "fully disabled." Jimmy lived in a crack between law and medicine.

In order to upgrade his payout every month, Jimmy participated in a VA experiment that used virtual reality to look inside the mind of a person with PTSD. The experiment's creators put Jimmy on a bus and surrounded him with the sights and sounds seen and heard by a person with extreme mental tensions. Instead of helping Jimmy better understand and manage his condition, the experiment created visual hallucinations based on real war experiences Jimmy had provided forty years earlier, upon his return from Vietnam. The experiment worked to reinforce his horrible memories and keep them in real time, so that every day, at any time or anyplace, the least little trigger caused Jimmy to remember the worst episodes of the Vietnam war. In living color. For science. For money.

And, as his custom, before he tries to sleep, in his trailer, in June of 2023, knowing he has to get up and drive the DAV van, Jimmy stares at the old photograph - the one with the three hats, and he tries something new...

. . . Staying awake. Remembering. On purpose. In order to control the story. To heal.

CHAPTER 10
Excitations

With only a week to go, and it may be grudgingly, but the retirement home staff is abuzz planning the centenarian birthday celebration for it's chief ninety-five-year-old curmudgeon. Moiselle asks a few of the retirement home residents (the respected, the virtuous), along with the beloved eighty-five-year-old floosies (Delene, Christine and Felicia), to form a committee to help her plan.

Celeste is called in to consult.

Mo organizes an afternoon meeting with coffee and donuts, suggests displaying pictures at the party to show off everything Dan has done and enjoyed over the past one-hundred/ninety-five years.

"There are his military pictures, pictures of his gun collection," Celeste says.

"What about pictures of his family?" adds Delene.

"And pictures of the old asshole's family, no offense, Celeste," adds Delene.

"None taken," says C, unsure.

"Well, there can't be pictures of the three of us broads. We were just his mistresses. There have to be pictures of his legitimate family. Wife, children, grandchildren," Felicia insists.

"Dad has no grandchildren, his wife died under horrible circumstances, and his son is missing."

"Still missing?" "Oh I forgot all about that." "Awful times."

The worst topic just had to come up. The bane of C's existence.

C explains to everyone in the room, or reminds the three old ladies of something they already know and have forgotten. "Tad's been missing in action from Vietnam for OVER fifty years. The military has never been able to find him. Of course, it's entirely possible that finding him was a low priority, considering the number of ongoing wars we remain engaged in."

Moiselle changes the subject. "Buzzer, wrong topic. Okay, what theme, what colors for the party?"

"Dad likes red. Blood red."

"BUZZER again. Purple! Let's decorate in purple," Moiselle decides. "That's what all the party books say about a one-hundredth birthday party. Purple."

"As in 'Purple Heart.' Purple is the military color for 'you got yourself shot, dumb ass.' It's a terrible choice," Celeste says.

"Purple Heart—Dan's 'Imma too slow' award," Felicia adds, giggling.

"Well damn," says Christine, "the military just ruins everything, even party planning."

They laugh at the disrespectful humor. Recognizing each other as fellow patriots who love and respect their nation and the armed forces that protect it, the topic is still ripe for humor. Everyone needs a laugh in 2023.

Well, not everyone. The virtuous, respected, evangelical members of the donut meeting find the jokes offensive. Huff makes everyone feel uncomfortable by declaring, "The sacrifice our veterans made, 1.8 million Americans who paid the ultimate price don't think your so-called jokes are funny."

"You people are fucking awful," chirps Old Lady Lurlene, who is fucking awful herself most of the time, so nobody cares what she says.

Sometimes the television set is not necessary in these offensive transactions between old people. These are some hard ass old ladies getting in some faces.

Because jokes beget opinions, too.

"Alright, then we'll do red, like his classy red jacket, his pampered scarlet leather," Moiselle decides. "Settled. Now for a theme?"

"How about 'signs that you've lived too long,'" Celeste suggests. Mo laughs. Of course she's the lone laugher, the only one to laugh at something that was not meant to be a joke.

"Don't laugh, Mo. She's being serious," Delene says.

Celeste enthusiastically offers her true opinion to the now somber group.

"My father has lived too long."

The group jeers. This statement meant they've all lived too long.

"Buzzer. Okay. We'll ask Dad to tell one of his famous war stories at the party." (Moans all around.)

"You know there might be a story he has yet to tell, Celeste," Mo says, in defense of Dan.

"Ha! I never dreamed I'd be planning a birthday party for that old horndog," Delene says.

"I wanted to smother him more than once myself," Christine adds.

"I almost cut his thing off," Felicia one-ups.

"We'd only need bang-trimmin' scissors. Last time I saw his wee it looked like a seahorse. And that was twenty years ago."

And the old women giggle like school girls.

They giggle even louder when Christine reminds them of how Dan used to make a quacking sound in his sleep. "He was fast and furious in the bedroom, nothing fun about it. Finally told me all he was interested in was relaxing enough to go to sleep! So after the three minutes, he'd be dead to the world, quacking in his sleep."

Nobody notices or cares that Celeste is hearing this personal and embarrassing tirade about her father.

"Stop this inappropriate talk." Moiselle is constantly surprised by how crude and crass old women can be, even though her mother had warned her when she first took the job at the RRC. "Old people are just rude," her mother warned. "And the older they get the nastier they are. They lose their filter. Even as Christians. Especially as Christians. Jesus stops censoring them. He lets them yap. Damn, shit, the C-word, MF, all sorts of bad words." Moiselle laughs at the memory. She had waited all her life for her sainted mother to utter even a single expletive.

"What a wonderful thing to hear you say a cuss word," Moiselle had said to her mother.

That turned out not to be entirely accurate.

The next swear word Moiselle's mother spoke was a result of misery. Her cancer-stricken mother prayed to her Lord God after a night of agony. "Help me, goddammit," she cried. When Moiselle overheard her mother using the Lord's name, as they say, in vain, she cried out in shock, "Mama!" Her mother, eyes wide, said, "Mo, I am not using the Lord's name in vain. I want Him to DAMN MY PAIN. He knows exactly what I mean when I say the words 'God. D. It.' God please, if you love me, if you are my Father, damn this horrible, horrible . . . pain. God damn this pain!"

And with that her God acted in mercy, and her mother closed her eyes and fell into a sound sleep.

"Dan Kellar was the worst boyfriend I ever had in my life," says Delene. "We should be telling stories on him."

That settled it. Theme: Floozies roasting Dan. Color: Red.

Celeste gathers her belongings, walks to the door, turns to the group and says, "Yes, he was awful, and there are several women in this room who know it as well as I do. But now he thinks he needs forgiveness. Before he kills himself. Which we cannot let him do. We should work to convince him of his true worth and make his birthday a celebration of all he accomplished."

Nothing curbs a conversation like the mention of someone threatening suicide. "You three floozies," Mo says, "take notice. There will be no harassing Dan Kellar on his birthday, or before. God dammit to any ill will towards that man, let the man have a great birthday, whatever his heart desires."

Near tears, moved, Celeste barrels down the hall to Dan's room, and finds him asleep. Taking a lovely, peaceful nap.

The war hero has nothing left but sad memories, grief, and shame, and yes, he was awful, but at this moment, C thinks to herself, *Why can't he just die easy in his sleep?*

Cause he's my Daddy.

There is a tornado warning, and the wind is beginning to whip up outside.

C prays for the tornado to be the mishap that lands right on top of her Daddy's head, and ends it all for him. An easy end for this bigger-than-life war hero, both her Daddy and her nemesis.

C opens the top drawer of the nightstand to look for Ativan.

But she finds a photograph of three little boys and an old '45 record. "Ode to Billie Joe." She thinks, then decides: *nothing about me.*

PART **TWO** . . .

CHAPTER 11
Walking with the Wounded

Celeste

Poor Celeste, if she had to write her own obituary.

She can't sum up her life with reports of marriage, travel, education, raising children, philanthropy, career advancements, artistic accomplishments, successful hobbies, or hanging out with a tribe of good friends. Not even a life of crime. And yet time flew by. It is surprising to C 'how fast life flew by when nothing happened.'

Born, grew up. Her twenties turned into her fifties, and her fifties to her seventies. With the exception of a few evenings every week for decades, when she would blow off some steam at the Porterfield, and meet up with a stranger, or some newly-divorced guy she knew from high school, Celeste was the child who never left home.

She found Jesus Christ in her late forties, but pretty much dropped Him when she was fifty-five. That's when her father moved into the RRC. Finally alone in her childhood home, she was able to do whatever the hell she wanted to do—which was nothing—and she didn't need Christ for that. And by then her hormones had stopped working, so even the random man wasn't of much interest.

At seventy years old, Celeste was still in the bedroom she'd had from birth. With no hormones. And a shower that's broken.

This is nothing anybody would admit to in an obituary.

Going back to her fifties—a defining decade filled with triggers. C always says about her life, if asked, "I had hardships. Don't let anybody tell you that the middle of life is easy. It ain't." She generally speaks in a Texas rancher dialect reminiscent of Mercedes McCambridge in *Giant* but, depending on how inebriated she is, she might slur into a syrupy southern accent that brings to mind

Morgan Freeman.

"My fifties, ferchrissakes," she'd say. "Didn't feel like the end of dreams then. It felt like a last chance, though." Her fifties. If she didn't move forward, she knew she would die in that house. She wasn't old, certainly not young, but still able to slam down a bunch of margaritas, spend the night with some rando man, get up, go to work the next morning and get there on time, looking good. Still young enough to love romcoms, to still want her own hot pink landline (long out of style), and foolish enough to believe there were Hallmark Christmases.

Hallmark Christmases. Romcoms.

Twenties to fifties.

C hoped to marry one of the many men she met late nights (secrets) at the Porterfield. She especially wanted to marry Wayne. Before Wayne burned his draft card and hitchhiked to Canada, C tried everything to get him to marry her. Her daddy knew all about it. Broke his heart, if you want to know the truth. Her daddy knew all about what men do with women they can easily have. And Wayne was a cookie-cutter of Dan where women were concerned.

Twenties to fifties. Celeste squandered thirty years screwing around by night, and as secretary to the funeral director at Rupert's Peaceful Pines Cemetery by day. "You see, obituary, nothing happened!"

"But then the absolute weirdest thing happened in my fifties. A turning point. Maybe I was normal enough before this, but then, I did this thing that's weird, and nothing was ever right again."

There were two beds in Dan's room. One was a queen, one was a day bed. Corrie wasn't in either bed, because she was dead by then. But her pink landline phone remained.

Celeste coveted that phone. Celeste was never allowed to have her own phone and finally, in her fifties, she'd stopped asking, just gave up. But Lord, she wanted her own pink Princess. C claimed she needed it because Dan was a drunk, and an old one, at that, and that she worried when he was out late. She tried to convince him that if the phone were to ring in the middle of the night, if the police called, if Dan managed to get himself killed in a bar fight or a car accident, Celeste would not be able to take the call unless she had her own phone. In her room.

Her father was unmoved and refused to add another landline. Now, she had been working for decades, had her own money, was perfectly capable of going out and getting a phone, but . . .

. . . something snapped inside her. She took to sleeping in that day bed, in her father's room, to be near the pink landline.

She knew it was odd, sleeping in the other bed in her father's room, just to be near a landline. She complained to Jimmy about not having her own phone.

"Well, it is the 21st century, and the rest of the world has a cellphone," he said.

At the time, Jimmy, also in his fifties, was practically homeless, living under the radar and off the grid in the old hotel, suffering intensely from PTSD, but even he had a cellphone. "Git yourself a goddam cellphone, C, like every other grownup," he'd say. "And figure out how to use it."

To be like everyone else was a goal. There was a Dee's Cellular store downtown, right by the old hotel. She'd drive up there, park, and just sit. "No, I don't want a cellphone. I want a pink princess phone," she'd say to herself, then drive away.

C was finally diagnosed in her sixties. She had suffered for decades, as much as Jimmy did—or any other soldier of war, or crime victim—with PTSD.

It didn't really show up until her fifties. Before her fifties she always paid her bills on time. She cleaned her room. She cooked meals. She drove a car. She didn't take drugs. Her promiscuity and her alcoholism didn't seem to reveal PTSD. But when she moved into her father's bedroom, that's when she knew she needed help.

Strange, the cause. She *didn't* make a phone call that she should have made.

In 1978, when her father shot Wayne, she'd found him lying in the sludge. She ran back to the Bar to call the police, but her mother and father were fighting and she failed to make the call. Even after she, and Corrie, and Dan, had left the Bar to go home, and her parents went to sleep, she lay awake, wanting to call the cops, but she had no phone in her room. She couldn't make the call from the kitchen; she was afraid her father would hear. And the only other phone was in their bedroom. It was the pink princess landline that she fixated on for years after, an object that represented pain and regret. Again, nothing for an obituary.

Fifties to seventies. The shower is broken at the house, and it's become the bane of her existence. Celeste washes her hair in her dad's shower at the RRC. It's the perfect place to cry, and it serves him right if her alligator tears clog up the shower drain. She thinks of Peaceful Pines, where soon she'll bury her father. Now that's a weird thought to have in the shower, because he is immortal, overwhelmingly immortal.

Still, the shower is also a punishment, one she repeats. Every time she steps into her father's shower, she hears him say something he didn't mean to say, but he did say, years ago . . . and still says, now . . . "Give up on men, C. They don't want ya. In fact. Don't get married, C. Marriage is terrible. Your mother and I barely existed. Maybe your mother didn't run up credit cards. Maybe she kept the house nice. Maybe she didn't mess with my earnings. But she cheated. You know, with Briggs. You look enough like me, right? That should be enough. But it isn't enough, is it? Look, I'm grateful to you now that I'm old, that you take care of me."

C is crushed more each time she replays this awfulness in her head. It really happened. He said that, and she cried. "You asshole. Are you trying to say that you're not my real father? Are you saying that Briggs might be my father?" Dan shrugs, doesn't care how much this hurts her.

"And Tad?"

"Well, of course Tad was mine. No question about that."

C hits herself in the face to stop the memory. She tiptoes out of the shower, stares at her napping father for a very long time. She knows that when he is sleeping, and for all the rest of his life, the few days he has left, she will look at his hands and hope to see her own in his. She will compare her aging hands to his gnarly old one. She will look at his earlobes, hoping against hope that his ears look like her ears. And someday, when Dan is long gone, another letter from the militarywill come to her, and she will send in her DNA and pray that it perfectly matches up with Tad's DNA, thus proving that Dan is her father. It is a particularly painful thing to be unsure that the man who caused you a lifetime of grief may not be your dad after all.

More and more, as she ages, her mind cycles faster and faster. She worries that she has more of a mental illness than PTSD. Bipolar? Crazy? She wants to scream every day. Throw something. Why does she allow his past abuse to haunt her? For God's sake, she's seventy now, not the twenty-something who found Wayne in the woods and never called the cops, who let her father off the hook for a crime. At least at twenty it is acceptable to suffer mental illness for a time, but not at seventy! At seventy she should be in control of herself. She is worse than ever. And she is still a coward, covering for her dad. Qualms taking on her dad, that's why. He never hit her, but what about Corrie, and Tad? She saw Dan kick Tad with steel-toed boots when he questioned the morality of the Vietnam war. He threw Tad into a glass door, shattering the door, knocking Tad unconscious when Tad first mentioned the idea of dodging the draft and the possibility of going to Canada with Wayne. But that wasn't the first time. Years before, he had pinned sixteen-year-old Tad to the bar's porch stairs, punching him over and over in the face, because Tad had dirtied the shower stall by using an egg as a hair conditioner. Tad cracked the egg on his hair. Most of the yolk and white goo got stuck to the shower pan, and Tad forgot to clean it up. Only a dirty mind would have judged it to be semen. Or a damaged mind. Her mother's dirty mind.

Corrie asked what the substance was in the bottom of the shower? Tad answered "egg, just egg for my hair." Corrie laughed, and asked again. "What nasty thing you been doing in the shower?" That triggered a response from Dan, who ran into the bathroom, saw Tad cowering beside the toilet, and interpreted Corrie's signals to mean "punish the kid." In their tiny, dysfunctional family world, "punish = abuse." Punching.

Yelling, name-calling. More punching. And slapping. And Corrie smirking all the while.

Evil.

Celeste feels sick. Dirty. She grabs her backpack, vowing that the next time she steps into her dad's ADA compliant bathroom again, she will bring a carton of eggs. She will lock the outer door, before Briggs returns from his Mexican Train game. She will throw each egg into the shower stall, smear the egg yolks, the whites all down the walls. Let Briggs find this shit. Let him report her dad for this offense.

Cycle. Cycle. Then a feeling of calm. Respite from the terrible storm. Slowing down to think. Well, no, she won't throw eggs. She would worry her father would be sent to a stricter home. With his birthday coming, the end is coming, and soon it will all be over— their horrible union as father and daughter.

C removes her clothes. Turns the shower on again, the second time in one day. She looks in the mirror, thoughtfully examining more than a few scrapes and bruises on her arms, her neck, her chest. Obviously she pounds her own fists against her body often enough to bruise herself. Opens her backpack, removes a dried piece of donut that she doesn't remember putting in her backpack, a plumber's business card, a fresh pair of panties, and a piece of cardboard. She pulls out her toothbrush and travel sized containers of shampoo and toothpaste. She steps into the shower.

 Hot water is heaven on earth. She stands, zombie like, under the water. Then twists the showerhead, aiming at this wall, that wall, the floor, washing imaginary egg away. They're just symbolic reminders of trauma, you know. That's all the eggs are. Casually, she pours shampoo into her hand. There's nothing wrong here, nothing to see here.

The door to the bathroom opens and her father appears. He peeks in. "Funny, I thought I heard you in the shower earlier. Turn that faucet off good when you're through."

"Ok, Dad."

"Celeste, I've written the first, a most satisfying first line for my obituary. You wanna hear it?"

"Sure," she says, one hand covering her breasts, one hand covering her privates.

He reads from a piece of paper. "Dan Kellar, a true American, a man of his times, a hot tea drinker, made do with the hand he was dealt, but he sometimes concocted the life he wanted for himself with his riveting stories, while dressed spectacularly."

"That's great, daddy."

"Of course there's more to tell."

"Yep."

"Another thing, C. I want you to invite Wayne to the party. I want to tell him I'm sorry."

"Yep." Water pouring over her, all around her, water. Water.

"Okay, I'll let you get back to your shower then."

"Yeah, thanks."

Wayne. The very last time she'd seen Wayne Herd, he was burying his son at Peaceful Pines. *Well, no, that's not really true. She booty called with him many more times after that. At any rate* . . . It had been well over twenty years since she'd seen him. She was almost fifty then.

"Almost fifty." Celeste had believed there was nothing to celebrate at fifty, that she was sexually invisible, socially irrelevant, and stupid. She struggled with hormone shifts, alcohol, depression, and weight issues at fifty. Embarrassed, even now, Celeste remembers that she had taken several days off from work back then to prepare for seeing Wayne, to go to Liam's funeral. The first day off was a "mental health day" she had called it back then. But this is now. She might see Wayne soon.

She faces the shower head, water smacking her face, sharply, tingly. She hadn't taken a mental health day in twenty years. Maybe she needed one. Lord knows she needed something, something for HER.

On the mental health days that defined her forties and fifties, Celeste performed a ritual she'd read about in some drug store self-help book—burning a scented candle, writing down her heart's desires on a piece of paper, placing that paper into the flame, saying a prayer while it burned. "Please God, let me lose ten pounds overnight and make me attractive to Wayne Herd when he sees me." (As if his focus would be on her at his only son's funeral.) Celeste's belief in the workings of the Universe, however, meant that she would be instantly gratified with self-knowledge and self-respect, as well as receiving the miracle the Universe promised to all who put their written desires into the flame of a candle, much like "God's forgiveness" worked for the Christians she knew and had abandoned.

Referring to self-help books, rituals, prayers. They were the best, perhaps only options for coping with her emotional problems without the expense and embarrassment of professional help. These resources helped her make an honest assessment of all things bothering her that day, and all things that influenced her self-worth every day. And because Celeste had a terrible opinion of herself, it was a busy day. She was truly fucked up.

If she was lucky her father would be gone for the whole day so she could cry, emote, scream out loud, and burn stuff. She tread ever so lightly into the arena of self-assessment. The ritual always began with coffee and time spent writing down and defining her current motivation for the ritual. She wrote, and mind you, she was almost fifty, "Wayne Herd, the love of my life, is in town for his son's funeral service."

Allowing herself then to fully experience the resulting churning in her stomach, she gave herself a thorough examination in the mirror. She had definitely let herself go. She looked for any evidence of acne or redness in her face, plucked those odd hairs on her chin and around her lips, scanned her teeth under a bright light to determine their whiteness, and measured that against a color chart. Finally, she determined whether or not the gray of her roots demanded a refresh.

She could dye her hair when Dan was home, so she brushed past this and onto writing down "the problem of the day."

She wrote, "I am too fat for Wayne Herd to want to marry, but this may be my only chance to see him, since I have not seen him for twenty-five years. And after the funeral he may go away forever, so please give me confidence to at least have a sexy romp with him, which I desperately need and want." A bit embarrassed by her mid-life libido, so intense it kept her from sleeping most nights, Celeste was happy that she would be able to make this wish disappear by tossing it into the great universal flame.

If she couldn't have Wayne for real, she thought, she could lie to herself and hope to at least provide him (and herself) with some physical comfort in their mutual time of need.

She suffered a trio of agonies on a regular basis that she called "The Three H's." So she wrote, "Give me the means to overcome the three H's sooner than later."

When plagued with these horrible symptoms of menopause, her hormones drove her crazy, steered her to the freezer in order to cool off and kept her from sleep, her mind working incessantly. They often propelled her to the refrigerator for food. Hot flashes and hunger were the two mainstays, but it got worse. The third H would show up unannounced and ornery as hell. No matter where she was, what she was doing, or time of day or night, Celeste could suddenly be one or all three of "hot, hungry and horny." Then add a fourth "H." "Helpless." Look, she could walk naked in front of a construction site, and not a single man would turn his head to look at her. All this suffering at once. At fifty, life for Celeste was fraught with insecurity and self-hatred.

Sometimes the three (or four) H's happened at work, which was the worst location and timing for such an attack. She ate donuts to counteract the hunger. She kept a fan on her desk for the heat. But curing the third H was not possible at work, and she was utterly miserable. She was like a drug addict looking for heroin at a Build-a-Bear party. Needing her fix, a simple pounding or two with some sex-craved man, any man, made her ashamed. She was, after all, raised a Christian. Standard menopause, a biological phase every middle-aged woman in the world experienced, made her ashamed. The three (or four) H's held her hostage, and she didn't know what to do about it. The "rituals" sure stopped working.

Eating made her fat, and soon she was an insulin dependent

diabetic, told never to drink alcohol again, and as far as she was concerned, life would have no meaning without alcohol and sex, so death was surely on its way. Occasionally she spent time trying to figure out how in God's name she might find a man who'd spend quality time with her, tolerating her many flaws and insecurities. She couldn't spend time at Bigelow's (her father's favorite dive) hoping to catch even a one-night stand among the drunks who frequented the place. Someone would either tell her dad, or worse, he'd be right there watching. OR WORSE, he'd be listening.

If she had sex in the house, even if Dan was sure to be gone for hours or days, weeks, she always felt he was listening at the door. He held that kind of power over her life.

So Celeste lit yet another candle and sat in meditation for a few minutes focusing on Step One in most self-help books—"Accept, Value, and Love Yourself the way you are." Fat, sweaty, horny, and hungry. And there was so much MORE wrong with her.

Step One, Number One. Celeste was allergic to all cats and most dogs. A most unfortunate trait for an almost fifty-year-old woman who fit the mold for "cat lady."

Number Two. She drank a little, the MOST unfortunate because she drank alone. And not just a little.

Number Three. God dang it, Celeste despised herself for being fat.

Step Two. "Wisdom lies within you and at all times." Okay, so she could do better. She could dress better. She could . . .

Celeste didn't consider herself to be fashionable, but she was no Walmartian either. Or was she? She took all her meals off that metal tray next to her worn, but comfortable recliner in the front room. She watched network television and soap operas from the time she got home from work until she fell asleep in her chair. With her weight at an all-time high, Celeste hid in the bathroom stall and cried every day. Then she came out of the stall and ate donuts.

She fat shamed herself constantly and brutally. THIS was her problem. But there was nothing, nothing, nothing Celeste could do about it. Nothing.

Step Three. "Abandon your fear of rejection." Deny that you

were ever abandoned by anyone you loved. Celeste, of course, lived with her father, still called him "daddy" most of the time. And he had the big bedroom suite—he never let her grow up and switch rooms—to the other big bedroom that had a nice bathroom and large shower.

Celeste maintained her childhood bedroom, down the hall from the smallest bathroom, which she reluctantly shared with any guests who happened in. The OTHER big bedroom, the one denied to her, belonged to her missing brother Tad. Celeste's mother, Corrie, refused to entertain the idea of changing the room, even though Celeste begged for years to convert the room into a small study for her art projects, quilting, scrapbooking and books. Corrie has been dead for decades, but Dan never allowed Celeste to alter the shrine.

The suburban ranch style home begged for change. ANY CHANGE would have helped. But nothing ever changed. At fifty-five, alone in the house at night, Celeste lived alone in a eighties style kitchen with floral fabrics on every surface, including the walls, and some of the walls were PADDED!

How many times over the decades had Celeste been tempted to tear off that awful fabric and pads and bare the actual walls of the house! Surely there were warm colors underneath! But there were also German knick knacks crowded around, a frugally repurposed wooden table and chairs, a wooden pie pantry, an old fashioned metal stair stool. The cabinets were still decent, though, and there was lots of space to work. She could do so much with this kitchen if only her Daddy would just DIE!

And now his death is at hand. Standing in the shower in Dan's room, now shared by her father and old man Briggs, who could be her father, she is crying. Jesus Christ. Fifties to seventies. Fifties to fucking seventies. And she's crazier than ever. And looking back she sees where she was still trying in her fifties. To be somebody normal. To be loved.

Celeste has washed her hair twice today, cried buckets of

tears, stood so long in the shower that she's pruny. She rinses her hair, slathers conditioner on the thin strands. A glob falls on her thigh. She stares at it, wonders how it would feel if she slathered it onto her private parts. Then she remembers that she's seventy and dry as the desert. If the third "H" came along these days, it would not only be a surprise, it would be a horrible frustration. Her gynecologist can't get anything more than the size of a pencil up inside her anymore. Dry as a goddam bone, she can never have sex again, not ever, not after her father stops listening at the door, not even after her father dies, not ever.

Once out of the shower for the second time, C digs out deodorant from her backpack. She puts on clean underwear, smells the garments she took off before her shower, and puts them on again. She wishes she had died in her fifties.

CHAPTER 12
. . . Friend of the devil . . .

"I'm glad you're back, FN, it's been three days, but I forgive you," Dan coos as the two of them take in the delights of the dry terrain from the porch.

"Thank you, Dan. I just needed a few days off."

"Were you getting laid, I hope?" Dan asks.

"Not hardly your business. By the way, how are you and Briggs getting along?"

"Ugh. That's how," Dan answers.

The two of them watch early morning traffic pass by. It's gonna be a scorcher of a day. Across the street, a flock of ducks makes its way across a tiny water hole. Dan bites his lip.

FN can read his mind, of course. "I know you have a duck story, and a yellow dog story, and a hundred war stories, Dan. I've heard 'em. And Briggs, so far, threatens that he has only one story to tell, about you, but you're a far better story-teller, so I would prefer hearing that one story from you."

"You need to hear my stories from me. My stories are embellished for effect but Briggs outright lies. Anyone else be telling you my stories?"

"Jimmy, who drives the van. He's good looking but my God, the old boy loves tellin' Dan Kellar stories."

"Jimmy telling my stories, huh?"

"Jimmy Ramirez, said he was like a second kid to you."

"You stop dating him immediately, you hear me? His first wife, Sarah, she was . . . "

" . . . You start telling me Jimmy's old stories, I swear I'll call in sick again . . . Dan, Dan, don't you even start telling a Jimmy story . . . I know I haven't lived here all my life, don't know a thing about him, but I need to give the boy a chance."

Dan smirks, then giggles. "Jimmy was born and raised here. Otherwise why anyone comes to Rupert is a mystery to me. Why are you here, FN?"

She hesitates. Finally makes a little small talk. "Oh Dan, come on, look at me. I wear too much makeup. Smoke too many cigarettes. Always late to work. Sometimes I sleep in my car because I'm drunk. But somehow, once I get here, I'm a damn good nurse. So are you from Rupert, Dan?"

"No, I was born in Arkansas, but we moved to Hot Springs when I was ten. In the Depression. *Why?* My father was a cobbler, and started some shoe shine services, for hotels. My mother was a waitress, and then Daddy moved us to the Porterfield, and we all worked there. I tended bar, then signed up. Went to war. Came back in one piece. Lucky. The rest of 'em all died. Mom and Dad died. Nothing to do when I got back, so I bought my own bar. And you? You stay with Jimmy, he'll want you to stay in Rupert."

There is an unexpected breeze on the patio of the RRC. It's dawn, during the lull before the rush of the day. The Texas sun just beginning to come up, six degrees above the horizon, a few stars still visible. FN is singing under her breath and counting stars, anxiously watching for Jimmy's van to pull up.

It's about the time in any relationship she usually gets dumped, so she'll dump first. She tries not to be too needy, too slutty, or too tormented by failures for someone to love her, but country songs could be written about her, she knows that. Songs one old boyfriend made up about her to the tune of "You Are My Sunshine." He thought he was really cute when he sang . . . *"Your four abortions/your STDs dear/ six bouts of Herpes/ bring me a beer/ You're a celebrity/ a famous ho here/ all things that endear you to me.*

"I'm just from Seppenville, down the river yonder, working around here since the Pandemic. That was a good time to start over, don't you think? Especially with staff shortages ever where . . . Makes it a little easier for this old drunk to keep a job. I like it here. I like working with you. Especially since you're not nearly as scary as I thought you were at first. I could stay here. Should I?"

" . . . his first wife, Sarah, well, he beat her."

Sure enough, Dan woke up alone the next morning, no nurse. No C. His "Hello world, dammit" went unheard. So he grudgingly dressed himself, got into his wheelchair, and rolled himself out into the hall, gasping and wheezing for breath the entire time. About to turn the corner to the main lobby, he could hear Moiselle whining and complaining to the Administrator about having to raise money for Dan's birthday party. He stopped cold and eavesdropped. "I have to put everything on hold and go door-to-door pleading with the residents for cash. For this damn party. Most residents scream at me about how they are on social assistance or at the very least have fixed incomes and, in truth, hardly want to contribute to any party, especially Dan's. They hate the bastard."

She continued. "I've got to put on a show. Cause he's famous, you know. Hero of THREE wars. La dee dah. Food, alcohol, entertainment, cake, balloons, and activities suitable for everyone—it's all fucking expensive."

Dan held his breath. He could hear Sue, the Administrator, grumbling quietly. Mo went on loudly. "Well, the old fucker complained that I had overlooked providing security for the party. The old fuck has a history of shooting out a few windows in government structures, so he thinks he needs security from some made up SWAT team he thinks he sees. I said, 'You're not so famous you need security, get over your old self.' He's so much more trouble than he's worth. I don't care how many Nazis he killed."

These were indeed the words a shocked Dan overheard Moiselle tell the blonde bitch Administrator.

So much more trouble than he's worth. Even though he killed hundreds of Nazis. Hell, Dan made the world safe for democracy practically single-handed. Mo continued, shrieking louder. "Dan Kellar is a big pain in my ass. Secretly, I wish he would just die in his sleep." Said out loud, and not so secretly, this proclamation shocked Dan even more than it pleased the Administrator. And boy, did it please her. That big boobed, fake blonde laughed her botoxed ass off.

"But," Mo went on, "demanding security like he's the damn president of the United States. I can't collect enough money for security. I can barely collect money for a cake. I tell the dementia group several times a day about the party. They just stare at me.

I tell the bingo group about the party. They act like they can't hear. "What? What? "Party, party, p-a-r-t-y, P-100!" "We ain't contributing to no party," they yell back."

The Administrator is in stitches.

"I say to the actual hard-of-hearing group. "WE ARE TAKING UP A COLLECTION SO WE CAN HAVE A BIG OLD PARTY FOR DAN KELLAR." "IS HE STILL ALIVE," they ask? "YES, YES, HE IS," I scream. They sign back. "THAT'S NO REASON TO CELEBRATE."

Both women are in hysterics at this point.

"You're as good a story teller as Dan is," the Administrator says.

Dan was incensed. *Well at least one nice thing was said about me, but you oughta be ashamed making fun of your paying clients who can't hear.*

Moiselle continues. "Can't hear you," said crotchety old Mr. Briggs, "but I damn sure won't be donating to his damn party. I already have to live with the nasty old, peeing-in-the-sink, walk-around-half-nekkid man who hates me." "Hates you cause you screwed his wife," I said." The Administrator howls.

Dan figured old Mr. Briggs was furious about Dan getting a party. After all, they're the same age, and Dan Kellar is his nemesis as well as his superior. Dan Kellar, war hero, killed Nazis while old Briggs was drafted to drive trains. Briggs was a British American, his father from London and his mother from Fort Worth. Briggs came here with her and went to work first running the Super Chief, and then bought up a coupla old railroad cars from the NW Railroad, and parked them in Rupert long after the war was over. Crazy coot just lived in 'em for years like they were tiny houses. Briggs was instantly smitten with Corrie, and for awhile there, Dan worried about her growing friendship with Briggs. Since Corrie didn't care for trains, Dan felt certain she was faithful. Boy, was he wrong.

"Let's do happy hour tonight, Sue," Mo says to the Administrator. "Gotta go beg for money."

"I'll go with you, Mo. Hey, maybe they'll actually donate if I'm with ya."

"Maybe they'll donate if we tell them we're hiring strippers."

Dan fumes over these two women having a laugh at his expense. *And how dare Old Mr. Briggs not donate, regardless of past ill will. He's got more money than God. Old Briggs, he'll want a party someday. Briggs is popular. It's that damn British accent of his that women love.* It irks Dan so much. Briggs is a train operator turned train collector, the coolest hobby on the planet. He buys up everyone's slices of cheesecake at dinner time, then wins the money back by playing "Ticket to Ride" against the three eighty-year old floozies, Delene, Felicia and Christine (who Dan screwed back in the day, all three of 'em and anybody else in a skirt). They all start drinking wine after six p.m. And by eight, they don't care if Briggs smells bad and is pooping on himself, which he is. After all, it's ten women to one man in the nursing home. Choo choo! And Briggs has money. Damn.

Dan rolls down the hall, talks to himself, and hears all. Dan's party is the talk of the RRC, but not in a good way. "A party during LOCK DOWN?" . . . says the pruny Daphne Huff, mother of Mayor Huff. Dan tests his memory—grandmother of Sergeant Huff, of the Rupert Police, and great-grandmother of Huff Huff, love child of her granddaughter, Buffy Huff, who also lived in the retirement home due to a debilitating car accident, and was the first in the home to die of COVID.

"I'm not gonna wear a mask to a party," says Margaret Mouser, who is married to ninety-five-year old Clyde, and who constantly obsesses about the ten women who try daily to entice her husband to partake of some sex cardio in a dark corner of someone's boudoir, under a heated blanket. She also has a tremendous fear of COVID and won't go anywhere without a mask on.

"No more masks" confirms Sue, the big boobed Administrator. "It's Dan Kellar's one-hundredth birthday party, the pandemic rules are over, and young men are coming! Men in the raw, all male. Men who look a whole lot like . . . like Magic Mike . . . or that actor Jack O'Connell from that TV show *Godless*."

Dan is gobsmacked. Male Strippers? Godless, all right! Administrator Sue, laughing so hard her big boobs bounce, slaps one hand over her mouth. "Jesus Christ, Mo, we're gonna kill these women with heart attacks."

Under his breath, Dan explodes. "Who is this party for anyway, you two dummies?" *Wants to scream out, "get girl strippers. Girls! This party is for ME!"* Deflated, Dan looks down at his crotch and frowns. *Oh well, my old crotch doesn't need a party.*

A group of half-drunk crones surround Sue and Mo. "Male strippers? Moiselle, is that the truth?"

"Meeeennnnnn, I say. Lots of men for everyone. You know, 'what is your real name, men? What will you give me for this five-dollar-bill, men? Do you have a girlfriend, men?' MEN. You get my drift? Only if I can raise enough money for Dan's party. Then we can have strippers."

"I'll help you collect," says Margaret Mouser.

"We're having La Bare night," shrieks Daphne.

"I need to give you a raise, Moiselle!" says Sue.

"Not to worry, girlfriend. The Italian Stallion will give me a raise. Or I'll give him one."

Mo raised over a hundred dollars in two seconds.

Plus, there were the aforementioned women who, years before, Dan Kellar had conquered and degraded who now lived under the same roof with him. *Jesus, talk about small town luck.* His conquests, the floozies, now hated men through no fault of his own, but Dan understood very clearly why each had no motivation to pay for any part of his birthday party.

"Please contribute," Moiselle begs. "I know Dan was awful. But it was SIXTY years ago. And honey, all men were awful sixty years ago."

All afternoon Mo begs for money. Dan, on a mission, followed her but kept a distance and held up a mirror so he could peer around corners. *Who's giving the most money for my party?*

Delene Walker gave a quarter.

Christine Falcon forked over a dime.

Felicia Blackmon spit on the floor!

And it got worse from there.

Unable to contain his frustration any longer, Dan rolled himself into the day room and made his presence known. "I'll pay for the damn party myself, Moiselle," he yells.

The spitting stops, grumbling stops, silence ensues. Dan squares off with a roomful of grumpy old women who do not like him. He outglares them. Most start to walk away. Then Delene forks over a few more bucks. "But only for the strippers." "TRAITOR!!" the other floozies holler, then lunge at Dan with an unexpected ferociousness. They drag him from his wheelchair, screaming obscenities.

Mo intervenes, furious.

"Dan, you do understand that Hell hath no fury like a woman scorned. But I forbade this kind of behavior around your birthday. I asked God to damn it, as a matter of fact. So I'm making one exception, today, just one. In order for there to be peace, you can all watch the news." Mo aims the remote.

Dan drags himself toward the television in the day room, motions for everyone to get out of his way.

He hears the roar of a helicopter, a fire fight. Rolls closer to the tv. It's not news, it's even better. It's a documentary about Vietnam. Lord, he almost pees himself.

"Saved by Vietnam," Moiselle giggles under her breath. Dan figures Mo will eventually hijack the remote, but while the documentary is on, Dan Kellar is in heaven.

On the TV, "*A disaster, a war that was never declared, killed four million Vietnamese and over 58,000 Americans.*" Music to his ears. "*And ideologically, the Vietnam war ripped the country apart.*"

Dan salivates, his soul on fire. Now THIS is his kind of television programming. Delene Walker cries and begs for the television to be turned off because she feels forced "against my will" to see the images of napalm explosions.

Vietnamese civilians on fire, protesting college students, draft dodgers, and armed national guard. "This is NEWS, for God's sake, NOT ALLOWED," she screams.

"Oh gosh dammit, shut up, Delene," Dan wails. "I never get to watch any good television. Bad enough we can't get national news, or cable, and now even stand-up comics, because of damn . . . everybody arguing over politics."

Delene continued to raise quite the ruckus. "Dan Kellar, have you not met the crazy kid who works in the kitchen????? He's a gun nut. He's a weirdo. I ask him for French fries, he goes off on the French. I ask him for oranges, or lettuce, he goes off on the illegals that pick 'em. Once he warned me that someday my social security would be taken away and I would be out on the streets, and shot because I'm old."

"None of us here are going to fight over Vietnam, Moiselle. The war in Vietnam has been over fifty years, this is not news, this is history," Dan pleads. "It's just a television program. And I'd give up my birthday party just to watch some relevant television! Please. Please."

"That's very tempting, Dan, but we've all agreed that Vietnam is a subject that is off limits in this home," Moiselle argues.

"It's been fifty years! I swear I won't get mad."

Moiselle takes pity, but reasons with him. "Dan, you know darn well why we do not talk about Vietnam or anything political."

Dan knows. The elections of 2016 and 2020 are only two of the many reasons television is off limits. Football, basketball, even *Dateline* causes problems. Old people can't curb themselves, and when furious and arguing, the canes become weapons. The insults fly. And Vietnam is still fresh in some old folks' minds, especially those without short-term memory. Since Dan's son went missing in Vietnam and was never found, and since any memory of this set off a "Dan tirade" that upsets everyone, television is limited to the Macy's Day parade at Thanksgiving, *A Charlie Brown Christmas* at Christmas, *Chicago Fire* and *Chicago Med* at any time of day or night. (Moiselle, from Chicago, draws the line at allowing anyone to watch *Chicago PD.)*

The TV on at this point in the day causes a stir. Normally, the television serves as background noise while residents wait in line to sign up for social activities. Every day, Mrs. Walker and Mrs. Falcon are the first in line for bingo and "Mexican Train." They watch bits of *Leave it to Beaver* and *Andy Griffith* while they wait. This is indeed censorship at its most extreme.

Lately though, they had permission to watch the weather

report. Not caring about the local weather, however, the floozies opt for YouTube to watch weather in New York. Why? The weatherman there sometimes takes off his shirt to announce "Heavy rains will be affecting our commute this afternoon." This is dumbassness at its most extreme, but the floozies are after all, floozies.

"Unfortunately, got to turn that shit off, I said news only."

"Oh MO!" Dan resumes his argument. "All right, I'll compromise. No Vietnam. World War II was a good war, Moiselle. Come on, let's turn on some Hitler. Everyone in this room agrees on Hitler. Always know what to expect with the Hitler channel! Please! Make an exception for Hitler!"

Mo grabs the remote, punches buttons. Fox News. Big mistake.

"Oh Lord, not Sean Hannity," Mo shrieks. But it's too late. Here's Sean Hannity, showing some "disturbing video, a clear and present danger" of "migrants, thousands of them, on the Texas border!" Just the sound of Sean Hannity's voice sends the old folks rolling down the halls trying to get to the TV—some so they can grumble and fear-monger with Sean, some to shake their canes at his rantings, but most to make themselves so mad they feel alive. Judge Judy has the same effect. Dan places himself square in front of the TV, takes the remote and successfully turns it off.

"Thank you," Mo says.

"You're welcome," he answers, "We don't need the news. I can solve all Texas's problems in one fell swoop, starting with the border." Mo begs everyone present not to ask Dan "the old windbag" how he would solve Texas's problems, but everyone indulges their craving to talk "news," their longing to ruminate about politics, maybe even their hankering to belong to a group or a cult. They ask.

And now Dan has an audience.

He rants. "You start with some poor migrants ready to swim across the Rio Grande over to Texas. On the other side of the river you bring in the destitute Americans, the people who urinate in public places, the panhandlers who beg for money, the homeless addicts, and you put them on a bus and take them to the southern border. Construct minuscule boat shelters and house them inside the boats. Since they're all drug addicts, the Mexican cartels then gather in the middle of the Rio Grande, in yachts, or even on foot in some low places, and sell drugs whenever they want. Hell, they don't even need to enter the country with their meth and cocaine. Why, you ask? The homeless row their boats out to the middle of the stream, where the cartel waits, get their drugs, row back, get stoned, and stink up the border. Don't forget the illegals waiting to cross the border. Well. These migrants will then swim over and discover who genuinely resides in the United States. And they'll say 'me no wanna live there. Those American people are icky.' And they'll go back home. They won't want to live here. Solves three problems at once. Homelessness, drugs, and migrants."

Dan pauses, waits for applause. Nada. Laughter? Nope.

"I oughta have my own show, right?"

Briggs has been in the wings, patiently waiting for his time to dig at Dan. Now he speaks up, with his important sounding British accent, "I really do see Dan's point. It's very clever. However, I have a better idea. Ditto on the boats, and the drug dealers wading halfway from Mexico to Texas to sell their drugs. But instead, halt the cartel in its tracks and exchange our drug-addled Americans for the good migrants from Columbia seeking better lives. Just hand over no-good Americans in exchange for decent brown people."

Silence, while the audience ponders... brilliance?

Dan says, "But I'm thinking the decent brown people wouldn't want to move here. Would you wanna move here if you encounter all of Texas' drug addicts and panhandlers on the border? If I were Republican, I'd say the homeless would be a very effective border patrol, and if I were Democrat, I'd applaud providing shelter for and giving homeless Americans the responsibility of rowing out to get their drugs, too. In fact, make 'em use their drugs out in the middle of the Rio Grande, so they don't bring the drugs in."

Briggs muses. "Of course they'd bring their drugs back. To their boat shelters. They want to use their drugs in the privacy of their homes. It's the American Dream, so that would never work. And another thing. These destitute drug addicts are Americans,

American citizens, are they not? And isn't the whole point of border control to keep out who we don't want to come into the country, particularly those who are not Americans? Wouldn't it be easier, Dan Hannity, if we just bombed all the schools in South America where people get swimming lessons? Then they couldn't cross the border at all, except in the places where they can walk across the Rio Grande. You know, the places where the drug dealers from Mexico are waiting. With their AR-15s."

Mo. "Jesus H. Christ. I've never in my life . . . "

"Neither of you are no Sean Hannity," says Delene.

"Thank God you two have no power in this country because you are both idiots," says Christine.

"Oh but Dan and I, we two white men, have all the power in this country, I have less, of course, because I'm British, and an immigrant," Briggs answers. "But White Dan is especially powerful. War hero. Killed Nazis. And gooks, isn't that what you called them?"

"Turn it to CNN," begs Felicia, "for two minutes- we need a palate cleanser."

"Some of us prefer the truth, Felicia," says another old bag. "And Sean tells us the gospel. Turn it back to Fox."

"TWO MINUTES. CNN," screams Mo, grabs the remote.

She turns it to CNN, takes one glance at the screen. "Oh Jesus H. Christ," she says, exhausted. "It's the border again."

CNN reporting that Texas Governor Abbott put migrants on buses and sent them to liberal and sanctuary cities for those mayors and governors to deal with.

"I think Dan's plan is better, as far as bus service goes," says Felicia.

"On another note, Mo . . . " Felicia hands over a twenty dollar bill to Mo. "For the strippers, before the devil outlaws 'em," she adds.

CHAPTER 13
For What It's Worth

Midnight. Her voice looms in his brain. "I'll fill in all your sins in your obituary, not to worry, Daddy." Celeste threatens more. "And however you die, I'll fill that in, too. I will tell the truth."

Dan realizes that the assignment is a ruse, that Celeste will indeed write her own version of his obituary, so Dan resolves that he will take control of his death, and pass out printed obituaries prior to his suicide—an obituary more to his liking. *Suicide? There you go, then.* He had passively considered killing himself during his midnight chats with himself, but had remained undecided. Until this moment.

Mostly he had wanted to worry C. But then he realizes that suicide is the stuff that makes writing one's own obituary truly fun. Internal conversations, planning, preparing, creating a great story—this task could inspire him right up until the intended last day of his life—his birthday, only a week away.

Dan writes a sentence that gives him chills. "Dan ended his life on the night of his birthday party. He died on his own terms, using Ativan and a Glock." It's brief, to the point, and badass. And bigger than the recent suicide of his very last girlfriend, Shell Jensen!

But if the proclamation to kill himself gives him a high by day, the intensity of the fantasy succumbs to fear during his midnight musings. *Who commits suicide? Mentally ill, destitute, frightened, raging, tortured human beings? Or confident, self-admiring war heroes? Self-admiring war heroes who were okay fathers, okay husbands, okay Christians, okay alcoholics?*

If he goes through with this, this suicide, Dan might simply become a number. At one of those interminable health lectures sponsored by the RRC, he learns that thirty percent of all suicides are committed by old people because of ill health, loneliness, or grief. And Dan can't stomach having anyone think of him as old, or sad, or lonely. And if he writes about his suicide in the obituary he intends to pass out at his party, then he'll give his plan away, and they'll lock him up before he can ever pull the trigger. *Shit.*

Once again he entertains the possibility of Rapture, but Dan knows he has little control over God's action. God might just leave him behind, pun intended. He believes in God's impeccable timing, but he never liked flying, so he shudders at the thought of angels carrying him to paradise. Dying in his sleep from a chocolate cake induced coma would be ideal. But just in case he can't make himself die a natural death, during sleep, he will keep the gun close by. Yes, Glock, if only he can make a solid decision and stick to it! Ativan will give him numbness. He just won't care if he lives or dies.

Editing. 'Old Dan Kellar died by his own hand on the night of his one-hundredth birthday party,' *will be the opening line of my obituary.* 'And not because I was lonely' *will be the second."*

Nobody listening, all alone to muse.

Adding. "A white man in America. A manifesto as well as a tribute." Completing his manifesto will reveal, with clarity, this white male's personal story, starting with Dan's own victimization. "I, like other white males my age, am guilty of sins—sins I didn't know I had made for the first nine decades of my life."

A manifesto and an obituary! Oh, so much to do, so little time . . . just a week! Dan is not a man who can just stare mindlessly at the stars. He has to challenge his old brain on those summer nights before the birthday party. Ninety-five-year-old Dan forces himself, midnight after midnight, for the few days still allotted to him, to go back to the mundane, forgettable nights at his old bar—ordinary days of life. It's more than nostalgia, he knows. He asks his old brain to recall any memorable incidents that might justify the man he became, and give him something to work with here at the end. And it turns out his new obsession is praying for forgiveness for the one thing over which he felt a wee bit of remorse. Shooting Wayne.

But first, in his mind, he replays the sounds of 1978.

Telephones. AM Radios. Window units. The Star Spangled Banner playing at midnight at the end of the television day. The clinking of bar glasses on a busy night. A percolator brewing.

Timers set for ovens. The punching of timecards at the beginning and end of a work shift. Lockers slamming as part-time workers changed clothes to begin their shift.

And Corrie, who was tragically placed on a leash due to her dementia, as she posed a constant risk of injury. (No "life alert" in those days.) *Shit.*

Dan spends his days alone in his room, working non-stop on his obituary. (Briggs is away, still assisting the police in their investigation into Shell's suicide.) He blissfully entertains the idea of writing that, upon his glorious demise, SOMEONE (who will find him first? Briggs? FN? Celeste? He ponders on this briefly, then moves on to the more thrilling parts) will discover a Glock 22 (a forty caliber semi-automatic handgun) in his grasp. Of course he knows that carrying a gun is illegal in general. He is a felon after all. When he was younger he did his utmost to conceal that fact. But at ninety-five he discovers that he doesn't actually care who is aware of his criminal history—he'll just leave out the felonious details. *Ahhh, the splendor of advanced age.* Dan adores being tasked to write about his actual death in advance of it. But it's tricky. "Death is so intriguing to plan," Dan whispers to himself between fits of coughing. "Dan enjoyed a large piece of chocolate cake, two bottles of wine, and six Ativan pills before blowing his head off in front of the partygoers," he writes. *Hmmm. Too much information?* He rethinks: *It's inconsiderate.* He scratches that out and rewrites. "Dan enjoyed a large piece of chocolate cake, two bottles of wine, three rounds of casual sex, and six Ativan pills before lying down in his bed. He said his prayers, placed a gun in his mouth and pulled the trigger, not leaving a mess." *Well, that's obviously a lie. Of course there would be a mess.* Did he think he could do it, could even write about it? The threat that C would write his obituary sealed his fate. Suicide, painless, lovely suicide—on his birthday—is how it will all end. Only thing left is to decide whether to do it in front of everyone, or alone.

Dan is sorely aggravated one afternoon because C is really

in the room and looking over his shoulder, monitoring the writing. Aggravating. So Dan nicely asks C to take the afternoon off. She dallies.

He does what he has to do to get rid of her. He insults her weight, her irritating voice, and reminds her that, once upon a time she had wanted to become an actress. "Only you couldn't act," he says. C runs out of the room crying. Success. She roars out of the parking lot, music blaring, sings along to some Taylor Swift, who also understands man problems. Her father watches her from his picture window. The car stops. The driver's side window rolls down. She turns the song up, and . . . Dan hollers *blah, blah, blah,* slams the window shut.

Sometimes, when Briggs is sound asleep, FN joins Dan in his midnight musings. She wants to pick his brain about Jimmy. Her relationship with Jimmy is still new, scary, strained. There are moments he goes all dark. Crazy. Dan had hinted that Jimmy used to beat his wife . . . maybe she should have listened. Sometimes, after their dates, she'd lie and tell Jimmy that she had to work the night shift. She figured he might spy on her, so she took to going back to the RRC on those nights when she lies. Just to hang until she felt it was okay to go home.

She'd take her bottle of wine, sit on the patio. Sometimes she'd catch Dan all weepy. God was moving ever closer to Dan. And He demanded an accounting.

Go deeper, Dan, God says. "God tells me to go deeper, FN."

"Well, I'm no therapist, and that's what I think you need, or a priest, but I'm here. I'm listening. Go to the night when you shot Wayne Herd in the back, if you're not finished with that story," FN suggests.

Nothing makes Dan happier than to tell his stories.

"In the few days I have left, forget everything Briggs says, or Jimmy says, about that night, and just listen to me, FN. Now, about shooting Wayne. Well. John Wayne would have justified the shooting as 'patriotic.' Dan sighs.

So. Long. Ago. But Dan's long term memory is excellent.

"Well, FN, bear with me while I light my pretend cigarette." Proceeded to mime tapping the pack, lighting the match, taking in that first great, bitter-tasting puff.

"First I guess I need to fess up about Tad."

Being the son of Dan Kellar, a hero of three American wars, Tad—Thaddeus Kellar—was destined to be a soldier. His heritage demanded that. Tad didn't have to hold out for the draft. He was expected to volunteer. Dan never doubted for a minute that Tad would ever think of doing otherwise.

But at some point in 1967, Tad started slanting left on the subject. All that hippie crap, you know? At the dinner table, fights were fought.

At the time, Dan felt confident that all Americans valued the troops and supported the war. The only exception he knew of was Wayne Herd.

One night Dan confided to FN. On the porch. Smoking their one cigarette. "I vowed that Tad would not follow Wayne's example. I told you Corrie was hard, but I struck my only begotten son across the face when he suggested going to Canada with Wayne. I slammed my Tad into the patio window, shattering it, injuring him. The following day when Tad joined the Army, his face was covered in stitches."

"Jesus Christ, Dan, that's pretty damn harsh," FN says.

His eyes fill with tears. "That was then. I remember being proud of my son for doing the right thing, even though I had to beat the shit out of him to get him to do it. I generally leave that part out when I tell this story, but now, at the end, I know it was wrong. To hit him, I mean. I used to say 'The boy is John Wayne (spoken in Dan's best 'John Wayne' voice.) Courage is being scared to death but saddling up anyway.' My boy saddled up."

The first time FN met Dan, only a few weeks before, he was all southern gentleman. Charming. Put together. He was sitting on the sofa reading the Bible, hair combed, teeth in, nice socks. She had expected a drooling, ranting, raging bull after her training sessions with Destin-ee and Celeste. And she knew that the team had already been called in several times to discuss moving him out of assisted living and into a more secure environment, or getting him a responsible roommate. She couldn't imagine why at the time. The man was sharp, with a kickass vocab, and was a master storyteller. For the first two weeks she hung on his every word. She also knew that part of her job was to listen politely to an old man tell the story of his life. After awhile it seemed to her that the story he most needed to get out was the one about shooting Wayne.

Then there was the Dan crashing bottles on the sidewalk, threatening her with death. This Dan, the bad father, is a whole different animal. But tonight FN sees the vulnerable Dan, the one who seeks God's forgiveness.

"Shooting that boy hurt me bad. I loved that boy. Wayne, along with your Jimmy, was one of our family. The little tykes used to don Daniel Boone caps, cowboy hats, and toy army helmets. Play army. (choking up, heavy intake of air) The three boys, Jimmy, my Tad, and Wayne, I swear the boys wanted to be just like me. Every word I uttered was the gospel to those three.

"All three boys were drafted to be sent to Vietnam. Your Jimmy went without question. He couldn't wait."

The sum of this old man's story was told over his last few midnights. As sharp as he was, sometimes his patter would slow down, he'd struggle to remember words. It was torture for Dan —paid torture for FN. She feigned listening, worrying the whole while. "Let's go inside, Dan. You need to wind it down." She checked his vitals, changed his sheets, his clothing, guided him to the toilet. She would wait outside the door, and listen to him pee in the sink—all the while droning on and on to try to finish the story.

"Wayne, on the other hand, was tow-headed like a girl, a star football player and ladies' man, whose upstanding stepfather "Mr. Chapman" had a chain of gas stations and had amassed quite a bit of fortune. Admittedly Wayne had the most promising civilian future. "If you would just enroll in college," Mr. Chapman begged him, "you could be anything you wanted to be." Wayne wouldn't budge. "And you could evade the draft." I wasn't fond of that attitude, but looking back, I guess I . . . but Wayne had no interest in going to college or fighting in Vietnam. He was just worthless, despite my efforts to bring him up right. So his stepdad cut him off, believing that a lack of money would force Wayne to do one or the other. Turns out the local Draft Board assigned him to go to Vietnam, so Wayne's only choice, in his opinion, was to run away to Canada when his number came up. And it did come up. And he did run.

"I helped Jimmy all I could. Lived in a small, shabby, slab house. His father was shot to death in the front yard. Shot by a lady who was "not his wife.""

FN was gobsmacked. "Jimmy's father was actually murdered?"

"When Jimmy was fourteen years old. Became the head of his family, and they were the poorest family in town. Eleven brothers and sisters, a mother, a grandmother, all living in that shack. Jimmy spent as much time with me as he could. We hunted and fished, and talked. He longed for the day when he would be an American soldier, and since he was fit, poor, and Mexican, he was guaranteed a tour in Vietnam by our local Draft Board. I was proud of that boy."

"Dan, Jimmy certainly never told me that his father was murdered. That explains . . . So much."

And it wasn't long before FN was having second thoughts about her new man. After a few more scary episodes with his temper, FN went from being late to calling in sick just to avoid talking to Jimmy in the parking lot. But avoiding him was not wise, she feared. He was damaged, and a lot more than Vietnam did the damaging.

Chapter 14
. . .The Devil's Herd. . .

"Dammit. Hello, you old consarned world. (giggles) Dan. Ninety-five. Birthday in a little more than one week. Joe Biden is President. I feel tangled, strangled, mangled and jangled, and I shot someone for show."

Now that was an odd sentence to blurt out. *Slow down Dan's brain, think things through.*

FN asks. "You shot someone for show. Do you remember that you were a soldier?"

"Yes, of course I remember. Three wars."

"Which wars were they?"

Dan stares for a long time before answering. He knows that he knows the answers. All of the answers are on the tip of his brain, but he is slow to retrieve them. Finally. "Nazis."

Noticing her look of dismay, Dan panics. "Joe Biden is president," he offers.

"Do you know who was president when you fought Nazis?"

Uhhhhhm. Not sure, but whatever. "Truman."

"Are you sure? What year did you go to war against the Nazis?"

"It's in my head, just let me work my way there, FN. I couldn't make change that day at Walmart. Today when I woke up, I realized I had needed four quarters, two dimes and three pennies to pay for my eye drops and my Brylcreem. I had two buddies and we called ourselves the Brylcreem Boys until we found out that was a name for RAF guys. And when I signed up in January 1945, Roosevelt was president, not Truman. World War Two, that's what it was called. World War Two."

"Dan, you can't always remember long-term things the older you get, true, and you can't always have control over what you blurt out all of the time. You said you shot someone for show. Did that mean anything?"

"Embarrassing."

"Feeling embarrassed is a good thing. It means you are aware. Concerned. Healthy! 'Tangled, strangled, mangled and jangled' is how you felt before you shot someone. I get it. Good work today, Dan."

Celeste was always there when he woke up, he remembered that. But on this day he had forgotten she would be there, in spite of the fact that she had been there every day for fifteen years, take or leave the Pandemic years, and panic overcame him. Celeste knows his secrets, and with his memory going, how terrifying it is to have a hostile daughter who knows his secrets, and who could even make some up, if she catches onto his forgetfulness. He looks around the room. His daughter staring out the window. At first he thinks maybe she has not heard this exchange with FN, but she's chewing the inside of her mouth, so he knows that she is aggravated about something. Once the nurse leaves, Celeste stands up, her arms crossed. He holds his breath and waits for the verbal abuse. It doesn't come. All she says, "you just got the wars out of order, Dad. Korea was before Viet Nam."

"Yes, Nazi. Korea. Viet Nam."

Dan is breathing rapidly.

"I covered for a slip of the tongue. I shot Wayne, I shot that Wayne Herd for show," he adds.

"Yes, you did, I remember every detail, Daddy. Trying to *wow* the bar's bloodthirsty customers that night."

"Yes, at the bar. I shot him near the bar. I didn't mean to."

"I remember every detail of that night, Daddy. January 1978."

He stares at Celeste with impatient disgust. At the moment, he hates her.

"That was so long ago. Let's not talk about it. I want to do something different today, C."

"Oh yeah?"

"Yeah, I want to be alone. I have things to think about."

"What things?"

"My obituary."

"I can help with that."

"Oh no, I remember things one way, you remember them

another."

"And of course your side of the story is all that matters."

Dan pounds his face with his fists and screams.

C shivers. Maybe it isn't mild forgetfulness, but the mood altering beginnings of actual dementia. At the very least the demons in her father are stronger now at the end of life. Maybe her demons will be even stronger than they are now, God forbid, when she reaches her own end. She shivers again. C wonders whether she makes her old Dad nervous. She's caught him talking to himself when he thinks he's alone, and he's lucid. But he's often tongue-tied around her, can he be fearful of how she remembers things? C knows that she remembers the truth of things.

Dan talks to his Maker out loud now during his midnight musings, needs Him more than ever. God gave Dan the gift of having regrets. He mourns how ignorant he was when a young man of seventy-five, at his worst at fifty, filled with bravado at seventeen, and how embarrassed he is about all that past foolishness now.

"How can I redeem myself in your eyes, Lord?"

While he smokes his one cigarette he recounts each day to his Lord, Jesus Christ, who seems closer to him than ever- as close as the Blue Moon can be to earth. Dan peers into the heavens with awe, seeking out the Milky Way, constellations and star patterns, as if he has never seen them before. Suddenly Dan wants to see the Northern Lights and panics that he will never get to travel again.

Of all the things Dan should be praying about, as judged by anyone who knows him, attempted murder, violent temperament, lies, selfishness, terrorism, "Lord," Dan prays, "will you let me live long enough to take a trip around the world? How horribly fast this life goes by! It rushes by. Brakes off! And then you're old. Forgive me, God, for wasting so much time! I didn't travel! Except to kill our enemies." And now a peace comes over Dan. He feels grace, the unearned bliss of grace, forgiveness by God to the point where he has no need to confess his heinous sins anymore.

The law, and Celeste, may not pardon Dan's sins, but God surely does. All you have to do is ask.

Celeste watches over her father while he naps.

Moments before he'd drifted off to sleep, Dan ordered Celeste to ask Moiselle to put in a good old John Wayne movie in the DVD player in the day room for later on in the evening. Celeste smiles at the nostalgic memory of her father, her mother, brother, Jimmy and Wayne, all settling down on a Saturday night to watch a patriotic John Wayne movie. "Nobody will argue about watching a John Wayne movie after supper," Dan adds, sure that Moiselle will agree.

She doesn't.

"Well, think again. It's 2023. I make the rules and I say no. No John Wayne."

Celeste then asks Moiselle to allow her to go through the collection of DVDs. "Most everyone in here loves John Wayne movies, Mo, even if you don't."

Moiselle growls. "I said hell no. Ain't nobody in this establishment gonna watch John Wayne."

Celeste laughs. "Whatcha got against John Wayne, Mo?"

"If your Daddy wants to watch John Wayne, let him do it on his phone," Moiselle answers.

"You know Dad can't figure out his phone."

Mo snaps. "Well, too bad cause John Wayne is off limits in this place!"

"Are we really arguing over John Wayne?"

"Celeste," Moiselle says, "times being what they are, people have changed, even all these old people. I work both sides of the world quite well, C, the past and the present. John Wayne is cancelled. And rightfully so. I am embarrassed myself that I loved his movies when I was growing up. I literally feel sick now. Pretend cowboy, fake soldier, phony patriot, made up name. Nothing about John Wayne was real. And in real life, he was a racist and he cheated on his wives. Well, it's just toxic masculinity. That's all it is. If someone were in his way, he might kill 'em, Pilgrim. He didn't go much for education, nah, had six or seven words in his vocabulary:

horse, gun, communist, Jap, dog, sawbuck and Pilgrim."

Celeste is tempted to be tickled by Moiselle's comedy act, and usually Moiselle loves the laughter she earns when she's putting her foot down on the use or viewing or hoping to date things or people she considers to be cancelled, like Bud Light, Tampax and Leo DeCaprio, none of whom or which mark high use or viewing or fantasizing about in the old folks' home. Unfortunately, this time she is serious.

Moiselle begins strutting her stuff, steps up the performance. "John Wayne got mean if someone sat on his hat or was rude to a horse. He only killed men who deserved it, then got out a Bible and buried the poor sumbitch proper. He could take or leave a woman, unless she happened to become an Indian *accidentally*, in which case he wanted her killed. Oh my God, that one where Natalie Wood is kidnapped by Indians and he wants . . . "

"*. . . The Searchers!*"

Moiselle's expression takes on a menacing undertone. *"The* effing *Searchers.* The worst."

Celeste is no longer laughing.

"Moiselle," Celeste challenges, "he was an actor, that's all."

"John Wilkes Booth was an actor and look at all the damage he caused," Mo razzes.

"Mo! *The Searchers* was our family favorite. It's a movie about imperfect family values, which we all have. It's a movie about how racial inequality and the desire for vengeance fuels more violence for generations to come. Oh my God, Mo. My brother and I were raised on John Wayne. My Dad was, *is* John Wayne. I love John Wayne movies."

"Your Dad was, IS John Wayne?" Moiselle teases. "I'm so sorry."

Celeste chuckles despite her indignation at the slam against her aging father. The one thing C still admires about her father—he's John Wayne-ish.

C needs a break from this argument and gets up to check on her napping Dad. Dan is sound asleep. She stares into his face, which she rarely sees in repose. Between his brows, there are deep concern lines, and in spite of having a luxurious mane of hair, his hairline is thinning, and there are age spots there. He appears to have dozed off just as he was about to squeeze tears from his eyes. His eyes are tightly shut and C's heart aches at the sight. He will be gone soon, and it will be too late to fix everything wrong with the two of them.

Moiselle is somewhat remorseful, follows her to Dan's room.

"I'm sorry, C." Moiselle apologizes but adds, "sometimes I forget how conservative you Kellars are."

"You don't know anything about us."

Moiselle purses her lips.

"You seem to be bracing yourself for a fight," Celeste says. "Don't. You don't even know what you don't know."

"Well, I'll be frank. FN has expressed concerns that you are reporting the news to your Dad every day."

"I told him about the Titan. I never talk to him about politics. Because he and I think very differently. AND I know there is a policy against the news."

"We want them shielded from the news. Period. This country was torn apart on January 6th and there are dozens of trials happening right now, trials that could end with a bunch of white fuckers getting away with near murder? You know, like your father did. Twice, I believe?"

This roar of rage coming her way takes Celeste by wide-eyed surprise. "Nobody I know, and certainly not my Dad, had anything to do with January 6th."

"You mean, *the insurrection*. But *generally speaking* your father is on the right and *generally speaking*, your father got off without going to prison. For attempted murder. Twice!"

"Mo, why are you trying to pick a fight with me?"

"Your father triggers me. He triggers a lot of people. Remember his speech to solve the border problems? All homeless are fucking drug addicts? Well, he didn't use the word 'fuck' that day in his crazy 'how I would fix border issues' rant. But fuck him anyway. And FN tells me he refers to Jimmy as 'being able to take the Texas heat, because he's Mexican, brown, brown,' he's a racist pig, your father is. And sometimes I watch the news at home. It just makes me so damned mad at everyone. Especially all those old white assholes. It's never been fair in this country."

"I have no way of knowing whether our racial experiences have been different or not, Mo. I don't know where you come from, or what your heritage is. I don't care. I respect you. I just want to understand why this hostility over a John Wayne movie. Dad was probably all the terrible things you imagine him to have been, so was John Wayne, but he's old now, and he's changing. And John Wayne was a . . . nothing more than a movie star."

"Your father. Like the Nazis at Nuremberg. Get to the end and pretend to change to keep from being executed. Lies. Only your father wants to go to heaven. Bullshit. I call bullshit."

"How can you compare my father to the Nazis at Nuremberg?" Celeste is calm, but shocked at what she is hearing from someone in power at the retirement home, someone who put rules into place that forbids her father and others from being exposed to any kind of national news. Someone whose job it is to care for her aging father, no matter what his political beliefs, or his past. The hypocrisy is glaring, but Mo doesn't see it. *Mo wants to hate.* C is not sure why.

A somber Celeste confides what she knows will be the biggest regret in her life—the lack of a loving relationship with her father. "I cursed the man to hell a million times in my seventy years of life, Mo, as you well know. How many times have we gone to the bars together, and confided in one another. I thought we were friends. But he's ninety-five, he's worried about his soul, he wants to go to heaven and that's where I want him to go."

"God don't want him, Celeste. He's too ornery and he's a Republican."

"You do not know how he votes. And God surely does not discriminate between Republican and Democrat."

"Okay, I hear you, loud and clear, old people get a pass, even Republicans," Mo says.

One last word from Celeste. "Okay, he voted for John McCain. Not that it is any of your business. He voted for Reagan. But he also voted for Obama, Mo. I'm just saying, warning you, there's much we don't know. About anyone. So shut your mouth and I'll shut mine. You have no idea why he wasn't punished for shooting Wayne Herd, didn't go to prison, and you have no idea why he thinks he wears an ankle bracelet. He wants to watch a damn John Wayne movie once more before he dies. I want him to have this one simple thing and I don't care who or what John Wayne may have been like in life. He's my Daddy and he's going to watch a GD John Wayne movie tonight. Now go get the DVD player, Mo, and you and I will put this to rest."

Wherever Dan is, in slumber, he smiles upon subconsciously hearing those words from his child.

From his wheelchair later that same day. Dan's holding a DVD in his hands. *The Shootist*, John Wayne's last movie. He scans the residents, the staff of the RRC.

For most of Dan's life, John Wayne was his hero. But *Saving Private Ryan* is Dan's all-time favorite war movie. When that movie was released, he was seventy years old. "Earn this. Earn it." Those are Captain Miller's last words before dying at the end of the movie.

Dan believes these words are the guiding principles that he and his mythological hero, John Wayne, have/had always lived by, that all their conduct had been in an attempt to "earn" the sacrifices made by American veterans. Everyone around Dan was held to this high standard. Dodge the draft? Not earning it. Not paying taxes. Nope. Drug-dealing, vandalism, car-jacking? No.

But these were all about being a man. Like the morality of his beloved country, the inclusion of respect for women came late.

Chasing women, using them, underestimating them? Hell, that's just being a man, though he would never use the "c" word, or refer to anyone's private parts as a "p" word.

Dan looks around the RRC and sees that a lot of men who believe they are "earning it" "have earned it" are men who treated women badly in the middle of their lives. And he was one of them. At ninety-five, Dan knows it's almost too late to be a better man to women. He doesn't know how he can make it up to the floozies in the home. He knows he should treat Celeste better, for example. But he really doesn't like her, or does he?

It always happens around midnight of the days when Dan does not feel God's grace upon him that the ninety-five-year-old man's mind is inundated with recollections of his own foolishness, aggression, bigotry, and just plain awful behavior. He has a brand-new issue—regret—that is making him contrast the importance of his life with Captain Miller's parting words, "Earn this. Earn it."

"Regret" reminds Dan of God's existence, the necessity of repentance, and the mystery of the afterlife. Faux Christian Dan, who never gave God a thought when he was younger, is now counting on the promise of the Bible that "He who has repented of his sins, the same is forgiven, and I, the Lord, remember them no more."

Dan Kellar is conscious of his past toxic attitudes, his scorn for any individuals who weren't or aren't in the military, and his general misogyny. He is adamant that God will not prevent him from entering paradise because of these things. All the men he knew committed the same sins.

Seeking justification for his transgressions requires recalling and critically evaluating nine decades' worth of wrongdoings. The simple targets are alcohol abuse, and, of course, his idea of what it meant to be a man. Hell, he could even blame his role models. But Dan concludes that his morals became clouded during Corrie's early stages of dementia, which had occurred ten years after their son, Tad, had vanished. Life hardened him. He misbehaved out of grief. God would understand. Nevertheless, he needs forgiveness for those years.

Once Dan is on his way to paradise, the truth, the memories, and the suffering will all be worth it. But for now memory is a hair shirt.

His terrible behavior was at its worst in 1978. The year he shot Wayne Herd. And sometimes God demands his accounting of such things. Dan knows he's got to face Wayne Herd, has got to get his forgiveness. The worst nights, the ones when God turns away from him, letting Dan feel fear, hopelessness, regret; these are the nights when He lets Dan stew on his greatest fear—that he'll do all this work to resolve his sins in this life, only to die and find out there's nothing after and that he should have stayed an atheist after all. But because he can't be sure, Dan gets himself worked up, in a panic that his end will be close, he'll be unforgiven by Wayne, by God, and will have to delay killing himself. So many long years without God, not needing God. So many years when he figured the misery with Corrie would end up with the reward of a long, peaceful sleep. It wasn't her fault. Before her mental decline, as the wife of an American soldier, Corrie had tried to fit in, tried to forget her struggles in Germany. She tried to be Dan's wife. They threw cocktail parties. She chattered endlessly in her German accent and laughed too loudly at the bad Texas small talk. But it was Hitler's accent, and the laughter of someone crazy. She couldn't make it work, not in Texas.

Nobody befriended her, except Briggs. The parties flopped, but no matter, Corrie hated them anyway. Everyone was doing the Twist. Or playing Twister. Or grinding their hips. Always flirting with vulnerability. Corrie and Briggs sat in the corner at the parties, sipping vodka and whispering. They slipped away once Dan started telling his stories. Dan, heart aching, would watch her go, but kept talking. Sometimes he didn't remember what story he'd told.

Briggs. Briggs was not the first sign that Dan's marriage was a sham. In fact, Briggs proved that Corrie had some life left in her.

Then, in a flash, after Tad went missing, Corrie's mental health declined. What with her grief, and the Alzheimer's diagnosis, Briggs bailed on her. She started setting fires. Any chance she could, she'd run out to the porch and grab the full gas can Dan always kept on hand. Try to start a little fire. She'd dance around it like it was some kind of healing ritual. He'd take it from her, trying to keep her and the bar and town safe. He started leashing her to the piano, but she'd find ways to escape. And then one day. One horrible day. She managed to pour gasoline all around without his knowing. Lit a match. And just like that, Corrie was gone. Now, at ninety-five, he wants to die and rejoin her. He longs for the misery of life to last eternally. Not just the blurring of days, one after another, but the dark nights and the loneliness of old age.

He had hoped that death would come easy for her, but it didn't. Eight years of dementia, and then she set herself on fire. Like a martyr. Maybe it was an accident—burning away her grief, her pain. *Death has to be better for me*, Dan thinks, as he thrashes around the Temper-Pedic, flinging the pillow onto the floor, flopping around with restless legs, tinnitus blaring, and neck aching. She had a horrible death. He's hoping that death for him will be like the excitement of Friday night at five, when the work week is over and it's party time with perfect weather.

Because Dan needs to die easily, he has to; he's too scared, he's too old, and he cannot imagine being ready. He knows he won't burn himself, and he figures he'll never be sick. He managed the Covid years without Covid. He managed the war years without being killed. He managed jail without being someone's bitch. He wins, every single time. He cannot be destroyed easily. But he's not invincible; he has to die. And he fucking always has to pee. He gets up too fast, dizzy, feet on the floor, tangles himself again in that goddam pillow case. This time, he hits chest first, BANG, hits the nightstand on full ribcage, and lands on the hard floor right on his temple. He's breathless, maybe injured. Knocks him out completely. Thinks he's dead for sure. White light. God! Well. He sure has a thing or two to say to God.

Yet even unconscious, the man can tell a story.

CHAPTER 15
. . . *Hey, Joe* . . .

Time was running out anyway. Then Dan fell, hit his ribs, and his head. Now he's in the white light. He's between life and death, and Dan knows enough about God to know that God (and maybe God's entourage, His Son, and The Holy Ghost) wants answers. An accounting for his life. Over the course of the three earth days he was unconscious, his injured brain became fixated on one story: He shot Wayne for show. Now to tell God all about it.

"I know, I believe that You're here. Let me say, though, there's an unsettling aspect to the color white. I feel alone in this white light. Nobody has come by to welcome me. Not my parents. Not brother Rick. And not Tad. Or Corrie. It's eerie.

"I figure you want me to account for why I shot Wayne Herd, and that's why we're alone." As soon as he speaks, the white descends into a vortex and suddenly there's a movie sprawled across a mighty heaven. It feels to Dan like being on a roller coaster coming to a slow stop in the station. And suddenly there he is, at his destination. The movie is silent, but in color. Like an anamorphic movie shot on an old Panasonic, "mit" out sound.

Dan narrates, but the images are so marvelous to see, after fifty years, that he easily trails off, staring, tears coming to his eyes.

SUPER: 1978

"It was a gritty, small town roadside bar for hard drinkers. That was my bar, Kellar's Bar—where Corrie and I served our community before, during, and after the Vietnam years. The full name of the bar was "Kellar's Born to be Wild Bar," and the perfect place for it to be was where it was—on the outskirts of Rupert, Texas. America. This was John Wayne's America, too, almost entirely Caucasian, although being Texas, a significant number of citizens were of Mexican heritage. And that was okay. It was a place for heterosexuals for sure. The town managed to avoid homosexuality until the 1980s, and it was not okay, but nobody really got upset over it, you know, by the light of day. My bar was very masculine, some today would say 'toxic.' So you gotta remember, Lord, this was way back in time. Please don't judge me by what those woke people say today. The bar itself was kitschy, and dusty, and ill-kept, although it was always in a state of being cleaned up and painted. It was a bar with a Juke box from the nineteen-fifties and there were cool neon signs, it became a bar where everyone drove either an American-made pickup or a basic Harley.

"It was a man's bar, Lord, though women were welcome as you can see. (This fact is evidenced by a dilapidated "Red, White, and Blue Bicentennial Wet T-shirt Contest" sign on the wall.) There was a casual area, sort of like a Starbucks of today, where men could come of an afternoon, sit in a comfy chair, have a beer and some chips, read from the 'library' of sorts—books about everyone's favorites at the time: Hitler, the Mafia, I couldn't keep a copy of *The Godfather* in the bar, always someone taking it home—leaving books on hunting, and other manly things.

"Kellar's was definitely a ramshackle old building and it was set back a ways from the rural two-lane highway. Up on a high hill. Packed every night, though. I could unlock the door, look at, and see all the truck lights on the road leading up. You parked. You made your way from the parking lot to the steps and up onto the rickety old porch. That's where I kept my grill. And a swing. Instead of coming into the bar, you could choose to head to a large patio off to the right of the porch. Lots of people gathered there, drinking, laughing, hollering at me, if I happened to be grilling that night, to "turn that beef now, don't let it burn." The roof leaked sometimes, drenching the porch, but inside it was homey. To come into the Bar, there was a screen door. I can still hear that door squeak and slam shut. I can still hear people's voices, "Hey there, Dan!" "Hello sweet C." C worked the bar, practically all her life. Patrons come in, sometimes, well, always they were stapling things to the walls—bras and panties sometimes, silly, I know, high school playbills and old TV Guide covers, black and white movie star pictures, especially John Wayne, funny things.

"The electrical wiring was always iffy in the place and you never knew when you might have to run for a fire exit, or any exit, because what with all the smoke from the cigarette smokers, in a bar where everybody was a smoker, and all the smoke from the barbeque grill outside on the porch, and all the smoke that spewed from one or two of the electric outlets, well, you get the picture, Lord.

"That bar represented when America was great to me 'cause we could smoke cigarettes and laugh at anything we wanted to laugh at.

"Now I know America wasn't always great for everyone, women had it harder, blacks, sometimes religions were . . . at odds, but in 1978, the like-minded of us in Rupert all thought we were living the American Dream. We really did. Believe me."

Dan marvels at the trip through the Bar when it was at its height of success. He wants to add as many details as he can to prove to God how truly great it was just being able to congregate somewhere, commune with like-minds, drink all night if you wanted, smoke, dance, flirt, stagger home, and go to work the next day to earn an honest living.

"Along about any night of the week, except Sundays, you could find me outside on the porch pouring lighter fluid onto the grill bricks, slapping burgers and dogs around, and charring them to a delicious crisp. Everybody ate good at Kellar's.

"Course everybody drank. Alot. Drunk dancers populated the central floor inside the bar from about dusk until two a.m. I generally watched the dancing from the porch, and simultaneously I would be watching the goings on that always seemed to be happening in the huge parking lot out front. I did see some fights, some adultery, got no other way to put that, some puking from overdoing it; but you know, normal stuff. I may have judged it some, but I didn't butt into other's business, you know?"

Some of this confessing makes Dan a little bit self-conscious, after all, he's telling God his story. Not sure the way he's telling it is appropriate for God's ears, but God is not a child, so Dan goes on, albeit a bit uncomfortably. His voice rattles more, his throat is drier, his chest is congested as if he'd smoked a couple packs. He uses all of these things as enhancements to his storytelling, though, you know, like you do.

He was taken aback a bit when God looks at his watch and says to him, "get on with it."

"The bar was extremely boisterous (cough, hark), even raucous, on that very chilly January night when I shot Wayne. Everyone in town was inside the warm bar, celebrating the long-awaited return (long exhalation, nostrils widening) of young Jimmy Ramirez to Rupert, after his protracted confinement in a mental institution, (quick puff of a fake cig) due to his unfortunate service in Vietnam.

"It got so crowded, so smoky, so warm in the bar, that folks ventured out onto the patio. Now the patio had six steps leading down to the gravel parking lot. It was a big parking lot. And in the parking lot, there were maybe six rows to park in, maybe fifteen cars to a row. Really, the only eyesore was the industrial dumpster that we kept off to one side. Otherwise the parking lot came up against thick, beautiful woods. Ash juniper, live oak, a few hackberries. Most rose up to sixty feet tall. And by moonlight? Jesus, it was beautiful, just like You planned it. And during thunderstorms? Woop. (coughing fit, cursing)

"Now, on that night, there was a big thunderstorm in the forecast, and we were all watching it come in, and then we saw an odd figure darting in and out of the trees, behind the rubbish bin. To the east.

"Wayne Herd was back in town, and the bar was abuzz with that news. Scumbag (hack, hark) had been pardoned by the weakest sumbitch president the U.S. ever had—Jimmy Carter. Forget him building huts for the poor now. Jimmy Carter pardoned traitors to this country. I'll never forgive it."

Momentary oops . . .

"The locals cheered me on. Yep, from that patio, on that night. They figured my Tad was missing as a result of the same draft that this asshole, Wayne Herd, had dodged. So they figured Wayne and I had a showdown coming. And yes, I damn well expected to get away with justifiable murder. It was Texas, after all.

"Since you mention it, Lord, I had no regrets about sending Tad to battle. I grieved afterwards that my son fell out of that helicopter. It might have been shot down, and he may have been abducted, and starved. Killed. I never wanted that. I just wanted him to serve his country.

"The moments before I shot Wayne I was out there in the parking lot, sweeping up broken bottles. I think I was looking for him. Out in the woods. If You recall, I prayed to You, I prayed that You would keep Wayne away from me. That if You didn't, it would be a sign to kill him. And then I saw him running through the trees. And I thought my prayer was answered. I had to go through with it then.

"This is on You, Lord.

"Still, I wanted to make sure it was him. He called out "Corrie! CORRIE!" So I knew. Corrie was inside the bar. Heard her name yelled, perked up and ran outside. She wasn't dressed for the weather at all. She flew off the porch, ran past me. Barefoot, arms up in the air, she ran across the parking lot. I ran inside, called to Jimmy for help. Because it was a dark, misty, and cold to the bone night. January, for God's sake. "Jimmy, we need to rescue Corrie; she escaped," I said.

"I sped past the patrons in the bar and made my way to the place in the back where I kept my guns. I grabbed a rifle, loaded it, and barreled back to the porch. All the bar patrons yelling. 'Look, Dan's got a rifle!' 'Dan's gonna kill that sumbitch.' They smelled blood.

"They taunted me and challenged me to 'kill the draft dodger' . . . 'You got a gun, use it!' 'I got your back. We all got your back.' 'You're the one who should do it, Dan.' 'No jury would convict you.'

"Jimmy and I ran deep into the woods. I screamed, 'Look for her white nightgown!' That's all she had on. Because Corrie's nightgown was surely off by this point, drifting in the chilly wind. And then we saw her. Standing next to that gown, shivering, naked, and crying. 'Jimmy, put her nightgown back on her, take her back to the bar. I'll stay in the woods and . . . "

And just like that, God cut him off. Dan found himself in the tunnel again, alone. Never had Dan been so alone. And Dan believed he was left alone to face himself and his deeds on earth. It took a scary long while for God to return to Dan's sight.

Celeste later said that, on the third day of his unconsciousness, Dan's mouth kept moving, but no words came out. He was salivating, chewing. He twitched, his jaw clenched.

For a second there, Celeste thought he was having a stroke.

"Daddy, what's happening? Speak!" Tears were pouring down his face. Something broke, a reservoir, a dam. But Dan fell still as a corpse. Celeste called for the doctor.

Dan's brain made his heart pound (Celeste could see it, feel it), and Dan, semi-conscious, but paralyzed to stillness, knew that his damaged brain was racing. Random thoughts: *Will God reward me for killing a draft dodger, the lowest of life forms? Will God accept my actions as justified for the times? Or will He punish me for my deeds?* "This all took place half a century ago, you know. Morals evolve, times change."

Dan begged to stand before God again.

Celeste watched her father flatline.

And then all was white light once more for Dan and His most Mighty God made His presence known.

"I know I fired some shots, Lord. I didn't know what I hit. About that time I saw Corrie. She sprinted twenty-five yards out in the open, up onto the porch. I ran up the stairs, and followed her into the bar, watched her open the freezer, grab some ice cream and wolf it down like she was starving. She took a few more bites, then stripped herself of her nightgown again, in front of everybody in the bar.

"Butt naked, chowing down on ice cream, that was my Crazy Corrie. By now, everybody's laughing at her and asking me, 'did you kill the draft dodger or not?' I knew then I did it to prove something to those assholes in the bar. I had to avenge Tad, to account for why Corrie was so crazy, you know. It was grief got her in the end. I mean, under all that . . .

"I thought it was a justified killing. Like the atomic bomb was, you know, in order to end the war with Japan. I swear I wondered if shooting Wayne, a bonafide, proven draft dodger and a traitor, was a good thing or an evil thing, considering the changing times?

I mean, President Truman fretted whether he done the right thing, too. Sending them bombs."

Realizing that he's deliberately using poor grammar in order to sound stupid before God, Dan catches himself. *What the? Well, damnit, God needs to understand the times he was living in, the 'back in the day we did it this way' kind of justification.* Emboldened, Dan then makes a play to accuse God of being at fault. *You know, the 'God has a plan' thing.* "And what about the torture that YOU had already inflicted on my family? Losing Tad? Jesus, can it get worse than that for any family? Corrie lost her mind, for God's sake.

"And the leash, please don't make me account for the leash. I had to restrain her, Lord, had to."

Jesus, the memories hurt so much—Corrie torments Dan even now. In his white light. In the fog, she's dancing and dousing that damn gas everywhere, and he, still alive, dumbfounded in the white light. The light that everyone said would be his bliss, but is not. Pissed. Pisssed is he. This is horrible.

And now, after his terrible fall, when his body couldn't move, but his mind, his mind was on fire. Fucking unfair. Reliving the awfulness of over fifty years before. Defending it when he shouldn't have to. God oughta know American history, for God's sake. How things were. For the white man. "When Corrie was found to have grief-related dementia, and continued to hit me, I wondered how I could take the best of care of her. There was simply no choice. I had to leash her. Like a dog."

Changing the subject.

"I shivered through the night in the woods after I shot Wayne, feverish and freezing, and I dreamt of the little boys I loved. Little boys playing army, bows and arrows, wearing a cowboy hat or an army cap, eating cookies at my kitchen table. Tad. Jimmy. Wayne. Sometime near dawn, I finally felt some peace, like You'd forgiven me, given me a pass, because of all our family suffering over Tad. I really wasn't sure I'd killed him. Then I saw Corrie dragging Wayne's body through the woods. She was carrying a gasoline can.

"So I went back to the bar, Celeste was behind the bar, quiet, I put the rifle up, and just started to clean up for the new day.

"Celeste opened the closet to get a mop. She took a sideways glance at my rifle . . . all she said, "Lots to clean, Daddy. Nothing like a shoot-em-up to get the testosterone tumefying the balls of all your macho man patrons. We'll talk about what you did out there later, Dad. But Mama was with Wayne, Daddy," C said. "When you were out there with your stupid gun. Out there yacking about mountain erosion, how everything looked different after ten years of him being gone. Laughing in the rain. You fired that gun four times, Daddy. Four times. With Mama out there. Daddy, you coulda killed mama."

"Tore my heart out of me, her saying that I could have killed Corrie accidentally. Later on, I learned I had not killed him. And of course, I was glad of that."

When Dan opened his eyes, he was in his Tempur-Pedic once more, and C was standing by the side of the bed. "I'm so stupid, C. I forgot to ask God about Tad. What happened to Tad? Jesus Christ. How utterly stupid of me to forget to ask. I had God right there, and . . . I just forgot to ask."

"In other words, you were just telling God one of your stories."

C smiled while she said it.

CHAPTER 16
It's Good to be King

On Friday afternoon Wayne Herd woke up with his back stiffer than usual. "Funny how back pain makes you feel old," he told Celeste, who had called him again for the second time in a week, while he was still in bed. This surprised him.

And for her part, C was surprised that he didn't throw the phone down again. He answered, she breathed, he knew who it was, and he said, "I'm not going to your dad's party." But he stayed on the line.

What in the world to say to the love of her life when, in fact, she had not spoken with him in twenty years. So much time had passed since their relationship soured; not a word since their last, their greatest shag of all time, a shag that cured the third "H" for months, back in 2004 or 2005. The problem was that they never talked. Never really talked. They had not talked about things that mattered to him. They had not talked about the regret that plagued her, plagues her still—she did not visit Wayne in the hospital after her father had shot him back in 1978. In fact she ignored the whole event.

Good God, she was, wait, had been, a terrible girlfriend, wait, she was merely the initiator, of booty calls. She was never a girlfriend.

He answered the phone, that sleepy-head voice she remembered. Hello.

This voice drove her crazy wild ever since she was seven. Lowering her normally whiny pitch to (what she believes is) hot sultry in order to seduce. "It's Celeste." (Clear throat, buzzzzzzzz lips, cough) "I'm calling to invite you to a party," she says. "Please change your mind, my love."

"Funny how back pain makes you feel old," he answers, "especially when that back pain was caused by a bullet."

"We can set some boundaries, Wayne. About Dad. But I need

you to be there with me."

"I said no." And then an opening. "I'm not feeling so hot."

"Oh Wayne, Rupert girls as young as forty-five, still see you as a "hottie," C assures him, to which he responds, "I meant, my back aches. Say, you been talking to many Rupert girls these past twenty years?"

"Well, I do still live here, even though I keep to myself these days," C answers. "I need you, Wayne, hot or not hot," she says.

Wayne stands up, winces, and glances at himself in the mirror. "Maybe I don't look so old. But I'm seventy-three, so having wonky discs in my spine, and so little lubricating fluid in my joints, is discombobulating."

"I know how old you are, Wayne. I'm sure you're . . . like I just said, still . . . "

" . . . There are mornings," he interrupts, "when I look in the mirror and see a disheveled old man with a dirty face staring back at me. Almost look like I'm an old drunk. And you know I don't drink much at all anymore. You remember when I could kill a bottle with one hand, while opening another?"

"You off that oxy, too?"

"You were the cause of that addiction, cutie cute. I'm clean as a whistle. Nothing wrong with me a little sleep wouldn't fix. If I could sleep better, I would look better," he says.

"I bet you're still as handsome as ever, especially in your sleep," she answers.

Wayne was happy to take the compliment. But business first.

"Ok, enough. I'm hurting real bad. I hear you, C. I'm gonna have to decline your invitation to the birthday party."

Pain ravaged him, which sometimes did take a toll on his looks and his mood.

"I need you to go to his birthday party."

"You do remember that the man shot me in the back?"

He reminded her that he had been unable to walk for more than a year.

"I'm sure you're just fine now, just a little pain."

"JUST A LITTLE PAIN?" He reeled, dizzy, but he didn't hang up.

Many years had passed, during which he lay flat on his back, unable to work. He'd considered the man who shot him as a second father. "You do remember that man, doncha, C? Your fucking dad."

"He's old now and all that . . . he wants to apologize to you, and he's inviting Jimmy, and Nicolette. And Geddy. You do want to see your grandkid, don't you?"

" . . . Stop. I don't want to see anyone from the past. And nobody from the past wants to see me. Especially Geddy. Whatever, though, Geddy has the last laugh. I inherited twelve gas stations, 10,000 acres of undeveloped land in Texas and New Mexico. From an uncle. And all that will go to Geddy." He suddenly has an afterthought. "You should have tried harder to catch me, C. I got . . . lots . . . of cash." (twinge, wince, squirm, tears form in his eyes from the pain) Celeste is driving eighty mph while she chats on her cellphone, excited to be talking to the unrequited love of her life, even if it's not going the way she wants. But then he hints at catching him? She drifts into another lane, nearly colliding with a truck.

"I know you're a rich man, Wayne, course I know all that. Whatcha been doin' every day since we last talked? Since you got rich?" C flirts, while she veers back into her lane. The driver of the truck brandishes a gun at her. She waves an apology. He shoots her the bird, but thank God, he keeps driving.

"I mean, it's great that you got rich, and that you never got married after Liam's mother died, but I figured that you'd become some kind of great philanthropist."

He tells her well, no, but he gives back to the community in the best way he knows how, even though his activities tempt fate and could cripple him. Two days a week he pounds nails all over Texas for Habitat for Humanity. He remains a member of a motorcycle club that rescues pit bulls and donkeys. Most days he lives his true dream, as a guitar playing singer/songwriter, even though he has to live it while leaning against a heating pad. "I'm famous, I live like a king, I'm completely happy," he says.

Yep, he writes a coupla songs a week. Rehearses them. Performs them. He rides his motorcycle to various small towns on Friday and Saturday nights to perform them with his little band, The AARPs. "You oughta come sometime when I'm performing around here."

Celeste chokes up. She glances in the rear-view mirror at herself. Jesus Christ, she is too overweight to see the man of her dreams again. She hasn't dyed her hair in months. She's stopped shaving her legs, for God's sake.

She changes the subject. "You don't get nervous riding a motorcycle with your back the way it is?"

Wayne explains that despite the modifications he had to make to his motorcycle to accommodate his wounded spine, he simply refuses to give it up. Yes, he feels stupid riding upright and reducing his speed, but by God, there's no bald spot under his helmet, and his blue eyes still blaze with passion, or so he has been told by his groupies. "Groupies!" And most important, he can still sport a leather jacket with dash.

"You're not a bit conceited!"

He laughs. "You know I am. (super twinge) Ah, it hurts to laugh, C. I wish I could say yes to your invite, but I just can't. Your father did a job on me. I'm just not the same man I was in 1978."

"I'll take the one you were in 2003," Celeste sighs, remembering the amazing, one and only Wayne Herd, from a time when wearing a leather jacket with verve was de rigueur. As in high school, as in his twenties and thirties, forties, Wayne Herd must still be the most desirable bad boy. "In my mind's eye, you're still that curly-haired blonde, not too tall, not too short, not skinny, not fat, but perfect, with boyish, bad boy good looks."

"I am that, C. Not dead yet. And perfect for a geezer band's lead singer. I get to sit on a stool and sing," he adds.

"You're the lead singer of a geezer band? OH MY GOD," she squeals. "I've always wanted to be a backup singer in a geezer band!"

"Well, come on, then, I remember you had a real pretty singing voice," he teases, but continues his tale before she can respond. He had long ago stopped traveling by motorcycle in the rain or sleet. He mostly just rides during the "eleven and a half months of the year when it's hot in Texas." He pauses. Waits. Laughs at his own joke, then "Oh, wait until you hear this news! This just happened this morning."

Because he is wealthy, Wayne has access to other filthy rich Texans, who have access to some pretty big music superstars from the eighties and nineties. About ten o'clock in the morning Wayne was sitting on his heating pad, strumming and drinking coffee, when the phone rang. "We want to produce a huge music festival. You got the land! We want it."

There's room. Lots of wide open space. There are only three trailers on any of his properties. Two of them are Wayne's—one when he sneaks into Rupert. His main trailer is in the Hatch Valley of New Mexico. The other trailer is outside of Rupert and belongs to the only other human being Wayne approves of, Jimmy Ramirez. So there is indeed room for a music festival.

"It may have been Don Henley who threw out the idea that I could be the new Tom Petty and headline the festival. Said he heard me sing once."

Celeste's heart pounds. "Don Henley? WOW. And Tom PETTY!!!!"

"The truth is that I don't fall for much, but this offer is tempting."

"What boomer doesn't want to be Tom Petty in a Tom Petty cover band?"

"I told 'em. I said look, you're just messin' with me. You could bring in any number of great cover bands. You could bring in The Wildflowers, for God's sake. Jesus. I wasn't born yesterday, you want my fucking property for free, don't you, you rich bastards."

"What did they say?"

"They said. 'We want to buy your property, for its full value and probably everything around it. We'll use Rupert city services. We'll work with the City Council. Rupert will get rich, property values will go up.' This is gonna change everyone's life," Wayne says.

"Looks like I'm calling at exactly the right time!" Celeste

answers. "Time for me to chase you down!"

Now she's embarrassed, that was dumb.

"Well, there are no accidents, C. What have you been up to for the past twenty years?"

Celeste has to think quick because she has nothing to tell. She lies. "You know, the usual. Working. Book clubs. Choir practice. Philanthropy. In fact, I'm just parking the car for a very important meeting. I'll have to call you back, is that okay?"

"Sure. Thanks for calling. Sorry I can't go to the party." And click, he is gone.

Tears run down her face. Celeste turns onto the street where she's lived her whole life, and parks in the drive way of the home she shared with her Dad. There is no meeting to go to. No job. Celeste could write a book about being in love with an unattainable man. He teases her, but he doesn't mean any of it. Sometimes he needs a woman, but not for long. The last time she'd seen Wayne Herd in the flesh, he was backing his motorcycle out of that driveway and heading off into the sunset.

The phone call from C is a win for Wayne, though. He puts down the phone, and hums a new tune.

At his age, her call feels even better than the ego boost of a successful booty call.

He picks up the phone and calls his buddy, Jimmy. "Guess who called me? Miss C herself. Celeste Kellar."

Wayne brags that the benefits of being complimented and admired by someone who carried a torch for him all her life, with none of her expectations, made his day. In the past, any encounter with C had led to arguments, then to tears, then sex, which then led to guilt and more sex, which then led to her calling him twenty times a day, screaming, "You think I love you but I don't love you. I don't." All that led to threats to never see each other again, which led to meeting in person to set up new ground rules for their relationship, which led to more sex. More and more sex.

"She was great in bed," Wayne recounts to Jimmy.

"Uh oh. Watch your back," Jimmy says, then reminds Wayne that he was too much of a horn dog to pay attention to the warnings his back offered when he was thirty, forty, or fifty years old. "And now you're seventy. Better listen."

"My back wanted me to choose between motorcycles on slick streets and slick women on motorcycles."

"Your injured spine is an excellent justification for staying away from the Kellars. I recommend you stay away from all of them."

Celeste Kellar had been a huge strain on his back in the years long after her father shot him. The roughhousing she instigated and expertly executed back in the day left him scarcely able to move more times than not. And just when he would regret sleeping with her because of his back pain, she would jump him again and off they would go, over hill, over dale, over kitchen counters.

"Might I remind you that the Kellar family is the cause of all your heartaches in life, first the gunshot, then the opiate addiction." Wayne's back ached before; the pain nearly killed him after having sex with her, and neither aspirin nor cocaine could make it better. But he couldn't resist her so he took drugs. Oxy.

He could certainly never resist her in private. In public, he ignored her because she was plump. But Jimmy knew the truth. Wayne secretly loved her.

"Just what I needed today, Jimmy. You reminding me of what's important."

"And don't go to the party if you don't want to."

"Why would he even ask, Jimmy?"

"Something about her father needing forgiveness. He's trying to make things right with God. Did he ever make things right with you?"

"Now how exactly would he do that, Jimmy? He can't go back and not shoot me."

Wayne was so excited, though, about the prospect of being the new Tom Petty, and about the prospect that a woman might still be interested in him, that his back stopped hurting. That afternoon he sat down and wrote a complete song in fifteen minutes, which he sang for a large and very drunk audience that very night.

By all accounts, his Friday night performance at The Crusty Curmudgeon in the small town of Perryville was sensational. His band buddies could hardly keep up with him. He did a mean Elvis, and wasn't bad singing songs by The Kinks, The Birds, with a little Johnny Cash thrown in. But when he sang that new one, "When love 'em and leave 'em leaves you unloved," he knew he had written a true crowd pleaser.

(singing) "When love 'em and leave 'em leaves you unloved/ you pour one/ you drink one/ you read *Atlas Shrugged*/You sit by the fire/ the liar that you are/ you pour one/ you drink one/ you watch *Lonesome Dove.*"

Even though audiences in small town Texas were not hard to please, Wayne was elated at the success of his latest song. The audience cheered, rims of beer glasses met and clinked, couples kissed. "Inspired by an old flame named Celeste. Celeste, are you out there?" Wayne knew that she wasn't, but wanted to riff with the crowd while he figured out his next set.

When the crowd hushed, he bravely tried out a few of his favorite Tom Petty songs, and while the response was positive, he could tell he was no Petty, and said so, but like he said, "who is?" The audience flicked lighters and swayed when he sang the anthems, though, and sang along.

But no rims clinked. No one kissed. There were a few angry slaps. Not sure if he had a real chance at being king. When they asked to hear his original song again, Wayne was thrilled. If he wanted more cheers, he needed new verses. So he slowed it down, improvised some.

(singing) "When love 'em and leave 'em leaves you unloved/ you strum your guitar/ head to the bar/ look for someone/ You sit by the fire/ the liar that you are/ you pour one/ you drink one/ you get yourself stoned/ you leave with Simone/ talking out loud."

"But (in sprechstimme) I wanted Celeste! (cheers, applause) I wanted Celeste, but her dad shot my ass!" (more cheers, then back to singing) "Wake up all alone/ when love 'em and leave 'em leaves you / oh, so fucking alone."

His audience gave an ovation then cried out for more boomer bliss: Fleetwood Mac, Jackson Browne, Bob Seger. Smoothly changed to wannabe cover band guy. He sang a throaty version of

"Dreams," played air keyboards, stood up and pranced around like Stevie Nicks, putting his left arm on his hip and waving an invisible lasso overhead. The crowd went wild. Wayne was on fire. Finally he took a little break, handed the vocals over to his buddy, the unambitious Brick, who couldn't have written an original song if somebody held a gun to his head. He played and sang some "Twist and Shout" that got everyone in the place dancing.

Wayne stepped outside for a smoke.

It was hot, brutally hot, and the middle aged ladies who were out smoking were scantily dressed. Wayne grinned as he saw three women in their fifties and sixties (what boomers refer to as "middle age") sporting artificial eyelashes, botoxed lips, and a couple crop tops that exposed their drooping midriffs. One desperate, flirty doll, who was well past her prime, raved about the cover of Rush's "In the Garden" that he sang in his last set. Wayne interrupted her knowing she was about to share her Rat experiences. He extinguished his cigarette, said "thanks, no stories, please" and then further wrecked her mood by stating, "I wish I'd had that song for my kid's funeral back in 2003, though. Say! You wanna hook up?"

Womp womp. "No thanks, I didn't mean . . . and sorry about your son," she said, walking away.

"Maybe some other time, okay," Wayne announced to her lovely, toned backside. "Hey, lady. Come back sometime. I am so deeply moved by you, if you get my drift."

He picked up his phone and punched in C's number. No answer.

Bad boy's back started hurting again.

CHAPTER 17
. . . When the bullet hits the bone . . .

Wayne kept up a good front. First there were the three gunshots. Took his breath away and knocked him to the ground. Hit his head on something. Then it was raining hard, and he saw Corrie under the light of a full moon. She was naked, pouring gasoline on the ground. He screamed to her, but with such a rasp that she didn't hear. She danced in circles, chanting. He remembered being turned over onto his stomach, a searing pain. Something warm wrapped around him. He was being dragged. He remembered cold, swirling water. He remembered his body being lodged on a limb. Then so much water, over his head, coming up for air, gasping, choking, sinking again, finally passing out.

At long last he came to, disentangled himself from the tree limb that had kept him from drowning. He crawled out of the flood waters, tree limb by limb, dragging seemingly dead legs to higher ground. Surgeons found and removed fragments of two bullets in the area of Wayne's lumbar spine, wreaking havoc throughout the soft tissue. His lower extremities were too weak to use for nearly a year after the surgery. He suffered post-traumatic amnesia. He didn't know whether he had a family or not, where he came from, where he was going that night, and most important, who shot him.

But somehow Wayne had saved himself. He'd survived the punishment for doing what he believed was right. He'd risen from rolling waters and got himself back down the mountain and called the cops for himself.

Music intervention therapy saved him. Released back into the scary world, Wayne rented a one-room efficiency apartment in East Dallas, near Baylor Hospital, lived next door to a redheaded therapist named Amie. For over a year, in her spare time, Amie taught him guitar, drums, held him when he cried with pain, sang with him, talked him down from the ledges of suicidal depression. And she made him dance—first sitting in a chair, then holding onto a chair, holding up a chair, without a chair. He never completely managed the pain because the pain was never manageable, but it felt better when he sang. By 1980 Wayne was strumming guitar with a band and singing backup. He invited his stepfather to come to Dallas and hear him play and meet Amie. On the big night, Wayne's wife and baby showed up instead, and Amie moved on.

Nowadays, occasionally, Wayne still wakes up in a pool of sweat, victim of a panic attack. He's not sure what happens in his sleep to bring the attack on, so whenever something important, or hopeful, or exciting is coming up, Wayne Herd keeps himself awake in order to prevent waking up in that pool of sweat. He needs to stay focused, decisive, organized. He takes Adderall and adds a few other over-the-counter drugs. His self-prescribed cocktail pushes his heart rate, elevates his blood pressure, increases his breathing, but it's worth it. Worth it, except the cocktail produces some sort of pharmacologic mechanism that causes traumatic nightmares.

This time, he stayed awake for two nights, excited about the music festival, knowing he had to make that final call to sell his land. At nine o'clock sharp on the deadline day, he made the call, but had to leave a message. *Well, fuck.*

Then he crashed, and woke up ten hours later drowning. How long it took him to swim to the surface of the dream water and above he'll never know, but it seemed like hours that he floated above the water, looking down on his reflection. He was hideously ugly in the reflection, like Abraham Lincoln ugly. Then he suddenly became handsome, and young, like John F. Kennedy. Junior. Then a newspaper floated by. Headline. "One bullet all it took to kill." By then he was fully awake, sweating, panicking, rehashing what Dan Kellar had intended to do to him. One bullet fifty years ago, lodged in his spine, tore through his stomach, pancreas, gut, lungs, spleen. Mother fucker. *Wake up, gotta relive the damn thing.*

He thought he lay on the ground for hours after he was shot. Time being relative to the experience of agony, it was actually only a matter of minutes. And then he felt his body being dragged away and tossed like he was nothing into water. The searing pain, so much pain. He fainted.

The bullets still leach lead into his system decades later.

When the phone rings, he picks it up and sells the land, just like that. His brain is still foggy, but he's ecstatic. The only thing that can go wrong is if the producers are mounting the music festival on behalf of the Second Amendment, or some political candidate on either side. He panicked at the thought of hearing, "We want to be sure Texas gun owners have the right to enjoy the festival without fear of bans. And we're thinking a gun show nearby might accompany the festival. And we're talking to Kid Rock, Alice Cooper, maybe Nugent."

Wayne went back to bed, put his head under the covers, and cried. He wasn't ready to "burn a draft card" again and get himself shot by some conservative white asshole, but he also wasn't ready to stand for shit policies. *Guns. Bullets. Not again. Holy mother fucker.*

CHAPTER 18

I had too much to dream last night

"Dammit. Still here. Hello world. I'm ready for my damn birthday party. A week, I think? Sue still collecting money for male strippers? Joe Biden is President."

With the mysterious firing of the big-boobed Administrator named Sue, came the sudden arrival of a new Administrator, Ms. Charlene Attenborough, and her husband, the Reverend A. R. Attenborough ("A. R." standing for the words "assault rifle," or so he jokes in church the first Sunday he preaches at the Rupert First Baptist.) Mo announces that strippers will not be coming to the birthday party. Already outlawed. "We all be Christians here now," she says. A.R.'s appearance at the RRC is a bad omen that Christianity might get in the way of Dan's suicide. Dan is seeking end of life forgiveness, but he realizes, finally, that what he seeks is forgiveness, but not from God. He owes God nothing. He listens to God. That's what you do. Dan clearly hears the voice of God interrupting his thoughts at the most inopportune times.

And Dan and God argue quite a bit over the one of Dan's big questions—the idea of God as "redeemer" while acknowledging God as "creator." Dan believes the Genesis account of the creation of the world, but after God made things and saw that they were good, Dan sees no reason for the Old Testament to have continued. The Old Testament only makes sense to Jews, and Dan is a Christian follower of Christ; therefore he is no longer required to follow Old Testament laws.

Assault Rifle loves taunting the old man. "I wish I could be a fly on the wall of Heaven when you get there, Dan. You will see the glory and the truth on that day."

"Great. Well, you were all wrong about what happens in the white light. But not to worry, I'm still a believer in heaven. And I sincerely hope I'll get to heaven for real and then, finally, someone in the know will answer my questions, not one of you dumb ass preachers down here."

"Oh, you won't be asking questions in heaven, Dan, you will be praising the Lord Jesus Christ all day and all night," A.R. assures.

"I will not spend twenty-four hours a day in praise, no sir, but I will be looking for flies, and I hope I find some, spiders and snakes, too, because that will prove to me that God is truly all loving—something none of you have proven to me yet," Dan warns. "Surely God, the Creator, did not create all of the living creatures just so each could have a short, miserable life and them send them to a hell after they die."

"Christians are the only creation that matters in heaven, Dan. Creator God is for earth. Redeemer God is for Christians." Assault Rifle can't wait to redeem the old backslider, and every chance he gets he corners the old man to suggest various Christian truths. For example, at the end of life Christian understanding pivots around two central truths—first, the sanctity of life, because God gave each one of us life at our birth (coming in) and secondly, encouraged us to be fearless of death because God will be our companion at our death (going out). Dan argues once or twice that surely God has been around throughout his entire life, not just at birth and not just at death, to which A.R. loudly proclaims, "God is too busy to deal with us on a daily basis; therefore, free will is in place throughout our lives, except for coming in and going out when God is actually around."

"Man cannot control his birth nor his inevitable death," the Reverend states, to which Dan replies, "Ain't the same thing true about sleep? Try to keep your ass awake for twenty-four hours or more and see what happens. No. Control."

"Sleep is just a dress rehearsal for death," A.R. pronounces, as he is an authority on all things labeled 'Christian,' especially when the rule is hard to follow.

"Sleep," Dan answers, "is one place I'd better not encounter your irritating, annoying ass. Now leave me and everyone in this home to our personal beliefs."

"Let's go potty now, honey, and change the subject." Moiselle snaps her fingers in Dan's face to make sure he is paying attention.

A.R. smirks with glee. But Dan furiously rolls away from the Reverend, pulling Mo along. "What's up with you, Mo? You've never talked to me like I'm a child before."

"You gotta stop talking to that nutty minister, Dan. You're gonna say something gets us all fired. There is no more freedom here. Besides, I don't think you can hear me most of the time, Mr. Kellar, and I think your memory is starting to fail you. Let's go potty, okay?"

"Mo, stop it! I don't need to go potty. And I don't need to go potty with your help. Is this the new regime's way? Hateful condescension? I am not incompetent. Or incontinent. I follow all the rules. On Tuesday I put my trash out. When it's April 15, I file my taxes. If it's Christmas, I wear my red jacket. I know what I'm doing. Do you? (*afterthought*) Joe Biden is president."

Moiselle sighs and whispers, "Don't mention Joe Biden again except in the privacy of your room, just a word of warning." Then out loud, "I'm sorry, Mr. Kellar, but I've been ordered to accompany every person over a certain age—especially those who are prone to falls, and those who were unconscious for three days—to the restroom twice a day to see if their magic panties need to be changed."

"Oh my God," Dan cries. "Magic Panties."

"Well, Ms. Charlene says you all hate it when I call them 'diapers.' She thinks 'magic panties' sounds funner. And that ain't all, Mr. Kellar."

"You mean it gets worse?"

"Later on this week all of the staff, even the janitors, everyone is going to wear these accessories all day to show us what it's like to be old, we're gonna wear thick gloves as if our fingers got arthritis, and funny glasses like glaucoma, and ear plugs like we're deaf. To show you we're on your teams."

"Will you be wearing magic panties?"

"Oh, Mr. Kellar. They tell us to talk to all of you as if you are all demented or deaf. Then they want us to wear goggles to see life through y'all's eyes.

"Our end of life eyes."

"Yes sir."

CHAPTER 19
A voice of rage and ruin

"Hello world. Dammit. Ninety-five years old. One-hundredth Birthday (hark, hack, hack) any day now. Since you asked, Mo, I've been gathering (snort, sneeze, wipe nose with toilet paper from the roll that he keeps on his night stand) the statistics of my life. There's nothing I can say about the years between 1979 and 2002—the dark years, tortuous. Shoulda gone to jail a few times. Other than that . . . can't account for . . . was too crapulous to remember a thing. Joe Biden is president."

Moiselle has taken FN's shift since she has not shown up. It's her turn to listen to the old man tell his stories. Dear God, old people origin stories are so important to old people. "My people lived hardscrabble. Ever one of us had TB. A bout of polio. It made us tough. You have TB and polio, and even when you get well and people let you in their homes, you find yourself drinking lemonade out of disposable mason jars instead of nice iced tea glasses. Children move their desks away from you. Or they cross the street to avoid you. I was not included in anything until I went to war. We drank after each other, out of the same cups, passed a canteen back and forth. Shared cigarettes. Nobody scared. My parents, Wyatt and Evelyn. I was first child. Rick came seven years later."

Mo listens, and wonders if she is supposed to be writing all this crap down.

"Walked four miles each way to school in the snow, no breakfast. Father abandoned us, so I was man of the house at eight years old. Dad came back later. Everyone had some version of this story in those days."

Mo's eyes were rolling back into her head from Dan's droning on about his life what seemed like a hundred years ago, Depression era stories, and his (wheezing) and his (harking) and his difficulties pronouncing certain letters, like someone whose dentures were out.

"Read storybooks to Rick. His favorite was about two ducks

hoping to start a family, who flew around looking for the right place to make a home, finally finding a perfect place in town at a park where they were fed peanuts everyday by good people passing by. A beautiful pond to splash around in. Everyone kind of adopted them ducks. Jack, Kack, Lack, Mack, Nack, Ouack, Pack, and Quack were born in that park. They started to grow up and they learned almost everything ducks needed to know about life in a park surrounded by good people, how to march and swim, and even to avoid bicycles."

(Phlegmy cough, hark, spit, wipe)

"Jesus, can you breathe?"

(Huffing, puffing, snort) Dan throws the toilet paper towards the trashcan near the night stand.

"FN says you quack like a damn duck in your sleep, Mr. Kellar. Even in your sleep you need to keep making noise."

"I know. The floozies used to complain I quacked in my sleep. But it's because I think about ducks, and Rick, every day, Mo, and I'll tell you why."

"Of course you will, Dan."

(Deep breath) (From both)

"It was Ricky's favorite story, Mo. But he was too little for it. See, the ducks in the story were always needing to get across the road, to get to the pond. The mother could not teach her tiny ducklings how to cross safely. They were too small. Only humans could help her little ducks cross the highway. And these ducks had to wait and wait and wait for a good human to come along and help them get to the pond every day. So naturally, one day, we were napping on the lawn and my three-year-old brother woke up, looked . . . saw . . . decided to help some real ducks cross the road.

"I heard the car tires screech. Ricky was so little. He didn't know how to cross the street by himself. He didn't know to look both ways."

Mo was struck dumb for a moment.

"Jesus Christ, Dan. That's awful."

"He died out there on the road. My mother blamed me for

it. I should have watched him better, she said. I was a lazy ass, sleeping all day. But you know what is messed up about that? Mother was the one driving the car. She killed her own kid, she did. And all the ducks, too. Mo? I'm getting peckish, wanna roll me down to breakfast?"

Mo pushes Dan in the wheelchair down to the dining room for breakfast and leaves him to fend for himself. Her RRC duties take over and she is happy to get away from the old man with his sad stories.

There he eats his crispy bacon. Drinks his hot tea. Tells his neighbors at the table how "everybody thinks I'm a coffee drinker by the looks of me . . . " After breakfast, he finds himself sitting alone. He notices that his right side is numb. He calls out. His speech is slurred. Someone alerts Mo. Mo comes running. She makes much of his symptoms. He begs to go back to his bed, and she lets him. He lies down, and tosses and turns, naps and tosses and turns some more, skips lunch and is tormented by memories even after the lunch hour, which is an unusually early torment time. By midafternoon he is able to force his weak, mangled, jangled mind to move the memories aside. He manages to get himself out of bed, and into his wheelchair. He wheels himself out of his room and down the hall to the day room. There he focuses on the window of the day room. He slowly parks himself in front of the window for a nice nap. He watches cars and delivery trucks speed past. He seems okay. Still foggy, like after a bout of vertigo. Getting sleepy.

Dan watches the gardener mow the lawn so late in the day, and the mower's repetitive movements enter Dan's brain and he has an earworm to battle now.

The beat of the mower circles and cuts, "boom a thump, thump, boom a thump, thump, mowin' the lawn I'm mowin' the lawn, boom a thump, mowin' the lawn." "Boom a thump, thump, Shot him for show. Boom, a thump, Shot at ol' Wayne." "Mowin' the lawn, boom a thump."

Dan panics. *What the hell is happening in my head?* His brain wants to spill the beans. No filter, no boundaries, no stopping his thoughts. He challenges his scared mind to find a comforting thought. Then he remembers. The great singer, Tony Bennett, had full blown Alzheimer's, and in his mid-nineties could still remember and sing all the lyrics to his hits. Short-term memory loss was not so scary if you could remember the songs from long ago, or the stories. So, Dan chooses the stories. Now, can he always tell a story? Would he always tell them the same way?

"I was only seventeen, manning the big gun . . . "

" . . . On the big tank!"

It was 1945, and I found myself in Leipzig. Had been at war for days. But I didn't need sleep, didn't need food. I shot a dog with my gun. My gun. My gun."

Dan looks around the room. His neck is stiff. Mr. Briggs is watching television, *Antiques Roadshow* or *Chicago Fire*, he can't tell from across the room. Doesn't matter, Briggs is fast asleep in front of the TV.

With a phone in her hand, Daphne Huff is also asleep in the rocking chair.

"Mama, I will call for a wellness check, do you hear me, MAMA?" yells the panicked voice on the other end of the phone line. If the cheesecake crumbs on Margaret Mouser's face are any indicator, she too is asleep, or is in a diabetic coma over there at the game table. In identical robes and shoes, Darlene, Christine, and Felicia are huddled together on the sofa. Everyone is fast asleep after a lazy afternoon of games and conversation.

So, nobody hears him say "shot my gun, my gun, my gun." Dan Kellar turns back to the big picture window and stares out at the lawn.

Outside, the gardener, Diego, notices the old man has been watching him mow. Diego nods hello. Dan points a finger gun his way. Diego wonders. *Why would an old man hand gesture like that?* He squints his eyes to see. The old man has a real gun?

"Jorge, get over here," Diego calls to his helper. Jorge hustles over, and Diego points. "Does that old man have a gun, should we tell someone?"

Seeing an elderly man with a pistol, or making a pistol gesture, does not worry Jorge, who laughs and says, "It's Texas, and it's just ol' man Kellar living his zenith again. Look now, he's already asleep."

Diego and Jorge move on to continue their lawn business. And Dan was, in fact, slumped over in his wheelchair, reliving his glory days, like in a dream.

His head droops, and he falls to the ground, banging his head on the windowsill.

And then his life is a movie. A big movie. A blockbuster. Technicolor. Words cross the screen. The SUPER.

Dan once lived the American Dream. Had a wife, owned a bar, and a big truck. Two kids—a son and a daughter.

The movie begins.

And Dan subconsciously worries that he's going to be facing God again in that godawful white light. *Instead, there's a real gun in Dan's hand and it's dropping as he hits the windowsill. The gun disappears under the chair. Dan collapses to the ground.*

Even unconscious, seriously ill, Dan knows he's suffering an aftermath from the previous injury, and that now he's having a stroke. He can't move, but he can hear. And it's not *Chicago Fire* he's hearing in his head. He's hearing a newscast coming from the sixty-inch flat screen in the day room.

The old man can only make out a few words of the newscast— "Vietnam" and "missing in action." He tries, but he's completely paralyzed underneath the windowsill, can't push his wheelchair any closer to the television. But he can hear, and he wants to climb out of his skin.

"The remains of a soldier have been identified a half century after he went missing during the Vietnam War. The disappearance was investigated by twelve separate teams over the years, but no clear identity was determined.

In 2022, a Vietnamese child found an actual burial site and alerted the United States authorities. The bones recovered there were consistent with those of four servicemen whose helicopter had crashed in 1968. However, the three other servicemen have still not been identified."

Dan rolls his wheelchair to the television.

SUPER: *That son went missing in action. In Vietnam. His name was Thaddeus Kellar.*

So, Dan dies again. On the spot. Actually dies, as flat as the previous flatline and maybe for longer than the time before when he knew he was in the White Light and talking directly to his God. He was dead again, but without the White Light, and this time . . . he's his own audience.

His body is inert. But inside his primal brain, well, with incredible strength, Dan comes back to life, gets to his feet, grabs up his chair, and throws it through the picture window, breaking both the window and the chair into a million pieces. Imaginary sirens go off, nurses and staff show up, and then a massive SWAT team arrives.

Dan Kellar puffs himself up to an even higher level of rage. He's flying, gonna hit the ceiling, has to hold on to something, thank God there's a chandelier. He grabs it. It's vibrating. Holds on for dear life. Gasping for air, his lungs fill. Opens his eyes, and feels a sharp pain in his head. Another part of his brain shuts down. He sees God. Harder this time to bring himself back to life. "Hold off, God, it's not time," Dan commands.

SWAT! Guns pointed at the old man.

A bit of a standoff, then . . .

Dan lowers himself to the ground, arms over his head. He lands on his feet. He gives up by raising his arms.

On cue, the newscast continues.

"Quang Tri City was a prime target of the North Vietnamese during the 1968 Tet Offensive. The newly discovered remains of the aircraft had crashed on the bank of the Ben Hai River, and the crew was taken prisoner." White. Flashing white. Now he understands. The All-knowing God is answering the question he forgot to ask the first time he was dead this past week. "What happened to Tad?" Doing it without making His presence seen, through the telecast! Dan is sure he understands what God is telling him through the miracle of the TV. Tad was alive, long after being taken prisoner fifty years before. Dan had lived on the hope that Tad had stayed alive after being captured, and had lived his life in bliss, in peace, in a faraway paradise, where there was no internet, no wifi, no phones, no way to let his old dad know that he was happy, that he was okay.

Like Fletcher Christian, in Tahiti, after the mutiny on the Bounty, Dan believed that Tad was somewhere founding a new generation of Kellars. That Tad did not die a cruel and heinous death, like the Black Hawk Down death that tormented Dan's mind when he was drunk or at his lowest.

Dan cracks. Shattered at this last bit of news. Remains found. The SWAT team leaders shake their heads in sorrow.

Then he explains what has happened to the imaginary SWAT team, pointing to the television.

"My son, looks like they found him." Dan sobs, and his pitiful wail disarms the SWAT unit.

His body hits the floor. His rigid arms are extended.

Dan strikes, screaming to the SWAT team, who now face him and are armed to the max, "The fucking Army can never find my son! When I hear the terms 'Vietnam,' 'pilot,' or 'missing in action,' I am enraged." Dan leans in and grabs onto a table to maintain his balance. In order to catch his breath, there follows a period of calm, but it is brief. Spry Dan battles with the tablecloth, dives under it, and emerges fighting with a wide variety of potent weaponry that the SWAT team somehow missed when they searched the day room. He shoots at the "enemies" while also taking out all the lights and windows. Bwoom. bwoom. bwoom. The fight lasts for a while, but he maintains control, and once he stands up from the floor, Dan Kellar hears the SWAT team (the ones who are still alive) praising his incredible peak form, especially 'for a ninety-five-year-old man.'

Dan saw the SWAT unit all down, some dead and some dying, and is surprised that nobody else can see the mayhem he has caused. He's shot his favorite SWAT guy. "Oh no!" Dan stoops down to offer aid and compassion to his favorite senior officer, who reaches out to touch Dan's cheek and speak to him before passing away. "Dan Kellar, you will always be my idol. You are our hero. You killed Nazis." "What a beautiful compliment," Dan answers, moved. "Did you all hear what he said?" No.

He repeats the compliment to be sure everyone hears. Dan offers a prayer over the deceased cop before starting a second struggle to stand. Once standing, Dan considers the collateral damage, including the damaged windows, dead SWAT personnel, busted furniture, and hundreds of shell casings.

Suddenly, dizziness struck! And it's real, too! Vertigo! It's not imaginary!

In severe discomfort, Dan staggers across the room in search of a chair. Dan pushes Briggs off his comfortable recliner and onto the floor. He prays as he falls into the recliner. "Please God. I am not afraid of anything in this world," says Dan Kellar. "Except vertigo."

Dan Kellar fought in three wars, heroically, brutally, and without an ounce of cowardice. But vertigo turns him into a baby. If life were vertigo, Dan would board the first train to hell.

Even in his dreamworld, Dan is old.

Snap. Dan wakes up. He finds himself on the floor. He opens his eyes. There is no dead SWAT team. He certainly has no sense of time passing, but it couldn't have been long. Mr. Briggs is watching television, the local news. (That explains the newscast he subconsciously heard.) If the cheesecake crumbs on Margaret Mouser's face are any indicator, she is in a diabetic coma over there at the game table. In identical robes and shoes, Darlene, Christine, and Felicia are huddled together on the sofa.

Everyone in the day room is asleep.

Dan takes a deep breath in through his nose in order to test his sense of smell. He smells something burning, like toast. His saliva tastes like metal. And his left side is somewhat numb. He's had a stroke. He knows for sure now. He somehow manages to maneuver his body back into his chair near the picture window. He sits very still, decides not to attract or call for any medical attention. He will pretend nothing has happened. He will just nap.

Dan barely catches the most recent Washington news story on the sixty-inch television broadcasting from Dallas before he falls into a sound sleep.

"Over six hundred species now have additional trade restrictions in place, including greater protection for sharks, frogs, and turtles. That concludes the local WFAA news. Reporting by Cynthia Izaguirre."

He is scarcely aware of Moiselle and the staff when they enter the day room, find him in distress, and, acting quickly, they transfer him from his chair to his wheelchair and push him through the day room and out into the corridor to wait for an ambulance.

PART THREE . . .

CHAPTER 20
About them mysteries

Nicolette

"This is Nicolette's first interview since the American servicemen exited Afghanistan," the moderator says.

Nicolette corrects her. "Lieutenant Colonel Mercer, retired, if you don't mind, and withdrawal, 'withdrawal' of troops. August 2021, a bit over two years ago."

"Oh! Ok," the moderator answers. "I can't thank you enough, Lieutenant Colonel, for being our guest today. And aren't you dressed to the nines in your little button-up shirt and those cute sneakers? Everyone, please give a hand to Lieutenant Colonel Nicolette Mercer, Army, Afghan War." There are a couple of thousand overdressed, overcoifed, and overpaid, well, wealthy members of the Tennessee megachurch in the audience. The moderator is not quite the Southern stereotype, close, or even 'Karen'ish. But anyone new in the audience this night might have had trouble figuring out which church was holding the event, one is right across the street from another megachurch, and that megachurch is right across the street from another. The audience stands to applaud the slight brunette who is billed as a "war hero." The topic of the special "Support Our Soldiers" event taking place on this day is "Faith and Freedom."

"It was 2003, twenty years ago," the moderator coos in her southern drawl, "when you survived a horrific IED attack that killed, um, your fiancé, I believe?" She looks at her notes.

"Yes, my fiancé . . . Liam . . . uhm . . . suicide attack . . . " The moderator glances at the audience to gauge its horror. A few mothers sitting in the front place palms over children's ears, and others shift in their seats. *Better get this back to God quick*, the Moderator thinks. She changes the subject.

" . . . God will reckon with that human being who killed your beloved, of course. And of course you're completely healed and married now to, ummmm . . . " (notes).

"Bob. Yeah, Bob Mercer, he's out there (waves), married seventeen years now (applause, relief), thank you all, thanks . . . "

" . . . And one child?"

"Yes, Geddy, has my name, Nicolette Turlo is my maiden name and I still use that, so Geddy Turlo. Almost nineteen. Geddy and I are heading out on a road trip together in a couple days. From here down to Texas. Rupert, Texas, where we will be attending a 100th birthday party for a true war hero, one of the Greatest Generation. We'll be heading back to the town where my fiancé, Liam, the one who was killed, was raised. Yeah, a war hero, one-hundred years old, I barely know him, I was a witness to some mischief he created that sent him to jail twenty years ago. Gosh. The town. Rupert. It has a haunted hotel."

"Interesting, of course you want to share Liam's roots with Geddy," the interviewer responds. *Seventeen years married to that Mercer guy. Nineteen-year-old child by another dude.*

She glances at the audience and notes that a few more Baptist panties are in a wad.

"So when you were first in the Army, and I believe you served in both Afghanistan and . . ."

"National Guard."

"National Guard? (Now she's disappointed.) That's like for natural disasters and stuff?"

"I supported military operations overseas," Nicolette explains, "but yes, the National Guard is often called for domestic events like disasters. It's federal and state."

"Yes, so let's go back to who you were in 2003, when you were actually a real soldier, but first quickly tell all of us who you are now and your exciting plans for the future."

"Well, after I entered civilian life, I began to teach music, which I plan to do for the next twenty years or so. And I just bought a car repossession business, a good investment, I think. People who don't pay their bills, shame on them, right?"

Nicolette smiles and looks into the bored, but fake-smiling audience.

"Uhm, so I'm a mom. Wife. Volunteer with various veteran

organizations. I've traveled the world with my husband since I retired."

She glances into the audience again and makes eye contact with a few approving women. They give her courage. "He's a franchise specialist for donut stores. (a few laughers) Who doesn't love a donut, right? (more laughter) And believe it or not, I sing in a garage band. (applause) I know, that's cool, right? Uhm. Of course. And… uhm... Another version of who am I? Wow, I'm not sure I know the answer to that. I was a soldier. Who I am today? Well . . . "

"And of course, you're a Christian," the moderator adds.

Nicolette nods and the moderator is pleased.

" . . . Yes, we want to hear about the attack that left you injured and your fiancé dead. What happened that day? Oh, the PG version, by the way. Lots of children here today." The moderator wags a finger in warning.

It is not just Nicolette's imagination that the lights dim and the mood shifts in the huge sanctuary. People seem to sit up straight, seem to lean in. The pressure of telling a great story is on. *Oh, how I wish I could tell a story like Dan Kellar,* she thinks.

"Well, it was at night. It was dark. Really dark. It was an insider hit- an Afghan gunman who had been working with all of us. Well, he was kind of our friend. More like our coworker. Our job was range training. Some testing, military munitions and explosives, weapon systems, training military personnel. And uhm, we worked with locals like this one, and we knew him well. The Afghans who worked with us were completely committed to the work. Alongside us. That's what we thought anyway. He just turned on us and killed several, my fiancé, Liam, and wounded several others, including me. He was wearing explosives, so it was a suicide mission, even though I can tell you there were others involved. Now, we started firing back. (noting some discomfort at the subject matter) I need to tell you about Liam, though. Liam was wonderful, he was a lover of music, poetry, he was funny and smart . . . "

The pseudo-sympathetic and overly-earnest moderator leans in. Interrupts, emphasizes, with faux gravitas. " . . . I'm sure he was a huge loss to the world. How were you after it happened and how are you now?"

Nicolette looks at the audience, aware that the PTSD she can so easily experience is upon her, pops her knuckles, pops her neck, takes a deep breath, rocks back and forth.

"It was a fucking awful experience, of course." (Uh oh, a mild clamor starts up with such language.)

Nicolette composes herself, looks up at the ceiling, into the rafters, spots a crucifix, remembers she's the guest speaker in a church. *Oh shit, a church. When my PTSD is happening. On a Sunday night. People bought tickets.*

"I'm sorry, I forgot myself. Where I was for a second. It's the PTSD. Forgive me, Lord. I see you up there."

Nicolette salutes the crucifix that is prominently suspended above the altar. She salutes as if Jesus is the Commander in Chief, then stops herself. "Jesus H.R. Biden, Jr." Nicolette spurts out. "Oh sorry, Lord. That's a joke, just a joke we . . . some of us . . . in service . . ."

The audience begins murmuring and shifting in their seats. Nicolette goes on. "I'm about to say what I think you probably don't want to hear, but for complete healing there are years of therapy and surgeries and you know, other difficulties. Mental, speech, memory, cognizance. Emotions. Frustrations. And then there are the moral injuries. The soul. And since the topic tonight is 'faith and freedom,' it's hard, but I can tell you what happens to your soul. Guilt and shame, feeling violated, feeling violating. Self-punishment, sabotaging relationships. Wanting to commit suicide, drug addictions, wondering whether you're serving the Devil or the Lord. Or just the U.S. Which could be like either. And our enemy of the day. Right? Watching people die, and killing people, liking killing people, hating that, it's . . . the damage to your morality, your soul. It's endless pain. I still love having served my country, but I'm not cocky anymore, which I miss, and there's no bringing back what's lost. But Liam actually showed me the way.

"Back to his love of poetry. Rilke, Liam's favorite poet, wrote 'Let everything happen to you: beauty and terror. Just keep going. No feeling is final.' The night of the attack challenged my soul. But I kept going. The fact that I knew him was beauty. That helped me so much. And I knew I would love Liam forever. And that would be ok.

"Even with Bob. And they are connected. The two men I love are connected. We are all connected, the loved ones who have gone before us, and the enemies we kill, too. They may be in some other heaven, but just like we're born, God is there, and whatever or whoever kills us, God is there. It's like why else would that enemy be standing there for you to shoot? Because God put him there? I believe that "the Lord shall keep thy coming in, and thy going out" but do I really believe that God put my enemy in the wrong place at the wrong time, for me to kill? Do I believe that God put Liam's killer on the earth to kill Liam? Hell no. Psalm 121. Right now there's trouble brewing all over the world, everywhere. Is God in control? Well, is He? Speaking of how we are all connected I would like to share another piece of one of Rilke's poem. 'How shall I hold my soul that it may not be touching yours?'"

By now, the audience has largely turned on Nicolette. The moderator looks at her watch, and, announcing the time, is interrupted by a poem.

"How shall I lift it then above you to where other things are waiting?" Nicolette recites and weeps.

"You and me—all that lights upon us though,

Brings us together like a fiddle bow.

Drawing one voice from two strings, it glides along.

Across what instrument have we been spanned?

And what violinist holds us in his hand?

O sweetest song."

"Yes, that was beautiful," the moderator says.

Nicolette proselytizes. "If God is the violinist, and He plays one tune for all of us, then truly we are all connected." Nicolette wipes tears from her eyes and smiles, embarrassed by her own earnestness.

"I always turn to that poem for comfort," she says. "I look forward to the skies opening up and seeing Liam again, but I know I have a life to live here, a life to love living while I am living it. You . . . you . . . you . . . " Audience and moderator are alarmed as Nicolette now offers up her special vocabulary that shows its alarming self only in times of PTSD, a combination of Touret's and speaking in tongues. "you . . . hetha, hippa, fucka . . . " (oh no, now the clamor really begins.)

The moderator hurriedly concludes. " . . . Summing up then, God led you to a new life with your husband, Bob Mercer, and that is the beauty of God's love. Praise the Lord. Thank you for sharing with us today, and everyone give Lieutenant Colonel Mercer a huge round . . . of . . . huge applause. Time for a light dessert buffet." (The audience claps, claps, there are a few shouts.)(Lights swirl, the music begins to swell, Nicolette is played off, like she's just accepted an Oscar and talked too long.)

Nicolette leaps to her feet. Caught in the spotlight, she is luminous. Other-worldly. She roams the stage, stopping the light applause, and the music. She points at different people in the audience, silencing all. She's so commanding that the audience takes their seats once more. " . . . THERE HAS TO BE A . . . There has to be a why and reason somewhere, in going to fight a war. When you sign up to go, when you volunteer, there is always a why, a reason to go. And then, after twenty years, like in Afghanistan, you'd expect some kind of win to make it all worthwhile. Otherwise what's the point of fighting? Right? Two things are said to me everywhere I speak. Asked in hindsight, of course. One. I am always asked if my sacrifice is worth it. Cause we lost. If Liam's loss was worth it. Cause we lost. People ask with condescension in their voices, because what they really want to say is, 'You loser, you fought and we didn't win.' How dare anyone think that, though. We don't fight wars here. There are no tanks roaring down our streets. No bombs going off over our cities. We fight wars everywhere else so we don't have to fight wars here. Because the same kind of tyranny can happen here, too. Evil can take over here, too. In fact, we're on such a slippery slope. We hate plenty of our neighbors here, don't think that hate can't go the way of what happened to Jews in World War Two. We take away rights every day here on this planet, in this country. May not be your rights, but your neighbor's rights. If we can. We take them. Some in the name of God. Christ. Everyone here always says we need to take care of things here first. Fuck the rest of the globe, they say. What the fuck, I say?" (Several stunned Christians pick up their purses and coats to leave, but Nicolette is undeterred—war taught her much and she is bound to share it all.) Before we left Afghanistan girls were going to school, women were in better shape, we left and the Taliban were right back in there. Killing and starving people. Not what I fought for, certainly not why Liam died. Fuck that, right? Definitely we lost that war. But here's the truth. We, Liam, myself, belong to This Country. We belong to America, who defends democracy on global fronts, and that's what he died for. This Country. And you know, yes, for the women of that country, who deserve the same rights we have here. And another thing, this second thing everybody does that fucking pisses me off. "Thank you for your service." What the fuck? If you don't know what you are thanking me for, if you think I'm a loser, don't fucking thank me. I have one more thing to say. It's about having PTSD. Half of you out there are saying to yourself, how the fuck did she make it to lieutenant colonel? Why is this nutcase on our stage? By working against my PTSD, that's the fuck how. I love this country and love the military. I love the soldiers. And I led the soldiers. As long as I could. But now. I can only come to places like this and talk about my life with people like you. And I am so grateful to say that people like you keep inviting me to speak."

She stops speaking, however. There is silence for a long time. Nicolette goes back to her chair, sits, smiles at the audience. Families get up, leave, uneasy.

In the corridors and the bathrooms of the megachurch, in the parking lots, there is chatter about the foul language, and more than a few comments about her obvious PTSD.

And "how in the world did she make it to lieutenant colonel?"

Apparently she had not answered that question well enough by bringing it up herself.

The audience, half gone. The moderator fake-smiles, removes her mike, then glowers at Nicolette.

"People like you? Seriously?"

The moderator leaves the stage in a huff.

For awhile, as people exit, Nicolette is afraid that she will be sitting there alone, that no one will come up to speak to her, ask her questions, thank her, just her and Jesus up there on the cross, saying things, standing for things that you can't unsay, things that get you crucified.

She looks up at Jesus and says, "You do spend a lot of time alone in here, don't you?" For a second there the letters "INRI" on the cross look like the letters "PTSD," which would explain alot, in Nicolette's mind.

Jesus had been through worse. That's why she believes in Him. His PTSD was at least as god-awful as hers.

CHAPTER 21
. . . Vacant and whitewashed and sad . . .

Twenty years earlier, FALL 2003

Dapper, at seventy-five years of age, Dan sports a masculine strut that belies that age. Dan Kellar is simply the "cock of the walk."

Corrie has been dead for years.

And his interest in women is finally waning.

Dan woke up proud of his service to his country, excited to head downtown first thing to view the Veteran's Day parade poster that honors him. Dan, the most prominent war hero in town, was always honored on Veteran's Day. It was his day. He hoped the town council had picked out a great photo of him for the poster.

But at nine a.m. came a surprise notification from JPAC, the Joint POW/MIA Accounting Command, the Command Center for POW/MIA servicemen. He knew it was about Tad. Hands shaking, he read the letter. No remains had been found, but, as the letter noted, "JPAC is searching for a special type of DNA from surviving family members of servicemen who remain missing in action." "Called "Mitochondrial DNA or mtDNA. Mitochondrial DNA is only passed on through the maternal line." "In a family tree linking the donor to the missing person, every link must be a female."

It was all he could do to keep from running to the liquor cabinet. He was incensed that he could not submit his own DNA to help identify future remains found, remains that might be Tad. So only Corrie's DNA, or C's DNA could link to Tad? Appalling.

He would never agree to digging Corrie up out of her grave at Peaceful Pines. Dan ran down the hall to the room that belonged to Tad; his room left empty for the last three decades; a room left seemingly untouched. The bedframe, the mattress, the chest of drawers, the night stand, all there. Surely there would be a comb he'd never found before, a hairbrush, something of Tad's, something with Tad's very own DNA on it. If he could find something, a hair, a nail, a used handkerchief, something from over thirty years ago, something else to send to JPAC, so that maybe someday he would learn the truth about Tad's death. But the drawers were empty, the closet was bare. Corrie must have gone into his room years ago, decades ago, and stripped it.

Dan cried as he dressed for the day.

The Army Recruiting Center (ARC) still operates in downtown Rupert in 2003, one of only a few surviving establishments in the failing town. Every other business shut down a long time ago. The ARC probably would have closed as well if 9/11 hadn't been such a remarkably unifying event. Each year since 9/11 over half the high school seniors signed up to go to war, even before graduation. The ARC is right across the street from the once-opulent, but now-condemned landmark hotel, the majestic Porterfield. Nowadays, crackheads and crackpots hide in plain sight in and around the hotel, scattered sometimes throughout fourteen stories of haunted, flooded, vandalized hotel rooms. Local law enforcement shew them out from time to time. Pungent odors drift out of the broken windows, so the townspeople call the hotel "the Majestic Turd." Even when there's a mass cleanup and fumigation of the site, the nickname stays. Sober Dan parks his old, big old red Ford truck on Main Street, in front of the Majestic Turd, gets out and saunters up to the picture window of the ARC. He's gonna look at his poster.

On this crisp fall morning, Dan looks sharp. His ironed flannel shirt tucks smoothly into starched, well-fitting pants.

He has dried the tears he cried upon receiving the letter from JPAC.

Two posters are plastered on the window of the Army Recruiting Center. One promotes the upcoming Veterans Day Parade. The other advertises the Annual Ghost-hunting Event at the Porterfield.

Dan admires his handsome reflection in the window of the ARC. He then turns to approve the picture of him that is plastered on the Veterans Day poster.

It is a contemporary photo, but one in which he is sporting his WWII uniform. The banner of the poster reads, "Dan Kellar, RUPERT WAR HERO of THREE AMERICAN WARS, including 'the good war.'" He looks past the poster to where the husky recruiting sergeant, Sergeant Gerard Gustavson Grissom, is talking to two female teenage recruits. Dan heartily disapproves. The gals are both cheerleader types with large boobs and blonde hair. Additionally, the Rupert rodeo queen and her blue-collar boyfriend sit in the waiting area.

Dan does not believe that women should be signing up to go to war; that's the crux of the matter.

He taps the glass to get Grissom's attention.

Grissom looks up.

Dan nods and points at the two girls.

Grissom mouths the words "what do you want?" In response, Dan mimes an hourglass shape with great big breasts. He points to each girl, then, using one finger, draws a line across his throat.

Grissom bolts to the door, hollering at the girls to get under his desk and hide. Grissom steps outside, and says, "You need to back away from this office, old man. Now."

"You are recruiting girls. Stop it now."

"What?" Griss stands in disbelief, then bursts out laughing, embarrassing the old veteran.

"Just look at your poster and move on. You just threatened my applicants with your inappropriate hand gesturing. What the fuck, old man?"

Launching his complaints, Dan starts out with the most contentious. "The defense of our country does not need two young, nubile girls. Three, counting the rodeo queen. Cyndi, I believe her name is."

Grissom stares at Dan for an uncomfortably long time.

Finally he speaks. "Dan, anyone can volunteer to be in the military. You, peeping into my office windows at seventeen-year-old girls, and basically hand signaling that you are going to slit their throats if they join the Army. And the fact that you know a high school girl's actual name is pretty darn pervy. Now go home or I'm gonna call the law."

"Do their parents know they're here?"

"Oh, for Christ's sake. Are you just dumb as a fucking rock?"

Dan feigns real shock at being talked to with such disrespect.

"You are a terrible representative of our Army, Sgt. Grissom. Girls in combat? In harm's way? Compromising situations? Enlisted men who haven't seen a curvy wonder in a very long while. What do you think can happen to them girls overseas? It's obscene."

"Well, it's 2003, sir. Times have changed."

"They sure have. But men haven't."

Dan turns and ceremoniously points across the street. "The Turd has been compromised, right under your nose."

"Compromised how?"

"Look up at the fourth floor, the window with the tattered sheet for curtains. There's definitely a light inside. Someone is living up there, not supposed to be. Someone is stealing electricity, too. You can see the wire coming out the window, running along over to the fire station. The firemen must know this but are surely in cahoots with whoever is living up there. The thing I cannot figure out is how this person gets in there. Maybe he goes in underground, under the swimming pool, or up through the spas. Maybe one of the old elevator shafts? Somebody needs to do something about whoever is living in that old hotel. Do you know who the criminal is who is stealing from taxpayers and living in a condemned building?"

"It's not my concern and shouldn't be yours; go away, leave us alone, and do not come back," Grissom answers.

His formerly friendly demeanor gone, Grissom goes back inside and pulls the blinds.

Incensed, Dan strides furiously down the sidewalk in the direction of the only other brisk business, Bigelow's, the downtown bar. He knows he will find many citizens who sympathize with him at the bar.

But he's already formulating a plan to get back at the Army.

CHAPTER 22
. . . *Tears in Heaven* . . .

Dan confidently pushes through the door to the Bigelow bar. It's a big pub-like bar, the only other successful establishment existing in Rupert in 2003. He is ready to rant about girls joining the Army with a barful of like-minded men. Instead he walks into dead silence, since the generally boisterous bunch are mid-toast, with their heads bowed. Looks like a funeral. In fact, it is a wake. Flowers. Photos. A big table of eats. There's a man in uniform standing on the bar, holding up a beer, shushing, ready to speak.

"First off prayers and salutes to all the American soldiers fighting in the 'Armed Conflict' taking place in Afghanistan." The second round of tributes is much more personal. "As you all know, The Pentagon identified some soldiers killed in an apparent insider attack at a base in the Afghan region of Paktia. One of those soldiers was our own—Liam Chapman. Only twenty-three years old, he died while on his second tour of service." He went on to say that Liam had been recruited by the Rupert Army Recruiter a few weeks after 9/11, when Americans were united and at the height of their need for vindication. "Grab a bulletin on your way out. Liam's detailed obituary, pictures, all that. But an anonymous benefactor, hopes you will enjoy this afternoon of food and drink, and stories. To Liam!" Raising a glass.

Dan bellies up to the bar. "Is this a private party?"

"Ain't a party, it's a wake," answers Big Bill, the bartender/ owner. "But you're welcome to be here."

"Dead kid from here? I must have missed that on the local news."

"Yeah. Dead kid from here. Liam? You know . . . Liam Chapman . . . never mind."

The bartender is evasive for good reason. Liam Chapman, raised by his wealthy step-grandpa, was the biological son of Wayne Herd, but nobody really connects the draft dodger to Liam anymore. Wayne is long forgotten.

"His family here?" Dan asks. "I'd like to pay my respects."

"Nope. Liam's mother, Canadian chick, long dead. Cancer. Breast cancer. Only thing I know."

Big Bill hands Dan a beer. Dan moves around the bar and puts himself smack dab in the middle of the wake, listens to a few tributes, drinks a couple or ten more beers. With booze rushing Dan's blood stream, the ugly heads of outrage and indignation emerge. *Another dead soldier, Liam, lived only 9,000 days or so,* Dan thinks. *But at least he's been identified, at least he is being buried.* Dan, being Dan, has to take over the conversations, forfeiting truth, if necessary, angry words slur, reminding everyone who will listen of things they already know. They don't listen to him long.

"My son, Tad, he's been missing in action—presumed dead— for thirty-five years. Incompetent Army writes me every few years, just got a letter from them today, asking for DNA, because they keep finding bones. But they're never Tad's bones. I've supplied DNA from his mother, and his sister. Several times. That's hell. At least Liam's people have answers," he begrudges. "I don't have closure."

A few of the nicer drinkers slap Dan on the back and say (to shut him up) "the Army will find your kid someday; never give up hope, old man." "Going home to pray that the Lord brings your son home." A few of the not-as-nice say things like, "Well, this is Liam's day, not Tad's. So shut the fuck up, old coot." They stare him down. He has no idea why.

One particularly honest human corners Dan at some point in the day. "Obviously Liam is a hero. Damn, I get tired of seeing your old mug on the Veterans' Day poster year after year. I vote for Liam to replace your fucking ugly mug on our poster!" Then the guy holds a vote. Sets himself in the middle of the bar patrons. "Who votes to replace Dan Kellar's ugly old mug on the Veterans' Day posters with Liam Chapman's face? A new hero!" A roar of approval, cheers.

At seventy-five years old, Dan isn't prepared to be replaced, not now and not ever. But he will change the subject, drink to Liam, and profess a mighty toast. He yells for silence, so he can toast the "great American hero." He says . . .

"Drink, drink, drink, so's not to think, think, think."

On Big Bill's cue, the men in the bar lightly tap their glasses against the bar in a ritual showing respect for Liam.

"To Liam Chapman!" "A brave soldier." "A good man." "Gone too soon."

Dan sidles up to the bar to join a new, somber group of veterans, who haven't humiliated him yet.

"To Liam."

"To Liam."

And to closure. And so they drink. Two by two, one by one, the veterans pay their respects, and leave, going home to dwindle away more ordinary days.

At noon, the High School Rodeo Queen, Cyndi (whom Dan had previously seen in the Army Recruiting Center) arrives to help out during her high school "vocational training" class.

She catches Big Bill's eye. Says, "Too many surly drunks in here, on a Tuesday. I'll have to put it on my school report and they won't let me work here anymore." Bill reassures her she will be safe, that it is just a wake. "It is a bar, Cyndi, the high school knows that," Big Bill says. Then he stations himself in front of Dan Kellar and announces . . .

"Sober up, folks! The kiddies are here to work! STORY TIME everyone." Pointing at Dan. "I'll be buying this man a drink, and he will entertain us with a story." That pronouncement did some good as the surliest drunks turn to see who has been given that special honor. Dan, the honoree, nods at each man.

Bill continues. "With respect to our Liam, let's turn it to Rupert's previous hero, of three American wars, Dan Kellar, my friends!" When there are only grumbles, Big Bill glares at a row of drinkers, slams free beers down in front of them, changing their tune. He then pours Dan a bourbon straight and slides the glass to him. "Best storyteller in the state. Do it, Dan."

Dan acknowledges the gift, and toasting all the bargoers, adds . . . "I aim to please."

The bartender slams down a drink for himself, and settles in for a story. Taken aback, startled, Dan asks, "Oh, you mean tell a story now?"

"Of course," says Big Bill, "one of your happy ones."

Always one to help a bartender, Dan Kellar announces . . . "Then that would be my favorite story. "How I Met My Wife.""

"That's the one, Pilgrim, that's the one."

Dan holds court, two full whiskeys in front of him.

"In the long ago past, when only men were allowed to fight wars, I was only seventeen, manning the big gun . . . "

" . . . On the big tank!" say the newly enthusiastic bargoers in unison (enthusiastic due to free beer, and not because they have heard this story before).

"It was 1945. And I found myself in Leipzig, Germany. Had been at war for days. But I didn't need sleep. Didn't need food . . . "

"He's an American soldier of the Greatest Generation!" hollers the crowd.

Taps glasses against the bar.

"That's right. I've told this story before?"

Dan kicks back a whiskey. And like a movie narration, he begins.

"Picture it. Granted, the Third Reich was in its death throes . . .

"General Ike had decided not to advance on Berlin, gonna let the Soviets have it, so we were sent in to capture Leipzig. Leipzig, of all places. It was April 1945, and our forces were gonna meet up with the Soviets there. The sixth largest city in the German Reich. Fifth largest in Germany. A critical railroad junction. They had a plant that manufactured airplanes. Only the best of American soldiers were sent to handle Leipzig. Let me describe the sound. There was the deafening sound of an M3 tank mounted with a .30 caliber machine gun that rumbled past a burned out fragment of a wall, but I'm cool as a cucumber. Almost superhuman. Say it with me."

"I'm THE American soldier of the Greatest Generation."

"That's right. My black hair is smeared with grime. My blue eyes are bloodshot. I scan the rubble.

"The tank stops.

"I leap off, with disregard for my own safety.

"Two cautious buddies have their rifles at the ready, but

'Fearless Dan', yeah, that was my nickname, Fearless Dan, doesn't need backup."

And now Dan mimics the moment that he senses a movement somewhere in the rubble. "I scream 'DON'T MAKE US BEG! COME OUT, YOU NAZI MOTHERFUCKERS!' I smell a Purple Heart! I may be young but I'm certainly at the top of my game! (sniffing the air) I tell my buddies 'I'm going in!'

"One of my instincts—well, I can sniff an opportunity for heroism and I found it there in the rubble. There was a grand piano leaning precariously against the bombed wall. I approached, rifle ready. My eyes caught a beautiful, frightened blonde. It was Corrie, she was eighteen, huddled underneath the piano. I said . . . 'Not gonna hurt you, ma'am.' Then my buddy said . . . 'Don't trust her, Kellar. She could be a Nazi.' Bullshit, I thought. I reached for her hand. And at that moment I fell in love with Corrie. The most beautiful woman I'd ever seen. I said to her, 'You can trust me. I'm an American.' To which my buddy replied . . . (Dan waits for his bar audience to respond) "To which my Buddy replied . . . "

(listeners in unison) "She's definitely a Nazi!"

"You know it! I didn't care. I had to coax her out. I said, 'It's okay. I can help you. We have something in America called The American Dream. I can take you to America. You'll be safe there'.

"Corrie looked behind her for a long moment.

"Finally trusting me, she nodded, decided what to do and reached out to me.

"I pulled her out of the rubble. My buddy said "Now what are you gonna do with her, John Wayne?"

"I said, "We gotta get her out of here before the Russians move in because . . ."(and the bargoers scream their answer, on queue.) "The Russians were real motherfuckers."

The Bartender adds. "They still are."

Dan continues. "That's right. They still are."

And after some heavy tapping of glasses by the listeners, heavy enough to break one or two of them, and loud curses against the Russians, Dan continues his story.

"I took Corrie's hand and lead her to the tank.

"Corrie looked back at the debris, and I followed her gaze. Then I ordered my buddies . . .'Just take care of her, okay?'

"I sensed something, that keen sense I have; I knew I had to go back and search her hiding place one more time.

"Corrie's eyes were wide with fear as she watched me search.

"I moved slowly around the piano to an opening in the wall.

"A badly injured Nazi was lying beneath the rubble. Belly bleeding out, probably dying slow. Useless limb. Obviously malnourished.

"Our eyes meet. 'Dammit. I'm gonna have to kill a Nazi today. Before lunch. Hopefully not in front of the girl.'"

Dammit was right. Dan Kellar stops telling the story, asks for another drink. The bar patrons wait in silence for Dan to speak again, but it becomes evident that he merely intends to brood and drink. They start up their own conversations, turn away from him, and leave him to stew in his memories.

And his contemplations. At seventy-five, Dan has yet to tell the truth about this part of the story. Did Dan murder an injured Nazi? Or just finish him off? One who was going to die anyway? Did Dan have a moment of compassion for the enemy and walk away? Did Corrie scream and demand that Dan leave her Nazi friend alone? Was the Nazi her lover? Her husband? Her brother? Her only connection to another person that she was not frightened of? Who was this Nazi?

The story Dan told always ended with Corrie jumping onto the back of the tank to ride away to her happy life in the U.S. of A.

Of course, the only person who knows the real truth is Dan Kellar. His made up stories are so much better than the truth. The truth hurts. He knows what happened to the Nazi. He knows that Corrie actually ran away from the three American soldiers. His two buddies lifted their rifles to shoot her down as she fled. Dan stopped them from shooting her. He wanted her. He posted notices in town. He made sure she could find him. When she responded to the notices weeks later, he married her. They had two children. And then, then . . . it all went to shit.

And at some point far in the future Corrie told another man, the lover she took, a man named Briggs, the true story of what happened to her after she fled and how she sought Dan out only to save her from starvation and homelessness, how she used him, in an act so desperate that it could only happen in a time of war, even in a time of 'the good war'.

Funny how someone can be dead for years, and still trigger . . . Dan signals the bartender to serve him another drink. He taps the glass against the bar. Tap, tap, tap, tap.

Customers tap along, and then the pub suddenly falls quiet, in anticipation. Dan takes a slow sip, deliberately stone silent, building suspense, until finally he speaks.

"And that is how I met my wife."

Downs the drink.

Slams the glass on the bar.

Applause and cheers.

There is a slight commotion among Dan's "fans" as he stands to go.

They all want to know. "Was she a Nazi?" "Did you kill her friend?" "You took him prisoner, right?" "You gotta tell us the truth someday, Kellar."

Dan sips, wipes his mouth, then responds, easing the tension once more.

He says, "The truth can never live up to your expectations, gentlemen. Or mine. Good night."

CHAPTER 23
... *The end of the line* ...

Later that night.

Dan staggers to the exit of his favorite establishment and barrels out. It is dark. He's been drinking heavily all afternoon and beyond.

He stumbles a few blocks, finally stops to rest in front of the Army Recruiting Center. Looks for his truck.

He notices the flyer for the "ghost-hunting" event. He throws up a little in his mouth. Ghost-hunting. What a sad epilog for the condemned hotel. Another fraud. The Porterfield used to generate nostalgic feelings of a glorious American past. *But it's a fraud now, and just maybe America's glorious past was a swindle, too,* Dan thinks. "Well, we all get old," Dan muses aloud. "I would toast you if I had a drink!" Dan says to the Hotel. "I'll toast you nonetheless." Raising a pretend glass, Dan says, "Porterfield Hotel, you're not a virgin but that's not a sin, cause you still got the box that the cherry came in."

Nostalgia. Remembers that his son, Tad, was a tour guide back in the day. Walking tours around the Porterfield, when everyone called it "The Cherry Box" and not "The Majestic Turd." "The cherry box," he'd say, "with its four hundred rooms, once hosted celebrities from all over the world. Roy Rogers, Will Rogers, even Kenny Rogers—were just a few. John Wayne, however, never visited their great hotel. Sadly.

"... The Porterfield's patrons came to partake of the mysterious spa waters that ran underneath the hotel—waters that healed the sick and eased the mentally ill. Mineral water. Liquid lithium."

Oh, well, of course John Wayne didn't need any of that.

Dan considers the ghost-hunting event, and the hotel, an embarrassment. Every year the Rupert Banner newspaper repeats and publishes a commentary bashing the ghost-hunting event. Dan can practically quote it. "The ghost-hunting event is a moneymaker affair for Rupert, but one that the entire town dreads. RVs. Campsites.

People and porta-potties. A bunch of loud weirdos, lovers of horror and gore, pot-smokers, psychics and para-normals with their candles and their flashlights, cameras, two-way radios, with recorders trying to capture other-worldly voice phenomena, walking around with EMF meters to detect electromagnetic fields, or ghosts, all over downtown. Just like America in the sixties. Disaster." Locals loved reading the rumination. They agreed with the sentiment, by and large, but loved the money the event brought to the town. Dan turns, feeling dizzy as he looks upon the fourteen stories of gloom where the ghost-hunting would soon take place. In preparation for the event, workers are tearing down the fences that protect the Porterfield from vandals. Tearing them down. Letting anyone in. *It's dangerous, and Rupert cannot handle such an onslaught of humanity,* thinks Dan.

"Just start with the police force" the article continues. 'The fire department. City services. The hospital. What can Rupert do to prepare for visitors who will undoubtedly be seduced by the dilapidated hotel, finding it horrifying and ominous, pathetic and anachronistic, but still picketing for its revitalization and renewal?

"Pot-smoking strangers walking around lamenting the sad state of Rupert, Texas, passing judgment on the voters and the City Council for allowing the Majestic Turd to fall into ruin, looking for the vegan restaurant that doesn't exist?"

He notes, with the intensity of sadness that can only be brought on by intoxication, that ghost-hunters turned vandals from last year's event had stayed to further the damage heaped on by the turned vandals from the year before. Most recently vandals have cut through the huge chain-link fence that surrounds the hotel and have broken into the entry doors of the old beauty. A terrible breach into the magnificent lobby. They'd set fire to the most spectacular set of stairs in all of Texas. And in just a couple of weeks, a new crop of worthless humanity would be invading the beautiful condemned doll, although some of the inferior crop of dumb humans would have cash on them, which is why this nightmare repeats itself year after year after year. Capitalism.

Dan thinks, along with most of Rupert, that all of the ghost-hunters that turn vandal should just be shot.

"Homeless have also taken over the pool, and are quite territorial. And mean. It is empty and nasty, sure, but home to these vagrants, and soon will be the wannabe home to new unwashed residents fresh from hell. Crime will be rampant. And the smell will be noxious."

Dan then recalls, repeating in his mind, a fact that the article has not included in this year's repetition, a story that is surely noteworthy; the wires running from the fire station to the hotel's fourth story, which are stealing electricity from the taxpayers. Now that affects him, as it affects everyone, surely. That's his business. Dan contemplates, *what if an illegal alien, some dirty mofo who swam the Rio Grande to get here, has taken up residence in the Majestic Turd?* Dan is prepared to assault the fire station in a fit of rage and demand that the wires, which, again, are being used to steal electricity from the taxpayers, from legitimate Americans, be stopped from entering the hotel.

Suddenly Dan notices a familiar face. Up on the fourth floor. *Who? The man in the window is old . . . Jimmy? Jimmy Ramirez? Let's see, Jimmy must be . . . he must be around fifty-four now, fifty-four! Tad and Wayne Herd and Jimmy, all those little boys I practically raised would be fifty-four years old,* he thinks. *How can that be? Jimmy!* Dan surmises that, if that is indeed Jimmy up there on the fourth floor, then Jimmy is the lone occupant of the old hotel. Peering with old eyes, Dan sees that his Jimmy now has burn scars on his face and neck, though Jimmy is still ruggedly debonair. This pleases Dan very much. Jimmy may be nuts, but he has the look of a real man.

To gain a better view Dan moves closer and takes cover behind a huge tree on the lawn. His Jimmy wears a mix of thrift store rejects and old Army issue. This attire definitely confirms his identity. *Yes, Jimmy would dress exactly like that, even at fifty-four, Jimmy!* Now he is certain of it. His Jimmy is living in the condemned hotel. *Thank God, it's Jimmy. Still a Mexican. But not an illegal!*

"Oh, there's my truck," Dan announces to himself, and stumbles away.

Jimmy's illegally occupied hotel room is well lived in. Fully equipped with all the luxuries a surly loner could possibly need.

A coffee pot, two cots, a bong, booze bottles, some empty, some not, as well as a few dirty glasses and empty tv dinner packages. And a scrumptious chocolate cake.

There are a few photographs of better days, and a few black and white photos of his war buddies. A couple of pictures of himself, with Corrie and Dan. With Tad and Wayne.

Jimmy.

Jimmy spends his days at the window with his trusty binoculars, watching ambulances speeding through town heading toward the big hospital on the outskirts, followed by firetrucks, on a big night. Just a normal day for him—decides to watch an old war movie, one Dan Kellar had introduced to him when he was just a boy.

Jimmy tears off a chunk of cake, makes himself comfortable on the cot in his room on the fourth floor.

Aims his remote control.

On the TV—*Battle of the Bulge.*

And the movie starts.

Jimmy relishes the first visual. Pilot Joe (Robert Woods) and Kiley (Henry Fonda) flying low in a WWII era airplane over German terrain, buzzing German soldier (Robert Shaw) while he drives down a dirt road. Robert Shaw, Jimmy's favorite make-believe Nazi. His favorite King Henry VIII. His favorite grizzled ship captain. Robert Shaw. All hail!

And the war. The high point of American History—defeating the Nazis! Heals his mental wounds every single time he watches the movie.

Jimmy knows this movie by heart and quotes along. He narrates along with the film's narrator.

"December, 1944 . . . (Jimmy following along in his best narrator voice) This is their story."

Jimmy slaps his pockets, feeling for a cigarette.

Doesn't find one.

On cue his old yellow dog gets up from his resting place in the corner of the room, saunters to the night stand, and picks up a pack of cigarettes with his teeth.

The old yellow dog delivers the cigarettes, then trots back for a piece of memorabilia of Jimmy's childhood, the old Daniel Boone coonskin cap that he had constantly worn as a child, (a mixed bag there—would the cap bring back good memories or would the cap represent the loss of his childhood friends? The dog wasn't complex enough to figure out the end result.) The dog put the cap between his teeth and ventured forth. Brave dog.

On this night Jimmy is not triggered by the cap. Jimmy pats the dog on the head and both settle down for the long movie. "Good doggie," Jimmy says. Doggie immediately falls asleep, his duty done.

Intermission. Jimmy takes a stretch.

From the fourth floor window, Jimmy scans the horizon with binoculars so to see the town from every angle.

Satisfied that the town is fine, Jimmy opens the dingy, tattered curtains wide, reaches for his crotch...

. . . and eases into a long piss out the hotel window. Back to his spot to finish the movie. Content. Another long piss to come around one a.m and then . . . hopefully, sleep. The end to another ordinary day.

But right before bedtime, when Jimmy would typically undress, feed and water his old yellow dog, get into his cot, cover up, and put on another old John Wayne movie, Jimmy notices a Greyhound bus stop in front of the hotel. He takes his customary piss out the window, and muses.

Zipping up, Jimmy picks up the binoculars once again. Something is up.

The pneumatic door of the bus opens.

The bus driver steps off and opens the luggage hold.

The luggage compartment is nearly empty. Only two duffel bags and a garment bag remain.

The lone passenger. A girl, a frail girl wearing Army BDUs, steps off the bus. She is perhaps twenty-five years old.

She holds a folder in her hand marked "Nicolette Turlo. Walter Reed Medical Center."

She, too, watches the bus driver unload her luggage.

The bus driver checks his watch.

The bus driver is ready to roll, on a schedule.

"We're in Rupert, ma'am. Your stop."

The frail girl struggles to lift a duffel bag.

"Slept on your arm for three hundred miles."

Her speech is as slow as her exit from the bus.

"You watched me sleep?"

"Sorry. Anyone picking you up?"

"On my own. And I'm okay."

"Well, thank you for your service."

She drops her bags as the driver steps onto the bus.

"You're welcome."

The girl scans the landscape, with her gaze finally landing on the immense hotel.

Four stories up, behind the tattered curtain, she catches a movement.

A few sputtering sparks show a wire connected straight to an outdoor power line.

She moves closer. The bus driver, almost ready to depart, hesitates to ask, but asks anyway . . .

"You got anywhere to stay the night, miss?"

"I do. Thanks," she says.

The relieved bus driver drives away. She's left staring in the direction of the dilapidated hotel, directly at Jimmy, in fact, which alarms the hell out of Jimmy, who slams the window shut, yanks the curtains closed, and disappears.

The same notion crosses both their minds at the exact same time. "What in the hell?" Synchronicity.

What the hell, she thinks, *is a man doing in the window of an abandoned hotel,* and *what the hell,* he thinks, *is a wee gal fresh off a bus doing out there in front of the hotel at midnight?* For a second there, he is curious, so curious he yells at her out the fourth story window. To ask. "What the hell are you doing here?"

He learns that she's ridden the bus all the way from Bethesda, Maryland to come to this crappy little town called Rupert, Texas, to bury her fiancé, a war hero killed in active duty.

"You sure you're in the right crappy town? Dallas has the hero cemetery. We sure don't." Jimmy says and shut the window.

Exhausted, Nicolette parks herself on the curb, not sure what to do next.

After graduating high school, Nicolette enlisted in the Army. She completed military basic training followed by specialized combat medic training, and went right to work.

She met Liam during her first tour of duty in Afghanistan. On her first day, while stationed at the base in the province of Paktia, she saw him and heard that syrupy voice of his. He had the slightest drawl, and a smile that changed her life. Nicolette Turlo, big city gal from Chicago, a brown eyed buxom beauty, didn't enlist in the Army in search of love, but love for Liam—this handsome, tall, blonde, smiling soldier from Texas—found her.

He was standing in a turret and bouncing along in a Humvee, riding past her like some sort of deity. She was Greek-American, dark haired, gorgeous, slim, fit and smart. Such an exotic beauty would have been impossible for Liam to resist. He spotted her, said "Well, hello, miss." And she knew. He was the one.

It was six months before she saw him again. He showed up in her hospital unit, injured and unconscious. She was determined that her stunning brown eyes would be the first eyes he saw when he awoke. He woke up so slowly, and slowly they got to know each other.

Sometimes she skipped out on her duties to make sure he was okay. Once, when an attack was imminent, they both heard a mortar go off. She ran from her duties to his bedside to check on him, and he grabbed her hand. Tight. Stared into her eyes. That was their first real encounter. She crawled right into his bed. Together they felt terror, fear, excitement, anger, rage, and a welcome wartime, adrenaline filled lust that was wildly stimulating to Nicolette, though Liam assured her that wartime lust couldn't compare with peacetime lust. "Whatever that is," she murmured. He smiled. "You'll find out. Come home with me. Marry me when we get outta here."

Of course Nicolette was taken aback by a proposal of marriage at such an early stage in their relationship. After all, the man was badly injured, "not out of the woods." But even from his hospital bed, a night here, a night there, he proved that he was very much out of the woods in ways that she knew she was never to forget long as she lived—wartime lust combined with peacetime hopes and dreams for a future that might not ever come. This was heady stuff. Liam reassured her that she was his true love, whether he lived or died. She blatantly spent as many nights as she could by, or in, his bed, and was constantly marveled by his performance. He had no sexual dysfunction despite injuries. And he marveled how the two of them were able to avoid being caught screwing around like rabbits—even though consensual, improper sexual conduct could result in court martial.

The sex was intense and dangerous for both of them, which made it even more marvelous. Oh God, oh God, oh God.

She felt bad asking God to prolong the danger. It was like taking a risky vacation every day—somewhere strange, unfamiliar, and wild. At first, like going to where there are travel advisories. But as he got stronger, Liam took her to the back side of the moon. Mortars, gunfire, screaming, orders to evacuate, adrenaline rushes, all intensified the pleasure of sex with Liam. She was afraid that marriage would stop everything in its tracks! "I want you, but I also want to be Turlo, and only Turlo, forever," she told him. Every time she thought about, and every time she turned down his marriage proposals, it was in favor of wildness. After all it was a great big world.

And she ran to the dangerous places always. Where wars have been and will always be. Crazies. Terrorists. That warmth. That force. Then one night there was a particularly frightening episode of warfare and she got scared.

So she ran to his bedside where he was sitting up, putting on his slippers, ready to find her and he asked her again, "marry me," when mortar fire came in fast and hard, and she'd had enough of bullets flying at her, and got scared, in fact, sensed something terrible was going to happen to them.

She screamed, "Yes," without thinking or hesitation. "I'll even get married in Texas." He laughed. "I think the Army would have something to say about that, Nic." She said, "I just know something bad is going to happen to us, Liam. We need to do our time and not re-up, just leave, go home." She started crying so hard that Liam was shocked. "Okay," he replied. "I'll finish my tour and be done with it if you agree to marry me."

She'd better find someplace to lay her head for the night.

From the fourth-floor window, a strange blinking of lights, like Christmas lights, with sparks, blazed.

Jimmy had slammed the window too hard and jammed some wires. He had to open it, which meant making another contact with this . . . this . . . girl outside.

Nicolette jumps on the moment. She leaps up from the curb, sure that her problem will be solved.

"Hey! Is there another room in there that I might possibly use to set up camp for a few days?"

"Looked to me like you've made camp in the yard."

"I'm cold now."

Nothing could have triggered a worse response in Jimmy than a strange girl showing up in the yard of the Porterfield wanting to stay there. He almost puked his guts out at the thought. But she said she's cold. Jesus fucking Christ.

He yells from the window while trying to quickly disappear.

"No electricity. No working bathrooms. No elevators. No stairs! No place for girls."

"I don't care," she answers. "I'm used to a little hardship. Hey, I'm just in from Afghanistan. It's just for a few days, man. Come on. Tell me how to get on up there. How did you get up there? Please. Please. I'm broke. Tired. Cold. I'm a wounded veteran! What all do I need to say?"

"You need to go to the fire station; they can take care of you."

"I want to stay in this old hotel. I mistakenly thought it was still open for business."

"It's haunted."

"Even better."

Jimmy, more and more agitated, knew that if he let this girl in something very bad would happen.

"I can't let you in. I'm here because I work in security. I am the security guard, I am armed, and I am the only person permitted in this area. Now go away before I have to shoot you."

"Okay, I got it. I'll go to the fire station. Jesus. Hey, will they feed me at the fire station? I'm starving."

"Best eating in town," he replies, slams the window shut, but still watches surreptitiously.

Nicolette picks up her bags just as she hears the rumble of a lone motorcycle as it eases to a stop at the Main Street intersection.

Curiosity gets the best of Jimmy, too. He peers out, intently. Hyper. It's like they all "knew."

Jimmy. Nicolette. And now. The third human.

The man riding the bike looked to be in his fifties, with a thick beard that could pass for a disguise, and dirty blond hair. He's definitely hot for an old dude, she thinks. The hot, old biker had his fair share of bad boy magnetism.

"Oh shit, he's probably armed, too. Goddam Texans," she says under her breath.

But then blonde bad boy speaks, yells over the sound of the motorbike. "YOU NEED A RIDE SOMEWHERE, BEAUTIFUL?"

"No," Nicolette answers.

"Suit yourself."

As the light changes, the biker happens to look up, notices the man on the fourth floor. He salutes him. Like he knows him!

The hunky biker speeds off.

Alarming indeed. Jimmy's binoculars follow the bike as it roars down Main Street. A close call averted. But wait . . .

Jimmy spots the customized "Colorado" license plate on the bike. Jimmy is able to get a better look at the distinctly curly blond hair that he now recognizes as belonging to an old, old friend—one he never wanted to see ever again. Jimmy gasps out loud, and says "Colorado. Mother fucker, it's fucking Wayne Herd," and looks back at the coonskin cap the dog had brought to him. "Mother fucker. Jesus Christ, Wayne wore the army helmet and I wore the coonskin cap, and he's come back." Seeing someone from way back, someone he is supposed to hate, but still loves like a brother from another mother, Jimmy retreats to the safety of his bed. That blonde pecker is an old friend turned coward turned enemy. But dang he misses him. Puts his head under the covers.

Alone in the cold and the dark, Nicolette wishes she had taken the gorgeous man up on his offer. *It's so fucking cold here*, she thinks. But he's moved on, so . . . Nicolette traces the route of the electrical wires from the fourth floor room to the fire station, picks up her bags, and heads that way.

She's stopped by a potent burning smell and a sizzling sound. At that very moment, a huge explosion occurs and the entire electrical line catches fire.

Then—whack, a big whacking sound coming from the sky. Thunderstorms like Liam used to talk about. Big. Loud. Angry. Texan. Huge sudden burst of rain.

She runs, but her feet get tangled up in a pothole and she falls flat on her face in front of the fire station.

She is found drenched and unconscious the following morning. The firemen gather around her, and assume 'she must have been dropping off an unwanted baby Moses in the Safe Haven box,' as young, scared women often do in that small town. A brief hunt for the missing child is launched.

An ambulance takes Nicolette to the hospital where the Emergency Room doctor who examines her has a cigarette in his mouth. The ash on the cig is two inches long. After a half-assed examination, he skims the documents in her folder from Walter Reed Hospital.

He reports to the firemen. "I can confirm that you can quit looking for a missing baby. She's still pregnant."

CHAPTER 24
. . . In the mouth of a graveyard . . .

The road to Peaceful Pines Cemetery is a familiar route for the bad boy on the motorbike, but Wayne is distracted by grief and misses the entrance. He pulls over to the side of the two lane highway to gather his thoughts.

It had been two decades since he'd been in Rupert, since he'd driven this road. Twenty years since he'd last seen his boy, Liam. Seemed like yesterday that Liam was three years old, and carefree — catching butterflies for his mother. It never occurred to Wayne that his son would feel abandoned by his father, or would come to know death before his father. If it had occurred to him, Wayne wondered if he would have done anything differently.

It had also been twenty-five years since Dan Kellar had shot him in the back. That was back in 1978. He never used that as an excuse for not returning, but he could have, you know. Getting shot, becoming a father while recovering, then forgetting your wife and child.

Every day since 1978, though, these twenty-five years, Wayne relives the night of the shooting, though, recalls driving to the old bar, Kellar's Bar, where his friends were congregating—friends who may or may not have forgiven him for dodging the draft. Dodging the draft is what got him shot.

He remembers parking at the back of the parking lot, near the woods, getting out of his beat up Pinto, and hearing such a ruckus of drunken rowdiness inside the bar that he went chicken, changed his mind, and just ran into the woods. He remembers encountering Corrie. He remembers hearing gunshots. He doesn't remember lying in the woods until the sun came up, like they say he did, or the rescue team or the care flight or the weeks in the hospital in Dallas. Back then he struggled to remember his own name, and most important, he had no ID on him. He figured whoever shot him removed the ID when they dragged his body to a nearby crick.

It's a cool fall day. Wayne sits on the immobile bike, lights up a cigarette, and inhales. The mechanical excavator has already done most of the digging. The gravedigger crew is on the ready with the support frame.

When the grave is complete, Wayne throws his cig on the ground and starts the bike back up, but he is suddenly physically overcome . . . he has to vomit. His heart is pounding. The onset of grief surprises this bad boy, because he barely knew his son.

He wants Liam buried next to his mother, though. Liam's mother, Alaina, deserves that honor. It seems the right thing to do after a lifetime of never doing the right thing.

In Canada, Wayne had met and married the beautiful earth mother named Alaina. She played guitar, and grew vegetables and herbs. She made her own compost and raised goats and geese. She could kill a goose. Scald and skin a goose. She could dress a goose. But she could not kill the goats. She loved them like pets. Alaina was gentle and perfect. So, of course, after President Jimmy Carter pardoned the draft dodgers, Wayne packed his bags to head home to Rupert, temporarily, but he never made it back to Canada. He intended to return to her, sure he did. But Dan shot him, and that changed all his plans.

Alaina did show up at the rehab center in Dallas. He was glad to see her. In fact, he was so glad to see her that they started a new life in Texas. At some point she got pregnant. They tried to make it work for three years. It didn't. Wayne bailed. Then Wayne's stepfather took Alaina and Liam in, adopted the kid, renamed him "Liam Chapman," and raised him there in Rupert. Alaina died early of breast cancer. She'd refused treatment, figuring she could give up sugar and heal herself.

There's regrets. And there's been change. A consciousness. Wayne knows he doesn't deserve the 100k death gratuity the government gave him for Liam's death. But he wants something selfless, something good to come out of the money, not for himself, but for someone deserving. He asks the God he never prays to for forgiveness for abandoning his wife and baby. He begs to be forgiven for allowing his stepfather to raise his son. He can't make it up to Liam now, but if he could, he would. He assures himself that he would, over and over.

When he gets on his bike to head back to Rupert proper, a grey dove appears in his rearview mirror. It's got to be a sign. The last time Wayne saw a grey dove, he was visiting friends over at Peaceful Pines Trailer Park! Okay, well, there's the sign! And so quick, too. *What does the sign mean? What about buying a trailer? And giving it away?*

With a spring in his step, Wayne heads to the cemetery offices for a meeting with the funeral director. He enters the office with his checkbook already out, a pen in his hand. The funeral director bids him sit down at a large table, pushes Kleenex into his general direction.

"Will his mother be a problem?" the director asks.

"She's dead. So nope."

The funeral director slides a shiny brochure across the table.

"I am obliged to inform you that the military does offer a very nice stone free of charge. And there's a beautiful National Cemetery near. In Dallas area. Also free. My service department can handle the arrangements."

Damn this guy, Wayne thinks, suddenly triggered. *He thinks I'm poor. He thinks I'm stupid.*

"No. I want him buried here. And I want the biggest and best tombstone."

The funeral director hesitates. "Well, We don't normally bury soldiers here since the national cemetery is so close."

Oh, to hell with this creep's condescension, Wayne thinks.

"What the fuck did I just say? I want him buried here, with a big fucking headstone. Jesus!"

"Yes, sir. Okay, sir. Ok. I hear you loud and clear. It is an honor to bury your son here, sir."

"How much do I owe you?"

"Eight thousand eight hundred and eighty dollars."

Wayne writes a check for the full amount, slams it down on the table, and leaves without taking the receipt.

Impulsive now, before he has second thoughts about giving the money away, his next stop is the Oasis Valley Homebuilders office. Wayne steps into the lot to view what he hopes will be a long row of 'top of the line' manufactured homes to choose from. His long blonde locks, his gruff exterior, his tanned skin, and that nice hog attracts every salesman in the joint. Wayne is a mobile home man if ever they saw one.

Lester, the top salesman, is the first to approach.

"Purchasing a manufactured home is probably the most important decision you will make in your lifetime, sir, and you have come to the right place."

"I'm definitely interested in a mobile home."

"Well, okay then. Let me show you around." He ushers Wayne down the concrete. "First, here's a Horton, 28 x 70, 3 Bedroom 2 Bath. This home is very well built with all 2 x 4 construction 16" O. C. It's a split floor plan with a living room, dining room, den, fireplace, sliding glass doors, carpet, ceiling fans, glamourous bath, stove, microwave, dishwasher, and central air. We offer a VA discount."

"Yeah, I like this one. Paying cash."

"Cash?" Wayne follows the excited salesman into the office. "Cash, good. You sure you don't want an RV instead, maybe visit all the national parks with your lady friend for awhile, see how things go?

"Nope. I want that Horton. How much? When can I get it?"

"Well, you got land to park it on, I'm hoping."

Slapping his checkbook onto the desk, Wayne answers, "I'm gonna park it on the lawn of the Porterfield Hotel."

CHAPTER 25
Stairway to Heaven

"Missing in action. No closure."

Awake, dreaming, in a coma, dead. Dan is never sure. Sleep is such a strange thing. And everybody sleeps, dreams, dies. And the long nights add up, decades, days. Like a silent scream.

Tad was still missing on the night Dan shot Wayne. He was still missing when Sarah left Jimmy, when Jimmy lost his firefighting job, and when the yellow dog brought the Daniel Boone cap to Jimmy to ease his mood. He was still missing when Wayne purchased the trailer. No closure underneath it all. Every fucking thing. For Dan. For C. Jimmy. Wayne.

Wayne planned on delivering the trailer to the Porterfield lawn, but wait, no wait, seriously, wait, sure didn't take long to find out that the City of Rupert was never going to allow that to happen. So, of a morning Wayne woke up, took the 50k he had left from Liam's death benefit, and bought a parcel of land with utility easements on the outskirts of Rupert, and set in motion plans to park the trailer there.

That done, it was time to face burying Liam.

The next step in Nicolette's journey was to greet, *Jesus, what a horrible term, greet, greet?* Liam's body when it arrived from Afghanistan, and to attend his funeral. *Jesus Christ.* She'd missed the wake at Bigelow Bar. The firemen told her it had been massive. A great send-off. What about the funeral? No, won't do both, can't get away from work. Went to the wake, all we could do. *What the fuck?* She wasn't invited to the wake. She guessed nobody knew about her.

All she knew was that she and his estranged father, Wayne Herd, were set to . . . greet the coffin. Nicolette dreaded meeting him.

They might be the only two to attend the funeral service, too, even though an Honor Guard would be there. Nicolette waited outside the fire station for one of Rupert's finest, someone named

Officer Trout, to pick her up in his police car, to take her to the funeral home. She got into the front seat, said nothing, looked out the window, and braced herself for the arrival of the coffin to its final, sad destination, podunk Rupert, Texas, USA.

However sad the final destination seemed to be to his worldly fiancé, the journey to bring Liam's treasured body home was ritualized and respectful. Liam Chapman's honored remains made a carefully orchestrated 8,000 mile trip back to Texas.

Liam's Afghan killer, on the other hand, was laid to rest within a day of his death. The terrorist was buried in his home village, under the hot sun, in a hastily dug grave carved out by a pickax.

Liam's body was recovered, in pieces and parts, as much of it was humanly possible to recover. He was placed in a bag, transported away, with an American flag pinned to the bag. At some point he was placed in a transfer case, with a protective aluminum cover, and flown to Dover Air Force Base. The pieces of Liam's body would spend five days there, being readied for the trip home. A length of red carpet was rolled across the platform at the airport. His body was met by the President of the United States, George W. Bush, and Honor Guard–seven total. Six men carefully and lovingly carried the draped coffin, and one followed behind. His coffin was painstakingly placed into a waiting hearse, and once Liam arrived at Dover, he was carried first into the E.O.D. Room, or Explosive Ordnance Disposal Room, a room with foot-thick, steel-reinforced walls built to withstand blasts, where his body was scanned for unexploded bombs, ammunition, or booby traps. None were found. The technicians unpacked Liam from the case, lifted his body bag onto a metal table and digitally photographed and archived his various body parts. They bar-coded every part of him so that none of Liam, and nothing that belonged to him, such as a ring or watch, could be lost.

Experts examined Liam's fingerprints. Technicians took dental and full-body X-rays.

DNA samples were obtained to match to the blood samples

drawn before Liam's deployment (lessons learned by the military that were not known at the time of Tad's service—get the DNA before you send the kid off to die.)

Finally, the experts officially identified the remains as those of "Liam Chapman." And then the autopsy began. Every war brings better autopsy methods and information. At Liam's autopsy, the Medical Examiner noted that he had suffered traumatic injuries consistent with proximity to an explosive device. Liam's death was deemed instantaneous. His body parts and decapitated head were examined to determine the extent of his wounds, which were documented and entered into a database.

Liam had died with his beautiful blue eyes open. The eyes were closed in preparation for burial. His bodily fluids were replaced with embalming fluid. His remains were wrapped in gauze, sealed in plastic and tucked inside white sheets, carefully closed with safety pins—the head of each safety pin faced in the same direction. Liam became a cocoon. He was carefully wrapped in a green blanket and a full, pristine uniform was pinned on top of his remains.

Liam then became the responsibility of an honor escort, who accompanied him on the flight to DFW Airport, where his remains were transferred to a hearse, which then completed the two hour drive to Rupert's Peaceful Pines Cemetery, where his remains would be delivered to the funeral home for arrangements.

There, another Honor Guard, the family if there is one, and the Funeral Director, would greet Liam's remains.

"This is my first funeral," Nicolette says to Officer Trout as they walk the grounds of Peaceful Pines.

She and Trout are escorted by the funeral director to the place where Liam will be laid to rest. "His father should be here shortly," the funeral director says.

She runs to the grave space as if in a rage. The plot is a football field length away from the parking area. She increases her speed, screams expletives, and hurls herself, almost flying, for the last few steps. She flings herself to the ground, near the open hole, screaming.

The funeral director grabs his cellphone. "Need assistance at

Garden of Eden, Lot 20 . . . " When she later repeats this behavior at the funeral service, flinging herself onto the coffin before the service, and draping herself with the American flag that adorns his casket, the funeral director will retreat, the Honor Guard will stand statue-still while Nicolette rages, unruffled because they have seen this behavior before. Trout will take his cues from them and allow her to seethe. He will remain near the squad car until other mourners arrive. Then he will find the courage to approach.

But on this morning, once she composes herself and gets up off the ground, Trout comes closer. She is still angry. "I just had to rage at the Lord a little," she says. "Now I want to see what God has done, up close and personal. Please take me back to the funeral home and open the casket for me."

"They can't do that," Trout answers. "I'm sorry, but no," the funeral director adds.

"I want him to see me!" Nicolette is rabid. "I want Liam to know I'm here."

"He knows, Nicolette."

"He knows you're here. But we can't open the coffin."

"HE DIED IN MY ARMS. I KNOW WHAT SHAPE HE'S IN. I want to see him."

"Well, the Army won't let them do that."

"Not funeral policy in these cases, ma'am."

And in her madness, hallucinating, suddenly there Liam stands on the other side of the hole in the ground where he will reside forever, so real, gorgeous, in uniform, slightly drunk, an alcoholic drink in one hand, a karaoke microphone in the other, singing Tom Petty's "American Girl" to her, apparitions of other soldiers cheer him on.

A desperate moment when he crept back in her memory.

The loud roar of Wayne's motorcycle entering the parking area interrupts the horrible, magical moment. At the sound, Nicolette shakes herself sane.

Wayne parks and gets off the bike, spots her, curious, removes his helmet, and concerned, walks the long walk to the burial area.

He looks into the hole, looks back at her and says, "Who are you?"

Nicolette turns to face him, and when she looks into the man's handsome face, she gasps.

Then she speaks. "You offered me a ride, remember? Last night."

"Who are you?"

Wayne does remember the stray gal in front of the Porterfield at midnight, but is embarrassed—he'd offered her a ride because she was good looking. Thought he might score, actually.

"Again, no, who are you?"

Trout looks to Nicolette for her response, and hopes he is misreading her face, because it seems to him she looks at Wayne with more than a little lust.

Wayne asks, "You know my kid?"

"Are you Liam's fucking father?" Nicolette says.

"Excuse me?" Wayne looks at her, peering into her face, and she turns away, red-faced. He can't hide his conceit and obvious assurance that she is attracted to him as much as he had been attracted to her in that brief moment at that stop light.

"If you are who I think you are . . . " she sputters.

"I belong here, who the fuck are you?" Wayne snaps.

"Your son's fiancé, you asshole. He hated you." She stares at the hot older man who spawned Liam. Her breath is quick. The tears are hot on her cheeks.

She says, "Can't you bury him somewhere honorable? I had to take a long-ass, miserable bus ride to this podunk shitty town to see him thrown into this ugly hole. There's not another soldier's grave anywhere near here. It's disgusting. He deserves better."

"His mother is buried right over there. Liam will be near her. Near her and near his grandpa."

"Fuck that, dude."

Trout steps in between them.

"Stop it, ma'am. Stop it now. I'm sorry, sir. She stayed at the fire station last night. They asked me to . . . This is Ms. Turlo, I guess you met last night, but then she fell, hit her head, spent the night in the emergency room, I dunno if she's okay."

"I'm okay," Nicolette answers. "Just fucking angry at the world."

Now in palpable grief, Wayne's eyes fill up with tears.

"Oh, fuck you." Nicolette stomps her feet, screams, "FUCK YOU. FUCK YOU. FUCK YOU. You cannot possibly be grieving. He didn't even know you."

Trout pulls Nicolette away.

"We're getting in the car," Trout orders.

Dragging her by the arm, she still continues to taunt Wayne.

"You wanted to fuck me last night, didn't ya? Yep, tried to pick me up."

"We're leaving, sir," Trout says. "I'm sorry about all this."

Nicolette pulls herself away from Trout and continues her rant while in retreat to the squad car.

"Liam deserves to be buried at Arlington!"

And she adds, "He didn't even keep your name! Ha! He hated you!"

Trout opens the car door and pushes her inside the vehicle.

"Get in and leave the man alone," he warns.

Nicolette let go one last loud scream, buckles her seat belt and crosses her arms. Trout starts the car. But Nicolette has one more taunt left in her. She rolls down her window to scream one more insult.

"Fucking coward. I know you were a draft dodger!" Trout almost backhands her to shut her up.

Trout looks in his rearview mirror and can see that Wayne is helpless in grief. He sobs like a five year old as he walks back to his bike.

As Trout enters the highway, he sees Wayne get back on his bike and ride away.

CHAPTER 26
. . . Rider on a train going nowhere . . .

Dan speeds towards home, with Officer Trout in pursuit, horns and lights blaring.

He doesn't stop until he is in front of his own house. The old truck skids over the curb, into the yard, and Dan saunters out of the truck, leaves the door wide open, and stumbles to the front door. Trout sidelines him just before the porch light flickers, then goes out. Dan can't manage the key to the front door so he sure can't manhandle Trout, or save himself from being mauled by Trout, and especially at the same time, and in the dark. The old man stumbles backwards and falls on his ass out into the yard.

"How dare you!" Dan yells. "We had a few, maybe too many drinks, I tol' 'em we ssshhhouldn't do it, too fast, on an empty . . . they made me drink, in honor of our wee, little soldier killed in Afghanish . . . threatened to replacsh me on the poster, they did . . . and they got all up in my business about a Nazi I shot . . . "

"The wake was a couple days ago, Dan. You have clearly been driving and drinking and driving for days."

No concept that days or nights had been lost. "I bet you woke my daughter up . . . but, honestly, they kept buying me drinks. It just happened. I swear." Officer Trout orders Dan to stand up and threatens him with a field sobriety test, but Dan convinces Trout to let him go. "I'm seventy-five," Dan slurs. "Not only will it take me ten damn minutes for me to stand up, I can't stand on one leg, and I can't balance. Your test won't prove . . . " "All right, all right, sit back down and just sit there," Trout answers. Gives Dan a ticket. And a lecture. Then helps him to his feet. And that was all.

Sure enough Celeste is awake. Dammit. She steps outside to talk to Trout. "Jesus Christ, daddy. Couldn't anyone drag your old ass out of that bar before you got so drunk?"

"I don't want to stand here and listen to you and Trout discuss my conduct," Dan screams. "You assholes. I'd rather kill myself than listen to you lecture me. I'm going in to bed."

Once in the house the old drunk tosses the contents of his night stand drawer—twenty pill bottles—onto the bed just as Celeste knocks on the bedroom door. Dan does not want to answer, chooses to let her fret, but dammit, she opens the door anyway, in spite of the hard and fast rule to never enter his room without permission.

She sees the pills—various meds he takes daily for blood pressure, diabetes, cholesterol, hypothyroidism, restless legs, insomnia, plus a few basic happy pills—but taken as a whole they could kill him. Celeste, afraid of her bigger-than-life Dad, risks much when she challenges him. Not that long ago, in this same scenario, drunk for days, then pills, more booze, he'd smacked her so hard that he busted her nose, and several times he broke a few pairs of the reading glasses on her face. In the 1990s he hit her so hard that he caused her to suffer a retinal detachment.

But Dan doesn't smack the cowering Celeste this time. Instead he sloppily barrels down the hall, opens the fridge, grabs a six pack of bottled Heineken, throws one against the wall, holds a bottle shard against his own neck, then against his wrist. Celeste relents. Shuts the heck up. Starts cleaning the wall. Mopping the floor.

Dan throws the shard and bottle into the trash, goes into his room, and puts on the red, polyester blazer. He combs his hair. He smells his breath.

He staggers past Celeste and out the front door.

Dan heads out once again in his old truck to slam a few more drinks down with some of the very late night regulars at Bigelow Big Bar. "The bar you've been living in, daddy? The bar you just left?" Celeste chases him outside, screams at him, goes inside when a few neighbor's houselights flick on.

Trout was barely away from the house, in fact, was still at the stop sign on Dan's street. He witnesses Dan swerve and hit a curb. Looks at his watch. Quitting time. Does nothing. Dan roars past.

Somehow he arrives safely, now back at Bigelow's to keep company with the late night regulars, all seasoned listeners.

He'd rehearsed one of his favorite stories while he'd driven like a madman—a narration of movie-like events he knew well and had told often. Swerving left and right, still drunker than shit.

"SOUTH VIETNAM—1967 (BEACH)—DAY

"A blue, smoke-filled sky and the sound of a dozen or more COBRA attack helicopters defensively dodging rapid enemy fire from the earth below.

"I might have been forty, but by God I could still jump from a helicopter, and so I do, but just as I do the helicopter explodes and falls toward the ground, (car swerving around him, honking). But I managed to land on my feet, ready to fight. I was exposed to withering enemy fire. I look over to the left and see that my fellow soldier, John McCain, is taken prisoner. I want to save him, but I feel an intense pain. A North Vietnamese soldier has stabbed me with a bayonet. I pull it out, screaming at the gook that done it."

Happy with his rehearsal, Dan parks his old truck, sideways, outside the lines, trots up to the bar, a little vertigo in tow, squeezes into his usual spot at the bar, orders a drink and starts talking to/ at some of the regulars who have been there all day and all night. Drunks hear the first words of the story they'd heard before, smirk and laugh at the old soldier, only this time they move down the bar to get away from him.

"He yanks out his own knife," one scoffs. "He kills the gook, the nip, whatever we called them then. Some ugly term."

"Yes, I did," Dan responds to the slights, "but then I fell to the ground from my injury. Life threatening."

Losing the confidence of his audience, Dan insists . . . "I was injured, you see, bad. And I was not a young man!"

The barhounds ask. "Was this Korea or Vietnam?"

"It was 1968, for God's sake," he answers.

They ask again. "Was this Korea or Vietnam?"

Surprised at how dumb his audience is about American history, Dan wants to condescend, but answers with "Vietnam. I don't have any stories from Korea. Hell, nobody does."

For a moment, though, Dan does reflect on his time of service in Korea. He rarely allows himself to remember his time there, or the thousands of other soldiers that come to his mind, Army, Marine, and UN forces. They were all heroes who froze, sometimes to death, in sub-zero temperatures. They survived with little food, no shelter, and were surrounded on all sides by a fierce, invisible, invincible Chinese military force. There are stories (of course there are stories), but Dan holds South Korea in his heart in silence for a reason. He will never speak of Korea, never. His time in Korea is sacred. He'd served the world and fought for freedom, truly. Because of Korea Dan loathes mountains and winter—and most male Asians. He truly hates the feeling of claustrophobia, and being surrounded, and living in breathlessness. He recalls that in Korea he was most alive and yet most afraid. He prayed there, and he cried there, and of his quiet service in Korea he was most proud. "American Assholes not educated enough to know the difference between Vietnam and Korea make me sick." Dan is most afraid that these treasured memories, the secrets of his heart, will scud away like ghosts and dwindle into nothing to be proud of (as his brain ages, and as popular opinion changes in these United States—to embrace diversity). "Hate the Asians, and now . . . and now . . . "

"Time to call it a night, Dan," says the bartender. "Not a good night for your offensive stories, Dan. And they sound like lies tonight."

"I'm not making up shit," Dan insists. "I served in three wars, three bloody-ass wars."

"Yeah, and we've heard all of your stories and never before have we heard about you pulling a bayonet out of your own heart."

"It might not have been my heart exactly."

And suddenly Dan has no audience and no booze.

"Everyone loves my stories," Dan laments.

The bartender shakes his head and laughs. "Yeah, when everyone had a hero to honor the other day they loved your stories, but tonight everyone is just 'business as usual.' Nobody wants to hear 'em. Go home."

Near dawn, the old man arrives home once more, and finds C sleeping in the day bed in his room. He knows she's been awake since he'd staggered past her, that she'd been waiting for the phone to ring, figuring he'd be drunk, and have had a wreck. He knows she's checking up on him, but it's not endearing. *She's treating me like I'm the child.*

"I'm awake, Dad."

"I know that because you're not snoring. Will you make coffee? I have a busy day ahead."

"You acted like an ass last night, Daddy, pills, booze, then leaving drunk."

"So you're not making coffee?"

"Staying out all night again at your age." Celeste pads into the kitchen to make that coffee. She chastises herself for her cowardice regarding her father. Why she allows him to trap her into a life in his house is a question that even therapy never answered.

Celeste pours Dan a cup, delivers it to his nightstand, and retreats to her own bedroom.

But there he is, standing in the bathroom doorway. "I'm going to go round to the old bar today and burn trash."

"NOW? Before the sun rises?" She can't help herself, she mothers him, and they both wonder why in the hell does she care where he spends his day. Celeste follows her Dad to his bedroom.

Dan gathers nice slacks, a shirt, and a tie from his closet.

"Is that what you are going to wear to burn trash? A tie?"

Dan panics. In just seconds he has completely forgotten his intention to burn trash. "What the hell. Celeste, you're gonna have to back off me, please. I'm a grown man, can take care of myself, you just stay so damn nervous all the time. You're making me crazy. I'm gonna go and . . . " Trailing off.

"Dad, you said you were going to burn trash at the old bar. You forgot what you said four seconds ago, didn't you? You're growing older. Dad, you have got to someday give up your whiteknuckled grip on your white man power and just take it easy, let me just keep you safe, and out of the way. And quit drinking."

Dan discards the tie and grabs appropriate clothing—donning a scotch plaid flannel shirt, some stylish cargo pants.

He clumsily dresses and heads to the hallway.

"Leave me alone, Celeste. You harangue me nonstop. I wish to God you had some kind of life without me. I was just thinking about going to the VA after, that's all. I'm dressed okay now."

"You have my permission to go burn trash. If you don't forget to put on socks and shoes."

Dan, mortified, ashamed, looks down at his bare feet.

"Here, let me," Celeste kindly suggests.

Dan allows Celeste to finish dressing him. But begrudgingly.

CHAPTER 27
. . . Another overload . . .

The old, shuttered bar, "Kellar's Born to be Wild Bar," is neglected and worn. Hasn't been in business for a decade at least. Dan's beat up truck is parked haphazardly near the big dumpster. The bar patio is now a hoard of furniture, dead plants, and all the old memorabilia that used to adorn the walls of the bar. Boxes of rummaged-through old books, child's toys (GI Joe's, plastic guns, fake Indian headdresses, bows and arrows) grace the planks of the patio. Lots of keys, wallets, newspapers, a thermos, and Corrie's old beat-up gasoline can rest on a rusted table. And a storm is coming. He has to work fast today.

Dan hates coming to the bar. He hates the memories it conjures. But every Saturday morning, hungover, sick, arthritic, doesn't matter, he comes to the old bar, parks his truck, and starts working. The place has to be cleaned out before he gets too old to do it. It needs selling. The bar will not get much money because it's a death trap, but maybe the property will. Whatever it sells for will not matter. It will be his little money. The house is all paid for, so he intends to buy some new place for himself, a place for older people, using the proceeds from selling the bar, and social security, and Corrie's life insurance money. That way he'll finish out his life in comfort and peace. He drags a filthy throw rug to the dumpster. Then back up the steps for more junk for the dumpster, then back up and down again, and finally he slogs up the steps to retrieve the gasoline can. Dan pours gasoline into the dumpster and lights a match. Within seconds an utterly calamitous, a mismanaged occurrence, an all-out disaster happens. A dumpster fire.

Maybe too much gasoline. But at least the wind is blowing away from the hills. From the trees. Toward the roof of the bar, though. The neon sign bangs against the wall of the porch as the wind picks up. The wind scatters burning embers as the dumpster fire grows. Still, not too bad. Dan decides to free one more throw rug from under a table, throw it into the fire. Maybe the rug will kinda tamp down the fire. But dammit, the table is heavier than he remembered it to be. He lifts, not budging it.

The stronger the wind, the faster the wildfire. Of course. And since heat rises, fire moves more quickly and up towards the porch. The dumpster fire grows quickly to include the whole damn bar. Dan loses his balance and falls off the porch. Lands on the edge of a step, knocking the breath out of him.

The first responders rush Dan's gurney through the automatic sliding doors, through the waiting room of the empty Emergency Room.

He is immobilized while being examined for burn wounds, evidence of smoke inhalation, toxins that may have damaged lungs, deprivation of oxygen level, soot around the mouth, on the tongue or pharynx, burning of the face, or in the nostrils, irritation of eyes, throat, or bronchi. Finally the medical team confirm that Dan fell down the steps before the fire got out of control. "I don't see evidence of smoke intoxication," the doctor pronounces. "Probably alcohol intoxication, though," muses one of the nurses while hooking Dan up to oxygen and hydration. "He was doing a dumpster burn. It's funny cause his wife, she was the craziest woman in town, she used to set fires all over the place. Total arsonist. Runs in the family."

The doctor disapproves of such narrative by a gossipy nurse, and quickly orders up an x-ray of Dan's sternum. "We'll need to watch his heart."

Dan is semi-conscious and responds to commands, even though he can not communicate well. The activity in the ER becomes mute and blurry when Dan sees a bright light crash through the ceiling and hears the roar of a Cobra helicopter.

The body of a soldier floats down through the light, falling fast, the wind buffeting his Vietnam era fatigues.

The body plummets but never hits the hospital floor.

The vision brings a smile to Dan's face.

The doctor shines a bright light into Dan's eyes.

Dan thinks . . . *Am I dead?*

As Dan's consciousness increases he is aware of the doctor asking him questions.

How old are you? What year is it? Who is the President of the United States?

"How old are YOU?" Dan replies.

The doctor chortles, happy to see Dan doing so well so soon.

"I'm seventy-five," Dan says. "It's 2003. George W. Bush is president. And when my son went missing in action Lyndon B. Johnson was president. Then Nixon, and Ford, who pardoned Nixon, and Carter, who pardoned the draft dodgers, then Reagan, Bush 1, and then that womanizer who shall remain nameless, and now, in 2003, it's W. Bush, none of them, not a one of them presidents have been able to find my son and bring him home. Am I dead? No. Would I like to be?"

The doctor nods. "I understand."

CHAPTER 28
. . . Nobody inside . . .

The VA shuttle bus, well, basically a large van, no, a mini bus, stops at the curb near the Porterfield Hotel to pick up a few veterans.

The driver, Laney, looks to be in her fifties, still pretty, pleasingly plump, quite lively and cheery. She is whistling as she opens the pneumatic door.

Nicolette, fresh from her screaming tirade the day before, and another night of hysteria that got her kicked out of the fire station, boards the bus and sits down in a seat up front, directly behind Laney. "You are my first injured combatant from the Afghanistan war, and it is a pleasure to have you on board," says Laney.

Then Laney repeatedly turns the pages of her Manifest, finally having to ask . . .

"What's your name, hon?"

"Turlo. Nicolette Turlo."

"Hmmmm, not seeing it, any other name you use?"

Veterans and several of their wives are boarding the bus by this point. They fill the aisle, blocking Nicolette from Laney's view. Nicolette observes that the really, really old guys are probably from World War Two and the Korean War era. Those old guys are the better clothed, better maintained, and more joyful of the passengers. They converse and laugh as though they are all longtime friends. The second group of old soldiers are somewhat segregated, quieter, more solemn, are dressed considerably more sloppily, with their hair largely uncombed. *They are obviously younger than the really old ones, so they have to be the Vietnam bunch,* Nicolette thinks.

Everyone is looking at her, so curious about her being on board.

Nicolette is relieved when Laney says "Well, we'll sort out why you are not on the Manifest later. Welcome aboard. Every person on this bus is one of America's finest. Loyal to the VA Hospital may be their only flaw. The VA hospitals are unbelievably backed up, in case you haven't found that out yet. A few of these men will wait all day, tell their war stories, never see a doctor. And then next Thursday, they'll get on the bus again. Sometimes I think they just like to get on the bus and talk to each other. At least they are patient as they wait for doctors to come available. Do you actually have a doctor's appointment?"

"I am scheduled to be admitted again to Walter Reed."

"Well honey, the VA and Walter Reed, they are definitely separate systems. So maybe that's why you're not on my Manifest today."

"Maybe. I . . . Please don't make me get off the bus. I need to see a doctor right away. I need help. I'm . . . here for a funeral and I'm sick."

"Well . . . they are different systems. Are you still in active service?"

"I'm still active, yes. I might be deemed disabled, I don't know yet."

"Let her stay" someone kindly requests from the back of the bus.

Nicolette scans the bus and spots an old guy called "Buck." Buck looks to be in his seventies, and is so average you'd never notice him, except for his fantastic huge smile. The man is made of lily white straight teeth!

He is so upbeat that Nicolette is compelled to smile back at him right away.

Suddenly Laney is distracted. She is on hyper alert, checking her hair and makeup in the rear view mirror. "Turlo, stay right where you are," Laney snaps. "Royalty coming on board."

Laney is referring to sweet Jimmy, who is trotting across the Porterfield lawn toward the van bus. Jimmy waves to Laney.

"We gotta give him some cash," Laney confides. "Jimmy only comes out to see me and the veterans when he needs a handout. And we are all so glad to do it! Let's give Jimmy a little something this morning." Laney smiles her biggest smile and pleads with the veterans on board to open their wallets to Jimmy. "We still haven't convinced him to get on the bus and leave that claptrap hotel behind," she adds. "He needs medical help, he does."

To catch Nicolette up, Laney turns and speaks to her directly. "Turlo, Jimmy is the town nut, and we love him so much. War hero, but went crazy after serving in Nam. His wife left him, then he was a fireman, but once there was a huge old fire and he only saved the pets, not the people or the kids, so that job didn't last long. If it were not for the kindness of everyone here, he would be completely homeless."

Jimmy hobbles closer.

"Course the hotel is awful. You know that old hotel is condemned, nobody allowed to be in it. Ever. It's not like we want him to live in squalor, hun. We don't. I guess one of us could have taken him in, given him a real home. But you know, he lacks certain manners. But it's right and good that someone live in it, otherwise, there wouldn't be a window left. Vandals, you know. And he can pee out the window all he wants."

Nicolette strains to see Jimmy up close and personal the closer he gets.

Buck collects cash and bags of food from the other veterans.

He holds the bag out to Nicolette for her contribution.

She opens up her wallet and finds zip.

"Sorry, I don't . . . "

" . . . I'll put in a little extra for you."

Buck reaches into his pocket and pulls out a five to add to the stash of money before handing it all over to Laney.

"Thanks. That's so nice."

"You don't have to pay it back. Thank you for your service." Opening up his wallet a second time, Buck takes out a twenty to give to her. "For lunch."

"Oh no, no thank you. I'm fine," she answers. "I have money coming."

Buck puts the twenty back into his wallet, hands the bucket to Laney, and retreats to his seat in the back.

Jimmy waits at the bottom of the steps, smiling as he peers into the bucket of cash and snacks.

"One of these days you're gonna ride this bus with us, Jimmy, our love," Laney assures him.

Jimmy points back at the Porterfield.

"I hate to leave the old girl alone that long." He makes a point to connect with Nicolette. He offers her a tip of the hat and a timid grin.

Laney hands over the loot.

"Thank you! THANKS EVERYBODY," Jimmy tips his cap again.

And then he's suddenly embarrassed to get a little money from the other warriors, especially since he seems to take extra notice of Nicolette.

"See you next week, hon," Laney says.

Laney shuts the door to the bus and starts the engine.

But before the bus moves, she instructs everyone onboard to bow their heads. "Let's all pray to the Lord for Jimmy."

Heads nod in the affirmative.

"Dear Lord, we ask you to keep poor old Jimmy in your constant care. We ask that somebody good give him a home to live in. We ask you to keep him healthy and sane, clean and groomed. We ask you . . . "

Conversations resume among the soldiers long before Laney is finished praying . . . .

"They got an old A-7 in real good shape in Albuquerque . . . "

"We were there last month, visiting our daughter . . . "

"I flew one of them wild weasels."

"They had one of them, too."

Finally, Laney gets the hint. "AMEN! Assholes. Sorry Lord, you better not whisper when you come to rapture these assholes or they won't hear you," she adds for Nicolette's benefit.

Laney puts the bus in gear and merges into light traffic.

The bus circles the Porterfield Hotel to start the trail through a unique mix of homes, the first being the Haunted House behind the hotel.

"It used to be a brothel," Laney announces as if she were Nicolette's tour guide. "Now the Porterfield hotel is mightily haunted, but this house. Oh my Lord, nobody lasts through the night here."

"Do they die?" Nicolette is impressed that there might be anything of interest in Rupert.

"No, mostly they run out screaming, scared shitless, you know. People hear things, like ghost voices telling them to get the hell out!

Some of the ghosts throw things, they scratch people, they even bite sometimes. Make the chairs rock."

One of the old veterans comments, "And this is just 1st street!"

"Jesus," Nicolette asks Laney, "How many streets are there?"

"The Hotel, of course, most haunted. Something like twenty-nine mysterious deaths there, and ever one of 'em linger around haunting people."

"I love haunted houses!" Nicolette says.

"Well, hang around, girlfriend. The Porterfield opens up ever once't in awhile for a ghost hunting tour. Gonna have one in a few days, in fact. People come from all over to get inside for one night only. It ain't safe in there at all, but for one night the whole town comes out to stand guard over the old girl."

"What will happen to Jimmy that night?"

"What? Oh, I never thought about that. WHAT WILL HAPPEN TO JIMMY, EVER BODY?"

Amongst the grumblings, a veteran states that nobody knows what will happen to Jimmy that night, then points out yet another of the amazing sights of the town of Rupert. "And to your left, take a gander at Noah's Ark." Sure enough there is a big reproduction of the Ark in somebody's side yard, big enough that only a flood could lift it out through all the tall trees. "And down here, two Statues of Liberty in front yards."

"Don't we need to get on the highway to Dallas?" Nicolette asks.

"We got to pick someone up," Laney responds.

"Uh oh, I heard that someone might not be allowed to drive around anymore after he burnt down his bar the other day," offers up one of the veterans' wives.

"Dan Kellar has an appointment today." Well, that starts the gossip going. The bus is lively with gossip now.

"We're picking up Dan 'Put-a-leash-on-her' Kellar?"

"Hero of three wars."

"No kidding!"

"Yep. The very one."

"Get ready for some stories!"

Moans and rolling of eyes from several veterans.

"More like lies."

Nodding in agreement and joking around continues until Laney drives the bus onto Davy Crockett Avenue, where the few well-to-do residents of Rupert maintain their own expansive lawns for their red brick ranch homes with their vibrant front doors and white pillars. Suddenly Nicolette notices a strange tension on the bus. She watches veterans bury themselves in books or feign to be asleep as they drive deeper into the neighborhood. Seems like everyone kind of dreads this Dan's appearance on the bus. "Uh oh," says Laney. "There's trouble lurking. Looky yonder ever body, ummmm . . . Trouble . . . Town."

The bus slows down. Nicolette strains to see a motorcycle parked on a side street, and the blonde rider of the motorcycle looks extremely familiar to her. *Oh God, it's Liam's father.*

"Shit, everyone. That's Wayne Herd lurking on that bike," Laney announces, and is gratified by whoops and whistles from the riders.

In fact, Wayne Herd is indeed waiting at the end of the block, just sitting on his motorcycle.

"Hope Dan Kellar doesn't see him skulking around down there," someone says. "He'll come out of his house shootin'."

Nicolette, wide-eyed, is anxious for more information.

"Um, Laney, newcomer here. Spill!"

"Honey, there's two men in Rupert are mortal enemies, the gorgeous man on the bike, and Dan Kellar, hero of three wars. Well, hang on everyone. Trouble awaits," Laney adds, as she stops the bus in front of Dan Kellar's house.

On the large front porch, Dan is prepared and waiting for his ride. His stylish red blazer is draped over the railing. Dan has no idea that a motorcycle, THE motorcycle, is parked at the end of the street, HIS street.

Dan sips from a cup of tea while gently dipping the black tea bag, despite the fact that, as he reminds everyone who catches him drinking tea, you'd anticipate him to be the type of man to consume strong coffee. Dan is deep in private thought, still furious at the thought of having to ride a bus anywhere.

He believes he can hear Celeste's snoring through the window. But she is faking it. Celeste is actually watching her father from the bedroom window in anticipation of the moment when the VA bus arrives, when Dan gets on that bus and will be gone for the better part of a whole day. The better part of a whole day is time enough for C to get laid. By the hunk on the motorbike. That's her plan anyway.

Celeste intends to get laid while Dan is on the bus to Dallas. If she's lucky. She thinks if Wayne Herd is game for a romp with a past booty-call gal, who has gained a few pounds and maintains a fairly low self-esteem, at a time when he is in terrible grief, then she's in luck. *Oh God, please let Daddy have gotten his appointment right. Today. Please, bus. Come.* Yes, Wayne is paying her a visit to catch up with his old friend, mostly to talk about Liam, he hopes. When he called her, and was actually crying, she couldn't help seeing it as a huge opportunity and immediately began plotting how to get her life-long unrequited love into her house and into her bed. The bus to the doctor appointment in Dallas is a gift from God. Dan having to take the bus means a long, long, longer drive than if he could drive himself. A two hour drive at best. Then appointments, which can take all day at the Dallas VA Medical Center. Then a ride back, dropping everybody off. Jesus Christ, the wonderment of an almost whole day alone with a man, even if that man is in terrible grief, having lost a son and burying him tomorrow, makes Celeste giddy. Timing. Bad. But doable. She feels guilty that she is so joyful about her father being injured, because otherwise her Daddy never goes to the doctor, but she is also thankful for the possible reprieve from at least one of the "H's". The nagging lack of shagging "H" is a Perfect Storm in the most spectacular way, and C is the captain of the raft. If she guides the raft properly, gets Daddy on that bus (and he is out there ready to be picked up), listens to Wayne with the greatest of sympathy (because of course he'll want to talk about Liam, who can blame him, my God, she has to be patient) she'll take out the "H," the itch that has simply got to be scratched.

"Thank you God, and Officer Trout, and Dr. Whoever, that Daddy can no longer drive as of yesterday."

The bus stops in front of the house. Celeste squelches a scream. Dan puts his cup down, carefully saving his tea bag in a small plastic baggie. Laney bounces down the sidewalk to assist him.

"Mr. Kellar. Welcome!"

A quizzical look from Dan—Do I know you?

"Remember me? Laney? My parents used to go to your bar when I was a kid. I told my Dad you were on my bus today. He said . . . "

"I can get on the bus by myself," Dan interrupts.

Celeste dons binoculars to be sure his ass gets on the bus.

Dan breezes past Laney and positions himself behind the driver's seat. Laney boards the bus, and by the look on her face, her feelings are obviously hurt.

"Daddy is an asshole, bus lady," Celeste says out loud to herself. "But please don't bring him home early."

Dan looks around to see the disapproving faces of his fellow veterans. He sighs and wonders what in hell he has done wrong so early in the day.

Not exactly apologetic, and sorely unskilled at apologies, Dan smooths things over as Laney starts up the bus.

"Who's your Dad?" he asks.

Laney hesitates, still licking her wounds, but Dan stays put. Finally, "Mr. Clayton, who owned the . . . "

" . . . Jesus H. Owned the gun . . . " Dan retorts with excessive friendly fervor.

" . . . Owned the gun store and the skating rink." Appeased, Laney smiles.

"Your Dad on the bus today?" Dan asks as he pulls the corner of his mouth to the maximum in a painful grin and looks around at the veterans as if to demonstrate to them how he 'got out of that one.'

"No. He only rides with me when he wants to squat."

"Squat? What's that?" Dan asks.

"Doesn't have an appointment, not sick. Gets on the bus just to ride and tell old war stories to his buddies."

"Oh! I like that! Nobody has better stories than I do."

Dan goes to sit down next to the "purty gal" in the front of the bus. But she, Nicolette, scoots away as if he smells bad. He turns to look once again at the veterans on the bus, expecting approval.

He doesn't get it.

In fact the passengers have gone radio silent. The squatty bus picks up speed on the roadway. But Dan roams the aisle.

"You must be seated while the vehicle is moving, Mr. Kellar," Laney stresses to Dan.

Dan scans the riders, looking for anyone he can call a friend. They are all listening, eavesdropping, making eye contact communication with each other, but none of them are looking Dan in the eye.

His eyes pause on Buck's face for a beat.

A little queasy from the swaying of the bus, Dan walks down the aisle towards Buck, points at Buck's attire— lime green polyester slacks.

"What are you reenacting now, Buck? Last time I saw you . . . you were wearing Confederate britches. Playing a Civil War soldier."

" . . . Our hosts usually refer to The Civil War as The War of Northern Aggression," Buck smugly replies.

"Well no wonder they lost," Dan jokes, thinking he's funny. "They didn't even know the name of the war." Dan looks around and voila, does see a couple of grins.

Pleased to be winning, Dan continues. "I've seen you wear those pants before, back in the seventies, wasn't it?"

"I need to do laundry, Dan. I'll swear to Gawd . . . couldn't find my Confederate britches, or my blue britches, or my nice grey slacks, this mornin'. Couldn't find my keys. Retraced my steps. My keys were in these lime green britches. These are my leisure suit britches, worn only as a last resort. But for some reason my keys were in 'em," Buck explains.

"Well, when did you last use your keys, Buck? 1978?"

"I can tell you exactly how you would remember these old britches. I wore these britches the night you shot Wayne Herd, wonder if any of us have seen him around lately? Anybody hear about maybe him coming back from Canada?"

Dan notes a collective gasp. *What's that all about*, he wonders.

Finds a seat in the back and sits down.

It sorely bothers Dan that Buck mentioned the long-forgotten Wayne Herd after all these years. Dan's mind cycles faster and faster, trying to remember and suppress the memories at the same time. So. 1978. How to recall that memory. In his mind, he rehearses the official story. The Texas rain poured down that night, the weather was terrible, and nobody except Celeste knew who fired those shots. C and all the hateful bar rowdies.

Dan wanted to burn Wayne's body after he'd shot him. He knew it was tricky burning up a body to ash with such a rainstorm sure to put out the fire, but Corrie's gasoline can was nearby and he had to risk it. Disregarding the rain, Dan wrapped Wayne up in an American flag and set him afire. The police would naturally think "if there's a gasoline can, that means crazy Corrie had gotten out of the bar without anybody seeing her, and she done it." Nobody would put Corrie in prison. It was a no-brainer to let her take the blame.

(Actually, the rain put the fire out before Wayne was even singed. But Dan didn't know that.)

Dan was a safety risk as he moved back down the aisle of the bus to find a seat up front, and get away from Buck.

"The bus is still moving, Mr. Kellar," Laney warns.

"I know when something as big as a minibus is in motion," is Dan's smart ass rebuttal.

"Then sit down, please!"

He maneuvers the aisle, searches for a seat, and discovers that every desirable seat is taken. Dan will have to sit next to Nicolette, and she yells at him this time, "Oh fuck, no!"

Laney and the veterans are amused by her outburst. Dan lowers his rump in the direction of the vacant seat despite feeling a little surprised by her reaction.

"Oh fuck, I said," she repeats. "Don't sit by me!"

Dan chooses the seat anyway, taking care to keep as much space as he can between them.

"You might like me if you give me a chance," he says as he clicks his seat belt.

"But then again, you might not. Because I am the asshole everyone says I am."

Dan leans forward, eyes wide, and points to a flock of ducks crossing the highway ahead.

"Danger ahead, Madam Bus Driver. Mind the ducks."

"I see them."

"I think you need to pull over."

"On a tight schedule, Mr. Kellar."

"Man of Action" Dan removes his seat belt.

"I order you to stop the bus," he says.

"Stay in your seat or I'll call for backup!"

Laney reaches for her mobile phone.

But Dan is up, out of his seat again.

He jerks forward, and grabs the steering wheel.

The bus swerves as Laney momentarily loses control.

Half of everyone on the bus cries out, "Holy shit!!!!"

Combat Soldier Nicolette is quickly up, too. She pulls Dan back.

The bus straightens, and a shaken, furious Laney pulls over to the side of the highway.

She turns to face Dan.

"I'm reporting this incident. Sit your old ass down while I make a call to my superiors."

Dan obeys, but not without snark. "Call your superiors, they'll agree with me."

"I've never run over a single duck," Laney states, puts down her phone, and decides to keep the bus moving. "Got a schedule to keep, so . . . " Dan grins at Nicolette, she shakes her head in disapproval and thinks, *well, white man, soldier, always wins.* But she says, "Wayne Herd was almost my father-in-law, and you're the man shot him? Tell me more."

And so he does.

But on the bus that day, Dan Kellar felt for the very first time in his seventy-five years that his life had taken a turn. 2003 would prove to be the year that old age sank in. Being the storytelling hero of three wars did not automatically give him the respect he craved among his fellow veterans. There were other heroes on the bus and some of them were girls. The world was changing before his very eyes.

Dan notices that Nicolette's right hand is shaking uncontrollably.

Dan is quiet for a moment.

Finally he speaks, "You don't have to respect my service. But I damn sure respect yours."

"Leave me the fuck alone about my service," Nicolette warns.

Dan is suddenly curious, wants also to change the subject. "Okay. I know I'm old now and out of touch. But what does the phrase "leave me the fuck alone" mean?"

"We have veterans on the bus today who may not appreciate such language, Mr. Kellar," Laney alerts.

"Oh shut up, Laney. She said the "F" word first. I just think that particular phrase makes no sense and I want to ask this obviously intelligent woman what she means when she says . . . "

" . . . She means leave her the fuck alone, Dan. Leave everyone alone." Laney yells.

Dan notices the long scar on Nicolette's neck, running from below her collar to deep into the hairline.

He wants to ask about the scar, but doesn't. He just stares. Her scar, and her obviously bad temperament, confirm his opinion about girls in combat. It should never happen.

"What the fuck are you looking at now?" Nicolette screams.

CHAPTER 29
... *Lightning strikes, end scene* ...

Well, there are always second thoughts to be had. Wayne hadn't seen Celeste in twenty years. He found a house key rummaging through some old drawers. Poor C. Why in the world would she have given him a house key all those years ago? Oh.

He'd had to force himself to stay away from her. He'd never really dated her, even before the shooting. Just sometimes when she was around, he would, on occasion, show her a little affection, so she was necessary and irresistible. After the shooting, however, a round with Celeste hurt his back. Bad. And it would never be just one round.

Dang, that woman was seriously gifted in the sack.

Oxycontin came into his life to manage the pain of C-sex, and the oxy finally replaced her. He dumped her for a long time. His guitar, singing, and oxy kept him going for years. Then oxy addiction got the best of him. Getting off oxy was even harder than getting off C.

Wayne takes off his helmet, brushes a couple fingers through those blonde locks, and walks up the sidewalk like he owns the place. But he's anxious—walking right up to Dan Kellar's house scares him.

A windy morning and Wayne's hair blows in the breeze, but it is just right, a little bang over one eye. He catches a glimpse of himself in the window of the door as he knocks. He is content with his appearance because in thirty or forty years he has never really changed. Or so he thinks.

He knocks a second time. Nada.

"Answer the fucking door, Celeste!" Wayne knocks again, wondering if C is having second thoughts about seeing him.

One night, decades ago, Wayne and Celeste met in the woods. He was going to leave for Canada the next morning. Celeste almost talked Wayne into letting her run away with him, too. But by dawn, when she was sound asleep in the dewy grass, Wayne fled. Left her sleeping. When she woke up she was alone.

The people he abandoned and hurt. He has regrets. "I'm only knocking one more time," he says, just barely loud enough for anyone to hear. "MY SON DIED, C!"

Celeste had fallen asleep in her recliner but she finally heard the knock.

She checks herself in the mirror. Her hair looks okay, her makeup is fine, her teeth are white. She smells good. Her breasts are full and boastful in their positioning inside a tank top which is tucked into an emerald green broom skirt. She wears knee highs underneath, instead of panty hose. Wearing knee highs under a broom skirt means 'don't go out in the wind.'

Opens the front door.

Takes in the blonde bad boy, still gorgeous.

Waits.

He doesn't puke at the sight of her. *That's a good thing.*

"Wow. You are beautiful, Wayne."

"Saw the asshole get on the bus."

"Lucky you, and lucky us, he got on the bus."

"When is he coming home?"

"Tonight. Headed to the VA Hospital in Dallas. Long drive, long day there, long drive back."

"You want me to move my bike somewhere else in case of the neighbors?" Wayne offers.

"Oh, hell no. I love it when the neighbors talk. Step inside, big boy." Of course, as soon as she says anything remotely flirtatious, she feels really dumb.

Wayne grins, steps inside, looks her up and down and says, "You aged okay."

"Thanks? Damn you."

"What took you so long answering the door?"

Celeste gives him a sort of halfway hug, mostly just to get a sniff of him, this kind of 'cigarettey, been out in the sun, wind blowing through his hair on a hot day' kind of smell of him that's as sexy as it gets.

"I guess I can tell you. I needed to change clothes. When I got dressed I, well, I put on knee highs and a pair of ill-fitting bikini underwear. I never have company, so . . . "

"What kind of underwear do you have on now?"

"All my underwear is ill-fitting. I took my knee highs off . . . you want some coffee?"

"Okay, you want to sit down somewhere, C? I can't stay long."

"Sure. Let's go into the tv room. I don't wear this skirt often, dumb me so used to putting it on with knee highs instead of panty hose. Once I wore it to a job interview in Dallas, I really was gonna move there once, and walking through the parking garage, the wind came in and blew it clean over my head. Two women burst out laughing. One man just kind of stood in shock. I'm guessing he'd never seen knee highs under a skirt. Plus the ill-fitting panties. Not my best moment. And it was caught on CCTV. I kept walking towards him, trying to make sure my skirt fell back down to cover my privates, nothing I could do to change the fact that I had been caught in public almost with my panties down. I passed him and I said 'Hello. Windy day today.' And I kept walking, even smiling at the CCTV cameras. Haven't been back to Dallas since."

Wayne lands on one of the recliners, feeling uncomfortable as hell, both in the well-worn recliner and with the conversation.

"I'm heavier than I've ever been in my entire life, Wayne. I know you have eyes, you can see that. And I'm sorry. But you want some coffee?" Celeste kisses him on the cheek and turns toward the kitchen.

"Coffee would be great. You still live here! Surprised to see that."

Celeste slowly turns back to him and takes his hand.

"Believe me, I have screwed every man I want in this very house. My Dad is not a problem. So if you are into fat women, then come on. I'm ready to roll." And with that she tosses her hair and swaggers into the kitchen.

Celeste, feeling stupid, notes that Wayne doesn't seem to quite know what to make of her ridiculous banter.

"Whoa horsie. Whoa!" is all he manages to say.

Celeste shrugs, she is moving in on him too fast, her actions governed by a very strong bout with her most powerful "H" and the fact that she has loved him all of her life. She pours two cups of coffee. Wayne pushes his aside. "Why not? Let's do it for old times sake." He drags Celeste down the hall to her bedroom. "Your dad's not home, C." Wayne, snickering, like he's fifteen years old instead of fifty-something. "We can get in a few rounds before my back starts aching," Wayne says. "It might make me forget . . . "

Over the course of the morning, if Dan had somehow come home earlier than planned, and been standing on the front porch, where he could have heard everything going on inside the house, he would have heard more than a few sounds emitting from Celeste during her romps with Wayne. It would not have been her snoring. Dan would find it difficult to identify the exact sound. He might have known that C was with a man. But he'd have thought . . . *was that a moan, which is a low sound? Or was it a whimper, something that sounds submissive?* And then he would wonder if the sound he heard was a grunt or a groan, neither of which sounded very polite, and Celeste is nothing if not polite, even if her nervous chatter verges on inappropriate and off-putting. *It isn't a squeal*, he'd think, *maybe a yelp? The cry may have been shrill, so is it a whoop? No, that's too enthusiastic.* Finally Dan would correctly identify the sound. "It's a squawk or a quack, like when ducks are scared," he'd say, because he has this thing about ducks. But then there's another sound—*a hiss, a puff*, which Dan would undoubtedly identify as coming from a male.

Good thing C's dad wasn't home.

Celeste actually WAS squawking. Loudly. And then, like a miracle, the satisfying finish that meant no more "H" to plague her for a while. She had taken the lead, so Wayne is happy and numb, pain-free for the moment, and grateful for it.

It was later that day, after several rounds of mindless, mind-blowing, desperate sex, that Wayne finally tries to confide his grief to her, connect with her, and hold on tight to her, emotionally, like a real couple, but Dan interrupts their connection with a frantic phone call from the VA Hospital, which C answers, and which, as always, takes priority.

He waits for the call to end. Wayne watches the clock even as he makes himself at home in Dan's house.

When the call ends, Wayne stands. "Liam's service is tomorrow," he offers up to Celeste, a few moments before Dan intrudes with another frantic phone call. "I hope you don't think I came here just to take some kind of advantage of you, Celeste," Wayne says.

"It's okay. Please don't leave. *Hello daddy?* I want different things now . . . *What? Why are you yelling, daddy?* . . . than I did back in the seventies . . . or eighties." Celeste lies. Her heart aches because her heart knows full well that that Wayne is indeed only here for Liam's service, that he came to see her only because he had no one else to befriend him when he needed a friend. Celeste longs for a stronger and more lasting connection to Wayne. He is still the great love that got away. But she is damaged. She cannot connect. At least she got laid, though.

"You deserved so much better than you got," Wayne adds.

"I got nothin', you're right about that." Celeste turns to look Wayne square in the eye. "Not your fault, is it? And wow, you just made up for it, you know."

"You never got married or anything?" It was Wayne at his most disgusted with himself for being a jerk to everyone who ever loved him. Here is this woman he occasionally met up with, hooked up with, over a very long period of time, decades. He has always known of her great love for him. He has never cared. But in this moment he felt remorse for that. The "or anything" is particularly pathetic.

She disconnects the call from her daddy.

"You thinking about marrying me, Wayne, late in life?"

"Just making conversation, C."

"Do we have anything at all to really talk about?" They both ask the question at the same time, then laugh.

Wayne looks at the clock again, starts talking faster. "Hey, guess what I did? Bought a trailer. That trailer park used to be near Plentiful Pines? It's gone." Not quite what Celeste expects to hear, and she has to wonder if this is promising. *If he stays, if he moves into a trailer park, what would that mean for her, for the two of them?*

"Gone. Plentiful Pines went bankrupt. But there are other parks nearby. If you're thinking of moving here, oh my God, Wayne, please think about moving here."

Sadly, Wayne doesn't ask about any other parks. Instead he leans forward and says "Listen. You wanna talk about important stuff, let's talk. Let's talk about Liam. Let's get some talk in before your daddy calls again."

Liam. Celeste says a quick prayer and hopes she will be sympathetic and kind, unselfish and not needy. It is not her time of need, after all. And she really doesn't want to leave the possibility of another friendly romp to talk about death. But Celeste always gives in to what she thinks a man wants.

They stare at each other for a long time. Finally Wayne believes he can talk about it. "It was an insider . . . So at the base, Liam and his fiancé, this Nicolette girl, were training, and this Afghan who was working with them, in a flash turned on them and killed Liam . . ." But in fact, Wayne isn't ready to talk. He is rendered speechless with grief; tears pour and turn to wailing. Wayne at his most vulnerable. "I deserve it, losing a kid, but you never deserved all you had to live with after Tad and . . . "

And this is when the ring of the telephone interrupts the story and the wailing. Celeste panics but answers the damn phone. Again.

"*Sorry, Wayne.* Hello. *It's Dad again.* What happened, Daddy, are you all right?"

Utter resentment crosses Wayne's face.

Celeste puts the phone down on the table, her father's screeching can be heard by both. Celeste reaches for Wayne's hand. "I'm sorry. I have to take his call. I can't help it."

Wayne answers. "I understand."

But he doesn't understand.

"I just lost a son, Celeste." Wayne reminds her.

"Well, but you didn't really care about him, Wayne," she snaps back.

CHAPTER 30
. . . Through the jungle . . .

Laney is ready for a break and, in fact, is first off the bus when they arrive at the Dallas VA Medical Center. Stiff from the long ride, the veterans and their wives take their sweet time moseying off the van and down the long walkway to the hospital.

But one person stays on the bus. Nicolette.

Dan Kellar is the first to see a doctor. After meeting what he considers to be the "dumbest doctor known to man, a dumbass girl doctor," he heads back to the bus to wait for the others. To take a nap.

The minibus is locked.

Dan paces back and forth before deciding to call Celeste. She answers quickly, irritated.

"I just had my checkup. God dammit, Celeste, I can hardly catch my breath, and now they want me to see a shrink." At this point Dan notices that Nicolette is still on the bus.

"Unlock the door, girl soldier." Dan orders.

Nicolette motions for him to "go away."

"Did you see your doctor already?"

Nicolette turns away.

"Nicolette, did you see your . . . your . . . fucking doctor?"

She shoots him the finger.

Dan pounds on the bus door.

"Come on, get out of there. There's no heat on in there. And no bathroom!"

Nicolette moves the few rows to the back of the bus.

"Open the damn door, soldier!"

She opens her purse and pulls out a gun. She shows the gun to Dan, sorta teases him with it, crazy-like. Finally, she points the gun. At her own head.

"NO, oh my God, stop it. Open the damn door."

She starts screaming . . .

. . . and won't stop.

Lots of people walk by, shake their heads and hurry past. Lots of crazies surround the VA Hospitals at various times. Apparently.

Her screams attract some attention. VA Hospital security quickly surround the bus. But she's locked in.

When the five-man security team leader locates Laney, they get the keys, and board the minibus. Nicolette is railing, and brandishes the gun like a crazy person wanting to commit suicide by cop, but she is quickly subdued and cuffed by two hulking man cops. Dan, still on the phone to his confused daughter, steps back as the security officers drag Nic off the minibus. They look like a SWAT team to him. He holds the phone to his side, steps into the middle of the chaos, yells "What the fuck are you planning to do with this girl?" *Oh, the power of that expletive. Felt really good to scream such at someone in authority.*

Laney reprimands Dan. "Go back inside the waiting room, but don't say anything to the others, please. I don't know when they'll let us back on the bus."

Dan hangs up on C, pockets his phone, does as he is told. He enters the waiting room, now packed to the brim with animated soldiers sharing their complaints and war stories.

He scans the room, a sea of infirmity occupying most of the large room. Everyone looks so old. He pauses a moment to listen to the stories being told by the old soldiers—accounts of war wounds and the medals they received. Dan knows the loud mouths are lying. He should know. He's a loud mouthed liar himself.

He locates Buck. Acts like they're friends.

"Let's take a cab home. I'm not waiting all day to see that other doctor they want me to see."

"They've been calling your name, Dan!" Buck answers.

"Screw them. Let's go."

"But I haven't seen a doctor yet!" Buck says.

Dan assesses the chaos inside the waiting room. "Come with me, Buck. I'll make sure you see a doctor today."

Dan and Buck approach the receptionist window and its

overwhelmed occupant, a young woman of college age. "My friend Buck here needs to see a doctor right away. It's urgent. He needs his neck looked at. We have dates tonight. Don't want him dancing like this." Trying to be funny, Dan performs a crick-riddled jig that is not well received by the receptionist.

Turning to Buck, Dan says, "You thought I'd forgotten about the Veteran's Day dance."

"Well, you did, Dan, the dance is not for another week."

"Does your friend have an appointment?" the receptionist asks the deflated Dan.

"No, but, he needs to be able to dance. Waltzes, tangos, two steps. By next week."

"I can't help you, sorry, everyone has to have an appointment today," she states.

Dan grabs her wrist as she tries to close the window and pleads, actually warns, "and once the old folks go on to beddy-bye, then it's good old country music. Line dancing. Please. Get him in to see someone. Please. I want to go home. We want to go home and know that we are going to be able to go to the dance. Next week."

The receptionist, who has seen it all, is in no mood for this. She snaps her wrist away, glares with menace, shuts the window.

Buck steps up. Knocks on the glass. "I've never been a patient here. I don't know the 'drill'. What do I do? My neck does hurt bad."

The receptionist reopens the window and answers the old man with the toothy smile. "You have to have an appointment, we need your military papers and then you wait."

"Well, darn . . . negative. I never actually served. So I sorta don't have papers."

She smirks. "You have to have papers. We don't know who you are."

Dan interjects a new tactic. "He never actually served in any legitimate war. Okay. Buck here served in the 'War on Fashion'."

The Receptionist slams the window shut. Dan knocks again, and makes himself heard.

"He served in the War of Northern Aggression. You and I, normal folks, call it The Civil War. They didn't have papers back then."

But she's gone. They've gotten nowhere.

"You never served. I did not know that. And you ride the VA bus because . . . ?"

"Because I like the stories. I'm lonely."

"Well, you just made me look like a fool, Buck."

Every seat is filled with a waiting veteran. There are at least two dozen veterans, dazed, dejected. Wandering.

"Look at the 'Nam crowd, Buck. They used to be the young ones. Now look at 'em. Jesus. They all look like old groundhogs."

Dan thinks perhaps he has drawn the attention of security as they enter the room. "I'D BETTER SIT MY OLD ASS DOWN BEFORE THEY THROW ME IN THE CLINKER. Unless they're looking for you, Buck, because you are not supposed to be here at all." It takes the two men several minutes to get their asses down onto the floor.

But the security officers aren't interested in Dan or Buck. They are accompanying Nicolette and Laney into the waiting room.

Nicolette moves very slowly, a long, painful trek. As hard as it is for him to do, Dan places both hands onto the floor, and manages to hoist himself up on his knees. After catching his breath, Dan hurls himself up to standing and approaches the receptionist once again.

"Ma'am, I would appreciate it if you would at least get help for the young lady coming in."

Just as the receptionist opens the window to witness what is happening with Security, the room goes noticeably quiet, in a sort of reverence for the seriously impaired young woman.

The receptionist has seen the crazies before, sees them every day, and well, today is no exception. "I'm way too busy for this bullshit," she says. She trudges back to her cage as Laney delivers Nicolette to the window.

Nicolette has her folder from Walter Reed Hospital. She holds it out for the receptionist to see.

From her cage across the room, the receptionist says, "I'll need you to fill out some forms, ma'am. Just wait there."

Nicolette, tears brimming, is impatient. "Can you just look in your database? I filled out like a million pieces of paper in the past few weeks." She drops the folder onto the desk.

Dan approaches the window, butting in, as he does.

"You got a . . . magic machine . . . a computer, don't you? Look her up. YOU ARE ALL THE SAME SYSTEM, RIGHT?"

Nicolette shoves him away.

"I do not need your help, Mr. Kellar."

"Are you transitioning out?" the receptionist asks her, as she moves across the room, disinterested.

"I don't know yet," Nicolette replies. "I am thinking no."

"She has an appointment," Laney adds.

"I was referred by my doctor at Walter Reed," Nicolette whispers and points to the folder. Then talking on top of one another, the receptionist asks more questions like "what is your birthdate?" and the loudness of her voice, and Dan's voice, and her own voice screaming in Nicolette's brain, sets her off on another crying jag.

The receptionist is at her wit's end and searches for her pack of cigarettes. She lights up right there in the waiting room, realizes, says "Oh shit!" and snuffs it out after a quick puff.

And later, somewhere in the hospital, Nicolette, hooked up to what seems a thousand wires, is flat on her back in the hospital bed. A soft rain is falling outside her window. Someone, a nurse practitioner, examines Nicolette's ever-shaking hand.

"Maybe I can sleep in this rain," Nicolette offers.

"Are you having difficulties sleeping? Because you're going to need good sleep, with this baby coming," the nurse says.

"So I'm still pregnant. Thank God."

"Not sleeping at all or? Are you experiencing more than the usual irritability?"

"I'm irritable by nature."

"Are you fine if we just talk a little bit, Nicolette? I'm assigned to you and I'm skilled as a psychiatric nurse and..."

" . . . Psychiatric? Okay. I want to talk. Because I have zero chill fizz, no tranquility. I want to be able to go to back to Walter Reed without being depressed the whole time. Suicidal. Crazy."

"I understand you are in the area for a funeral. Another soldier.

Is the deceased the father of your child?

"Yes. Please don't judge me. I can't take it."

The nurse closes the notepad, and nervously asks what she is not supposed to be asking of her patient. "What are you going to do? About the baby."

"I'll look at my options. I don't want to talk about it."

The nurse moves closer, leans down to whisper to her patient.

"Don't wait long to decide on abortion, because you will be lucky to find an outpatient facility and a doctor willing to perform, let alone talk about an abortion."

"I'm not considering abortion, unless it's medically necessary."

The nurse considers her response, then confides. "The baby is probably fine. Traumatic brain injury can affect your pregnancy in many ways, including possible miscarriage, but if you . . . I recommend going to Routh Street Women's Clinic, or Planned Parenthood, not to any other kind of . . . not to a church . . . between us, woman to woman, this is Texas, you know, pro-life no matter what."

"I'll go back to D.C."

"Listen to me, I could be fired for talking to you about this, even as your personal nurse practitioner, but President Bush gave a speech this week, that babies come from the Creator of life. In other words, screw Roe v. Wade. End of story. There are more abortion bans and restrictions coming every day. You and your baby are not protected everywhere."

"But Roe v. Wade is the law of the land."

"Doesn't matter what rights you have if you can't find anyone to help you."

"I am not a likely candidate for abortion."

"Well, that is surely a good thing. But you will need support. From someone. So." The nurse moves back to her bedside chair, opens her notebook, continues. "Have you become . . . hyper-vigilant?"

"Scared all the time. Because . . ."

Nicolette slowly considers what she wants to say.

"Take your time," says the nurse, who looks at her watch.

The first thing she says, "Liam's head landed in my lap! Of course I'm going to have his baby."

The nurse, on the edge of the hospital bed, places Nicolette's hands in hers. Nic continues letting it all out.

"Liam and Manon, his name was Manon, were beside my truck. I was inside my truck. We had all just been laughing over a story about soccer, Manon was our friend, he was Afghan, and seems to me he was telling this story and laughing really hard but from where I was sitting I could see something inside his uniform when he laughed. Now I know he was wearing some kind of suicide bomb. I remember realizing and Manon looking at me, and then . . . I remember thinking that I had not even gotten to tell Liam that I was pregnant. The explosion was so loud. I went deaf. My brain jangled round in my head."

"Thus the TBI," the nurse concludes the obvious.

"The next thing I know was they were cutting my pants off, and a medic was taking Liam's head from my lap and wrapping it. His . . . his head. The rest of him was gone."

The nurse gasps, calms herself. "We can only hope they had already removed him from the area. I'm so sorry. So, so sorry."

"I felt numb. I feel numb. In my toes. In my hands. In my asshole. Every fucking where. And I'm afraid how bad it will hurt when the numb wears off."

"I understand. Nicolette, it will hurt when the numb wears off. On another note, please do not tell anyone that we talked about what we talked about regarding . . . rural Texas and all that." Nicolette nods in agreement.

In notes, the nurse has carefully written down her concerns about Nicolette, including medical concerns about her pregnancy, which were later shared, and perhaps altered, in committee meetings with a panel of professionals. "The cortisol levels in Ms. Turlo's blood are off the charts high, her brain images show that she remains in constant high alert, scanning her environment for danger as a survival mechanism. She suffers from extreme threat bias. She lacks the ability to make complex decisions and her IQ test results show a severe decline from the time she enlisted. She is a suicide risk and could perhaps become violent. But these risks can pass with treatment and rest."

And one other note, not altered. "Nicolette Turlo should be allowed to decide her own fate regarding impending motherhood."

"Sure she can," doctors agree. "We sure don't need to be anywhere near that situation. Let's get her to Walter Reed as soon as we can. Get her out of here."

Later, after Nicolette is told she must leave immediately, before the funeral, without further assessment, Nicolette waits for the doctor to leave, pulls out her IVs, finds her street clothes, escapes the hospital. Nobody notices. She doesn't get to the minibus in time. She watches the bus leave. But she figures there are other buses back to Rupert. If not, she'll hitchhike. She's not going to miss the funeral. She and her baby are not. Going. To. Miss. Liam's. Funeral.

CHAPTER 31
. . . I can't get it out of my head . . .

Laney put the pedal down on a smooth highway heading back to
Rupert, Brad Paisley on the CD player, then a huge switch to Bob
Dylan, dark clouds on the horizon, windows down, the smell of
ozone from the coming storm.

Buck and Dan are the silent passengers on the long ride home.

Dan opens the bus window, sticks his nose out. Big, full sniff,
as if he still has the lung power of a twenty year old. His head feels
a bit woozy after, but he inhales again.

"I still love the smell of rain. Freshly mowed grass. Tobacco."

"I can't smell anything, so I ain't got nothing to list," Buck says.

"When life is no fun anymore, I say end it, Buck."

Laney smiles as she listens to all three philosophers of life—
Buck, Dan and Bob Dylan.

"Laney? Would you ever consider killing yourself?"

"Nope. I would, however, consider killing someone else."

Buck laughs.

"We're close to your old bar, Dan."

The old dilapidated bar is just visible on the hill.

Dan releases his seat belt.

Laney hears the click.

"Mr. Kellar, buckle your ass back up."

Dan stands up.

"Stop the bus."

"I cannot let you off until I get you home."

"Stop the bus."

"Buck? Talk sense into your friend, please?"

"I'm just mindin' my own business."

Laney looks in the rear view mirror, makes the decision,
pulls over.

Opens the pneumatic door.

"Do you need an umbrella?"

"I was in Korea when hell froze over," Dan says. "It was minus fifty-four degrees most of the time. And wet. I do not need an umbrella. You are coming with me, Buck?"

"Nobody waitin' anywhere for me, so I'm comin' with you." He stands up slowly.

Laney looks Dan square in the eye . . .

"I will not be responsible if something happens to you two dumbasses, do you understand?"

"We have cab money," Dan snarks.

"And it don't matter what happens to me," Buck adds, walking toward the steps down from the bus. He's breathless after a few strides.

Buck and Dan, left standing alone, see the charred, loose sign from the road—KELLAR'S BAR AND GRILL. An ominous sound from afar, a roar, thunder, and the sign flaps in the wind. There's a storm coming.

They look at each other, alarmed, then back to the road, but the bus is well on its way back to Rupert. Dumbly, they stare up the hill—the bar's a bit of a hike.

And now the sky spits.

Cocky Dan takes off his shoes and socks, determined to beat the rain. He takes off in a sort of sprint.

The rain becomes heavier and the lightning moves closer. The air is thick with the smell of ozone and wet dirt. Dan can hear the sound of hail in the distance. *Oh shit . . .* but doesn't stop to smell or listen. "Easy peasy, Buck," he says. "We can walk up there just fine if you can't run like I can."

Buck walks a few yards, then finds a place to hunker down, a cleft in a rock.

"I'm waiting right here. You go on up if you want to."

Dan soldiers on. A few slips and slides, a couple of hard landings, but he doesn't give up. Then a turn on his backside lands him in a muddy heap. Buck laughs at him.

Dan stops for a moment, breathing harder than usual, and turns back to Buck. "Well, hell, I served in rain, hail, wind, ice, heat, in mountains and swamps, Buck, and now look at me, I'm suddenly old, and you, well, your excuse is that you never served this country. Never got soldier fit."

"Heck, John Wayne never served his country either, and I guess he was fit enough."

"Different."

"Hey, nobody's more patriotic than me and John Wayne, to this day I never talk down this country, and when he was alive he never talked down this country, probably to make up for the fact we didn't, couldn't go to war like everyone else. He had a big family to support. I was 4G, couldn't go."

" . . . 4G? How?"

"Lost two brothers early on in the war, Dan. You know that."

"No I didn't."

"I clearly remember talking to you about it after Tad went missing."

"Not the same, losing brothers is not like losing a son."

"You ever have a brother you love?" Buck taunts.

"Yeah, I did." Dan replies angrily.

"Sorry, okay."

Dan attempts another trek to the bar.

This time, Buck comes up from under the rock and follows Dan inside the bar.

Flames, heat, smoke, water and ruin are all that is left of the old bar. If he hadn't fallen on his ass that day he'd be under investigation for arson.

It wasn't a cleansing fire. Dan knew it was the 'beginning of the end' kind of fire.

The charred, soggy remnants of furnishings and the piano remain. But what good are they ever going to be again? Restoring any of what is left of these possessions has no appeal to the old man.

So why does he want to get in so badly?

Dan forces the bar door open.

Buck waits outside on the shaky wooden porch. Despite taking careful measures to enter the bar, Dan's weight alone on the groaning wooden planks forces one board out of its roost. The neon sign is thrown directly up into the air and strikes the burned porch hard before coming dangerously close to Buck's head. It seems deliberate. Something ungodly.

Weirdly uninjured, Dan and Buck enter the gloom. They walk slowly, carefully, toward the back of the bar. Once they pass the piano, tears form in Buck's eyes. He follows the trail of the dog leash —still tied to the leg of the piano.

"What are you looking for, Dan?"

Guns. I might kill myself. On the floor nearby lay photos of Tad, Jimmy and Wayne. Dan scans the photos a second time, figuring that he can call them the reason he wants in the bar so badly. Photos.

Vague memories begin flooding in—of a lively, crowded bar in it's heyday—lots of couples dancing to the country music that's playing on the juke box. Memories of Dan holding court, telling his stories. " . . . What do you mean get off the 'copter. Said you gotta run five miles and drop" . . . "and when one of 'em bayoneted me . . . " "I said 'oh no you don't, pilgrim . . . "

Memories of Corrie, going nuts, holding onto her gasoline can, her eyes wild, her lipstick smeared.

Memories of Buck himself when he was a young man, bringing drinks to his beautiful wife, Mary Jane, dancing with her, twirling her around, both of them trying to include Corrie in their couples dance.

Corrie leashed to the piano leg, dancing, laughing.

In the back room of the bar, Dan searches shelves, pulls rotting things down, throws the nasty things onto the floor. He opens a trunk and finds exactly what he's looking for—an armory of guns. They are all intact, and pristine. Buck gasps at the sight. Lots of guns. *Gun collector? Conspiracy theorist? Scaredy-cat?* Guns. Lots of guns. And lots of ammunition on the shelves above.

"Don't remember you having so many guns, Dan! Did we come up here in the rain so you could fetch up all these guns?" Buck backs out of the room, suddenly nervous.

Dan is overwhelmed by the size of the collection himself. Guns he hadn't touched in years; he'd sworn off guns after what he did to

Wayne; he couldn't shoot; the guns represented past horrors more than past glories. Not sure he can ever fire a gun again. *Unless.* But now, Dan lies to Buck. "Come on back in, Buck," Dan says. "I only want photos. What I am looking for is my old film projector."

The search is desperate. He throws things around, breaking some. He searches drawers which fall apart. He looks in closets.

Finally he finds the old Keystone projector, along with a treasure trove of strips, and a hat box filled with pictures. Not sure what he's going to do with them, but he figures he needs to take something out of the bar since he made such a point of coming up that long hill, something nostalgic seems right.

With the dusty relic, as well as Buck in tow, Dan navigates the old stairs to the parking lot. Buck has to stop, breathless again, and coughing.

Dan asks, "You got a cold, or you been smoking out here?"

"Allergic to something this rain bringing down. Or it could be this damn bar filled with dirt and soot."

"Or you've been smoking."

"Nope. Mary Jane made me stop smoking ages ago. I've been out here crying. Hit me sudden. We had some great times here, remember? All of us, and Corrie and Mary Jane. Hard to remember."

"Buck, Mary Jane was one helluva gal. She was good to Corrie, too. Me and her, we looked for Corrie day and night, all that running off Corrie did after she got demented, starting little fires. And when Corrie died like that, all burnt up . . . that little nightgown all . . . burned off her, Mary Jane cried like a baby at the sight. Mary Jane was a fine woman who . . . "

" . . . Liked to break Mary Jane's heart when Corrie got burned to death. She fretted that Corrie didn't know she was burning. Didn't know her hair was on fire." Buck wipes away tears. "Dan, we shoulda known a fire would get Corrie. She started so many of them."

Dan, stoic as ever. "Mary Jane was a good woman to care that much."

Dan beams as he presents the projector to Buck. "Family. And you two were family. Take this on back with you and see if you can find old movies of all of us."

Buck turns away. "I don't know how you can look at those old films, Dan. I can barely look at pictures of Mary Jane without crying. You take it home with you."

The two men step off the porch, and begin the long trek downhill to the highway. About halfway down, Buck stops again. Bending from the waist and rubbing his knees, he says as he gasps for good breath, "Walking downhill should be easier, but you hit the ground harder, and at an angle that does your knees no favors."

"It oughta worry you that you can't breathe so good going downhill. It's uphill oughta be the hard part."

"Going uphill we had a mission, Dan. Without a mission, everything is just downhill."

And so Dan and Buck try again. Downhill. Dan hits a patch of loose rocks and topples over, rolls about fifty feet and lands on his ass. The film projector scurries to the bottom of the hill.

CHAPTER 32
What direction home?

Even though a dozen chairs are set up for Liam's graveside service, Nicolette, in her dress greens and coat, and Officer Trout, in his police uniform, are the only two mourners. The funeral director waits at the podium, patient, but visibly uncomfortable.

Finally, the motorcycle roars up.

Wayne, clean shaven and well groomed, removes his helmet, and walks to the closed coffin. He whispers to the coffin, privately. He chooses the chair farthest from Nicolette, and with a nod of his head, signals to the funeral director that it is time to start. He looks at his watch, hoping to give it a few more minutes . . . but . . .

The funeral director and honor guard take their positions, and the three mourners stand for the folding of the flag of the United States of America.

Two dozen stragglers show, looking confused by the fact that the service has begun without them. Not taking seats. Feeling awkward, like they are intruding. Standing so straight, respectful, glad to be there, and finally, sympathetic to Wayne, in spite of their sensitivities. Wayne and Nicolette watch the ceremony with pained expressions, their eyes shimmering. The ache of their hearts on their faces, grieving so profoundly, the price one pays for love, letting go, holding on, lost identities, no longer a father, no longer the great love, empty futures. They both sit absolutely still, afraid to move. To move would dishonor Liam so much. They are protecting the stillness to share the stillness with him, if only for a moment. Slowing down time and turning inward, trying to breathe.

They listen to the playing of "Taps" by audio recording.

During the song Nicolette leaps to her feet, just as before, lets out a moan, runs to the coffin. Wayne is up, this time comforting her, and she clings to him. She lets her heart break open, and he does, too. They share their grief. Seeing grief up close and personal feels like the assault of a nuclear wave on the stragglers. The mourners burst into tears en masse, grief connecting these human beings with one another. The loss of a child is so profound to ponder, regardless of the history of the family, and the murder of a true love? Jesus.

How does any human being keep from crying when witnessing grief?

Quite late, but during "Taps" one more mourner shows up—Celeste, looking like a million bucks. She sits, even though she's the only mourner who does so. Tearless, sorry she is late, but still . . . looking like a million bucks and hoping Wayne notices. Pathetic.

As soon as the service ends she gives Wayne a quick hug, and apologizes for having to run out on him.

Daddy needs her.

She leaves without Wayne having acknowledged her appearance.

The next day Celeste is driving Dan to the Dallas VA hospital. They both dread the meeting with the resident authority on Alzheimer's and Dementia, Dr. Horne. He hopes he doesn't blurt out how much he wants to turn a gun on himself.

Dan and C enter the hustle and bustle of the VA Hospital waiting room.

The veterans rumble about the inefficiencies of the VA system, talking only amongst themselves, never wanting to complain for real. Long wait times. Inefficient use of resources, complex procedures for registration—all tedious. Veterans give up waiting and just leave, then another leaves, and another, and the remaining veterans rumble again, about not getting the necessary healthcare, which can lead to a poor outcome. "Hope old Marvin comes back and gets that blood pressure under control," the veterans might add, and then go back to their grievances.

Finally, the receptionist holds an interior door open and invites Dan in. Dan had been warned by other veterans in the waiting room about the initial meeting with Dr. Horne. "You think seeing Nazis up close was scary, wait until you meet Dr. Horne!" There will be neurological exams, cognitive and functional assessments, brain imaging, and then Dr. Horne herself.

They are directed to the examination room, where three

different people come in and out to ask questions and do tests on Dan over the course of a few hours. They perform some simple medical tests on Dan: blood pressure, temperature, oxygen levels, pulse, swelling of lymph nodes, looking into the ears, listening to the heart and lungs. The questions directed at C are fast and furious. *What kind of symptoms have you noticed? When did they begin? How often do they happen? Have they gotten worse?* Celeste is scared about how to respond without upsetting her father and without risking further intrusive tests, such as MRIs or scans, that will surely be required if she were to disclose his drinking and his threats to take pills. She worries that Adult Protective Services might be contacted to have her detained and imprisoned for elder abuse if she lies. C is all alone taking care of her father, and she wishes she had a sibling who could judge her and correct her caretaking mistakes. But she knows that, in a family, there's usually the old folk, and the siblings, and among the siblings there's one child always caretaking, and the others breezing in from time to time to judge the caretaking one—and that child taking care of the old one lives in fear of the other siblings calling in Adult Protective Services. Maybe she's lucky Tad is not around.

"What kind of symptoms have you noticed?"

C chooses her answer carefully.

"I have only noticed a little memory loss of names and sometimes he comes into a room and forgets why. And maybe he's a bit calmer than he used to be? More reflective. He used to be much angrier than he is now that he's older."

Dan's nostrils flair slightly, which means he is getting mad. But he remains quiet and refuses to look at Celeste. He stares straight ahead, with a hard look on his face.

Oh my God, he is furious.

A quick review of medical history, psychiatric history and history of cognitive and behavioral changes, current and past medical problems and concerns, list of any medications being taken. Celeste has carefully copied down each and every medication name, dosage and instructions so that she will have them all straight—for blood pressure and cholesterol and bladder and mood. But she is crying and blubbering so much as she delivers this information that Dan howls loudly, and knocks the paper list from her hand. The list of medications falls to the floor. Celeste reaches down to pick up the list. Dan kicks the list away from her. Terrified, Celeste is so distraught that she can't control her tears.

Questions about other family members and their medical histories, about diet, nutrition and use of alcohol and drugs. Dan's reflexes are tested, along with his coordination, muscle tone and strength. His eye movements, his speech, his cognitive, functional and behavioral tests—all these are done to evaluate memory, thinking and simple problem-solving abilities. Dr. Horne herself is a neuropsychologist and so she personally conducts tests to evaluate executive function, judgment, attention and language.

She looms over him and asks "Mr. Kellar, do you know the date, time and where you are?"

"Of course I fucking do," he answers. "It's almost Veteran's Day, 2003. I'm in at the VA. I'm in the hell of realizing that a day like today, a month like this month, might be what I recall on the day I die, when my life passes before me. Jesus Christ. Kill me now, if this is my story!"

"I'll give you a list of words," Horne continues. "Can you remember a short list of words?"

"Give me the words."

"Apple. Table. Cell. Plugs. Color."

Dan rolls his eyes. "Oferchrisakes. Apple, Table . . . "

"NO," Dr. Horne sharply reprimands. "I haven't finished. I'm going to tell you three more words to see if you remember them later on. Razor. Kitchen. Calculator. Now draw a picture of a clock at 7:20 and when you are finished repeat back to me the two sets of words." She pushes a piece of paper and a pencil to Dan. He draws, embarrassed as he draws a round clock with hands and numbers and two little ringy things for an alarm. He feels five years old as he pushes the drawing back to Dr. Horne. "And the sets of words?"

"Apple. Razor. Crop?"

"What is six times twenty-four?"

"Stand up, turn to the right, touch your toes."

Finally Dr. Horne reviews some notes.

"You fell?"

"Yes. It was an accident."

"Do you remember how it happened?"

"Yes. I was trying to lift a rug out from under a table. I remember vividly."

"Who is the President?"

"George W. Bush."

"Are you depressed?"

"No."

"Well, you seem okay to me. I think we're done here."

Dr. Horne stands up to dismiss Dan and Celeste.

"Thanks for coming in."

Dan scoots off the table.

"He missed every one," Celeste says.

"Your dad seems pretty sharp to me and that's my report," Dr. Horne states. Dan faces Dr. Horne and says "What a waste of a day this is. I am sharp. But I don't want to spend the next twenty years telling idiots who the president is."

"What do you want from me, Mr. Kellar?"

"My son is still "missing" from Vietnam."

"And that is bothering you? Something I can do nothing about?"

"Naturally, you dumb ass. He went missing in 1968. I'm waiting for word about some new remains the Army found."

"You seem to manage well for someone with a loss of that magnitude."

This remark pleases Dan, though he doesn't trust it at all. He continues. "I take it on the chin, tell myself he is alive. But it bothers me. To the point that I am now thinking about . . . "

He pointedly stops speaking. Celeste holds her breath.

"About what? Suicide?" asks the doctor. "That would seem reasonable."

"No. The other night I went to bed thinking how I would like to shoot President Johnson for drafting my son in the first place."

Dr. Horne smirks. "Well, thank heavens you can't do that. Prsident Johnson is already dead."

"True," Dan adds. "And now Bush is president and we're in a different war. A "volunteer" war."

"Well, if you say you are thinking about assassinating a living president, I will have to . . . report . . . "

" . . . No, I'm okay with Bush . . . but there's this one thing I don't like. My son was drafted in the 1960's. Now they recruit. My town has one Army Recruiter. With a quota he can barely fill unless he recruits cheerleaders. Girls. Young girls. Our military is out there recruiting little cheerleaders."

"And what point are you trying to make?"

"I guess I'm babbling."

"No worries, Mr. Kellar. Men your age babble. We'll see you at your next appointment, in six weeks."

"Sure."

Dan and Celeste are outside before Dan turns to Celeste and says, "Do you understand what point was I trying to make?"

"Of course, daddy. You want Tad home. Dead or alive. It's why you drink, it's why you hurt people, it's why you're awful. Right?"

CHAPTER 33
Last dance with Mary Jane . . .

"So I'm gonna drive as long as I possibly can! You all shut up. Making fun of my britches and now my car? What type of car should a seventy-five-year-old man drive?" A tipsy Buck asks the bartender at Bigelow's, and adds, "A safe one. I love my car. Been driving it a long time."

"Driving a car." The bartender laughs. Well. Just about everybody teases Buck about NOT driving a truck in Rupert. "Bought my first Honda Civic Sedan in 1974. Beautiful little thing, pale blue, five speed manual transmission, drove it up to Kellar's and all I got was Dan Kellar suggesting that I was not patriotic anymore because I was driving a Japanese car. By 1974 you'd think he would have figured out we don't hate the Japanese anymore, am I right?"

"What did he know about hating Japanese?"

"That's right. He went after Nazis. Not like I drove up to his bar in a Mercedes-Benz 770K Grosser Offener Tourenwagen. Hitler's favorite. It was a Honda Civic Sedan what I drove."

"Not a truck." Hilarious.

"Not a truck. In Rupert. Bought this new Honda about ten years ago. It's comfortable. Affordable. Got a rear defroster and power brakes. Easy to steer. I paid $11,000 for it and I'm gonna get my money's worth."

"You were a trailblazing mother fucker, Buck. The first not to drive a truck in Rupert."

Buck throws out a few dollars, tosses them on the bar, and says his farewells. He jumps into his Honda Civic, starts it up, and pulls away from the curb, barely missing several of the dozens of cars parked all along Main Street. He muses out loud that so many cars are parked right in front of the Porterfield Hotel. Unusual. Of course! Veterans Day weekend! The busiest weekend of the year. Of course, so happens the Ghost-hunting Weekend is coming, and lots of tourists come early for that! The ten ft. high safety fence that always surrounds the Porterfield has been taken down in preparation for the Weekend. Temporarily replacing the fence will be dozens of security officers.

The Porterfield lawn is filled with construction materials for both events. Buck stops to gawk at locals busy at work. Surprised when Dan Kellar pops unannounced and unexpected into the passenger side of the Sedan.

Dan lands in the front seat. "Ain't tonight our dance, Buck?"

"I figured you forgot," Buck says, breathless. Dan is dressed to the nines. "I never miss a chance to wear my red jacket," Dan crows. "Tonight's the night. It's my civic duty at the Retirement home tonight. In my dancing reds."

Dan buckles up, ready to roll.

So. Buck merges into a bit of traffic, and becomes flustered. Hits a curb.

"Good God. You really can't even drive a little old car, Buckaroo."

"And you, my friend, ain't allowed to drive at all. Don't get your panties in a wad. There's alot of dang traffic," Buck says as he rounds a corner . . . sort of.

Buck parks the Civic in front of the Peaceful Oaks Home. The home is kind of a cross between a roadside motel and a rundown VFW lodge. Like the Porterfield, the home will eventually be shuttered and condemned, but on this night in November of 2003, the Peaceful Oaks is a busy, low-cost retirement home, and ready to party.

Dan fairly leaps out of the car.

Buck, however, is not overly anxious to enter the retirement home.

Dan leans in to chastise Buck.

"You act like we're moving in. We got years before we're that old. Time to dance. Crick or no crick. What's wrong with you? You're the one put Mary Jane in a Retirement home, so come on."

"I don't want her here. But I don't think about me. I think about her. And I know this is what's best for her."

"Then get your ass out of the car. Come on."

Buck hesitates.

"I do believe it is best for her, Dan."

"I'm sure you do. But for my money I would have never put Corrie in a retirement home," Dan challenges, pushing in the knife, so to speak.

"No. She'd have burned it down," Buck answers, bravely, crossing Dan, unusual for Buck. As the two men walk to the entry door of the retirement home, Buck feels the rousing effects of having just had a little bit of gumption.

Dan and Buck survey the scene before them.

The lunchroom, where the party is, is packed with elderly residents, their families, and some fans of the band, a singing quartet of boomers, with their karaoke machine full of songs from WWII all the way to Madonna. Veteran's Day decorations adorn the room.

Elderly couples dance, attempt to dance, some sit and stare, whatever their capabilities. The staff is dancing with other staff, or with residents in wheelchairs. Some folks are moving in rhythm to the music from their beds- beds that are parked in the hallway so that nobody misses the chance to enjoy the party. Others are waving their arms in the air, and a few are attached to oxygen tubing to help them breathe. Everybody who can raises their arms over their heads— forming "Y.M.C.A.," actually disco dancing even while gasping for life. By all accounts, it is a wonderful, inclusive celebration.

"Place smells like piss," is all Dan can say.

Buck spots his wife. Senile, white-haired, and plump, Mary Jane sits in a wheelchair, watching—Dan, suddenly "on," sidles up to her, flirtatious.

Buck takes it in stride. "Been married for almost sixty years and I am still competing with you for my wife's affections," he teases.

"Well, what do you expect? I'm a stud muffin," Dan boasts.

Dan holds his nose and scoots onto the dance floor. He picks out and shuffles around with a blue haired lady in a wheelchair who clearly doesn't know she's in the world.

The home's receptionist boogies up to Dan, forces him to take a turn with her on the dance floor. He is happy to accommodate.

Later on, the place is still alive with happy, dancing staff leading the fun. Buck, however, is sitting next to the fairly unresponsive Mary Jane, with tears rolling down his face. He tries to distract himself from the realization that Mary Jane is not her usual self. Her usual self? Unresponsive always, but eyes usually not quite as vacant as they are tonight. He tries to enjoy Dan's antics as Dan moves around the floor, cock of the walk, catch of the day. Buck envies Dan's charm, even the mean part of his charm, and he is jealous of Dan's gregariousness.

Around nine, the band, and their overweight, scraggly roadie, are packing up for the night.

Still wanting to party down, the staff put out more ice cream, and turn on a boom box. Latin free-style music turns quickly to good ol' country music, just like Dan had told the VA receptionist it would. Even as he dances, Dan turns and fairly smirks at Buck, visually bragging about always being right.

Oddly, Mary Jane taps her toes when she hears the wondrous, reassuring and warm vocals of her favorite singing storyteller, George Strait, crooning, "Amarillo by Morning."

Absolutely delighted, Buck cautiously asks, "You want to dance, Mary Jane? You wanna dance to old King George?"

The smiling but still catatonic Mary Jane appears to hear the raspy, rural voice of her husband, but stares into space.

"Honey?" Buck implores.

But alas, nothing, no response to the sound of her husband's voice.

After leading a sad conga line, Dan is forced to shift gears, line dancing instead of jitterbugging. Bored, Dan returns to Buck when the music slows way down to true country twang.

"I don't think she knows me anymore," Buck confides.

"Well, she's old. Go dance with someone else."

"I want to dance with my wife."

"I'll sit with her."

Buck is reluctant and awkward, but he stands up, lumbers to the makeshift dance area, and asks someone, anyone, to dance.

Buck knows Dan is watching his awkward freestyle flirtations, and he is embarrassed. But Dan surprises him when he hears him say, "Mary Jane, your old boy just won't let go." Dan puts an arm around Mary Jane and pats her.

Mary Jane, suddenly lucid, and no longer smiling, turns to Dan and barks like a dog.

More barks . . . and howls.

"BUCK! What the . . . ?" Dan screams.

Buck comes running.

"What did you do to her, Dan Kellar?"

"I didn't do a damn thing."

Buck is flabbergasted at Mary Jane's odd behavior, but then . . . "She remembers Corrie on a leash. Only thing I can think of!"

Buck yanks at her wheelchair, hard.

"Buck, stop, you're gonna hurt her." Dan orders.

Buck, in tears, twirls the wheelchair, forces her to sort of . . . dance.

"Stop it, damn it. Stop, Buck."

Now Buck is attracting the attention of the staff and administrator.

"Stop it, Buck." It seems to Buck that Dan tries to knock some sense into him, smacking him on the back, pulling him away from her. But Buck screams, "She remembers you leashed your wife, but she doesn't remember who I am? What the hell did you do to her?"

"It's the disease, Buck. She can't help what her brain does."

Distraught, Buck kneels before his bride, howls in agony, but gets control of himself just in time to sing along to the current George Strait song on the boom box. He sings the whole George Strait song right to her. Dan is mortified for him. "You're embarrassing yourself, Buck. Stop singing. Stupid. Stop."

"It's her favorite damn song!" Buck argues.

Mary Jane is, unfortunately, now completely unresponsive, her head dropping to her chest.

"She doesn't remember, Buck. You've got to stop. Damnit, Buck. She's in terrible shape. If I were you, I'd . . . "

Buck stands up, glowers at Mary Jane, and pushes her wheelchair away, almost toppling it. The administrator intervenes, and asks Buck to leave. Hanging his head, Buck bursts into tears. Dan tries to lead him to the entry door to leave. As they walk past two old ladies, they hear one say to the other "it's the end when an old lady don't remember her favorite George Strait song."

Buck can see out of the corner of his eye that Dan laughs the loudest at the slight against Mary Jane.

It is an uncomfortable, silent drive after the dance. Buck cries like he is five years old. His heart broke, his spirit died. He needs a friend. And he picks Dan Kellar. Worst friend ever.

"You'd what? If you were me, you'd . . . what, Dan?"

"I'd . . . Maybe God will take her, that would be the best."

"I don't know what to do. I've lost her forever. I mean, her life is over."

Dan impatiently answers, "Take her home with you and put her on a leash."

"You're an asshole, Dan. It ain't right to put a human on a leash."

Buck stops the car in front of the Porterfield.

Orders Dan "Out."

Dan uses any tactic he can to ensure that he will not be walking home in the dark. Even Dan Kellar is afraid of downtown Rupert in the dark. He chooses a blithe rebuff. "Corrie would have run off if I hadn't leashed her, Buck. Be sensible."

"Get out of my car. You think you do everything right, Mr. War Hero. Maybe you do. I never went to war. Never had a son. Just went to an ordinary job every day. Never missed a day of work. Had a wife. But I could never put my wife on a dog leash. Just get out of my car. Get out now."

"All right," Dan warns. "But I guess that's it for us, buddy, and I've been your only friend for decades."

"I can do without you, asshole. In fact, how many decades since I seen you, till that day on the bus?"

Dan opens the car door. But before he steps out onto the pavement, in the scary dark, in front of the old hotel, he has to stick in the knife one more time. "You never went to war, never had a son. I went to war three times," he brags. "And that last time, Viet Nam, I took my son, my only begotten son, and lost him. If putting a leash on my wife to keep her safe is the worst thing I ever did, then there's nothing more to prove to the likes of you—you who never served your country—you reenactor, why you're so phony you hang out at the VA like you belong there, but you don't."

Dan is a master at averting blame or causing pain. He has always been a terrible friend and a terrible man. Why Buck had ever needed and wanted his friendship, he could not remember. But Buck knows that Dan has a point. Buck pretended in life, to be the things Dan really had been, the soldier he would never be.

Dan grimaces, and steps out of the car. He leans into the window. One more twist of the knife.

"Never went to war, never had a son. Since you never had a son, you can't possibly understand. God understands. I'm sorry that God leaves Mary Jane to suffer like that. If I were you, I might consider . . . well . . . "

Buck pushes Dan away from the window. Shoves him hard. Dan falls to the ground. Buck roars away from the Porterfield.

Turns out, though, Dan did have an impact on Buck.

The next stop Buck makes, a spontaneous stop, is to purchase two packs of over-the-counter sleeping pills, and a large bottle of rubbing alcohol at the late-night pharmacy. He speeds away from the pharmacy, runs a stop sign, skids on his brakes, coming to a stop in some shrubs. He's shaken, sobs, but backs out of the shrubs and onto the road. The next stop is his own home. He leaves the car running and leaps out, rushing into the frame house to the bathroom. He opens the medicine chest above the sink and grabs his half-full prescription bottles—Valium and Vicodin—left over from a recent surgery. He puts the drugs in his jacket pocket, and as he exits the bathroom, he glances to the shower stall. His brown Confederate britches are hanging on the showerhead.

Buck navigates a dark road back to Peaceful Oaks.

He enters the retirement home through the staff entrance.

The party long over, residents in wheelchairs still wait in the long corridor for assistance to their rooms.

Mary Jane among them, nods off in her wheelchair, tugging at her pants. She has wet her pants.

Buck pushes her wheelchair to her dreary, simple room.

Once inside, Buck opens the sack of sleeping pills. He announces how ironic a time he has chosen for both of them to die —the night before Veterans' Day, Dan Kellar's big day. He empties the pills onto the bed and divides them into two stacks. He walks to the sink, looks in the mirror, fills a water glass with rubbing alcohol. "To Dan," he toasts. Then he gently nudges Mary Jane, force feeds her some sleeping pills and some Valium, makes her swallow the alcohol, repeats. Repeats again. She swallows sixteen pills before she flings the glass away.

Buck refills the glass with tap water. He makes sure she can see that the glass is filled with only water. Mary Jane blinks her eyes and smiles. He hesitates to continue giving her pills when she has what seems like a moment of lucidity, but then again, he thinks, dogs and cats sometimes have the same response moments before they receive the proof of their owner's betrayal—the sedating shot prior to putting them down. Buck knows, though, that the truth is that animals do not process concepts like betrayal. And neither does Mary Jane. Buck counts out and gives her a variety of ten more pills.

Gives her another round, six more pills. Waits. She's still breathing. Heart barely beating, but . . . is she suffering? Grabs a pillow from the bed . . . *no, no, no, no, Jesus, stop me, Lord, make her die from the pills*. Waits. Endless wait. Pillow. Listens. Buck makes sure his wife is gone. "This is on you, Dan Kellar," he says.

Takes a handful, two handfuls of pills himself. And repeats. Pukes a little. Sobbing . . . repeats. Repeats . . . Re . . .

CHAPTER 34
Troubled Water in a Troubled Town

Perhaps God alone knew the details, well, God, and the half-drunk nursing assistant who was rummaging through old ladies' night stands during the party. Looking for valuables. Had to hide in a closet when he heard Buck's key in the door. Witnessed the whole thing. Told police he followed Buck to try to stop him. Jabber, jabber. Lies.

Of course, Dan had no idea about Buck on the day he decided to act out his own mania. If he had known, and especially if it had occurred to him that he may have played a role in Buck's last decisions, could he have enjoyed his favorite day of the year, Veteran's Day? All the sights and tastes and smells of a clear, crisp morning perfectly merging. Only a tiny hint of the nightmare to come. After events of last night, at the Dance, Dan's brain is cycling from "crazy visit to Trouble Town" to "off his rocker." He knows it. He can control it. Doesn't want to rehash it.

There's a newer, more important problem. Dan holds in his hand a new letter from JPAC, "remains have been found" and "need identification" . . . *fucking blah, blah, blah. Asking for DNA. Again. What the fuck?*

It is a beautiful, clear, crisp morning on the day that Dan Kellar, Honored War Hero, chooses to take out the Army recruiter. Understood. He has hit a new low. At seventy-five years old, he now uses the word "fuck" as often as Nicolette does. But the Army has also hit a new low. Girls signing up. Like Nicolette (and look what happened to her), and another fucking letter. Maybe Dan takes out Sgt. Grissom, maybe it makes national news. Maybe it draws attention to Tad. Maybe the Army will definitively pronounce his son dead, let him bury something, anything. Maybe the cops will come and maybe he will resist and maybe they will shoot him dead. Maybe his pain will end. Whatever happens today, the world will end. Is the world a better place because Dan Kellar had been part of it? Probably. He'd killed Nazis.

Dan is in an excellent mood, in spite of his brain cycling, while he waits on the porch, for a cab, watches the sun peek up, sips a nutty mocha tea, re-dips his tea bag, watches the tea ooze out and darken the hot water, inhales the smells of morning, a kind of mix of fresh apple, pear, and maybe a hint of pine, if you want to be specific. And Dan wants to be specific on this, the potential last day of his life if the cops end up killing him.

Definitely smells coffee all over the neighborhood, Sumatra, full bodied, low acid, as this is America, and most men like him are coffee drinkers, with a little touch of maple syrup smell, and bacon. Breathe.

Dan's growing problem with tinnitus prevents his hearing the sizzling of the bacon, or is it finally deafness coming on? Doesn't matter. As long as Dan can still smell, can still taste, growing older will be—wait . . . growing older would have been just fine. Until this last letter from JPAC, growing older might have been just fine. His attitude about life, about ordinary days, days alone with himself (the best days, the very best days). Alone. No family. None of their shit. Routine morning. Routine end of day. Nights when he wears his red jacket, is cock of the walk, stud muffin Dan. Days when his friends, like Buck, ask his advice and he gives it freely because he's lived and he knows things and he loves to hear himself talk, loves to tell his stories. Days and nights on the planet, in this country, when being a white man is the supreme gift from God, when being a soldier who killed Nazis is the height of accomplishment.

"Life is best when it's like an Oreo cookie, I'll take care of both ends, You take care of the middle," Dan generally offers up to God in his fake daily prayer of gratitude. But today the air is crisper, the wind snappier. Dan wants to be specific on this day. It's the most important day of his life, second to none save the day he shot Wayne (which he doesn't regret), or the day he found Corrie (which he does), or the day Rick was killed (for which he was blamed and it wasn't his fucking fault). This day he'll make his own destiny. No Dr. Horne shit. No slow bus to Dallas. No sidelooks from other people. No staggering out of the bar. No falling down drunk. No ambulances. No people telling him he can't drive. "Since You have seen fit to make sure I got this God forsaken letter from JPAC, I'll take care of today, Lord. But I thank You for this delicious tea or coffee, sun, the smell of freshly mown grass, though I miss the actual sound of bacon sizzling at the morning end. Sleeping easily, comfortably, pleasant dreams, no aches and pains at the end of the day. The cookie part of a morning, the cookie part of the start of slumber. Whatever happens in between, the sugar, high fructose corn syrup, soy lecithin, artificial flavor, and palm and/or canola oil part of the cookie, the middle, bad-for-you part, the part I usually leave under Your control, leave to You to command, ain't happening today. This is the day I HAVE MADE. It will be bad. Indeed. But. This is Dan 3:16 Day, Lord. 'You may so love the world, but I loved this country and I gave my only begotten son' to this country, and that means my life is awful. Awful. Today is special, Lord. I avenge my son's loss. But still, I thank You for the recognition and approval I am to receive today as a Veteran of War."

When the cab pulls up, he leaps in, eager beaver to settle into his seat and buckle himself in. His reward will be the praise of the nation on Veteran's Day, and the ending of the high fructose, corn syrup nightmare of his life. One way or the other.

The Veterans' Day Parade proceeds down the street in front of the Porterfield Hotel. Hundreds of people appear to be watching the march from the curb, which is rare for Veterans Day celebrations in small communities. Literally. Hundreds of people. Dan figures that it might still be related to 9/11. He cherishes the thought of having such a sizable audience.

He exits the cab and walks down Main Street behind a high school band.

The Army Recruiting Center, when Dan passes, appears busier than ever. Dan glances in the window. It is clear that the Army Recruiter is at the top of his persuasion game as he holds court.

Dan sadly observes numerous young women completing paperwork.

It is upsetting, but Dan has promised himself that nothing will bother him today, not until the end of the day. And because it's his favorite day, he walks away without admiring his photo on the ever-present poster, even after noticing that someone has scrawled the words "Fuck Dan Kellar" across his picture.

As far as he is concerned, he is still the hero of all of Rupert. What some asshole graffiti criminal thinks of him is none of his business. What his friend, Buck, thinks of him, is none of his business. Shit. Not gonna give that idiot a thought today. Not today. No, he has no idea that anything he says or does really impacts anyone. Bullet in his gun, gun in his hand, that impacts. Words? Fuck, no.

The beautifully decorated bandstand where dignitaries from the small town wait for Dan to appear. Shades of 1946, Uncle Sam, and Lady Liberty plastered on posters nailed to the trees of the Porterfield lawn.

1946, the greatest year in the greatest country in all of human existence for this white boy, America was great then—great in spite of the war effort rules of the day—rationing of coffee, sugar, gasoline, in spite of the terror of deployment, facing injury and death overseas, in spite of the loneliness of a new marriage, and the silent requirement of having to prove your patriotism over and over again because you married a girl from the country of our enemy.

Still mostly great in '67. But cracking. He thought of Tad—falling from the sky and landing behind enemy lines. Unconscious, maybe injured. Probably injured. Then dragged away by the enemy. How would Tad ever prove to the enemy that he was just one soldier, doing a job he didn't believe was right, a job his father forced him to do? He would have been harmed for his loyalty to the United States. Oh dear God, if only Tad had turned his back on his country then, assimilated into the culture of his captors, if he could have lived out his life in peace, it wouldn't matter one fuck to Dan Kellar at this point if his son had turned on the country. Just as long as he lived. Somewhere.

The gathering he observes on this Veteran's Day, at the age of seventy-five (as he keeps reminding himself) resembles the crowd he observed in 1946 after his return as a hero of that illustrious American war, WWII, when he was just eighteen years old. *No, hold on. It's untrue. This crowd in 2003 is unique*, Dan thinks. Many more folks are present, and so many women. Dan observes, um, judges, that these women on the Porterfield Hotel lawn are generally obese and unsightly and are not as neatly dressed or as thin as the onlookers were in 1946. Oh no, Dan really doesn't want to think such a woman-hating thought, so once more, he forces the judgmental idea of the deterioration of American female citizens' appearance out of his mind. Too late, he has already thought it. He doesn't understand why he cannot think obesity is unhealthy, sinful, ugly, rude, unsightly and uncalled for, but he's aware enough of the world to know he has to push thoughts like that from his mind. Those thoughts offend others in 2003. "Jesus Christ, how neurotic will we all be twenty years from now," he asks.

Dan takes a deep breath and yet can't help himself. He entertains the idea that perhaps the solution to the obesity problem in America is the rationing of sugar, as it was in the good old days. But can he say something like that out loud? "Would rather you didn't, Dad," his fat daughter, Celeste, would say. Hell no. He is no longer welcome to contribute to the conversation, even if he speaks the truth.

The mayor takes the podium. Mayor Richards. African American. Born in poverty in 1929. Worked as a waiter and a railroad porter prior to the Civil Rights Movement. Mayor Richard speaks. "Thank you to all of you men and women, young and old, whose service has kept our country and its citizens safe and free."

Applause. Loud applause. Loud and patriotic applause.

"We honor three soldiers today. One who honorably served in World War Two, Korea and again, in Vietnam during the Tet Offensive, where he fought alongside his own son. Dan Kellar, we applaud you, and your son, Thaddeus, but—wait until you hear this —I was just notified. Thaddeus Kellar was missing in action but his remains were recently recovered and are en route to the United States and will soon be home in Rupert. Finally, we can all cheer the news. Thaddeus Kellar is coming home."

HUGE applause.

Dan's eyes are as big as saucers.

Under his breath. "No, that's wrong." Dan is stunned by this off-putting, false pronouncement, to say the least, and he is shocked to hear that the lie is coming from the Mayor. It's a big lie, too. The mayor continues his speech.

"Thaddeus Kellar went missing in 1967, was presumed dead all these years, and our hearts still go out to his family for having experienced that heartache, very personal, but praise God Thaddeus Kellar's body will be coming home soon."

Another round of raucous applause. Dan smiles weakly and wonders if there is another letter waiting for him with this news. He must call Celeste and find out for sure before he gets on the podium and calls the Mayor a liar. *It could be true. I sure want it to be true.*

The mayor drones on. Dan prepares to take his place at the podium once the mayor fucking shuts up. "But the job of defending this country is never finished. I'd like to introduce you now to Sergeant First Class Gerard Grissom, who has met the Army's high standard of Recruiting Officer." The Army Recruiter receives even noisier cheers and greater applause than the false story about Tad.

The mayor steps aside.

Dan sours, and a chilly expression replaces his fake, though confused smile. It was his turn. *Now Grissom is up there?*

Sergeant Grissom, the Army Recruiter, who spends his days recruiting cheerleaders, is now taking front and center on the podium. The crowd roars so much he has to ask for silence. Then he speaks. "So we have much to cheer. Two sets of remains made and/or are making their way home to Rupert. Thaddeus Kellar and Liam Chapman. Since 9/11 over 500,000 men and women have enlisted in the armed services to fight terrorism, and most of those fought in Afghanistan. One of those, Sgt. Liam Chapman, came home from war last week and was buried next to his mother at Peaceful Pines. His fiancé, another soldier named Nicolette Turlo, is in town, was here for his funeral, but is still being treated for the injuries she sustained when Liam and other Americans were killed. We pray for her quick recovery.

"If Liam Chapman and Thaddeus Kellar could speak to you today, I believe they would both say that serving in the military was the greatest accomplishment of their lives. That they would do it all over again, and gladly. Welcome back, Soldiers of war, and gosh, look at the time, I'm sorry we have to stop. No time for Dan Kellar's speech, but be sure and let him know how happy you are for him that his son is finally coming home."

Grissom leaves the stage, stares directly at Dan, puts his index finger to his throat, and grins like a hyena.

He knows it's a lie. This army recruiter bastard just wants to die. But not today. And not tonight. Dan needs a nap.

CHAPTER 35
Where to now, St. Peter?

The morning after, the sun rose over the remains of the Veterans Parade and the beginnings of the Ghost-hunter Weekend. Overnight, carpenters had torn down the bandstand to put up tiny vendor shacks where the ghost-hunters could buy food, drinks, swag, candles, flashlights, batteries, booze, and special cameras. Painters had touched up the porch of the hotel, slathered creamy colors around the broken windows, and decorated with directional signs on the pathways.

The excitement was palpable as cars and RVs made their way down Main Street, looking for parking, or a space to tailgate.

The event organizers had it down pat. Better safe than sorry.

Hundreds and hundreds, even thousands of spectators, were always anticipated to show up for the event. To ensure the safety of the ghost-hunters, the entire police force and fire department descended on the Porterfield to protect and serve Rupert's guests, no matter how many showed up.

Attendance varied, of course. But real ghost-hunters, the professionals, were the predictable attendees who paid a lot of money to secure the few available tour spots. They were given access and tours to/of the lobby, the staircase, and the ballroom for two hours before the event opened, and then again, from closing until daylight. During that time they were free to tramp all but three rickety floors in relative safety, without being bothered by the amateurs. The special corridors they used, though lit, would still be dark and dank, and predictably scary.

If all went as planned, the chosen few, the real ghost-hunters, the professionals, would experience the full mystery and terror of the old hotel, without crowds. Footsteps on the granite staircase. Moving objects. Unexplained sounds and voices. Real ghost stories based on authenticated murders, suicides, and hauntings. If they were lucky, they would encounter the disembodied, freeze in the cold spots, and their infrared cameras might capture crazy orbs and auras that are invisible to the human eye.

The elevators remained in disrepair. Everyone had to climb the stairs, and if they were unable to do so, the gaily lit lobby was their delight from five p.m. until midnight. It was advertised that most of the hotel ghosts preferred the lobby anyway. Ooooh, also on the lawns and in the lobby—candlelight vigils, séances, and psychics.

The basic spectators remained out on the lawns from start to finish, even after midnight, smoking, drinking, laughing, eating, and still buying stuff. The most fun weekend of a given year is happening in Rupert, Texas.

Back to the numbers. Well, the ghost-hunters were joined by so many locals that the event organizers could always say that the "famous Ghost-hunting event of (whatever year) broke all attendance records. Thousands of visitors were . . . A good time was had by all . . ." Texans, as far away as Fort Worth, who read these statistics, would scratch their heads and ask, over their coffee, "Where do all those tourists stay in Rupert? That one-horse dump only has two diners and three motels? I think the trailer parks are even closed down."

What is never reported, of course, is that after midnight, some might venture inside (break in) to view (or further damage) the wrecked lobby and vandalized staircase. The empty twelve-foot pool is officially off limits to everyone for the entire event, but every year someone breaks into the pool . . . and falls in. Or pushes someone in. And sometimes someone takes advantage of the salacious nature of the event, and disappears.

A few crazies will head to Peaceful Pines Cemetery, and will break in late that night to search for newly buried, some hoping to be scared out of their wits, some with ill intent to violate new graves, just to see if they can.

Wayne Herd took precautions. He hired security to protect Liam's fresh grave. He's staying in town a few extra nights, a last minute decision, just to be sure that Liam's first few nights alone, next to his mother, in the cold earth, would go well. No, his son would not be violated by boozers with shovels and picks. Not desecrated by vandals. Wayne ended up waiting out most of the weekend close to the Porterfield, at the Bigelow Bar, because the whole idea of ghost-hunting made him physically ill after the recent burial of his son. But Wayne was ultimately drawn to the Porterfield. He knew that Jimmy would be there.

Jimmy, of course, despised the ghost-hunting weekend, though he put up with it. All the night and day before he'd watched the carpenters, and the painters, not letting them deter him. Right on schedule, Jimmy eased into a nice long piss out the window just a couple of hours before the crowd would show up. One of the carpenters hollered up. "You're gonna have to hold it till tomorrow, Jimmy! Or put on a white sheet, pretend you're a ghost, n' scare ever body." Jimmy nodded okay, waved and smiled. He hated missing his piss-time out the window, but it was for only one weekend, and that weekend was good for Rupert. The Ghost-hunting Weekend benefitted the city coffers.

It was also possible for Jimmy to remain anonymous and merge into humanity on ghost-hunting weekend. He ventured out late at night and cruised around the lawn like a vampire. Occasionally he even dressed like one.

Jimmy also felt free enough to walk about the lobby, and down to the spas in the basement, to peek outside near the pool, and to follow the secret pathways of the old hotel. The crowds grew each hour, but Jimmy knew all the hiding places in the old hotel. He could watch in peace.

At dusk, or "magic hour," the folks on the lawn grew quiet. A city official with a bull horn took over. "Hello. Everyone, pay attention. Check in is to the right. Everyone will be assigned to a specific group for safety's sake." That's when Jimmy would head back upstairs to the fourth floor, to the peace of his room. All night he would listen to the snickers and the gasps of the visiting ghost-hunters in his hallway. And he would smile. He knew that part of the fun for the tourists was pretending to be scared of the old hotel. Like Halloween. Childlike. And right on time, rain. Thunder. Hail. As the severe weather intensified, the crumbling mezzanine filled to the brim with tourists taking shelter from the storm. When the electricity went out, as it does during storms in these parts, flashlights surveyed the cave-like, water-stained lobby ceiling. The mood was festive as ghost-hunters quietly chatted and shared photos. The band for hire started up some "Thriller," some "Ghostbusters," and some Hitchcock theme songs. Thrill-seekers. These are the kind of folks who love the "rush" of excitement, the chemical release of hormones that label them "adrenaline junkies." The scarier, the darker, the better. Thunderclaps and lightning strikes just up the thrill level. The weekend was off to a great start.

After a long nap, and after dinner, Dan swigs half a bottle of booze, calls a cab, heads to Kellar's Bar to get the guns. Dan enters the bar in the pitch dark. "Damn!" He trips over debris, probably sprains an ankle, lucky he doesn't break a hip. Dan lets out a wail like a wounded animal, but he makes his way to the cash register, where he finds the flashlight.

Dan strides into the back room of the charred bar, with its dangling ceiling, and locates a large, faded OD Green duffel bag. He brings it out of the room, puts it on the half-burned grand piano. Now he's got a duffel on the ready and is running back and forth in the dark, loading up. He's raging to an invisible Tad. "Now, Tad, let me tell you about war. Where you're going is dangerous, son. There's little gook kids with grenades strapped to their waists. Your little toys, your little tv shows didn't prepare you for what you're gonna see. Daniel Boone. The Lone Ranger, none of them could teach you how to make the world safe, son."

Picking up ashes of his old bar's stuff, he fills the duffel and zips it tight. Now Dan's tearing closets apart until he can barely breathe. He opens the lid of the piano, thinking that maybe pistols are hidden in there. No. Just music. Sheet music. He's manic—talking to himself, or Corrie, or to the absent C. "I used to honor other people's sentiments. Your mother's sheet music, all burned up. She treasured her music. Now it has paid for my moral malfuckasense with its life. Did I flinch when these objects of unremembered sentiment to the mindless Corrie Kellar burned? No. My morality has diminished. Deteriorated, Eroded. It's the times. A kind of decadence. A call not to believe in the things we were raised to believe in. Vietnam ruined the American vision of itself, C. Tragic purpose for a war. Not worth giving Tad to that war. Why did I do it, C?" Then crying like a baby.

Dan checks his ammo, his weaponry. There's a Winchester 30-30 rifle, some M-1s, and a snub-nose revolver in the duffel. Enough to kill Grissom. Then maybe himself.

Weighed down by guns, Dan struggles to move with any speed. Adrenaline propels him, but the trek to downtown, on foot, is not easy for the seventy-five year old man. It's 1.3 miles by bird. He calls for one of the few Rupert cabs, but, by now, they are all on the streets transporting ghost-hunters from diners or the Sonic, from the Pines Bowling Alley that serves the best hamburgers in town, from the few motels and rented rooms to the Porterfield lawn. Nobody answers the phone. His call to Buck goes unanswered.

"I need a darn ride downtown," Dan says to the sky. But he sets off walking the parking lot until he gets to the long, steep drive from the bar to the highway. On the way he sits and scooches his way down. He pushes the duffel bag with his feet. When he gets to the bottom, to the highway itself, he has a mile left. It's a damn long mile.

Finally, around ten p.m., Dan stumbles onto Main Street by way of Hubbell Street. Close to the drug store, not far from the Army Recruiting Center, across the street from the Porterfield. He notes that something is definitely going on over at the Porterfield. There are cabs! There are vendors and a crowd of what looks like five-hundred people on the front lawn. Jesus Christ. Dan has long forgotten about the ghost-hunter event, but knows it's a terrible night to act on his plan if there's a crowd. Dan has no interest, though, in hauling his ass and his duffel bag back up the hill to the bar. He scans the lawn of the Porterfield.

He glances over and up to Jimmy's room on the fourth floor, where the ancient black and white portable TV with its coat-hanger antenna casts the only light. For a moment Dan considers hiding out up there himself. But common sense prevails. There's too many people around so he decides to walk another block to Bigelow's, and wait out the crowd. Once inside the noisy bar, Dan drops his heavy duffel to the floor, and orders a beer.

Now on the fourth floor of the Porterfield, Jimmy is up to—the inevitable John Wayne western, only in order to shake things up, this time it's dubbed in Spanish, with the volume way down. It's the one mysterious series of sounds he can contribute to the excitement that is already going on in the halls. Jimmy watches from his bunk, perfectly lip-syncing all the words. As ghost tours pass by his room, causing a ruckus, the tour guides "shhhh" everyone, stop to listen, gasp "Spanish! Sounds like Spanish!" Gleeful shrieks. "Does anyone speak Spanish? What is the ghost in that room saying?" "Lo que viste fue un dólar con el vestido de Lucy . . . what you saw was a dollar in Lucy's dress . . . " Jimmy snorts a laugh, hollers out. "A buck, dumb shit. A buck wearing Lucy's dress!"

"Sounds like two ghosts in there!"

The flamboyant tour group leader spins his well-worn tale. Jimmy listens at the door.

"The fire that finally did the hotel in was arson. The sprinklers were faulty by then, no alarms, as the hotel had long been condemned and closed down. The stairways were rotted. They think one of the firefighters killed in the fire haunts the place to this day. Some people have actually seen him and his yellow dog."

Some are swayed, some giggle.

"Sometimes, you can still hear the dog howl."

Jimmy looks down at Ol' Buddy, sound asleep. He considers making the dog howl, to add more mystery. The group moves on and another follows. And on and on and all through the night.

Outside on the lawn, there's a fresh chill in the air. Nicolette, with a corndog in one hand, a cold longneck in the other, takes a long sip of a beer, and joins a group of ghost-hunters.

Wayne Herd is also making his way up the dark stairwell. Around a corner, a door to another floor. Going up.

He counts the doors, thinking he knows where Jimmy lives.

He knocks softly, then one more gentle knock.

And hears Jimmy inside.

CHAPTER 36
Hello dark place . . .

From the fourth floor window Jimmy waves to the local pot dealer, a pungent-smelling teenager everyone calls 'Ripe-oh'. Ryepo is either a brave, or a stupid soul—down below selling his wares in plain sight of whoever and whatever. In Texas. He has gobs of cash in one fist, and visible knives stashed around both calves. Maybe has guns, too. These days.

Jimmy whistles for the dog. "Time to pee, Ol' Buddy," he says.

Ol' Buddy cowers. "I agree, Ol' Buddy, I don't want to be among the rabble myself, but we all must pee." Listens at the door, opens it to venture out. But because a strange blonde dude is sitting in the hallway, Ol' Buddy growls, barks, and howls, warning the intruder to leave.

Jimmy stops in his tracks.

Blondie speaks. "It's me, Pilgrim."

"By God. It is." Blondie's face is worn, older than the last time the two childhood friends had seen each other, but damn pretty for a dude. Wayne. Jimmy had spotted him on that motorcycle, sure enough, the night that girl got off the bus. That license plate. "Colorado." Jimmy chokes back sudden tears and settles into the fact of Wayne Herd sitting there in that hallway. Jesus Christ. Bit his lip to maintain an air of some Western hero masculinity. Memories of the greatest years of childhood are wrapped up in that blonde-haired, blue-eyed Wayne.

"Your back all right?"

"It's always hurting, but I'm okay . . . it was the kind of wound that never . . . "

" . . . that's good . . . Gotta take a piss, Colorado. Me and the dog. Be right back. It's okay. (in his best John Wayne) It's nice to see a smart kid for a change, Pilgrim. Go on in and wait for me while we do our business. We got lots of catching up to do."

Jimmy and Ol' Buddy head for the laundry chute, where

they both slide down, obviously, or, apparently to go take a piss somewhere. About ten minutes later they return. Jimmy saunters into the room, grabs the remote and mutes the tv. Still watches it. Wayne follows.

JIMMY

You come to start trouble, Colorado? You got a pair of pistols there. I hope you know how to use 'em.

WAYNE

I'm here to see my old friend. But if you've got someone you need me to go after . . . pgghew pgghew pgghew . . . got my make believe pistol right here.

Both men point at some invisible enemy down the hall, teaming up like the little boys they once were, to shoot it out, pgghew, pgghew, pgghew with their imaginary pop guns made out of fingers. Jimmy shuts the door, piddles around the refrigerator, looks through cabinets. Pulls out some booze, some crackers.

Wayne's heart is pounding with fear that his old friend might have second thoughts and turn him away. But Jimmy holds out a glass. "Let's forgo the darkness."

And some small talk begins. From Wayne, "So this is your home now?" And Jimmy, "Don't like living on the fourth floor, but can't live on the ground floor, vandals, break ins."

"The ghost-hunters all think you're a ghost," Wayne says.

Jimmy, reminiscing, "'Member how we'd sneak girls up to the ballroom, and almost get caught, and have to slide down the laundry chute, land in the sheets in the basement, creep up the butler's stairs . . . knowing how to slide my ass down the laundry chute comes in handy . . . Remember how in love we were with Keiko Ito . . . ''

Wayne interrupts. "Jimmy, I gotta ask your forgiveness, man."

"Why? Are you dying?"

"We don't have much time. I'm leaving tomorrow."

"I'm listening, Colorado."

"My son died."

"Liam? What the fuck?"

"Afghanistan."

"Jesus. Jesus Christ, Wayne, I'm so sorry. Well, makes sense you have been rethinking things."

"The games, Jimmy."

"We were just boys. I heard this shit from Sarah, ages ago, that our boyhood games caused all our shit to go wrong, I will not hear it from you."

"I'm not saying that exactly. We were just boys who would always be there for each other and I was not there for you or Tad when it came to Nam. I was scared and ran to Canada. And now Liam is dead and I deserve it."

"We always knew there would come a fucking war, Wayne. For every generation of male in this country. Women cry when they have sons in this country, you know that."

"I know."

"We trained all our lives for it. We knew it would come. You can't blame yourself for Liam."

"I know."

"Your stepdad was all about you, and certainly all about Liam, joining up, because there would come a fucking war for all of the men in every family. And then there's Dan Kellar . . . Jesus, we were doomed to go to war, Wayne."

"I know. But when we were boys. We drank milk. Had sleepovers. Got indoctrinated."

"Well, yes. Watched war movies. Why didn't we learn from them?"

"Where I'm going is dangerous, soldier . . . you can't trust anybody. Women, even kids with grenades strapped to 'em . . ."

" . . . babies running at you, screaming for help, but with hand grenades strapped to their waists."

"Our hero, John Wayne, never saw this in real life, I don't even believe Dan Kellar did, but you did, didn't you? I'm so sorry I abandoned you. And Tad, oh my God, what happened to Tad, we will never know."

"Tad, yeah . . . little American boys, wearing our little army helmet, our cowboy hat, our coonskin cap. Our little pop guns. We loved war, Wayne. It was fun. Black or white. We couldn't wait. I knew in my heart that I was destined to be a soldier. And then. I was asked the question, "would you, when the time comes, be capable of using a weapon in cold blood? On an enemy of the United States?" I was handed a sharp, long-bladed knife with a short metal hilt, modified by the U.S. Government to ensure that its use required specific top secret training in order to effect the appropriate covert destruction. It was a knife, I don't even remember if it was real, but it was a knife held like so, for sneaking up on someone from behind, not for stabbing someone in the back like a gutless chicken shit, no, for reaching around and cutting a man's throat. It was a knife intended for an American soldier, for a killer. It was a knife my Daddy gave to me for Christmas when I was five years old. I was five."

"Jesus, man. You oughta do a TED conference with that speech."

"It's good, right? I always thought I should write my memoir. But listen, seriously. My boyhood idealism, my patriotism, chafe with what I feel now, how scared I am all the fucking time. But I do miss war. Miss the brotherhood of it. Knowing who you can count on."

"Well, you couldn't count on me, that's my point," Wayne says.

Jimmy is immediately triggered. Anger. "But. I fucked everything up, because I couldn't count on myself. Sarah, the firefighters, all on me. I know you had to, you went to Canada, I get why, I do, and Tad fell out of a Cobra, he couldn't help that, and I was in the goddamn forest, and he was right out there in the open, for the gooks to slaughter. I couldn't save him. But I did not kill children . . . I did not kill women . . . I did not kill civilians . . . I did not become an animal in Viet Nam because you and I, and Tad, played with pop guns and wore coonskin caps and Army helmets and cowboy hats. I became an animal because I was told to. Expected to. I used to pray, too. I prayed when I knew I didn't know how to do it right. Didn't know why it was expected of me to burn all their huts down, their crops, kill their pigs. "Just start a little fire, burn their shit to the ground," they'd say. I knew I shoulda gone to Canada with you, and we shoulda convinced Tad to go with us. I am the one made the mistake. So I let it all burn. And never stopped. What illusions we grow up with, so comforting and safe. Kill the bad guys, burn their villages, so the world can sleep safe at night. But still. I miss war."

"I missed home. I wanted to come home. I must have been crazy to come back in '78. Whatever it was that captivated me as a boy, the wargames with you and Tad, whatever it was, the wonderment of living in the U.S.A., left me cold when the Vietnam war started. You can't call your cap a coonskin anymore. Jesus, Jimmy, wake up."

"I know that, asshole."

Later, Wayne walks around the room, sees the shrine of hats. Picks up the photo of himself and his two boyhood friends. "You saved our hats!"

"Yep. How about a milk, Pilgrim? We've had enough booze." The memory of cold glasses of milk enjoyed by two little boys after a busy morning of killing the bad guys brought tears to both men. They hug each other, crying, blubbering words representing an enduring friendship, finally settling down. Jimmy pours two glasses of milk.

"You have to leave tomorrow?"

"Yes. Heading back to Canada."

"You see Celeste yet?"

"I saw Celeste, and before you ask, yes, yes, we did do it, several times, you're my last stop," Wayne confides.

"Well, I'm no booty call, Wayne . . . flattered, but no thanks."

"I came by to give you something, Jimmy." Wayne takes a deep breath and smiles, pulls out the deed to the trailer.

Wayne opens the paper, and puts on readers, ready to make a great presentation of his gift to Jimmy. But the lights in the room blink off a couple of times. Then there's the disturbing, familiar sound—dut, dut, dut. Not too far away, maybe across the street. Dut, dut, dut.

"What the fuck?" Jimmy hears it, too. He heads to his window, grabbing his binoculars.

Incessant firing, more duts . . . GUNFIRE. Definitely. Jimmy ducks, carefully peers out the window, Wayne is behind him, they hear screams coming from the ghost-hunters, a few more odd sounds, a whrack, some concussive pops, then nothing.

"Wayne, call 911, some fucking weirdo out there shooting."

Wayne is on it.

"911, what is your emergency."

"An active shooter? In downtown Rupert, at the ghost-hunter event." But then two more shots! Jimmy's instinct now is to save the day.

Wayne answers questions, but watches while Jimmy dons a concealed carry jacket, grabs his holster, checks for ammo and arms up. He hooks one .44 behind his back, puts one in a pocket, Fuck, Wayne notes, Jimmy's practically salivating over this.

"Tell them there's no pattern, can't tell how many shooters. Tell them I can make it down there before they can. I can't make out who the shooter is so I'm heading out. God damn, I love this."

But the sound of a spray of bullets completely shattering what turns out to be the huge plate glass window of the Army Recruiting Center happens right across the street from the hotel. There's glass all over the sidewalk and street. Jimmy sees that one shooter is there —slipping and falling, yelling in pain.

He throws the binoculars onto the floor, ready to move.

Jimmy leashes the old dog, and heads for the laundry chute to slide down to the basement. He opens the chute and throws Ol' Buddy in. The dog flays his legs and lowers his head. He's an old pro at riding the chute. Jimmy follows, sliding on his side. Ol' Buddy knows the drill. He and Jimmy make a perfect landing. Out they go through the basement door. Jimmy and Ol' Buddy sidle along the fence to the pool.

Wayne follows, choosing to take the stairs, and bolts through the lobby, outside, to the street. Once out, he sees that Jimmy is barreling through the crowd. There's an explosion of some kind. The ghost-hunters are running this way and that, piling up inside the grand doorways, squeezing into the hotel lobby for cover. Wayne takes cover behind a tree.

Both men then travel like pros, people moving out of their way, against the crowd to the street. They dart across Main Street and enter the retreating melee. Jimmy, getting in front of the injured shooter first, is armed and ready. He aims at what appears to be a lone shooter now.

It's dark, but he has a clear shot at the shooter. Aiming, yelling for the man to freeze, Jimmy assesses and realizes that he is encountering an obviously prostrate old man. The old man is frail. And scared. Jimmy lowers his weapon as the old man lowers his body onto the ground, where he leans against the wall for just long enough to look up into the dark sky. There's no moon, just a street light, but the old man is lit up like a Christmas tree. "Fuckin' Dan Kellar????? Holy fuck, we were just talking about you." Jimmy turns to face Wayne, who is staring back at him incredulously.

Dan acknowledges both men. He forms his hand into the shape of a pistol, puts his index finger against his temple. He says, "Just shoot me."

"I'm not going to shoot you, but I'm going to hold you here," Jimmy says.

The old man puts his forehead against the sidewalk, and raises his right hand to stop Jimmy from coming closer. He places two guns on the sidewalk, uses both hands to get up to his knees, and holds onto the wall to stand upright. Defiantly, he reaches down, picks up one gun, then moves to the open window frame. "I told you not to fucking move," Jimmy warns.

"I'm just gonna check on the Army Recruiter. I think I shot him."

He looks back at Jimmy as he climbs inside, and disappears into the black hole of the Army Recruiting Center.

CHAPTER 37
WTF is playing in my head?

Dan sits in a dark corner of the Bigelow, planning, talking to himself, rehearsing the attack on the Army Recruiting Center.

For anybody in the Bigelow bar who cares to notice, they would see Dan Kellar with tears streaming down his face, pounding the back of his head against the wall. Over and over.

But then. Dan looks up. He sees a white light. Tad himself crashes through the ceiling of the Bar, hovers over him. Tad holds out his hands to Dan and releases a flood of blood into Dan's upturned face. Tad speaks to Dan from his place in Heaven, at the right side of Jesus. "Sometimes the only way to keep sinful people from doing great harm to the innocent is by going to war, but Daddy, war must end. Go to the place where war begins—the Army Recruiting Center —and be resolute in your actions." When Dan hears these things, he becomes outraged, but understands his heaven-sent mission.

He cracks. Grabs the duffel filled with guns. Loads up with ammo. Somehow gets some superhuman energy, and drives ninety to nothing back to town, only to have no place to park on Main Street. Cars and vans, RVs, and barriers. *What the hell?* Dan leaves the car running in the middle of the street. He jumps out, opens the duffel, arms himself, and aims, sending rounds of bullets into the air.

Nicolette is moving up the stairs when she hears the first shots. Skilled in detecting armed threats, she recognizes the sound of an active shooter. She makes her way outside to the lawn. By this time the ghost- hunters are scrambling, and she can not make out where the shooter or shooters are. She focuses, and tries to identify sounds as she moves from the lobby to the porch. Nicolette reaches into her pack for her Glock. She always carries a weapon. Better safe than sorry. Her pistol is always locked and loaded. She holds it with both hands, points to the ground, and moves through the hysterical crowd. She is not in any position to take a stance with so many people around. She works her way against the chaos around the Porterfield.

There is a commotion outside the lobby, but no shooter; even more outside the hotel and on the lawn, but still no shooter. She runs out onto Main Street, and finally hones in on the shooter's location —across the street from the Porterfield. Is he in one of the empty buildings? No, the Army Recruiting Center. She definitely recognizes more gunfire coming from there. She hears glass shattering. Like windows. Finally, Nicolette sees a fragment of broken glass from the front window. The lone shooter is breaking the window—seemingly to enter the building. He is within range, she could save the day, but Nicolette's aim is blocked by dozens of people running away from the hotel. They run so close to the shooter that he could easily turn toward the street and fire directly into the crowd. Instead, he steps through the frame of the window into the dark abyss of the recruiting center where Grissom is waiting, and armed. He spots Grissom and fires several shots. Now the whole street is filled with screaming. Dan barrels back into the street.

Nicolette lost her chance to save the day. But it doesn't appear to her that the shooter intends to hurt the crowd. She bets on a personal vendetta—someone against the Army Recruiter—she backs away, slides into the lobby of the hotel. Let it be.

Dan had fired off quite a few shots before realizing there were people everywhere, having long forgotten about the ghost-hunting event. *Where did they all come from?*

He's frantic to understand. *Jesus Christ, did I shoot Grissom? Lord help me, did I do it?*

Confused, and a little scared, an adrenaline filled burst of energy fortifies Dan. He runs through the dark, hauling the heavy load of guns, determined to get into an alley behind the ARC, where there has to be a loading dock door or back door he could enter. If he is going to do this thing, he needs to finish it. Somehow he makes it out into the alley undeterred. A failing Dan Keller leans against the back wall of the Army Recruiting Center, his heart near exploding. He rushes the back door. No Grissom to be seen.

His stash of rifles and the duffel now thrown on the ground beside him. He is in plain sight of anyone who happens by. He hears sirens and realizes the easiest thing would be to simply let the cops kill him. Then it would be over. Then he would know what happened to Tad because he would be in heaven, where all becomes clear. Surely. Surely God wouldn't deny him that. Dan raises the rifle and fires into the air, like a warning shot. Which is stupid; he should keep moving, locate Grissom and shoot the bastard. Finish the mission. A lowly sergeant who represented the inept Army, who represented killing and suffering and ending young lives deserves execution.

From the vantage point of the alley, Dan sees dozens of hysterical people running down the side street. They are running from a terrorist, some bigger than life, some crazy kid who had been radicalized, some foreigner, but nobody notices one old man with a duffel bag. Dan jumps up, slings a rifle onto his back, and, picking up his duffel bag he enters the fray. Converges into the dark recesses of the terrified crowd. Then he sees Grissom, a bit ahead. Now Dan is way beyond reason and self control. He discharges a blast in the general direction of the enemy, inhales the smell of gun powder, rubs his sore shoulder, which is almost dangling from the reverberation. The screams deafen him—he's almost trampled in the mire. But he keeps moving.

Dan marvels at the chaos of the moment. "I caused this." Everyone is running away from the Porterfield, away from downtown. No heroes in this bunch of chicken shits running around. They don't even know where they are going, or who they are running from, that's obvious, but he's going with them. For a bit. But there's nothing but empty shacks on dirt roads in the direction they are running. They'll run out of street, they'll stop to figure things out, they'll see his guns and someone will call the cops. Maybe Dan doesn't want death by cop after all. Dan figures it's safer for him if he gets himself back to the Bigelow Bar. There's a short cut ahead. He gets in step with a middle aged, flabby man who wears a camera around his neck.

Dan asks, "Where did all these people come from?" The man doesn't answer.

What luck to be lost in a crowd and be the only one who knows where he's going. *God must be guiding me,* Dan thinks, *because my ass is worn out.* Not sure whether he shot Grissom or not doesn't matter.

He's drained of energy, and hardly able to lift his rifle. His rage is satisfied. He finally feels avenged. Best of all, Dan is invisible in the chaos.

He works his way down side streets back to Main Street, turns the corner. The crowds have largely dispersed. There are a few cop cars, but no feeling of urgency. So he's done it. He's gotten away with something, but he is not sure what. He can head back to the Bigelow Bar. He turns the opposite direction from the Porterfield, toward the bar. But Dan Kellar, who knows the value of a great story, decides it cannot, will not end there. Other people will say that he lost his fucking mind. But he knows it's about the legacy, the story. He raises the rifle, and while making a bold escape, stupidly, fires again, blasting the windows out of other storefronts as he moves down the street. Then he turns around for some damn reason. Heads back towards the hotel. He opens the duffel, pulls out another rifle, and strolls over to peer into the opening of the Army Recruiting Center again, like a dumb ass. Oh yeah, there's that dumb fuck Grissom now, come back to the scene, looking around the dark office space, with a flashlight. Lift that rifle, aim at that light. *Easy peasy. Grissom, you mother fucker, you're a dead man for recruiting girls, for recruiting my boy, for bragging about my family pain like you know shit.* There's one blast. Then two. And then someone from behind, from the direction of the Porterfield, knocks Dan to the ground, puts a knee to his neck, and screams for assistance, but Dan's ever ready adrenaline rush makes an appearance. Full of blood thirst, thrilled, panting with excitement, Dan manages to free himself. The problem is when he tries to get onto his feet, he's tackled by a couple of men who are definitely weaker than he is. He lies on his back and fires into the air, bullets spraying the ceiling of the Recruiting Center. Finally, one gun is wrestled away from him. But Dan has another burst of superhero adrenaline. He fires once, twice.

Dan has managed to crawl to the window frame, and is now firing at the few remaining ghost-hunters.

He's surrounded by police now, and . . . Police Officer Trout is out there, but no Grissom, maybe he killed that motherfucker. At any rate, time to die, either by cop or suicide, doesn't matter. *Come get me, Trout. Or fuck no, I'll just end it myself.* Dan seats himself against the office wall, puts the butt of the rifle between his feet, and tries to force the barrel into his mouth. The barrel is too fucking long. Shit.

He flings the rifle aside. He's out of breath, all energy spent. His head spins, he's dizzy, his heart is skipping beats. He's old, he'll just have to give up.

And it's not just people running everywhere, now the skies are filled with choppers, with search lights! Dan sees a chopper lift off from the tall grass of the Porterfield lawn. He sees Viet Cong, a couple of dogs, little Vietnamese children, a few American soldiers. Noise and chaos surrounds him, but Dan makes a break for it. He climbs out of the window frame and runs toward a clearing, to be rescued, but the helicopter has already lifted off, now high in the sky. A dog whimpers beside him. Dan pats the pup, reaches into his pocket, thinking he has a dog treat there. Respite doesn't last long, because suddenly the area is crawling with shadows, vapors of the enemy. Dan fires as he sweeps his weaponry right to left, left to right. No clear target. Something causes a loud explosion in the sky. There's a huge beam of light, and a soldier, a U.S. soldier falls from the chopper, a Huey. No, a Cobra. One soldier. The only two things in the world. And then everything stops. The soldier hovers over him. "You think this is my last act?" Dan asks the floating soldier. "You think I don't know what this looks like?"

And then Dan's fantasy ends; he's facing Officer Trout, who disarms him. Handcuffs him.

"Where did all these people come from?"

Trout answers, "Those are all the people who are gonna own you."

Someone controls the crowd to make way for the firetruck, the ambulance, EMTs, stretcher, people running inside the Army Recruiting Center. Someone pulls Grissom out of the ravaged building. He's on his feet, and though shaken up, doesn't appear to be hurt too badly, just enough for Dan to be judged a felon. Dan's head stops spinning. Calm. Sane. Realizing. *Shit, what have I done?*

Smart enough to know his only defense will be insanity, aging, grief.

Not smart enough to know which part he actually imagined.

PART FOUR . . .

CHAPTER 38
Gimme a beautiful balloon

Dan's Party Coming Up, 2023

Nicolette's musical tastes always leaned toward boomer oldies because that's what Liam had liked. Her long-gone hippie mom used to say "our music was the best," and she agrees. Loves her some Beatles, some Stones, some Kinks and some Hollies, but then, her own generation's soundtrack appeals to her, and that era of disco diversion, so throw in some one hit wonders here and there, some "Funky Town," and some "Take on me" . . . add a little Babys, Bangles, a little Britney when Nic's drunk and happy and throw in a little Duffy, and a little Sinead when Nic's drunk and wanting to cry. Alone in the car, she sings to Barry Manilow and Dan Fogelberg. The road tripping—the trek to Rupert for Dan's 100th birthday party—means different music being fought over for days and days. Husband Bob's picks are blue grass and folk, some Allison Krauss, Billy Strings. Blech. Lots of fighting, though everyone in the Turlo-Mercer bunch agree on Tom Petty and the Heartbreakers. Geddy's tastes are all over the place—thank God for Sirius Radio. So, in spite of the fighting, Nicolette thinks it's the best part of a road trip. Singing with Geddy. Bob, on the other hand, sees hidden messages in all the songs Geddy chooses to play. Fuck Bob.

Turn that fucking shit off, Geddy. Are you trying to tell us you're a damn queer, Geddy?

Shut up, Bob. Get out of the car, you two go take a walk somewhere. I'll just sit here in the car and sing by myself.

The RV is loaded. Nicolette and Geddy are packed for an undoubtedly tense journey to and from Texas. Going to the Middle East to serve this country was nothing for Nicolette, but traveling in this divided country is terrifying because she is traveling with the human being she loves most in the world—Geddy. Her child, called a "male" at birth, is now neither son nor daughter, is just the beautiful being she tries to understand, whom Bob refuses to understand. In this country. In 2023. Jesus Christ. And heading to Texas. Nicolette is fucking terrified.

It's a mixed blessing that her husband, Bob, has decided to travel with them to Texas. He could provide some security, if he will. In any case, he's incredibly difficult to get along with and they strongly disagree about all things Geddy.

Geddy, who Bob says should be studying to be a lawyer or engineer instead of a fashion designer. Geddy, who Bob says should be experiencing heterosexual romance, and grown up responsibilities living on "his" own. Geddy represents a changing landscape in a country that, in Nicolette's experience, leans too conservatively, too religious, and too quick to condemn anyone with a different lifestyle, especially someone questioning his, um, their gender identity. But Bob has two enemies now. So simple, too. Nicolette represents careless wokeness and Geddy is chasing what's new and trendy and temporary. "He just needs to be a boy, Nic. That would save our marriage and get things back to normal." To some of her best friends, Geddy is considered to be, ummmm, "they are considered to be," Nicolette reminds herself, "a peculiar person." Particularly stupid adults who ought to know better—well, Bob, for one — have bullied them and called them freaky or creepy. Protecting Geddy has been a top concern, particularly as he moves, um, they move, drat, they, they, they, through whatever it is that they are going through. The pronouns are just so fucking hard to get used to. Nicolette works non-stop to navigate this new world in the most supportive and positive way she can conjure, considering that she finds their world confusing.

Because she's terrified for their safety, she wishes Geddy is "normal," like Bob wants, that they are in a first apartment or dormitory or even jail. Honestly, she wouldn't really care where, but Geddy is home with her, and Bob. Of course, it would be best if Geddy would just stay home! She lives in fear of Geddy venturing out into the world, ending up tied to a post somewhere, beaten to death like . . . like God bless him, Matthew Shepard, that fucking Wyoming bullshit mentality that killed that poor boy, or dead either by suicide, or shot in the street for any one of a million reasons, mostly for being queer, for landing somewhere on the transgender spectrum, and on the autism spectrum as well. If he, they would move away, on his, their own, drat, get the pronouns right, she might have some peace. She couldn't know where he was or what was happening to him. THEM. As for being queer, yes, he is, they are, in the questionable sexuality sense, though Geddy has never come out. Not transgender, either, so far. He's definitely friendless, and this saddens her. There is no way to imagine a future for this child. Her child, with all his, their complications, torments Nicolette on a daily basis. Soldiering is not the skill that helps her child. She's a soldier, a suffering mother, an evolving human being, and Geddy is her cross, her heart, her bliss.

So Nicolette goes on her speaker tours, to the very places where Geddy could face condemnation, to talk about her service to her country, if only to remind herself that she had a life before Geddy, a life that was maximum stress, by any standard. The traumatic events, the life-altering events still haunt her, and she lives with PTSD from the attack on Liam. Maybe it is her imagination, but nothing has ever compared to the stress Nicolette lives with as a mom to a vulnerable, sometimes nonverbal child/young adult with anxiety, one whose identity could endanger his, their life.

Nicolette talks about her PTSD, Liam's death, her injuries, but Geddy is off limits. She will not speak in public about Geddy. Why draw attention to Geddy? Hell, it's 2023, and it's a mean, motherfucking world out there.

Geddy does have a lifesaving trait. A miracle trait. He is, they are a total nerd—awkward, yes, but brainy. Loves some "normal" things —the space program, baseball, American History, museums. But Geddy's favorite passion is an extremely odd one, Nicolette knows, and the trip to Texas is planned to accommodate its weirdness. Geddy's obsessive love is of a sport called "extreme ironing." Nicolette has to explain this strange hobby everywhere they go, right after she has to explain that Geddy is not transgender as far as she knows. When Geddy inevitably brings it up, the day is saved. "I iron," Geddy says.

"It's ironing clothing in different, extreme situations like while climbing, surfing, rowing, hanging upside down, underwater, stuff like that," she tries to explain to the nosy stunned.

"You mean on an ironing board, with a real iron?"

"Yep, hauling a few ironing boards up mountains, you know, like you do. I do it, too. It's fun. I love it. We have the best time together, ironing." Nicolette no more loves extreme ironing than she loves wallowing in shit, but she does love Geddy. She'll do anything for Geddy. Extreme ironing is so odd that spectators who encounter Geddy in travels focus on the ironing, rather than the presumed transgender aspect. Geddy has long hair. Geddy is slim. Geddy's body is hairless. Geddy might wear a dress. Geddy might wear a tux. But their voice is deep. They could be nearing a reveal, that they're gay, or transgender, or just unique. It all worries Nicolette, and offends Bob. But so far Geddy has remained just Geddy, which is a relief since, in 2023, at least thirty transgender lives in the U.S. ended by violence committed against them. By hate. They were human beings who worked, had families, educated themselves, were activists, and helped others. And there were some who appeared to be one thing or another (like Geddy would be described), but who were extremely kind and willing to give you the shirt off their backs. As Geddy would say, "I would truly give you the shirt off my back, but I would iron it first."

The trip to Texas is an RV adventure with stops for fabulous meals of pizza, chili, and barbeque. It starts with Nic and Geddy, each ironing a white shirt while on horseback in North Dakota, continues by ironing under the light of the stars and moon in the Black Hills of South Dakota, ironing on top of Devil's Tower, ironing while rock climbing at Custer State Park, ironing on top of Mt. Rushmore (as close as they can get), ironing while dangling over a waterfall, ironing on a duck boat, ironing on a kayak in Nebraska, then ironing in the bed of a pickup going sixty-five miles per hour on rural roads in Kansas, again in underground caverns in Colorado, and then taking some time away from ironing to enjoy a Louis Tomlinson (Geddy's favorite) concert at Red Rocks, where another extreme situation blasts them—a tremendous hail storm that sends hundreds of people running for shelter. Several are injured, the concert is ended. Eventually huddled together in their RV, hungry and disappointed, Nic and Bob start arguing. Bob assesses what he believes is a broken bone injury and acts like a whiny-ass baby. Finally, the three of them get into a screaming match. It is the only terrible hiccup of the trip, and it is pretty terrible.

Instead of going straight to Texas, they detour to Santa Fe, New Mexico. Sans ironing boards. The change in routine upsets Geddy. Nic insists they take in "just gorgeous sunsets, mountain vistas, unique architecture, and shopping." Geddy broods in the RV most of the time they are in Santa Fe. Nicolette buys some Christmas ornaments, some kitchen magnets, some ironing board covers decorated with skulls or kias. Nothing appeases Geddy. They go to Meow Wolf. But Geddy hides somewhere inside the House of Eternal Return. For ten hours. Security saves the day when they find Geddy. The remainder of the drive is quiet, nobody speaking. Everyone is worn out.

"The middle of life is so, so hard, we need to find a way to enjoy our time together, enjoy Geddy being with us," Nicolette says to Bob.

"Geddy has only made life harder," he answers.

They get to Texas, stop in Fort Worth to spend the night before driving into Rupert. Nicolette is sorely dreading the Dan Kellar birthday party, tells Bob she's mourning Liam after all these years, and thin-skinned Bob goes off to buy an airplane ticket home. Alone. Needing a drink. She gets herself drunk, goes back, finds Geddy in the hotel bathroom, passed out in cold bath water, wrists slightly cut, just a few trickles of blood. Geddy rouses. Then screams. It was certainly a statement of emotional desperation, but not a definitive or particularly dangerous one. It's a scream for help Nic has heard before.

She dials 911, but the hotel staff is already on the alert.

EMTs to Geddy: "Do you know how old you are?"

"Nineteen."

"Do you know where you are?"

"Are we in New Mexico still, mama? I want to iron in a hot air balloon. That balloon festival thing."

"That's not until fall, Geddy."

"What month is it now, mama?"

"June. It's June."

"Oh good, well, we have time to get there then."

"We're going to Texas first, Geddy."

"I'll die there, mama. Don't take me to Texas."

The EMTs determine that Geddy is just fine.

CHAPTER 39
. . . *Whatever don't get lost* . . .

Dan awakens from his stroke to find that Celeste has not left his side. He sits up and says, very loudly, and in a new, slower cadence, "That's the besht . . . sshleep . . . I ever had! How long was I . . . asshleep, C?"

"About two minutes."

"Oh." A bit crushed.

He was convinced that some kind of metabolic insult had kept him in a deep coma for at least three days, and was highly insulted that Celeste would suggest that he was wrong. "Two minutesh ish not . . . enough time to account for all the . . . shi-ut I just went through. I was in a coma."

He tries leaping out of bed. The side bolsters are in the way, so Dan bangs the shit out of his side and thigh, and yelps his almost favorite word. "Dammit."

Scantily clad in frayed boxer shorts, and with his chest tightly bandaged, Dan pushes C away, and struggles to understand.

"Why are you lying to me, C? Damn, would take more than two minutes for somebody to take my pants off, and leave me in my underwear. That's just common sense."

Second day. *Hello world. Dammit.* Not yet four a.m. Dan is prematurely awakened by an active brain. Within seconds he's wide awake, but tired, irritable and groggy: sheer misery. "Dammit." No way to get a cup of coffee. *It's been awhile since I have been able to get a cup of hot coffee, come to think of it.* Coffee makers aren't allowed in common areas since old man Briggs burned himself while pouring a cup. And the water in the bathroom sink never gets hot enough for a tea bag. Jesus Christ, Dan wonders why he hasn't asked C to figure out something for coffee or tea in his room? Without coffee or tea there is no reason to get up.

Dan reaches for his meds and, once again, considers ending it all before the birthday party. Like now, this minute—this minute without coffee or tea. But alas, once again, he chickens out, puts the pills down, and hangs his head in shame. He falls back onto his pillow, his brain on fire. Hot coffee. Hot tea. Hot pizza with C. *Oh God, I made a rhyme. Oh my God, what I would give for a hot slice of pizza, hell, even a cold one. Those were the good old days.* It takes so little to be considered "the good old days."

He lies back and closes his eyes. He needs to pee, but the trek to the bathroom sink seems endless. Maybe he'll just pee in his bed.

Thus, another day and night pass after the awakening from the "two minute" stroke.

Sixth day? *Hello world. Joe Biden is president. Ninety-five years old. Birthday soon.* "Birthday schoon."

Celeste's squeal is so loud it reaches from her father's bed to the hallway, "Oh dear God," she shrieks, and calls for the nursing staff. "He's awake, you guys."

But the mouth, the tongue stops working. *"Holla whirl."*

"Daddy, don't try to talk. You had another stroke—a bigger one. You almost died. You should have died. Someone saved you. I saved you."

Celeste speaks with conspicuous relish. Dan utters the word "wheredaga," and he doesn't seem frightened, or thankful, at all.

"Wheredaga? Vertigo? If that's all it was, that's good. But keep quiet; we'll let the nurses handle everything, all right?"

Celeste is deflated by his lack of anxiety over the prospect of another stroke, and this time one that is even worse. She loves it when she can create some rare drama at her father's expense. He might really notice her at those times.

"C, seep."

"Daddy, I believe we both should remain awake."

FN enters the room, and shines a light in his direction. Indeed, he appears to be having an episode of vertigo since his eyes are flitting back and forth.

The question comes, "What is your name?"

Dan struggles. "Dan. Near mah mouf, mah face num. Seep." He doesn't have any drooping when FN examines him. But he is drooling. She wipes his mouth.

"Well, you're slurring your words, Dan. You surely had a stroke. But you feel you're just waking up from vertigo?"

"Gibme a seck."

Dan takes great care lifting his head from the pillow. He moves his head from side to side before feeling confident enough to sit up. He nods and points to his stomach, and signals for everyone to wait.

Finally. "Not watego. I would be sick to schtomach. But no stroke. Joe Biden is still president," Dan says.

"Yes, Dan, Joe Biden is still president." Relief.

"Ask me tuffa keston."

"He wants a tougher question." FN makes a "V" hand gesture to show concern and relief that Dan is still alive.

"A tougher question? Okay. Who is she?" FN continues, pointing at C.

Dan turns his neck to look at his daughter.

The vertigo must be gone, Celeste thinks, because her father is glaring at her with steady focus.

"That's Scheleste. She's the fambly historyan. She saw everthan. She heard everthan."

"I think your Dad is going to be just fine, but we'll need to get him into speech therapy," FN says.

Celeste doesn't trust him. She wouldn't put it past him to fake a stroke. He is such a liar. And that glare!

CHAPTER 40
. . . A beggar and his travels . . .

"Hello. Dammit. Biden. A little ague today. Feeling small. Feeling obdurate about something that C and I have been discussing. Heavy laden. I mean, it is, after all, the desert season of life. Tomorrow. Birthday party. God dammit y'all, Joe Biden is president, FUCK, gimme a break, stop asking me that question. Somebody get me my red jacket. I wanna make sure it fits."

"It's gonna rain, Dad, but no worries. Everyone is coming to the party."

"No preachers. Because I only have one more day to make my peace with God, and I don't want any preachers rucking it up."

"No preachers."

"Jimmy, Mo and FN?"

"Yes."

"All the floozies. Briggs? Did we have to invite Briggs? Nicolette?"

"Yes. Yes. And yes, she's bringing her kid."

"And?"

Dan notices that C smells particularly fresh and looks fairly put together.

"And yes, Wayne is coming. For me. He's bringing his band. We have a very special afternoon planned, Daddy."

"May I say, C, that your fat legs under your fat ass look particularly nice tucked into your new boots?"

Celeste has spent a week preparing herself, her physical self, for the party. Sneaking to Dallas. A light peel on her face. A little filler in the marionette creases by her lips. Some expensive foundation to create a soft glow. A lash and brow treatment. A little sapphire blue eyeliner along the edge of her lashes. Some rose gold eyeshadow, blended into a bit of cocoa color along the outside edge of her eyelids. Some highlighting of the hair. A trim. A blow dry. A new lipstick color, pedicure, manicure. Finally, a few outfits from the haute couture consignment store in Highland Park, hand-picked by a capable salesgirl named Brittany. Nothing black. Or too flowy. Cute white jeans (not "britches"). A poppin' maroon boat neck flowy blouse. A pair of gold cropped pants with a blazer to match, accented with teal. A buttery-soft faux leather jacket in pale blue, with fringe (for the white britches/pants). No elastic anywhere. Square-toe, perforated heel boots, one pair in taupe, one with rhinestones. The selections were bold, pricey, and not really "her," but Celeste left the store feeling like the most beautiful seventy-year-old in Texas.

Tom Petty blaring on her Sirius Radio, and she is singing at the top of her lungs when buyer's remorse hits. That particular reaction is usually almost instant, but she is determined to get her big Texas bling on, so she dismisses the unsteady feeling. But she stops—at the familiar Chico's at the Pavilion on Lover's Lane store, and it was SO gratifying there. Like home. There she purchases an orange silk blend shirt dress with leaf drop earrings to match, and a jewel neck tee priced at $29.00. She leaves the store, gets on I-30 to head home, changes the channel to something more mellow on Sirius FM, the Bridge. Outside of Fort Worth, she stops to get gas, pee and grab a Subway sandwich at the Love's Travel Stop. On her way to the register, she picks up a great bottle of a knockoff perfume that claims to smell like Giorgio. It is the single most elegant day of her life.

Jimmy hosts a party the night before Dan's birthday bash. FN, Nicolette, Wayne, C, and a slew of big drinkers, are invited to the trailer. By now the trailer is permanently parked on Wayne's property. A few additions have been made over the decades. Has a covered deck, a carport, a guest powder room. Lots of yard out under the stars. Room for everyone's trucks.

A barn.

A barndominium, in fact.

No neighbors for miles.

A pod containing a huge shipment of exterior acoustic panels for the upcoming music festival.

"Not too happy about that," Jimmy tells FN.

It is a grand night for Jimmy's party. Big barbeque spread. And fajitas. Taco Bar. Beer and margaritas. A chocolate fountain. But the best part is the music. Wayne does boomer covers with his band. Celeste performs backup and a few solos, including The Fifth Dimension's "Last night I didn't get to sleep at all" (in remembrance of the dreams she left behind) and Carly Simon's "The Right Thing to Do," which she sings directly, and boozily, into Wayne's face because, in reality, Celeste knows she will love Wayne tomorrow just as much as she loves him today.

She is reminded, *where in God's name did this memory come from and why is it intruding*, when she was a young girl. Celeste loved to sing. And she had a solo in a Christmas show. The whole town turned out. And she knocked it out of the park, as they say. There was universal applause and praise from the crowd. Even the newspaper critiqued "Rupert has a songbird." Dan couldn't believe it, though. When she sang, it sounded like screeching owls to her old dad. He covered his ears.

She felt like a peacock after the concert, walked around singing and professing that "someday I'll be a singing star!" Her dad said he knew such a dream would break her heart if he allowed her to pursue such. He sat her down and told her, "Celeste, everybody was just being nice to you. Let me tell you the truth, honey. You can't sing. So stop."

She did. No more dreams. Daddy killed them.

The more inebriated she becomes at the party, the louder she sings, and occasionally, sobs. One of Wayne's other girlfriends at the party express a desire to beat C's ass. White trash nights! FN attempts to sing "Blue Bayou"—Nicolette belts "Half Breed" for some reason. At the end of the evening, when things are winding down, Celeste takes Wayne aside and says "Glad to be with you, Wayne Herd, here at the end."

Nicolette breezes in just in time to taunt the man who would have been her father-in-law had life gone the way she wanted it to go. "Where's Geddy?" Wayne looks around.

"You know, Geddy is so tired out, sleeping, but will see you at the party tomorrow!"

When this night's party dies down, only Wayne and Jimmy, Celeste, and Nic remain, and they are listening to mellow classic rock on Pandora, and communing on plastic lawn chairs around a fire pit in the yard.

Everything slow, the mood calmer, so Jimmy gets up, goes into the trailer for a minute, comes back out with a box. He drags over a chair. "I must change the tone of the evening, sorry, everyone."

He places the old cowboy hat on the chair.

"Jesus," says Wayne.

"Cups to our beloved Tad. It seems appropriate to honor the brother, friend, and fellow soldier after fifty-five years. You, too Nicolette. Raise your glass. To Tad."

First Jimmy: "I loved being a soldier. I loved the stories. I loved serving my country. This country. And while we're at it, honoring Dan, too. He was my hero for a very long time."

Celeste raises a glass, and interjects, " . . . The flawed, never gonna change, unremorseful, Dan, lousy father, hero of three wars . . . And the damndest greatest storyteller I've ever known."

Jimmy again. "Anybody remember Buck?"

Nic screeches. "I remember Buck! He was toothy and sweet . . . "

" . . . Buck used to do his civil war reenacting on this property. He saw himself as a keeper of the stories as well, from a long ago, sad war. Sometimes I sit out here and I can see them soldiers wearing the blue and gray, reenacting, I even sometimes see the ghosts of the real soldiers back there, on the horizon, I see them now, all back there, raising their bayonets in salute to Buck. Here's to Buck."

"I guess he died by now, huh?" Nicolette raises her glass.

"Yes. All right, everyone, so this hat, this hat is for Tad. Tad, who, unlike Dan, unlike Buck, didn't get to tell his story of his life or war."

"Or his death." Celeste's red lips are pursed as she chews the inside of her mouth. "We still don't know what happened to Tad."

"Yes, we do, C. Of course, we do." Jimmy kneels before the

chair, before the cowboy hat. "I'm sorry, Tad. After all these years I just couldn't bring myself to tell your family what I saw that night. It was fucking Blackhawk Down, C. That's the story."

Celeste gasps.

And the drinking continues. The firepit crackles. Quietly. Nicolette asks for everyone's attention. " . . . I can tell you Tad's story. I never met him. But I know his story. His story is about that hat. That cowboy hat. And the hat is his boyhood, the hat is his great love for this country, for its history, and the hat is for the love he had for his father. His friends."

Jimmy reaches into a the box, and hands the Army helmet to Wayne.

Wayne pushes his hair into a pony, puts on his old boyhood toy. "Doesn't fit anymore." He squeezes it onto his head and laughs about that, but the emotion comes and he cries.

Jimmy then forces the coonskin cap onto his own head. "I didn't mean to torment you, C. He fell out of the Cobra, something we didn't count on when we were kids playing cowboys and Indians. I think he died right then, when he fell out, I do. I know he did. I saw everything. The thing was Tad had wanted to go to Canada with Wayne. Tad died believing that the war he was fighting, was wrong, was politically motivated, he knew it was based on a lie told by our leaders. I even kinda believed that, you know? But he came from where we all came from. Dan Kellar. Who went to war three times and would have died for any reason this country gave him. I don't think Dan ever questioned a thing this country asked him to do. But Tad questioned and dammit, Dan Kellar always wanted to die some goddam war hero, but Tad didn't. Nothing fucking fair about it. I know he was dead, C. I just couldn't tell you or Dan. He was dead, but to see them Viet Cong descend on him like they did, what they did to him . . . I could never tell it."

"STOP!" C shrieks.

Jimmy creaks up to standing. Salutes the hat.

"I love you, Tad. Rest in peace, my brother."

They each then step up to the empty chair, and kiss their fingers, and touch the cowboy hat, and shed some real tears. The ritual brings peace.

Nicolette was last to touch the hat. "Liam would tell us to remember Tad the way he was when he wore that hat, Jimmy. I know that for a fact. Remember I'm the girl who held Liam's . . . his . . . "

"STOP!" "STOP!" "STOP."

And then. "Sing us something, Nicolette. We need to stop our tears." And even though the song that comes to mind is a lie on its face, it manages to bring everyone peace. "I was thinking about singin' a song I used to sing to Geddy, about how I would protect everyone I love from harm, but . . . we know that . . ."

CHAPTER 41
White Dan for 200

"Dammit. Hello world. Still alive. Joe Biden is president. But today's the day."

C caught him at it.

With his amazing grip on the pen.

She peers over his shoulder. He writes legibly, and with ease. NOT like a stroke victim. He wads it up and hobbles to the bathroom, dragging one leg behind him.

The wadded obituary is right there on the night stand. She unravels it and reads. Not finished, but coming along. Still. *What stroke victim thinks to finish his obit?* C wads it up again while Dan pees in the sink.

Preceded in death by his wife, Corrie, and maybe his son, Tad.

As far as accomplishments—*Hero of Three Wars.*

But not a word about his crimes, his misdemeanors, his meanderings, his lies, his adulteries, his cruelties. C wants to tear the damn obit into pieces.

The 100th birthday party is in full swing in the cafeteria by the time C has gotten Dan dressed and his beautiful head of hair combed just right. She wheels her dad down the hallway.

When he enters the room, the orderly who is pretending to be a DJ changes the music. Dan rolls his eyes. "Of course, WWII music, my heyday, so they think, C." C smiles and sings along to sounds of the Andrew Sisters, Frank Sinatra, some Lena Horne, and some Bing Crosby tunes. Music is a great connector between the two of them, though Dan prefers C's music over the tunes of his own generation.

"Tell them to stop playing this old people music. But no glibby glubby, C! And no "Boogie Woogie Bugle Boy" either, please."

"The party is loaded with boomers, so you're probably okay," C promises.

"Did I ever tell you that the happiest moment of my life was standing outside your bedroom door when you were about fifteen and watching you sing to the mirror? Singing Skeeter Davis, I believe."

"That's totally creepy, Dad. You peeping at me . . . Remember when I used to stand on your toes and dance with you to Chuck Berry?"

"When I taught you to twist. You had no natural rhythm, so stiff you couldn't move your hips in a circle without falling down."

"You were never the right person to make someone feel supported in a new situation, Dad."

"Once an asshole, always an asshole."

Dan is wheeled centerstage, the music stops, time for the face Dan presents to the world to show up. The room full of partygoers blow party horns and yell "Happy Birthday!" "Speech! Speech!" He takes a deep breath while everyone quiets down. "Thank you. (clears throat, wheezes) Thank you for being here. I owe most of you an apology. I look around this room and I see (cough, sniff) many friends, and many caregivers, and so many of you who should have been friends, but I was too stupid, too ornery to make friends out of you. I see one man I shot. I cannot believe he's here."

"And he's gonna be doing the music, Daddy."

Dan notes that everyone laughs, except Wayne, of course.

"Aw, that'll be nice. So. Too stupid, too ornery to make friends out of you. Please accept my apology everyone, for all the bad, for all the stuff you think I did wrong. I want to be your friend. Okay, let's have a party."

And with that anticlimactic apology the birthday party begins.

After a couple of hours of grazing, sipping on punches, dancing to old tunes, Wayne and C gear up to put on their own show. Wayne makes the announcement. "We're gonna do two sets, and in between sets, we'll have prizes and surprises, and a special game Moiselle and some of the other staff put together just for tonight."

Lots of people coming in and out, practically everyone in town, a huge turnout of the uninvited, bringing food and beer and wine. "We saw the sign downtown. Party at the old folk's home. BYOB!"

Moiselle and the Administrator nearly have a stroke at the number of rowdy-types converging on the RRC. And the hippies. Jesus. The smell of pot wafts around the porch outside. Mo hates to get the police involved, but she's thinking might be a good idea to call Trout in, who is by now the Chief of Police.

Dan is the man of the hour, though. Everyone makes him feel important, seen, and heard. He tells a million stories, some in a microphone to the entire crowd, some privately from his wheelchair near the window. Most of the stories are prompted by the fact that his military discharge papers and records folder are in his lap for everyone to see, the bold marking "MILITARY SERVICE, THREE WARS" written in magic marker on the cover. As townspeople stop to wish him happy birthday, it doesn't matter that they've never met him, they notice the folder and ask questions that always begin with the overused statement, "Thank you for your service. Did you serve in the Pacific during WWII?" "Yes, killing japs, can't call 'em japs anymore, though, jalapenos are japs now," Dan says.

"Thank you for your service. Were you at Pearl Harbor?" "Yes, killing nips, oops, can't say that either," Dan says. "Normandy." "Yes." "Iwo Jima?" "Yes." "Were you one of those guys in the picture raising the flag?" "Y . . . no," Dan answers, realizing there's photo proof that he's lying if he said yes to that one. "Did you ever fly in an A-26?" "Yes." "Did you ever pilot a B-24?" "Yes." "Were you in a tank division? "Yes. Sherman tank." "Yep. Sabre." "Of course, yes. Fought with a Browning machine gun in all three wars, I believe." "Almost as decorated as Audie Murphy." "Solitary confinement, and tortured, yes." "Bayonet through the chest."

Briggs was next to last in line. "Thank you for your service, old man, with all this information of your amazing war service, I'm sure I can win the jeopardy game later today," he says.

"Jeopardy game?" Dan hasn't prepared himself for a game that will likely make fun of him and his stories, his many lives. He has to take the defensive quickly. "You never fought a war, did you, Briggs? I fought three. But I guess we're even cause you beat me in the love department. Good thing I went to fight Nazis, huh, or you wouldn't have met your favorite girlfriend, my wife. Glad to be of service to you, mother fucker. Now get the hell out of my birthday party, please."

Briggs mumbles a happy birthday and leaves the party completely, stopping only to fill a plate with barbeque to take back to the room the two old men still begrudgingly share.

FN is last. She is near tears. "I will miss your stories."

"I saved a war hero story just for you. Once I disguised myself as a tree trunk and captured thirteen Germans."

"How'd you do that?"

"I surrounded them."

"Now have fun, quit telling lies, and I'll plan on seeing you in the morning, seven a.m."

"More like eight, gonna stay up late, so why don't you stay awhile," Dan replies. "Get out on the dance floor."

A long line of grateful humanity passes by the old warrior that night. They love his stories, or pretend to. Dan is going to die a happy man, genuinely believing that he was, in some way, everywhere at once during all three wars, save from being that tree trunk.

Finally, Wayne kicks in the rock and roll he and C love so much. When Geddy and Nicolette finally show up, their first stop is the makeshift dance floor. Nicolette shows off some great "gams" with her military-style, short, pin-up girl, curve-hugging wiggle dress. In contrast, Geddy's getup is a breezy, hot pink, short corset dress, which they wear over black leggings with 3-inch espadrille wedge sandals. On one hand is a full set of acrylics, also in hot pink, and on the other hand are four knuckle rings. Geddy owns Geddy. Always the headturner, mostly the optimist, Geddy brushes off a couple of confused glances, one angry look, and a hundred smiles, as they and their mother dance freestyle to boomer hits—Geddy moving in club moves usually reserved for techno or rap—Nicolette merely "Stayin' Alive" on the dance floor.

Dan never quite gets the nerve to talk to Wayne, but the two men acknowledge each other. Jimmy and FN sit close to Dan, watching out for him because, after telling his embellished stories and outright lies, he becomes visibly agitated, perhaps in anticipation of the jeopardy game, or perhaps because he has every intention of dying after the party. On breaks from singing on stage, C hovers over him with an oddly terrified look on her face.

About two hours in, Nicolette and Geddy leave the dance floor. They've met everybody. Geddy has entertained by recounting ironing stories, but as townspeople get drunker, the snarls increase. Nicolette decides they need to scoot away pretty quickly. Tomorrow they plan on heading back North and East.

The two make their approach to introduce Geddy to the old war hero.

Wayne takes a break from his band to join, to protect, to go between Geddy and Dan. Cautious, fight or flight response taking hold, he stops Geddy, makes an up and down gander at the pink getup. "You sure you don't want to change your clothes, Geddy?"

"Wayne, be careful. Let Geddy do what Geddy is gonna do," Nicolette counsels.

"What the hell, Nic? Geddy is a boy. Not an ugly girl. We're in Texas."

"I know. I know."

Geddy leaves their mother and grandfather to argue among themselves.

"Why didn't you write me and tell me Geddy is doing that trans thing?"

"That's an offensive term, Wayne, you need to learn the vocab. Geddy is not doing a trans thing. Geddy is cross dressing. Maybe considering their gender identity. Do some work and learn about all this. For the sake of your only grandchild."

"How far is this going to go?"

"Not to the surgeries, or even hormones and counseling, as far as I know, but so what? It's Geddy's life and we, you and I, are damn well gonna back them, them all the way."

"Jesus Christ, Nic. Okay. So Geddy cross-dresses. What does Bob think about it? I mean. I'm not the one you need to worry about. I can handle cross-dressing, as long as Geddy knows he's a boy."

"Go on up to them, Wayne. Geddy may not consider themself

to be a boy today. I don't know. But you want them safe, right? And we are the ones who keep them safe by example. If we accept Geddy, everyone else will, at least, they will not act up."

Wayne mans up, catches up, shakes Geddy's hand, gives a shrinking hug, but has no idea what to say to his grandchild. Wayne is embarrassed to the max as he notices that everybody is staring at Geddy, or worse, trying not to stare.

Then. "Shit, Ged, you gotta get past Dan. Dan is an asshole, you know, old school, won't handle this well."

"It's okay. I can handle Dan if I can handle you. You call yourself a liberal, grandpa . . . and your knickers are all in a twist..."

" . . . I don't call myself anything... In the middle . . . Jesus, I get it, Geddy."

Nicolette leads Geddy to Dan's wheelchair, where he is still holding court. All the old fogies surrounding Dan look up at both Nic and Geddy and just smile. Just nice and friendly. But Dan. Dan. Dan looks Geddy up and down.

"Who's this? I require explanation."

"Geddy. You met Geddy as a baby. Remember, Dan?"

Looks Geddy over. "What are you? A boy or a girl? What do I call you?"

"Oh Jesus," Nicolette says.

"Cause you stick out like a sore thumb. You're one of those people don't know which bathroom to go to, right? I've heard about it, back when we could watch the news. Urinal or tampon dispenser all you need to know, I heard."

"Urinal, sir. I use a urinal."

"But you're wearing a dress."

Geddy grins, says "Happy birthday," and motions for his mother.

"Don't leave! You're the last person I will ever have the pleasure of knowing, Geddy. I only have one question for you . . . How do you plan to stay safe in this world, walking around in such a getup?"

Stops to consider an answer, Geddy rejoins Dan. "I plan on getting my own country, and inviting others to join me. I'll call it "Phagistan." "Transylvania" is already taken."

"Let's not get confrontational, Geddy. He's an old man,"

Nicolette intervenes.

"I am an old man, Geddy, but I want to get to know you, please, sit down. Just start over. What do I call you?"

Geddy nods "it's ok" to Nic, sits on the coffee table near the wheelchair, leans in to Dan and confides. "You call me by my name. Geddy. Obviously I don't remember meeting you when I was a baby. But I am honored to meet you, sir. I understand you are a war hero, three wars."

"Yes, that is what I am. But what are you?"

Nicolette is near tears.

"I know you are, but what I am? Right? Sorry." Geddy giggles back, which makes Dan glare, which makes everyone move in closer.

Geddy leans in to whisper to the confused old man. And Dan makes a serious effort to hear the person whispering.

"Does it really matter what I am, sir?"

"Yes, it does. And speak louder. So everyone can hear."

Okay. Geddy begins.

"Well, if inquiring minds really want to know. I'm Wayne's grandchild. Wayne Herd. Which means that I need to be thanking you for being a terrible shot. If you'd killed my grandpa, I wouldn't be here, right? I'm Nicolette's child. My father was Liam. I never met him. I am a singer, a music lover, a sports enthusiast, and my sport is called "Extreme Ironing." Have you heard of it?"

"No, what is extreme ironing?"

Geddy says, "I just explained it to all these nice people here at your party. But I'll explain again. It's a sport. It's an extreme sport in which people take ironing boards to remote locations and iron items of clothing."

"Oh dear God in heaven. That's a sport?"

"It's my living, too. I win contests. I do YouTubes. Interviews. I'm an influencer. I extreme ironed over at the Porterfield Hotel last night. Jimmy got me in there . . ."

" . . . so Jimmy knows you iron . . . And Wayne knows . . . "

" . . . and I was there for three hours, ironing, communing with the ghosts, the spirits, though they're losing their home since the renovation of the hotel began. And I talked to people who were walking past the Porterfield about the sport and about life. Then I post it all on social media. Here I am talking your head off, sir. Normally, I don't have so much to say. I really am quiet. Everyone has been so nice here. Happy birthday, Mr. Kellar. Mom and I have to go so . . ."

Dan smiles, and pats Geddy on the shoulder. " . . . We are a nice town, Geddy. I knew someone in the service like you. He wore dresses. He was also an influencer. Before you leave. My mother took in ironing. I was little. Depression era, everyone had to do whatever they could to make a living. She hated ironing, and had to distract herself, but when she ironed she would ask me about my day, have me chat at her, sometimes the neighbors would come in and tell her their problems. It was the only time my awful mother would sit and listen to anyone, and she did that while she ironed. I think it's my one good memory of my mother. Extreme ironing, and listening, yes? You're a good person, Geddy."

Geddy nods. "I understand you killed alot of Nazis and I thank you for that."

"Uh huh."

"I don't like Nazis. I think my mom and grandpa were afraid you might be a Nazi."

"I killed Nazis, but I didn't kill them so I could become one. Thank you for coming to my party."

Geddy pats the old man on the knee. "Mom, I think I'll grab some cake."

Dan smiles at Nicolette. "That's an extraordinary . . . "

"Human being," she answers.

"An extraordinary human being you got there, out there dealing with this mean, awful world. Dear God, I hope . . . Geddy survives," Dan says.

Marveling at the change in his heart, the acceptance, the respect he is willing to show, Dan realizes he has been gifted one last, one big lesson, the last one God intends for him to learn, before bringing him home to Heaven.

"Nic, I'm gonna die tonight. Geddy's the surefire sign. I really felt a change in my heart."

Nic smiles. "Well, okay. Happy birthday and happy dying day, old guy."

The glibby glub boomer music returns and Celeste joins Wayne in a set of magical boomer songs. She sings backup, duets, solos, her beautiful voice soaring again, the biggest smile on her face the whole time. Wayne and C perform mashups of "Come Monday" and "Monday, Monday," "House of the Rising Sun" and "Here Comes the Sun," then a duet of the two of them singing John Denver and Olivia Newton John's "Fly Away." *In this old world there's nobody as lonely as me.* Geddy stands center floor and beams.

"Sing some Rush, granddaddy!"

"Only if you sing with me, Geddy." Wayne smiles back, gets out an acoustic guitar, sings his heart out. Geddy joins and sings their heart out, too. One number, then another, until finally Nicolette rounds Geddy up and convinces them that it's time to leave the party. Geddy waves to Dan as they leave, throws him a kiss. Dan smiles and smirks at the same time, but waves back. "Poor Geddy, needs to be more boy," he mutters to himself.

DAN'S MIND FADES TO:

INT. BEDROOM—NIGHT

Three bunks beds, three little boys, Jimmy, Wayne, Tad, sleeping soundly. A young Dan Kellar, dressed for active duty, pats each boy on the head then turns to leave the room. Three hats hang on the wall. Cowboy. Army. Coonskin. It rushes over him. Dan will never know in this life what happened to his son. He prays, and he believes that at the minute he dies tonight, he will meet Tad in the heavens, and he will finally know what happened to the son he reveres. What a reunion that will be. If only Corrie doesn't come.

The memory is so real that Dan cries. He guesses God's big joke at the end is that, not only do you meet your last person (and someone who might be interesting, someone you might want to stick around to get to know, but can't), you also have to remember some intensely painful shit.

He doesn't want to be seen crying like a baby, so he rolls his wheelchair to the window, to watch the storm blow its way in. He feels for the gun that he has hidden under his seat (it's a real one this time). He marvels at the symmetry of this last day of his lifetime–that he receives praise for a life well lived, a chance to tell stories, give advice, apologize, figure out a regret or two, remember things from the past. And he gets to meet the newest of the new, someone remarkable like Geddy. Someone weird like Geddy that he can accept and like. All he needs now is for Clarence the Angel's bell to ring. Which reminds him. If he decides not to kill himself tonight, and if God doesn't take him after all, he's going to ask Mo if everyone can watch "It's a Wonderful Life" tomorrow night. Christmas in July. But of course, Dan does want Life to end. So as the storm brews, Dan watches the happy participants who are still enjoying the party, dancing, trading partners to dance some more, laughing, hugging. He sees Celeste looking at Wayne as if he's the last lemonade in the desert. Dan vaguely notices that a dozen of the partygoers are gathered around a blackboard playing a game. That "Jeopardy" insult. Well, he turns to face that humiliation.

Categories: WWII. Family. Quirks. *Something something*. What the fuck? Category: White Dan? *For real?* For real.

Mo is the Host of the game. Three contestants leap around like kids. Celeste is one of them.

"WWII for 500."

Answer. "Audie Murphy"

Buzz. Buzz. Buzz. "Yes, Jimmy."

Question. "Who is the second highest decorated soldier in World War Two after Dan Kellar?" Celeste laughs louder than everyone else in the room.

"'Merica for 400."

"July 20th, 1969?"

Buzz. Buzz. Buzz. "Yes, Jimmy."

"The date Dan Kellar landed on the moon."

"Wrong, Dan Kellar WALKED on the moon." Again, Celeste laughs the loudest.

Celeste. "White Dan for 200."

"STOP!" Dan is so mad, he's shaking. "White Dan for 200, Celeste?"

Now she's embarrassed. "It's your name."

"You were making fun of me, and my name made it easy to do."

Celeste. "No. White Dan for 200. White Dan Kellar is the answer. What is the question. What is Dan's name? My grandfather's name was Wyatt Dan Keller. He was nicknamed White Dan, because this was how his southern family said his name. Some of them probably spoke with a long drawl and said 'Whyyut' . . . but most of them just said. White. White Dan."

"That is the truth, but that's not what you mean when you call me White Dan . . . Is it?"

"Your race, and your entitlement, and why not? Old white men who are out of touch, and have always had all the power, which they hold onto with fingers clenched. You just spouted over not wanting to be a Nazi, acting like you care about Geddy, when we know... we all know...you would just soon throw Geddy into a plate glass window . . . "

" . . . I like Geddy just fine. He's never done anything to me. I just wanted to make him aware that there's hate out there, to keep the boy safe, that's all. When I look at Geddy, you know what I see? I see someone who has all future generations of his people inside him. Girls, boys, whatever. Geddy was meant to show me that I am forgiven for hurting Wayne. Thank God I didn't kill him. There would have been no Geddy if I had. See, he's proof that everything is okay. Hell, Wayne forgave me. He never pressed charges, and look, he sang songs at my birthday party, for God's sake. He wouldn't have done that if any of that mattered to him anymore. Who's out of touch? You are."

"Geddy comes along and see, you make it all about you, like you always have and like you always will. And I'm not talking about all white men. You. I'm talking about you."

"And we white men never want to contribute to the welfare of anyone else, we just love war, and love guns. We're terrible husbands and terrible fathers. White Dan for 200. Who says this? Who plays a game like this? Stupid people who know nothing, that's who."

Celeste is in tears.

"White Dan for 200. You're what needs to die out, C."

"You hate trees and ya hate immigrants and women, too," C blubbers. "Daddy, you've been my life, but I'd give anything if you weren't. You're really just an awful white man, who always, always, always wins. You're a bully."

"So go find another father. Some brown man."

"Racist, too. I'm sorry, Mo. I know I told you Daddy was really a good person, but he's not. He only thinks of himself, no matter what."

Mo, looking from Dan to C, from C to Dan, throws the list of Jeopardy answers into a trash can near her feet. There's no helping the situation. Dan and C are at a dead heat.

A stalemate. They stare at each other. Eons of judgmental and hateful memories flood between and around them.

Decades ago, White Dan used the term "Mexican standoff," which he learned he should never do because he is not Mexican, and he thinks he learned that only Mexicans should determine whether a standoff situation is a Mexican standoff. C taught him that. He learned. There are no Oriental rugs, no "dots not feathers," no barrios, no ghettos (despite the great song sung by Elvis), nothing gung ho, no nips, gooks, chinks. No butt ugly, No deformed. No retarded. No deplorables. No libs. And absolutely no Phagistan. C taught him all that. He learned.

"I'm sorry. I just don't see what I did so wrong by Geddy today."

"I'm sorry, Daddy. All your life you've asked for it. You can't make up for a lifetime of awful just by being nice to Geddy." C looks around for Geddy's approval, but doesn't see him.

"I am very old. I had to unlearn so many things, C. And I did change. I guess that don't matter to you."

Through the open window, Dan smells the crisp, clean scent of new rain, and wishes he was dead.

"You're such a fucking bitch, Celeste," he says.

He had the last word.

The party thins out quickly after this. It's late, and a storm is brewing outside. Everyone wraps up leftovers, says their goodbyes, and their solemn happy birthdays.

And leave. Jimmy and Wayne dismantle the band. Mo and her staff fold tablecloths and throw out the trash. C has retreated to a corner and cries. Geddy's forgotten the leftover cake someone had packed. Nicolette has another chance to commune with Wayne.

Dan, the tea-drinker, whom everyone would judge to be a coffee man. Dan, cock of the walk, hero, studmuffin, man of the hour, is no more. He sits alone at the window, and grapples with a complete loss of identity and confidence after the argument with C. He rolls himself to the very edge of the picture window, opens one side, feels around under his blanket for his gun. He'll roll himself around, maybe shoot himself and part of the window out at the same time, in tribute to the stunt in 2003 that earned him the moniker of "felon" and an ankle bracelet.

Now, where the hell is the ankle bracelet?

CHAPTER 42
Too long at the fair

Everyone is busy. Nobody paying attention to the old guy.

Through the open window, Dan smells the crisp, clean scent of new rain. The sky is dark and growing darker as the wind whips up. Static electricity sets Dan's hair on end. He senses a tingling sensation in his legs. As soon as he feels it, and recognizes its meaning, Dan tosses the pistol to the floor, rolls to the front doors, pushes the service button, and thrusts himself and his wheelchair outside to the porch. Nobody notices his escape. He feels the joy of freedom, and of winning. These are feelings he has not experienced since the rush of his war hero days. He has shrewdly taken advantage of the fact that the staff is distracted by party wine and party music and enthralled by the newly-returned Geddy, the only possibly future-transgender, or non-binary or gender-fluid human being any of them have ever met in the flesh. Because Geddy is so obviously the last person Dan is meant to meet in this life, it is time to die and, with the huge storm coming, God has provided such an easy way to do it! Now, Dan won't have to commit himself to suicide or wait for the Rapture. God, being the mighty God that He is, sent lightning. More than he'd ever experienced in Rupert, where lightning bolts were often trapped in low valleys during lengthy, violent thunderstorms, bolts boomeranging around trees, bouncing around homes and barns, terrifying children and horses, dogs and cats. This lightning is the greatest gift that God could ever give—this lightning could kill him on the spot. Dan steers the wheelchair to the top of the ADA-compliant ramp and rolls down the lengthy ramp's uniformed slope and onto the ground. Not an easy landing. The wheelchair topples and Dan tumbles from it. His head strikes a rock.

But ever vigilant, at some point, from inside the party room, through her tears, Celeste becomes aware of her father's disappearance. And the wheelchair is gone.

She signals to Jimmy and Wayne. "Have you seen Dad?" she yells at Nicolette. And then she looks out the picture window and sees him lying on the ground, in a heap. Geddy hears her scream. Both dash out the front door, into the horrible storm.

The picture window fills with the faces of spectators.

Celeste and Geddy reach the old man, who is lying face down on the ground. Dan is dead weight, but not dead. He screams with pain when C tries to gather him up in her arms. She lets go, and falls backwards, blinded. The mightiest of rain and wind is whipping around, but Geddy can see that Dan's legs are tangled in the wheels. Geddy grips the handle and lifts the heavy wheelchair off of the old man just as a huge bolt of lightning strikes the very largest, oldest tree in the yard. Geddy's body jolts and stiffens and blasts them a couple of feet back.

By now several people are taking on the storm, rushing to the rescue of all three fellow human beings, Geddy, C, and Dan. Dan, by some miracle, is unscathed, though confused. He's only dizzy. He knows he is experiencing vertigo so he motions everyone away. "Help someone else, and leave me alone, find Celeste," he orders.

The reverberation of the lightning strike has upped his ever-present tinnitus. Dan likens it to a bomb going off. He thinks he's in Leipzig again, or Nam. He raises his head just in time to think he sees Corrie running away, which makes him believe he is close to dead. *Success! He has done it. He has died!* Or is dying. On demand. Corrie runs into the rain, and disappears. He then sees his two war buddies at Leipzig rush forward, to shoot at Corrie! Dan manages to get up on his feet and stop his buddies from shooting her in the back. Suddenly Dan is floating, a few feet from the ground. Nobody is noticing. A group is gathered below him, around Geddy, who is sitting up and rubbing their head. Another group is gathered around C. She's rather lifeless, Dan thinks. She's lying flat on her back, her eyes wide open, unblinking, her mouth open, filling with rain. Dan hears someone yell "they were struck by lightning, all three of them, but the old man and the teen are okay!"

Dan's life is passing before him again, only this time, it's WWII. He makes his way back to the piano in Leipzig where Corrie hid the day he found her. The German soldier is still there, not dead, and he doesn't seem to be dying. He just seems to be terrified. Dan, not knowing what to do in this reenactment, aims his gun at the German, like the good soldier he is/was. The young German soldier points behind him to another hiding place in the crumbled bar, a hole that leads to a blackness where Dan is sure/ seems to remember/ or is sure other Germans are lying in wait for him. He aims his gun again. The German screams, yells in broken English, "My dog. Take my dog. Help my dog." He points to the hole again. Dan lowers the pistol, floats to the hole, and looks in to see a yellow dog lying in a pool of blood. The dog is obviously suffering from terrible injuries, probably caused by the bombings. Old Dan remembers now. His young heart broke then. And Dan's heart breaks again now, into a thousand pieces. He looks back to the German soldier, lifts his gun once more, points it at the dog, and waits for approval from the German soldier. To shoot the dog? Yes. So Dan fires one shot. The soldier wails at the sound. Dan makes sure the dog is out of its misery before stepping back over the German soldier. He floats back to the tank. He leaves the soldier be.

Dan comes to on the wet ground and feels confused when two ambulances pull up to the front of the RRC. It is still raining but the worst of the storm has passed. EMTs with gurneys fill the yard. RRC staff members cry all around him. Geddy is placed on one of the stretchers and taken to the ambulance, but Geddy is making jokes and trying to comfort everyone else, especially their hysterical mother. Geddy is all right. They say, "Mom, I told you I'd be killed in Texas. I was wrong. But . . . " Geddy breaks down. Wayne and Nicolette accompany Geddy in the ambulance. Dan feels slighted that Jimmy, at least, is not helping him. As an afterthought, he thinks, *Celeste is nowhere in sight. Strange.*

And then the EMTs tend to Dan. He thinks of Tad while the EMTs check his breathing, *Tad, he fell out of the helicopter.* Dan screams now in agony, broken ribs maybe, the EMTs hold him down to check his airway. His imagination finishes off Tad's story; Dan's such a wuss that a lightning strike gets the best of him, so the story of

Tad is an earworm to torture him for being the biggest pussy ever. Tad falling, hitting the ground, the enemy with machetes and knives, carving him limb to limb, but not killing him, just torturing him, then parading him about, people cheering his agony. The price he would pay for everything in his life was never knowing what really happened to his son and living instead with this fucking earworm he made up. The curse of having a talent for making up outrageous stories. Dan's heart aches, oh, it's just CPR, and then he sees Corrie again. She is standing where the first ambulance had been. He is glad to see her, if only because he knows he has to. "Please confirm. Am I dead?" He asks her, hopeful that he is, because if so, it had been an easy death, no real pain, quick. If he is dead, soon he will know the truth about Tad. He believes he must be dead or dying, at least. Corrie is beautiful and young again. He lifts up, looks down at his hands, pinned to his side, and is surprised to see only familiar aged ones. Someone pushes his head back down. *Fuck me*, he thinks, finally understanding the best context of the word, *still alive*. Dan barely has time to blink before Corrie is gone again. "You were kinder to a dog," she says as she flies back to heaven. "Kinder to a dog" is her judgment on his life. *But he had left the German soldier alive, wasn't that kind?* Dan knows he meant it to be kind. Or no, he just needed to get back to the tank. But, as Corrie had pointed out several times in life, to leave an injured man to bleed out, or starve, or be tortured if the wrong soldiers discovered him? That was the height of cruelty.

He put a sad dog out of its misery, why not a man? *Hell, who knows why a soldier does what a soldier does?*

Oh Jesus, now the worst parts of his life ARE passing in front of him. 1978. He had shot Wayne Herd in the back just for standing up for his beliefs, because those beliefs were not his own. 2003. He had attempted to take the life of a man just for doing his job, when times had changed, and women went to war. He had terrorized innocent people with a spray of bullets that could have killed or maimed any one of them for life, because he couldn't find out what happened to Tad, or because some women wanted to go to the Army. That same week he had talked down to Buck, treated C like she didn't matter, and leashed Corrie. On and on. It didn't matter what week. A lifetime he behaved in awful ways, represented so well in just two events! Life of nothing but stupid mistakes. And for what? So that he could be White Dan, fucking White Dan, the joke in a "Jeopardy" game.

At this point Dan isn't worried about getting his heavenly reward, he just wants to pass easily, and get these damn EMTs out of his way. God's forgiveness isn't enough to get him into heaven. He will also need to forgive God for putting him through this terrible hell of watching his life pass before him while being pounded in the chest by a couple of brutes.

"Where is Celeste?" Dan asks anyone who would listen.

"Where is my daughter?"

Finally, someone answers. Not one of the EMTs, who?

"She's dead, White Dan," Jimmy says.

Several days after the lightning strike. Celeste's passing—not from the lightning strike, but she'd had a massive heart attack out there on the lawn—her truly grieving father, *a little too late and not enough*, asks his beloved nurse, FN, to drive him to the little ranch house that he and his daughter had occupied for so many years, so he could choose her burial clothing.

But Dan Kellar was in no condition to be taken off grounds. The Administrator made this last decision after consultation with FN and Moiselle. Dan was humiliated.

"Mo or I can go to the house, Mr. Kellar, and we'll bring back outfits for you to pick from," the Administrator offers.

Dan shrugs in opposition. "No. Absolutely not. I don't want you whores in my house."

"Well, you cannot leave the grounds, Mr. Kellar, and that's final."

"Will you do it, FN?"

She will, of course.

Dan looks through the nightstand for the house key. He cries when he can't find it.

"You'll have to get a locksmith."

FN figures that Wayne Herd has a key. Not a day had passed that Celeste hadn't mentioned the man's name. FN keeps that information to herself, pats Dan on the shoulder, and leaves.

"I haven't been in the house in twenty years," Wayne answers, "but I have a key, it's sti . . . on my . . . here it is . . . we'll see if we can get in."

They step onto the porch of the little ranch style house. Wayne tries the key and it works, but the door will not open. Keeps trying. Again. "There's something blocking the door," he says.

"Let me try," Jimmy offers. FN stands back while Wayne and Jimmy take turns trying to force the door open.

"Oh shit," Jimmy says. "Oh my God."

"What is it?" Wayne and FN are alarmed. "What's blocking the door?"

Jimmy heaves himself against the door a few times, and is able to create an opening of a few inches.

"Oh my God."

"What?"

Wayne forces the door open wide enough to partially squeak through, the others close behind. All three smell a combination of rot, urine, mold, filth, and feces coming from inside the home.

The odor is offensive, like something has died, they slowly enter, and it is astonishing to discover an actual hoard within the house. Nobody knew that Celeste had been living in squalor.

They manage to get into the house. Each grip onto anything solid they can find to hold onto as they tiptoe across at least three feet of filth. It is so horrible to smell that each cover their noses and mouths, and come damn near puking.

The front area is a stunning formal living room with white sofas and white walls that are now stained with rodent dust and droppings. Even worse is the dining room, which has a mirror with gold inlay adorning the back wall. The mirror, which had always given the impression that Elvis Presley's personal interior decorator had ornamented the space, is broken.

A precise piece of glass hangs loosely from the mirror's center. The chandelier over the dining room table dangles precariously.

The kitchen is particularly hazardous. There are huge holes in the ceiling, and black mold throughout. Holes in the floor, upon further inspection, are obvious entry points into the house for living critters. Jimmy opens the refrigerator and shouts "Jesus!" before slamming the door shut. "Is there something dead in there?" FN asks. "I don't know. I don't think she was a serial killer, but she may have had some cats." As they enter the hallway, they step over urine-soaked periodicals, newspapers, and mail. It is evident that Celeste must have been sleeping in a makeshift bed made up of a soiled mattress jammed between the small walls of the hallway.

Wayne and Jimmy are horrified when they step into Tad's old bedroom. The three bunkbeds that belonged to the boys are buried under open food containers, cups and coke bottles.

Only Dan's bedroom is left untouched by squalor. His room is spotless, a shrine, both beds are beautifully quilted, ready for guests. The only clutter in the room? A hundred or more pink princess phones.

FN nearly passes out as she walks past the bathroom in the hall. There is a ceiling-high mass of trash. Paperbacks, skeins, soiled clothes, and other materials are stacked high in the bathtub. There is absolutely no access to the sink. From what she can see of the sink it had been a while since water had flowed there.

"How did she bathe, or brush her teeth?" she asks outloud. Wayne then adds, "How did she go to the bathroom?"

There is no sign of a toilet.

FN exclaims, "The toilet is gone."

Wayne says, "I found it," tears streaming down his face.

"Don't look in her bedroom."

Of course they have to look. Not imagining what they would be discovering, the three of them see that Celeste had been wearing diapers to manage her bodily functions. Boxes of adult diapers are stacked everywhere. But worse, one of the outdoor trash bins is in her bedroom, and crusty, used diapers are overflowing from it.

"Let's get out of here," Wayne says as he holds onto a wall. "I can't. I can't breathe."

"I have to find an outfit in her closet, that's why we're here," FN answers.

"Let's go buy her something, everything in that closet is going to be contaminated," Wayne pleads.

FN steps gingerly over piles of squalor to get to the closet. Several dresses and suits were nicely wrapped in plastic bags. FN grabs all of them and makes her way out of the room.

At the front door, Wayne asks "How did she not die in there? How did we not know?" FN answers, "I don't know, she took showers at the RRC, that seemed odd to me, but now I . . . but this is the Kellar story, right here."

FN, Jimmy and Wayne drive away from the home where Celeste had spent her life. Jimmy drove. Wayne rode shotgun. Both men are weeping, tortured by this outcome. FN is alone in the backseat, several of Celeste's outfits beside her. Still in their plastic dry cleaning bags, newly cleaned, and yet the smell of the hoard permeating the car. FN rolls down her window, looks out and sings a John Denver song under her breath. *"In this whole world there's nobody as lonely as she. There's nowhere to go and there's nowhere that she'd rather be."*

CHAPTER 43
I forgive it all

The Vietnam vets are now the oldies. In 2023, only a handful of WWII veterans are still alive. In fact, Dan Kellar is one of only one percent of all WWII veterans still alive.

Still, the world thanks them for their service. How long will that gratitude last? Remains to be seen.

The small VA bus parks in front of the Porterfield. Old, happy groundhogs, as Dan has long referred to the Vietnam era veterans, exit the little bus, bid farewell to their bus driver, Jimmy, and chat about the impressive work of the renovation of Jimmy's former abode. Jimmy bids the lads goodbye, locks the bus, then walks across the street to the parked limo that belongs to the RRC.

Jimmy waves to the old Porterfield before he gets into the limo.

CCTV cameras are everywhere now, and construction walls circle the Porterfield site, blocking any views, yet the restoration is already proving to be a boon for Rupert. There are several cute, touristy coffee shops, candle shops, t-shirt shops, vintage clothing stores, and one Army Recruiting Center in a new location and open for business now, as well as the hustle and bustle of delivery trucks stopping and starting up and down Main Street. Ghost-hunting tour posters are in every window along the bustling street, marketing the promise of a weekend of creaking chairs and moving beds, once again, with shadowy figures, disembodied voices, and especially the terror of going underground to the resort spa where murders, accidents and seances had taken place in the long ago past.

The 2023 weekend will include an escape room event (and the tickets are selling fast) where guests will attempt to save themselves from a realistic fire, recreating an act of arson that is said to have been committed upon the hotel by a half-crazed, grief-stricken German woman. At the bottom of the poster, in tiny letters, "See the famous halls and visit the rooms where famous movie stars met clandestinely in the early days of Hollywood." Underneath is a photo of the movie icon, John Wayne, who, of course, had never come to Rupert during his lifetime, so certainly was not a ghost there. And not everybody will even know who he is, of course.

But someone had taken a magic marker to the photo, defaming it, nevertheless.

Hello world. Not the world I expected to wake up to. Who cares who the fucking President is? Not me. Not anymore. Joe Biden will be the last President I will ever know about. Or care about. He's probably too old to be President again. No doubt, the next time this country elects a President it will be someone young, someone fresh, someone everyone loves. And all the old people in my home will get to watch the news again. Because nobody will be arguing over politics.

Dan is disappointed to wake up on the day of Celeste's funeral, but in fact he is awake, fully awake, and nothing matters anymore. Ninety-five-year-old Dan is an ancient man without a human legacy, no reason to concern himself with the future fate of the country he loved and fought for. He's glad he killed Nazis. That made his life bearable, meaningful. His service, and the service of millions of veterans of war made other lives bearable, in fact, gave Americans and other citizens of the world a future life, filled with possibilities and hope, perhaps even dreams of equality.

But so what? Waiting for death without C is unthinkable. He discovers that he loves her. Somewhat. More than he thought, more than he ever knew, now that she is gone. But underlying any love he has is the nagging, narcissistic question. *Who will help me in the end? Who will care about me or my stories?* Once upon a time Dan Kellar thought he would live on through C because C loved him so. And now nobody loves him. He dresses in his finest and waits for FN to take him to the funeral in the home's limo. While he waits he stares at the obituary on his nightstand. His own. So what? He'll have to finish it himself, without input from C. Well, there's one good thing to come out of this tragedy at least. He can write whatever the fuck he pleases about himself.

And as for today, Jimmy has another driving job.

FN sits in the front seat of the limo, with Jimmy. Turns out Jimmy has had twenty successful years driving various vehicles without a single negative incident—a far cry from the mishaps of the years before: the years of firefighting, soldiering, husbanding. He tells FN he thinks they should marry, that he's a fine upstanding prospect of a man at last.

Then there is the bane of Dan's existence—Wayne and Briggs —who accompany Dan in the limo. He buckles up, and stares hard at the two interlopers.

"I find it ironic and hellish that the three of us are together today, don't you?" Dan can't be pleasant, not now, not even on the ride to his child's funeral.

Wayne, with tears in his eyes, responds to the old man. "Dan, we gotta give her this one day of peace between us, man. C would want us to reconcile. She loved both of us. Her life was hellish because of us, and because of her mother." Dan nods, quietly conceding in agreement.

Briggs countered, though, his expression furious. "Her mother had a story, and like all stories, Corrie's story made her the way she was. I won't be hearing anything ill about her mother. If you knew her story, you would understand."

"I know Corrie's story," Dan snarls. "She was my wife until the day she died. I rescued her, you know, from Nazis."

They slowly make their way to the cemetery on the muggiest of days, dog days, suffering Texas summer days, in spite of icy cold air conditioning in the limo. Dan shivers with cold, knows he's likely to catch a cold with all these temperature changes in and out of the limo. In and out temperatures are hard on an old man. Texas summers are ugly anyway, and he catches himself thinking only of himself. He knows that his narcissism is the biggest thing he needs forgiveness for, and he makes a mental note to explain to God, when he sees Him again, IF he ever sees Him, that the narcissism is a result of his coming into the world to a family of origin—the family God sent him to—where he had to fend for himself. A mother who showed no interest in him. A father who ignored his cries for help. His original story, the one about his younger brother, Rick, being hit by the car his mother was driving, who blamed him for his brother's death. And his other childhood story, the one when he hanged himself from the rafter in the barn, and his father catching him, pulling him down, then pretending it never happened. It happened. He happened. He had to make his life matter. He told stories to make sure his life mattered. And if the stories weren't enough on their own, he embellished the stories. And the unembellished stories, the ugly stories, shooting Wayne, terrorizing the ARC, treating people the way he was treated when he was a child, discounting others, well, curse the day these stories turn out to be the ones that truly matter to God, who is obviously not damning them, but is forcing him to relive them on the day of his daughter's funeral, no less.

DAMN the lightning strike that struck down Celeste instead of him. They say it was a heart attack. Bull shit. It was God being God not even allowing Dan the closure of knowing for sure what killed his child—lightning or her heart.

They drive through the crazy neighborhoods, past the Porterfield, past the bowling alley. Dan asks to drive once more past the old Kellar's Born to be Wild bar. He asks Jimmy to park. He wants one last look.

Jimmy keeps the limo running while Dan moseys around what used to be the bar.

Wayne looks out of the window to the forest where he'd been shot so long ago. He opts to stay in the limo, though. Some memories really suck. After a few minutes, Dan saunters slowly back to the limo, and, buckling his seat belt, starts to tell a story.

Briggs looks at his shoes, trying to be patient. "This is where I brought Corrie after I rescued her from the Nazis. This was the American Dream I promised her. It was all bullshit. She was incapable of happiness."

It is all Briggs can do to keep his mouth shut.

Dan has his stories, the task of writing his obituary, and seeking God's forgiveness to keep him going. He began the long walk down memory lane to make sure that on the day when his life passed before him again, yes, again, no stone needing God's forgiveness would have been left unturned.

In the good ol' days he had his work. Soldiering. Running a bar.

He never wanted to retire. Especially without Corrie. It wasn't love, (well, it was "pretend" love). "Once upon a time" love. Truth? No embellishment? Grief over the loss of Tad, the unknown, is what bound them. And guilt.

And while Dan could create wonderful, embellished tales out of vague, mostly false memories, Corrie's scarred imagination had left her with little way out of the harsh reality of her own experiences.

So there were few happy memories in the Kellar family, but one memory dominated as the happiest of his life.

"Corrie was German," Dan begins. "Yes, we fucking know," Briggs says with his British lilt, "and I told you I don't want to hear a single ill remark about our Corrie."

"She never sang," Dan continues, ignoring Briggs, who is trapped in the limo, "and had no use for laziness. I was walking by C's room, heard her singing, "Another Pleasant Valley Sunday." I stopped. Well, Corrie spotted me eavesdropping. I smiled, tried to . . . but Corrie shit on the moment. She wanted C's room cleaned. "Quit wasting your time listening to her," she ordered, and opening C's door without knocking . . . "Turn that hippie shit off right now." Well, my heart broke when that music stopped, that singing. Is there anything happier to do than sing? But Corrie's awfulness ruled the house. She was damaged. And somehow she got a pass for being damaged. Even remembering it now is painful."

It was rare for Dan to consider the fact that others had their stories, too. That their stories influenced the outcome of their lives.

Dan's storytelling skills had always been the highest when he talked about how he met his wife. 1945. Leipzig. The fact that he left out Corrie's part of the story didn't matter to him. Until Briggs came along.

Finally, there, trapped in the limo, Briggs has heard enough of Dan's ramblings and can hold it in no more. "There is one answer that is waiting to be heard," he says. "One more story to be spoken today." And so he tells the story. It was a story Briggs regretted keeping to himself because, had Celeste known the truth, her life with her mother might have been different.

Corrie's story was the nail in the coffin of the Kellar dynasty.

"Leipzig, you rescued her. Well. The truth. Corrie ran from you, she had not gotten far so the sound of the shot you fired at her German soldier rang loud."

It was a dog, a shot at the dog, not the man. Dan knows he cannot defend himself to Briggs.

'She told me that she couldn't be certain that "Werner," the Nazi she loved, the intended victim of your shot, was dead or alive. But there was no going back to learn of his fate. The sun was going down and she . . . She had to find water, some food if she was lucky, but most important—shelter, because the Russians were close by and she knew what that meant for her safety, and the safety of the baby inside her body."

Dan gasps, sick inside that Briggs knew about Corrie's baby, but he remains quiet, listens.

" You know she was pregnant when you met her, Dan. You had to know. She was well into her pregnancy. By Werner. Well, Russian soldiers had the reputation of raping any German girl they found. It wouldn't matter to them that she was several months along in pregnancy. "They'll rape babies," her mother would say about the Russians. Corrie was eighteen years old and gorgeous. The Russian armies came in black helmets, in tanks, and on horses. And by now they were worn out and starving. The decent soldiers among them were unwilling to stop their fellow soldiers from stealing, torturing, and raping. Some committed rape with bottles of vodka.

"Corrie had managed to hide from these scenes more than once, but she had witnessed the atrocities first hand. She nursed her schoolgirl friends, their mothers, and even their baby sisters, after Russian soldiers abused them. Mutilated vaginas. Bloodied anuses. Their bones crushed and broken.

"While the city was under siege, she searched for shelter, finally coming across an abandoned Tiger tank. It was impossible to hide. She had to keep moving. When it got dark, she decided that if she survived the night she would try to find you, Dan, as a last hope to save herself and her baby."

The occupants of the limo sit in stunned silence, wishing such a story would end. But Briggs won't stop talking.

"She would go back the way she came and find you. She would allow you to protect her. She would do whatever was necessary for her survival. She stumbled upon a water-filled mine shaft and hid there that night. Corrie would only need to survive the night, each night, one night at a time, without being found by Russian soldiers.

"But she wasn't so lucky. When they found her their numbers were staggering, at least a platoon, she counted. She braced herself for mass rape, gang rape, and determined to survive. Corrie refused to scream or fight. Get it over with. Survive. They dragged her out into the open. And they lined up. She took it, like so many of her friends and their mothers did. She took it and filled her heart with hate and at the same time with hope for a better future in America.

"The vision of life in America got her through the ungodly night. The American Dream. Enough to eat. A warm bed.

"So she survived the attacks, and even slept afterwards, and one Russian soldier left a can of condensed milk and a few crackers . . . She buried her baby girl herself. Eventually she found you, and true to your word, you brought her to the U.S.

"And the first thing you wanted, she said, was a son. She told you that she would give you a son, but she also told you, "I will not give you a daughter. I could never love a daughter.""

Jimmy turns into Peaceful Pines Cemetery, traveling the long, smoothly paved road, down to a dirt road, where C will be in her coffin. Dan waits for Briggs to exit the car. Briggs holds onto the seat in front of him with both hands. Dan found himself staring at those hands, once again wondering if he was C's actual, biological father. As if that matters now.

Dan decides to sit in the car and watch the funeral from afar. "I can't hear anyway," he says, "my tinnitus is awful."

Regardless of any forthcoming revelation or confession that might have come from Briggs, another earworm saved Dan's day. It popped up, screaming through the tinnitus. C was in her twenties.

Her car had broken down and she had called her Dad to pick her up. "Triple A is sending a tow, Dad, but I need some air conditioning and good company. Come get me."

The two of them sat in his truck for the coupla hours it took for Triple A to show up, A/C running, CD playing boomer music, both of them singing at the top of their lungs.

Dan's best kept secret, the happiest moment of his life. And for a few minutes his tinnitus was overwhelmed by a lovely sound. A sound that had made life worth living.

On the drive home, Dan didn't talk, or listen. He thought. Celeste was alive for about 25,000 days. Her life had been restrained, like constant water dripping between her eyes, eroding her, hollowing her out. On the day of the birthday party, before the party, she came to help him dress, begged him not to kill himself that night, and then, frustrated by his lack of positive response, she prayed that Dan's passing, if he forced it, would bring an end to whatever reason had brought them together in this life. She was desperate to get his attention. Then they prayed together, Dan had to recall, and made a pact never to cross paths with one another again, not in any future life. "If there is a home in heaven," C said, "let us have separate homes in separate clouds. If there is reincarnation, let one be reborn on one side of the earth and the other of us reborn on the other side. For the rest of eternity, we prefer to be apart."

Dan answered her, "This is on God." God had made a terrible mistake making them a family. And Corrie had made it so much worse. They included her in their pact, knowing that she would agree. Some families are just bad together.

As C straightened his tie on the night of his birthday party, and helped him into his red jacket, as an afterthought, he said, suddenly, *figuring he would die that night, and wanting to get in one last familial dig,* he cruelly said to his daughter, the last words they would ever have alone, words made harsher when added to the 'White Dan for 200' disagreement at the party.

"C, I want you to know I finished my obituary. It's over on the table there. And since we agreed, in our prayer just now, I hope you won't mind that I left you out of my obituary."

C took two steps backward. Tears welled up in her eyes.

"Daddy," she said. "You have to put me in your obituary. I'm your family."

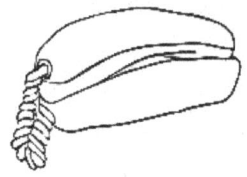

An excerpt from
LOVE LETTERS TO TERRIBLE PEOPLE
forthcoming by Angela Wilson

The first time I saw the train. I was maybe seven.

In my mind I can still see myself ambling along. . . because you know how fleeting a moment is . . . it's gone the minute it happens, and even at seven years old I knew I wanted to remember things vividly for the far away future, so any memory is blazed into my brain for life, if I choose it to be, and it's like a movie tracking shot, but in this case the eye camera—the brain camera tracks across a truly bucolic landscape and leads to a forgotten railcar that is parked in apparent perpetuity on an overgrown railroad track about three miles outside of town.

It's a Great Northern Railway 8 x 40 ft boxcar.

There is no crossbuck.

The car itself is graffitied with fresh "Peace and Love" "Make Love Not War" slogans. I remember the colors of the graffiti. And marvel at how clichéd it is now, looking back. "Peace and Love." "Make Love Not War." Quaint.

So . . . 1967? The slogans had been making the rounds for awhile and somehow made their way to Ponca Town, population 130, to be memorialized on an old, abandoned Great Northern railcar. So romantic, though. The old car had a past. Right? I hear the whoosh as it once zoomed along the tracks, headed to Amarillo, no doubt. The big city.

Woo Woowah. Woo Woowah.

Another image interrupts, penetrates. I'm nearing the car. Something stops me. Saves me. An angel? I squint. There. The footprints of a large man leading away from the railcar and disappearing into a great field of wildflowers.

A big man. I think I saw him from the back. Maybe smelled him, too. This is where it gets fuzzy, which is a shame, which is the way high emotional intensity works in a child. The hair on my neck stood on end, I remember that. I ducked. Under the car. I dared to look out again.

One of the wildflowers was blood-stained?

As the wildflowers blew in the soft breeze, there was a waft of the sound of a child singing, the words not audible to me during my walk, but there by the railcar . . .

. . . the singing became audible. It was a song we sang in music class at school. "Don't take my horse away?" Something like that. So this child singing? One of my schoolmates?

Take away my spurs
Take away my gal
Life's no good without my pal
So don't take my hoss away.

School. I was walking home from school, that's right. And. I have my pencil pack, my notebooks. I gotta write everything down, I somehow knew it. Like maybe I'd be a detective someday, or FBI.

Like yesterday.

The boxcar is corroded, red and dusty. The working parts probably don't work anymore, and the doors appear to be rusted and tightly shut, though I do manage to get inside. Through a . . . window. High up. I'm seven. I'm small. I'm . . .

But there is a wooden ladder underneath a small open window, an obvious way into the railcar. I climb.

And just as I place my little bitty hand on the car to push through, and drop inside the car, I happen to peek through one of the slats and see the bright blue eye of a small girl peeking back.

DISCUSSION GUIDE: twelve starter questions

Thank you for reading my debut novel. Please feel free to contact me directly at whitedanfor200@outlook.com and please review the book online.

Since so many people are reading novels and participating in book club discussions, below are some starting points for your discussions. Please let me know at the above email address what is happening in your book clubs.

Thank you!

Angela Wilson

Dan Kellar is struggling with the exhaustion and limitations of aging while exhibiting off-putting traits and lashing out harsh insults to his caretaker. How do you experience the aging process? What choices should Dan make at this age? Is there a Dan Kellar in your life and how do you maintain sympathy and empathy for him/her?

What are the challenges you fear you will face as a caretaker of your parent?

Were you surprised when Dan threw out the notion of committing suicide? Did you sympathize with him? If you were Celeste, how would you react to that?

How does being part of a family evolve over a lifetime?

What are the challenges to be faced by each member of dysfunctional family and are there takeaways in this novel to help family members cope with each other?

Is mid-life really the hardest time of life? How do you manage your personal mid-life crisis or to the mid-life crisis of your family members?

How did "parenting" go in the book? Dan to Celeste? Nicolette to Geddy? Wayne to Liam? What were turning points for each character? Do you relate to any character's parenting style?

Were there surprising outcomes in the book? If so, why?

Who is the villain in the story and why?

Should Dan have experienced bigger consequences for his actions? Did he experience consequences at all?

How do you relate to Dan's midnight musings with God?

Discuss Wayne's handling of his life decisions and the consequences of same. And the same for Jimmy.

GRATITUDES

To the town, the hotel, the hospitals, the old veterans, the crazies, the Recruiters, and the ghosthunter friends who served as inspiration for this fiction.

Pamela Warren Williams of Mercury HeartLink Press for invaluable expertise and much-needed cheerleading.

David Beebe III for your artistry and generosity.

Carl Savering for countless things, including support, advice, compassion, cheerleading and art.

Pamela Dougherty for asking amazing questions that got me to the finish line.

Kris Isom and Monique Mosher for invaluable help.

Keith W. Strom, ED of the Ernest Hemingway Foundation.

Yessenia Santos at Simon and Schuster.

A thousand times thank you to Bobbie Gentry, Universal/MCA Music Ltd.

Kailyn Lopez at MPL.

To Bert Pigg and Adriana Bate for producing the first staged readings of *Heart*, the play that led to this novel. To Joy Tipping, Juli Ericson, Susan Sargeant, Beverly Jacob Daniel, Paul Iwanski, Bruce Hennie (RIP), Jim Grant (RIP) for the second. Sherry Etzel, Thurman Moss, Jennifer Kuenzer, Lisa Cotie, and Jerry Crow (RIP) for taking it further. Megan Lane and Alexis Scott, thank you.

To my teachers in the long ago past, C.W. Smith, David McHam, Gretchen E. Smith, and John Carstarphen.

To the poets, Rainer Maria Rilke for "Go to the Limits of your Longing", and Bill Nevins.

To the actors who brought the characters to life in so many ways, Kim Titus, David Goodwin, Brenda J. Galgan, Laurel Whitsett, Anthony J. Ramirez, Stephen Seybold, and Linda Comess for *Heart*, Pat Watson, Bill Owen, Tung Tran, Sharyn Sparks, and Cynthia Hestand (RIP). The New Mexico Women in Film writers group for the countless read-alouds of *Blue Eyed Son*, the screenplay that influenced this novel. Jim Sea (aka James Charleston). And at the time of this writing, thank you to Lisa Fairchild, Carolyn Wickwire, Catherine Fridey, and Elly Lindsay. To Martin Holden for critiquing the main character all those years ago. To Tom Sime, Glenn Arbery, Jimmy Fowler, Mark Lowry and Lawson Taitte for putting me on the map and to Mike Templeton for putting *Heart* on the big stage in good ol' Mesquite, Tx.

Matt Hader, and Rosa Rajkovic, for spurring me on.

Susan Gladstein for providing expertise regarding when soldiers are missing in action, as well as the identification process.

To Randy Shiflet (RIP) regarding Texas law enforcement.

And to the American singer/songwriters who write our anthems (and are somewhat referenced in this book), and to the veterans of the United States of America who keep us free, there is no limit to my love and thanks. Please donate or follow my preferred charity https://www.garysinisefoundation.org

ABOUT THE AUTHOR

Angela Wilson was raised in Dallas. She and her accent now reside in New Mexico. She earned a BA in American History from UTDallas and an MLA from Southern Methodist University, where she also studied theater and writing.

Along with actor Carl Savering, she produced twenty-eight plays at their critically-acclaimed Theatre Quorum in Dallas. She wrote several of the plays for TQ and other theaters, but she also produced, directed, and acted in various, mostly obscure and underproduced plays by Lanford Wilson, Jeff Daniels, Joyce Carol Oates, and Thornton Wilder, with an emphasis on producing Irish playwrights. She taught theater, history, and humanities at several area community colleges.

She's been a member of several choirs, traveled "the world" with Credo Community Choir in Dallas and sings with the New Mexico Women's Chorus in Albuquerque. Though her unfulfilled dream is to be a backup singer in a geezer band, she is also proud to have been a recent "Last DJ" for Tom Petty Radio and to have been a "Can't Smile girl" for Barry Manilow back in the day.

She trained as a film and tv actor at Film Actors Lab. She is represented by Talent Trek Agency in the South and Presley Talent in the Southwest. Her love of film also led her to convert some of the plays to screenplays, and ultimately led to the writing of this novel.

Most important. Family. She is parent to the extraordinary Jennifer, and is very, very, very, very fond of cats.

Angela is also a foot model.

www.ingramcontent.com/pod-product-compliance
Lightning Source LLC
Chambersburg PA
CBHW060945030726
47503CB00003B/735